Praise for Doc Coleman

"Doc Coleman gives us a droll steampunk adventure full of engaging characters, from its unnamed narrator to the least spear carrier, nonstop action, and a lot of in-jokes (Lord Scaleslea, I'm looking at you.). If you love airships, adventure, humor and pathos, read *The Adventures of Crackle and Bang*."

Jody Lynn Nye
Author of View from the Imperium

"*The Perils of Prague* by Doc Coleman is worth every minute of your life to read and reread. I read my advance copy twice, and I fully intend on purchasing a hard copy. I'll be front and center when Doc does a book signing tour. I'm never embarrassed about being a fanboy over good art. The only thing better than this steampunk is the promise of more in this series, following these characters along on further adventures and character arcs. This is steampunk as it was meant to be!"

Aaron Spriggs
Piston Valve Press

Also by Doc Coleman

The Gift

"A Walk in the Park", published in the Special Steampunk Issue of **FlagShip**

Welcome to Paradox

The Cross of Columba

"The Shining Cog", published in **The Way of the Gun***, A Bushido Western Anthology*

THE PERILS OF PRAGUE

For Maria,

Adventure
Awaits!
Are you ready?

Published in the United States of America by Swimming Cat Studios
http://swimmingcatstudios.com

Cover design, cover art, interior illustrations, and book design
by Scott E. Pond Designs, LLC (http://scottpond.com)

Edited and proofed
by Jennifer Melzer (http://jennifermelzer.com)

Print ISBN: 978-0-9980151-0-1
eBook ISBN: 978-0-9980151-1-8

PRINTED IN THE UNITED STATES OF AMERICA

10 9 8 7 6 5 4 3 2 1

FIRST EDITION: First Printing—April 2017

The Adventures of Crackle and Bang: Book One

THE PERILS OF PRAGUE

DOC COLEMAN

Dedication

To my mother, who will never read these words.

You nearly died before I was born, and you told me repeatedly that God had saved you to do something special, and that I was it.

I've always remembered those words, and striven to be the best I could at whatever I was doing so that I could live up to that promise.

Now you have passed on, and I feel like I have finally started to understand what that purpose is.

I've always enjoyed stories, and I think I'm supposed to tell them.

Look, here comes one now...

Acknowledgements

This book wouldn't be possible without the help of a number of people who donated their particular skills and insights to improve my manuscript. So I'd like to take this moment to express my thanks to the following people:

Lucie Le Blanc - For questioning every phrase and idiom, so that I could make sure that my words were clear, even for those who learned English as a second (or third) language.

Kat Bowling - For catching the in jokes, and being concerned for my characters.

Denise Lhamon - For showing me I was both right and wrong, and that I could still make the book work. And for giving me the feedback I needed.

Jennifer Metzler - My editor. We didn't always see eye to eye, but your advice made a big difference in the book, and I hope it has made me a better writer.

Scott Pond - For making my book look beautiful, inside and out.

Scott Roche - For wanting to see the great book you know I will someday publish, and for being the first to volunteer.

Tim Salisbury - For checking the science, and sending me references I didn't even know I needed.

David W. Wooddell - For questioning everything, because that is how I knew I would have the answers.

Author Note

It started with a Halloween costume.

My wife and I went to a Halloween party dressed as a scientist and his lovely assistant. In keeping with the Steampunk trope, we wore goggles, and I wore a top hat. My wife soon got tired of her goggles and gave them to me to hold, and I quickly put them on my hat, above my own goggles. The look of the topper with two sets of goggles on it got to me. It seemed iconic. I started thinking about what kind of character would wear extra goggles on his hat, and why. What sort of world would that person live in?

And so, Crackle and Bang were born.

I have been working on this story and this world for years now, fleshing it out, and setting up the stories that come after. I hope that you will enjoy this introduction to the world of The Eternal Empress, and that you will follow the further adventures of Crackle and Bang as they explore their world and the wonders it holds. A place where nothing is exactly what it seems to be.

Enjoy!

Doc Coleman
Germantown, MD
23 March 2017

Chapter One

An Encounter at the Bohemian Opera

"Faster! Faster, man! *Macht schnell! Rychleji!*" I screamed at the driver as we careened around a corner, the carriage momentarily tipping up on two wheels as we narrowly avoided colliding with a wagon going the other way.

The horses neighed as the driver cracked his whip over their sweat-covered flanks. Pedestrians scattered from our path, leaping to the relative safety of the sidewalks and lobbing curses after us. *Little do they care that my life will be utterly ruined if I am late to the opera,* I thought. I repeated my exhortation for speed in broken German and even worse Bohemian. I wasn't even sure I used the right word, but it was clear from the driver's reaction he understood my meaning.

He understood English, of course. Practically everyone in the Empire spoke English in some capacity, with the possible exception of some of the most provincial farmers. My uncle Randolph, Duke of Bohemia by marriage, always said it was best to speak some of the native language when traveling abroad. It projected the impression we came to the country as partners, not rulers. He claimed it yielded much better results with the servants, or something of that nature. I honestly didn't pay much attention to him at the time. I only recalled his advice because of frequent repetitions. Who would have thought it would turn out to be useful? Since it had, I dearly hoped I remembered it correctly.

Uncle Randolph was the reason I was leaning out the window of his fourth-best coach, racing through the gaslit streets of Prague just past twilight, and admonishing the coachman for more speed. My lady mother sent me to visit Uncle Randolph and Aunt Katerina, allegedly as the first step of my Grand Tour to celebrate the completion of my university education and my emergence into high society as an adult. In reality, it was the next step in my parents continuing plot to dictate every step of my life.

From his behavior over the past two weeks, I deduced my uncle was charged with shaping me into my parent's idea of a proper member of the noble class. That particular experiment seemed doomed, as my best efforts failed to produce any hint of approval from Uncle Randolph. His critical frowns haunted me as I staggered my way through one society function after another. I much preferred the polite dismissal I received from commoners to the vocal disapproval I continually encountered from fellow nobles.

After weeks of my uncle's tutelage, and a series of unfortunate events, I found myself clinging to the roof of the carriage to keep from falling out the window as we galloped through the streets of Prague. A twisting in my stomach reminded me the evening was likely to be my last chance to gain favor in his eyes. If I conducted myself to his satisfaction at the opera, my uncle promised to forgive my past transgressions. If not, he would cancel my tour and send me packing home to England.

I understood some of my family's objections to my wastrel ways, but they drove me to it by controlling my every move. While I admit I made mistakes, they held me responsible for many things outside of my control. It was extremely unfair of them to hold the incident with Baron Berka's daughter against me. The woman was over a foot taller than me and strong enough to carry her own horse! Frankly, it is impossible to dance while one's hand and shoulder are being crushed in a vise-like grip. And the Comte du Langres positively reeked of cheese and onions. I wasn't being rude; I was trying to catch my breath.

When Uncle Randolph sent word earlier in the day to say he would not be able to take me to The Bohemian Opera that evening, I was momentarily overjoyed. My jubilation came quickly crashing down when I read his message further and discovered he wanted me to meet him at the State Opera House, on time and properly attired.

Dressing for the evening was a disaster.

I fortified myself with a glass or two of wine to prepare for the ordeal of another evening of "culture". In retrospect, that may have been a mistake. While the wine helped calm my nerves, it did no favors for my hands and I accidentally spilled some of the beverage on my shirt, forcing me to seek out a fresh one. I then dropped one of my studs while donning the replacement. Naturally, the errant piece of jewelry skittered away from me and hid under the bed, further souring my mood. When I retrieved the damned thing, the second shirt was ruined from a streak of dirt up the length of the sleeve.

I whipped the soiled garment off to put on a third dress shirt and then couldn't find my cuff links. I lost precious minutes searching for them before I found them hiding in the cuffs of the wine-stained shirt. When I finally managed to don a shirt without ruining it, I spent a good half-hour trying to find my dress shoes, and in the end settled for my next best pair.

By the time I managed to dress myself in something close to my uncle's standards, I was horribly late and desperate to make up the time. I charged my uncle's coachman to make all haste and promised him a great deal more money than I was able to pay should he deliver me on time.

I flung myself from the coach as we pulled up in front of the opera house, not waiting for the carriage to stop, but leaping to the street at a run, clutching my top hat in one hand and staggering to keep from falling and ruining my clothes, yet again. I raced up the grand stair, which fronted the State Opera House, abandoning any semblance of dignity. The august facade of the venerable building was unmoved, although I dare say some of the passersby were alarmed by the display. Fixated upon the consequences of arriving too late for the performance, I ran for all I was worth.

I caught the door as an usher in neat grey livery pulled it closed. He blocked the way with his body and said, "I'm sorry, sir, no one is permitted to enter once the doors are closed."

"But it is not closed," I replied. "Indeed, if you will stand aside I shall be glad to assist you in sealing this portal against those who would attempt to re-open it."

The man remained unmoved. "Sir, the performance is about to begin, and for the convenience of our patrons I must ask that you remain outside." He jerked on the handle in an attempt to wrest it from my hand and trap me outside of the theatre, but I maintained my grip.

I was not about to surrender so easily. "I am one of your patrons. Indeed I have a ticket!" I reached into my jacket to produce my ticket and the man nearly slammed the door shut. I slid my foot forward to block the door and he crushed my leg quite painfully against the jamb.

"Sir, please! I must close this door!"

His unapologetic violence raised my ire. So much so I did something I previously found distasteful. Pulling myself up to my full six foot height, I looked down at him and fixed him with my most harsh and steely glare, doing my best imitation the elitist prigs who made much of my life miserable. Summoning every ounce of self-importance I could muster, I leaned forward and asked, "Do you know who I am?"

"No, sir, I do not, and it would make no difference in any case. I must close the door!"

I told him.

The man's face blanched, the blood drained from his face as his eyes widened in shock and confusion. His hands fell limply to his side. He stepped backwards, his face transformed into a twisted rictus as he shied away. I pulled the door open and slid inside, pushing past the stunned usher. Tearing my own ticket, I dropped one half of the stub into the box with a flourish. Pointing to the open door, I told the man, "You should close that before some riffraff come in."

I turned and strode rapidly away from the sputtering man before he could gather his wits and pursue me.

It was the first time in my life I was grateful for my great-grandfather's perverse sense of social humor and the shockingly obscene name he saw fit to inflict upon me. It was not to be the last.

Desperate to regain time lost with the usher, I ran up the two flights of stairs to the level of the luxury boxes. I paused for a moment to regain my composure in the cool air of the foyer to my uncle's private box. If I entered before the performance began, I could count myself as punctual, but it would not do me any good to arrive disheveled, sweating, and panting with exertion. I inhaled deeply to steady my ragged breath and coax my heart to a more leisurely pace. As I did so, I drew my hands down over my suit to restore the lines of my attire to their proper state. Finally, I relaxed the crushing grip on my top hat and straightened the brim.

Thus composed, I opened the door to the box and slipped inside as quietly as I could. It took a moment for my eyes to adjust to the dimness, but my ears instantly informed me I had made it. I successfully arrived by an acceptable margin, as the orchestra was still busy with their pre-performance tunings. I closed the door behind me and turned to find myself confronted by a couple who were complete strangers to me.

I began to stammer an apology, thinking I entered the wrong box inadvertently, when the gentleman stood and turned, adjusting his spectacles with his left hand and extending his right as he declared, "Ah! You must be Reggie's nephew! I regret old Reggie has been called away on business this evening, but he was most kind as to allow Miss Bang and myself the use of his box. He did ask me to convey his regrets to you, my boy. Oh, do forgive my manners. I am Professor Harmonious Crackle, at your service, sir. And this lovely lady is my colleague and traveling companion, Miss Titania Bang."

Ingrained habit sent my hand out to meet his, while my mind and mouth were reeling and trying to cope with the man's statements. He was not precisely disreputable, but his odd appearance made him quite unlike anyone I could imagine as an associate of my uncle.

He was older than me, but no more than thirty, yet he had the manner of someone very confident in his position and abilities. He was two or three inches shorter than I, with close-cropped blonde hair and blue eyes shining behind his glasses. His clothes were neat, but he was obviously not dressed for an evening at the opera. He wore a tweed frock coat under a white laboratory coat, both left open to allow him access to the many pockets of his black and silver checked waistcoat. I wondered momentarily how he managed to slip past the usher in such outlandish attire. His accent marked him as a fellow Englishman, but it was the only thing about him to indicate an association with Uncle Randolph.

He shook my hand with a warm, firm grip. I attempted to gather my wits to question him about his relationship to my uncle when a motion to my right drew my attention. It proved to be the lady previously introduced, Miss Bang, stepping forward to present her hand to me. Even in the dim light of the box, the sight of her took my breath and dashed what wits I managed to recover.

To say the lady was beautiful was an understatement. She was clearly in the fullest bloom of youth, and by far the most attractive woman I had met upon my travels. Her raven hair was carefully piled upon her head, but still managed to frame her heart-shaped face. Her eyes were a warm, dark brown and her lips were lush. She was attired for the opera in a stylish gown of blue silk, which clung to her shapely form and artfully accentuated her full bosom. She appeared to be a few years younger than myself, perhaps twenty-four, and moved with the smooth, flowing grace of a dancer. She seemed as fit and appropriate to her surroundings as her companion was out of place. She smiled at me in the dim light and my heart leapt as her face lit up.

She extended her hand and I dumbly took it and kissed the top of her glove. "Such a pleasure to meet you, my lord. Your uncle has been so very kind to show us such hospitality." Her voice was likewise warm and sweet, and the sound of it made my knees threaten to desert me.

I struggled to form a reply, my mouth working on its own, but failing to produce any coherent sound. I was saved when the peculiar gentleman interrupted. "Ah, they are about to begin! Here, my good fellow, take the seat of honor along with Miss Bang. We shall have plenty of time to talk after the performance."

He took my arm and steered me to the front of the box with quiet authority. As I stepped forward, I became aware of the assembled gentles arrayed in the seats below, quietly awaiting the beginning of the opera. I felt extremely conspicuous as I stood there looking out over the audience, sitting in anticipation of the first notes of the evening's entertainment. I sat hastily, my hat still clutched awkwardly in my hand. Miss Bang gracefully folded herself into the seat beside me, the scent of her perfume wafting over me and further clouding my senses. Professor Crackle deposited himself in the seat behind me.

I struggled to make sense of the situation as the gaslights dimmed. What business had pulled my uncle away? Who were these strangers who appeared so unusual, but claimed the duke's acquaintance? I stole a last glance at Miss Bang before the failing light dropped us into full darkness. *Who was this gorgeous woman?* I wondered, *And how could I manage to get closer to her?* The thought tantalized me for a moment longer, before the first strains of music sealed each of us into our own thoughts and the performance began.

Chapter Two

A Most Peculiar Solo

I am told opinion is divided over the best place in the house to watch opera.

On one hand are those who view the performance as a theatrical presentation. For them the ideal seats are as close to the center of the opera house as possible so they may see the entire stage and the full play of the performers in their roles. This approach tends to have one of two drawbacks. Either one is seated among the press of the crowd, rubbing shoulders with the most common of theatre goers, or one is in a box in the back of the hall, and thus unable to watch the show without the aid of glasses.

Another camp, one to which my uncle adheres, places the most prestigious seats near the stage, so the notes are clear and crisp and one can catch the subtleties of the performance close up. Naturally, the drawback of this approach is one must sit either on one side of the stage or the other. From such a vantage one is unable to properly observe the action on one side or the other, and thus one misses half the performance.

Yet another following claims music is the best part of opera, and therefore the best seats are determined by the acoustics of the opera house.

The performance is best enjoyed by closing one's eyes and savoring the nuances of sound as they pour over you.

I have always been in a fourth camp. I believe the best place to listen to opera is in a cafe at least two miles from the opera house. One should be fortified with a few bottles of wine and some attractive female company. From such a position, one should strain to hear the opera over the lively music of a local band and completely fail in the attempt. Only in this way can one get the maximum pleasure out of opera.

I was, by my own lights, much, much too close to the performance, lacking the proper social lubricant, and failing abysmally at being unable to hear the orchestra or the squawking of the performers. The only manner in which the evening's entertainment was successful was in my female companionship, and even that aspect was marred by the presence of a chaperone behind me, and the lady's rapt attention upon the actual performance.

Under other circumstances, I would probably have contented myself to simply sit and admire the process of Miss Bang's breathing, allowing my imagination to wander along the curves and valleys of her form. Unfortunately, such entertainments were denied me. My awareness of the gentleman behind me continued to distract and unsettle me. My mind kept coming back to the ominous thought he was actually an acquaintance of my uncle's and able to dramatically impact my future freedom with a casual word of disapproval in my uncle's ear. The worry nagged at my mind, giving me little choice but to settle myself in for a miserable evening, punctuated by stolen peeks from the corner of my eye at my well-corseted companion.

Sitting in the dark, listening to the troupe belting out incomprehensible German lyrics, and fretting about how to approach Miss Bang without incurring censorship from her associate or my uncle, quite effectively dampened the excitement I originally experienced upon meeting her. After a few songs the soporific effect of the performance took hold of me and I found it difficult to keep my eyes open. I caught myself several times as I almost drifted off to sleep in my seat.

I held out as long as I could, but sleep claimed me at last. I woke to the soaring volume of the female lead in the midst of an aria, which I presumed signaled the end of the first act. I blinked my eyes open and straightened in my seat to see the two main performers alone upon the stage. The man stood frozen in place with a pained look upon his face, no doubt intended to portray some heartfelt emotion. The slim soprano pranced about in front of him, pouring her heart out to the audience in what sounded to my ears like a banshee wail. I am sure my face wore a pained expression similar to the man's.

Sleep firmly banished by her caterwauling; I attempted to focus on the performance once again. The singer struck a pose, her arms flung wide, and filled the opera house with a single sustained note. For a frozen moment, every eye in the house was on a performer at the height of her art. Even to me, it was mesmerizing, as sound continued to pour forth from her, unwavering and strong.

Then, her face... changed. Her right cheek dropped about an inch and the pitch of her note shot upwards several octaves, sounding more like a steam whistle than a human voice. Throughout the theatre, patrons sat forward in their seats and clutched their ears, trying to understand the strange transformation. The performers remained frozen in their positions, seemingly oblivious to the incongruity of the situation.

Professor Crackle surged to his feet. He crowded to the rail of the box, blocking the aisle beside me. "It can't be!" he cried. "I didn't think it was possible!" He was clearly as excited about the bizarre turn of events as the rest of us were puzzled.

While the situation was livelier than the previous entertainment, it still grated upon my ears.

"What is happening?" I cried over the keening shriek.

"I can't tell from up here," he answered. "I need to get down there!" He looked around briefly, as if expecting a stairwell to appear before him. He turned and leaned over me, snatching a cane from the seat behind Miss Bang. As I sputteringly protested his behavior, he climbed up onto the balcony rail using the cane to steady himself.

"Are you mad, sir?" I screamed, lurching to my feet, and reaching for him. Before I could lay a hand on him, he leapt from the rail, his white lab coat fluttering behind him. He dove into the thick velvet curtains at the edge of the stage. Grabbing a double armful of the heavy fabric, he arrested his fall and slid to the stage below in a controlled manner.

Miss Bang joined me at the rail and I shared a confused look with her, all thoughts of romance temporarily displaced by the chaos.

"What does he think he is up to?" I asked her.

She shrugged her shapely shoulders and spread her hands out before her. "Investigating, my lord. Clearly this is not a typical aria. Harmonious is always looking for such curiosities. I hope you don't mind if he takes a little of the evening to look into it." She smiled shyly at me. I opened my mouth to question her further but the words failed to come.

Professor Crackle skittered across the stage, still clutching his cane in one hand. He slid to a stop beside the soloist and peered at her deformed face. He reached his free hand out to touch her, but before he could make contact, her jaw dropped another inch, her mouth becoming a gruesome figure eight. The keening abruptly stopped and steam poured forth from the woman's nose and mouth, forcing the professor to stagger back half a step.

In the abrupt silence, the male soloist moved. Sinking down onto one knee, he braced his hands against the floor, and opened his mouth, projecting a single low, sustained note. I wondered why the man continued his performance in the midst of all the chaos for a moment, and then realized his jaw must have displaced itself, for it opened so wide it seemed to have fallen from his face. The skin of his cheeks stretched tight as he opened his mouth at least six inches, his jaw practically crawling down his neck.

The note he sang rumbled forth and seemed to reverberate back at us from the very walls and floor. In moments we heard the tinkling of the gaslight chandeliers as they shook on the ends of their chains. Everyone looked about in confusion. We could no longer hear the man's singing as a separate sound. The note blended into a background rumble permeating the entire structure. The building trembled and the chandeliers swung violently.

Professor Crackle returned to stand beneath my uncle's box. He yelled to us and gestured with his hands, but the sound of his voice was swallowed by the reverberating noise pulsing through the opera house. He raised one hand in frustration and almost smacked himself in the head with his own walking stick. He looked at the cane with sudden surprise and ran his hands over it, deftly twisting and pulling at the filigreed decorations on its sides. Grabbing a silver ring on the shaft, he slid it towards the ferrule and the sides swung out and bloomed into a large cone.

He raised the head of the cone to his mouth, pointing the wide end out over the audience. His voice projected clearly through the growing rumble, amplified by an apparatus concealed within. "Flee, you fools! The whole building is going to come down. Get out while you can!" For a split second, no one moved, then a section of catwalk crashed to the stage behind the professor, sending splinters flying. The falling planks hitting the stage snapped the audience out of their shock.

Frightened people leapt to their feet and pushed toward the exits. Panicked screams punctuated their progress, barely rising above the din. In an instant the crème of Prague transformed into a frightened mob.

I raised my hands to my mouth to call to Professor Crackle, but before I could speak Miss Bang stepped onto her seat, then jumped to the top of the brass rail and sprung off the edge. She caught the edge of the thick stage curtains and curled herself around it, wrapping the fabric around her, and taking her momentarily out of sight, before as she spun back and gracefully slid down to alight on the stage. She disengaged from the heavy fabric and stepped toward the professor, handing him a black top hat with two sets of goggles wrapped around the bulk of its crown.

The two of them looked up at me and beckoned for me to come to them, down on the stage.

I shook my head at the idea. I wasn't going to jump out of my uncle's box. I dashed to the door. The stairs would be crowded with other opera goers, but they were bound to be safer than a foolhardy leap to the stage. Grabbing the doorknob, I twisted and pulled, but the door shifted slightly with a squeak and stuck fast. I pounded at it, but it failed to budge. It was then that I noticed cracks spidering across the wall and dust pouring from the cracks. I realized the door was jammed by the weight of the building above it. The vibrations were eating away at the walls.

I ran back to the box rail and looked for another exit. Debris from the ceiling fell around me as the building shook. The box across the opera house from me pitched forward and fell into the orchestra pit with a crash. The orchestra had already disappeared, leaving behind the larger instruments they could not carry with them. The fallen box rolled forward demolishing the abandoned instruments as it broke itself apart. I imagined my box staging an encore of this performance and shuddered. I was out of time and options.

Feeling like a fool, I clambered up onto the vibrating balcony rail. The shaking grew stronger and I feared it would pitch me off. Miss Bang stood on the stage looking up at me and motioning for me to jump. The professor had returned to the man and appeared to be searching the soloist for something. I teetered for a moment longer. "Better to jump than fall!" I said although the rumbling swallowed my words, and I lunged for the curtains. Instinct drove my reactions and I clawed for purchase on the thick velvet, but as soon as I grabbed a handful of fabric, my own weight yanked it out of my hands. Instead of coming to a controlled landing as the professor did, I spun in the curtain's folds and slammed hard against the boards of the stage. I recovered my wind with a shuddering breath and tried to push myself back to my feet. Miss Bang appeared at my side and helped me rise.

The professor appeared next to us a moment later. I could scarcely hear him as he yelled to us. "The soloists, they must be automata! Machines made to imitate human life! A fascinating feat, but they seem to be broken and I can't deactivate them! Miss Bang, take our friend out the stage door before the building collapses!"

There was a brief flash of light as one of the chandeliers pulled free of its supporting chain, the burning gas flaring and going out as it crashed into the empty seats below. Some small spark must have reached the broken gas pipe, as naked fire blossomed far above the crowd and danced back and forth like an infernal snake. The hall was brightly lit, but the flames made the room look as if it sprang from some corner of hell.

Screams rang out from the fleeing audience. Those patrons who still sought the exits shoved harder against their fellows in an attempt to rush out the doors.

We struggled to stay on our feet as the floor heaved beneath us like a raging sea. Huge chunks of masonry detached themselves from the walls and ceiling, bombarding the abandoned seats and filling the air with chips of wood, plaster, and brick.

"Go! Now! Run!" the professor screamed, his voice barely registering in the commotion.

We tried to navigate our way across the stage, Professor Crackle close behind us, but holes appeared in the bucking floor as trap doors broke their latches and fell open in front of us. Waves of scenery and curtains crashed down around us, as the ropes securing them to the walls and ceiling of the theatre pulled free.

We held onto one another to stabilize ourselves as we struggled to cross the quaking boards without tumbling into a pit or being swept away by descending scenery. As we scrambled over the fallen curtains and tangled ropes, the pervasive rumble was broken momentarily by a thunderous crack.

I looked back towards the noise and witnessed the line of luxury boxes opposite us pitch forward and tumble to the floor with a tremendous crash. The tumult was so great I couldn't tell if the rushing crowd made good their escape, or if their screams were cut short by the crushing weight of masonry. A cloud of dust and particulates blossomed out from the impact, pushing past the still unmoving opera singers and briefly blinding me as it struck my disbelieving eyes.

I stumbled as I sought to clear my vision, the hands of my companions holding me up, and guiding me in the direction of the exit. I cleared my eyes with a hand and tried to regain my bearings. We moved to the back of the stage and could, at last, see the exit before us, but before we could take another step, the walls around us crumbled and the roof of the opera house came crashing down, casting us into darkness.

Chapter Three

A Voice in the Darkness

Pain brought me back to consciousness. My head throbbed, and my body protested the abuse it endured. I lay dazed for a moment before my memory supplied the reason I was in such pain: the opera, the strange singers, and a building collapsing on top of me.

The weight of debris piled on me made it difficult to breathe as I lay sprawled on my back in the midst of the rubble. Everything ached, but no part of my body screamed out in protest. Or at least, not too much protest. I took it as a sign that I hadn't broken anything.

I tried to shift to a more comfortable position, but my legs and right arm were trapped by detritus piled on and around them. I managed to free my left arm, with a rattle of small pieces of wreckage. I opened my eyes, the blackness remained impenetrable. There was no sign of light. I was completely buried.

My breath came in ragged wheezes and my heart beat against the inside of my ribs, attempting to break through and make its own way to freedom. Dust invaded my mouth and throat and I gagged and tried to spit. My knuckles battered against something hard and flat. "Buried alive! I'm buried alive!" I heard a voice, wailing in the darkness, ragged with fear and panic. It took a minute or two before I realized it was mine.

A fit of coughing cut off my cries as the dust tried to crawl into my lungs. I clamped down on my mouth and tried to will the spasms to stop. *Shallow breaths. Won't do any good to dig my way out of here if I end up with black lung from breathing in dust.* I remembered a mine disaster from my studies. The miners were rescued, but about half died in the weeks that followed from breathing in too much dust.

I finally let out a long, deliberate exhale, using the spent air in my lungs to blow the dust away from my face. My lungs burned. I inhaled as shallowly as I could, but I desperately wanted to gulp for breath.

I tried to force myself to be calm. There had to be a way out. I just needed to find it. I groped around with my free hand.

Splintered wood and stone lay under me. I crawled my hand back to my chest and ran my knuckles into something that was hard and smooth. It lay above me as far as I could reach in any direction. It must have been a section of roof or wall. It had fallen on top of me forming a small, protected pocket. I was lucky that I hadn't been crushed.

The weight on my chest reminded me that was still a possibility. I reached out again, trying to find a handhold. Perhaps I could pull myself out from under the weight. Several times I thought I had found a suitable grip, but each time the stone or wood piece that I grasped shifted or crumbled away in my hand.

I was trapped.

"Help." I called weakly into the darkness, still trying to keep from breathing in the dust. "Heeelp!"

A low groan sounded from the gloom and my heart leapt. Someone else survived!

"Hello? Can you hear me?" I called again.

A male voice replied. "Yes, Yes, I can hear you. Give me just a moment." I heard a strange crack, then another. What was he doing?

"Professor Crackle?" I replied in a hoarse, dust-choked voice.

"Yes. Yes, my young friend. Are you hurt?"

I hurt all over, I thought, but replied, "I'm trapped in a pile of rubble. I can't move. I don't think anything is broken, though."

"Good. Good. Lucky you. Just hold tight. I'll be along in a minute." The odd cracking sound repeated itself a couple times. Then I heard sounds of debris shifting.

"Keep talking. I'll follow the sound of your voice."

Of course. "Sorry," I said. "Did Miss Bang make it? Is she all right?"

"I don't know. I must admit that I'm worried about her, but let me get you out first." More sounds of shifting stone. "Keep talking. What brings you to Prague?"

The question was so ludicrous I laughed, although my laughter quickly turned into a coughing fit. "What brings me to Prague? Seriously? We've just had a building fall on us, and you want to know why I happen to be in town?"

He chuckled in response. "Yes, I suppose it does sound a bit silly. Talk about whatever you like, then. I need to follow the sound of your voice in the dark."

"You don't have a light?"

He coughed. "I had a torch of sorts built into my cane, but I lost hold of it in the tumble. It would certainly come in handy right now."

I listened to him making his way through the rubble for a minute. He stopped, and everything got quiet.

"Still with me, my boy?"

Oh, right. "Yes, sorry. I'm just trying to come up with something to talk about." My mind was blank. "Um, I, I guess I'm here to try to find some freedom."

"Problems at home?"

"More of a long-standing disagreement with my parents. They want to control my every action. Everything with them is about 'duty' and 'proper behavior' and 'not being an embarrassment'. I can't do anything without someone telling me that I'm bringing shame on my family name." I sighed. "I just want a chance to find my own way in the world."

"Surely it isn't that bad, is it?"

"Close enough. And it isn't even my fault. My damned great-grandfather went mad and started a campaign against polite society. He renamed everything. Made our county seat into an obscenity. Even insisted on naming me when I was born. Threatened to disinherit my father and myself unless he got his way. My parents gave in, and it has ruined my life. Left me branded with a name I cannot use in public."

"Surely that is an exaggeration?" he asked, sounding doubtful.

I snorted. "Do you really want to know?"

"Certainly, my friend. Reggie didn't actually mention your name."

I told him.

The sounds of Professor Crackle crawling about the rubble abruptly stopped. "Goodness! And here I thought I'd gotten beyond being shocked. Your great-grandfather did have a way with invective, didn't he?"

"And the law. He filled his will with so many clauses to rob me of my inheritance if I so much as recognize a nickname. I'm cursed to be known by an obscenity for the rest of my life."

The rattle of stone on stone came again. It seemed very close now.

"You have my sympathies. Sometimes it is those closest to us who can hurt us the most. Even our own families."

The weight on my ankle suddenly increased. "Ow!"

"Ah! Sorry about that, old chap. I hope I didn't hurt you."

"Felt like you stepped on my leg."

"Really, well, let me see what I can do about that." Loud thunks and the clattering of shifting debris echoed in the space around us as the professor dug at the wreckage covering me. The weight slowly lifted from my leg as he flung the broken remains off to the side.

"Aaaah!" a cry of pain sounded in the darkness. A feminine cry.

"Titania?" He stopped digging. "Titania? Was that you?"

Silence...

And then a moan, just barely audible.

Professor Crackle exploded in a flurry of motion. I couldn't see him, but I could hear as he flung himself in the direction of the sound, stone and wood scattering in his wake.

"Professor?" I called, but the only response was the sound of him scrambling away from me. "Professor!" He was leaving me? Leaving me to die?

"Titania, my dear, where are you?" He called, his voice receding as he went.

"Professor Crackle? I'm still here. Please don't leave me!" My voice cracked as I called out to him.

"Don't worry. I'll be right back. But if Miss Bang is unhurt, she'll be able to help me dig you out. Otherwise we may have to wait for the rescue workers. Providing they are willing to send any to find us."

"Why wouldn't they send rescue workers?" My words came out in a squeak.

"If they decide the collapse is too dangerous, they'll assume that no one survived and they won't risk more men looking for survivors."

"Oh." I began to feel very, very cold.

He called out for Miss Bang again as he searched, but if she answered, it was too faint for me to hear in my disadvantaged position. There wasn't much I could do but wait and listen.

Professor Crackle called out in surprise, "Ah, no wonder it is so dark down here."

I asked, "What did you find, Professor?"

"The curtains from the stage, they seem to be draped across some of the supports that survived. They've got us wrapped in darkness. I was wondering why I couldn't even see the stars."

I heard him struggling with the heavy fabric, trying to tug it out of his way for several seconds. "Yes!" he cried, followed almost immediately by "Oh, no."

"Professor?" I called, "What's wrong?"

"We are in great danger, my boy. There's a fire."

"But isn't that good? You can see now."

"Unfortunately, the opera house's chandelier and stage lights were all gas lights. Those gas lines have most likely ruptured in the collapse. If we are extraordinarily lucky, the lines have kinked and the gas leaks will have stopped. But it is much more likely that the gas is slowly leaking into the basement or sub-basement where we have landed, and once it reaches the flames there will be a rather large and uncomfortable burn-off."

"Can you put out the fire?"

"Unfortunately, I can't reach it. It is at the top of a steep slope of rubble. They best we can do is get out of here quickly."

"Then perhaps you'd better come back and help me, Professor?"

"I've found Miss Bang! I almost missed her. She's the same color as her surroundings. All this dust..." He fell silent for a moment. "Oh, thank God, she's alive!"

"Good, now you can come and get me, yes, Professor?"

He didn't answer me. I could hear him try to rouse Miss Bang. "Miss Bang? Titania? Are you all right?" She coughed hoarsely. "Are you injured? Can you move?" he asked.

She coughed again and I heard the clatter of small stones. "I've been knocked about a bit," she said, "but I believe I am none the worse for wear, Harmonius. Where is the Duke's nephew?"

"I'm here! I'm over here!" I called.

I could hear them scrambling over the rubble. Coming closer!

"Titania, you must find your way out immediately. I can dig out his lordship and we'll follow as fast as we can, but you must get out before the gas ignites."

"Leave without you, Harmonius? You know I can't do that. Besides, we'll make much better time if we work together."

"But if the gas ignites..."

"If it ignites, Harmonius, none of us will be in very good shape. Even with your resilient nature, you'll be just as trapped. I couldn't live with myself if I escaped only to leave you behind. No, we shall all leave together."

"But, Titania," he began, only to have her cut him off again.

"Harmonius, you're wasting time and precious oxygen, and we have much to do. Now, show me where he is."

"Yes, my dear."

I heard the clatter of their footsteps as they moved closer to where I lay, and I felt a tear slide down my cheek. They weren't going to leave me. They were coming back for me.

I wasn't going to die.

My body shook with sobs of joy as I listened to them approach. There were going to rescue me. We were going to get out and live to tell the tale.

If the gas didn't ignite.

Their footsteps drew closer and I tried to stifle my sobbing for fear that they would hear. The streaks the tears left on my face I could explain away by claiming dust in my eyes, but I would hate for Miss Bang to think me a coward, no matter how extreme my situation was.

"My lord? Are you hurt?" she called out to me.

"It's mostly my pride, Miss Bang. Mostly." My head felt light and the air smelled odd and thick. "I don't think I'm seriously hurt, but I can't move, and it is getting hard to breathe." My head continued to swim. The atmosphere seemed stale, but did not smell of old air. Perhaps it was the dust, but it felt as if something was missing from each lungful.

"Steady on. We'll have you out in no time," Professor Crackle called, and then I could hear stones and chunks of masonry rolling off of me. The pace of the noise increased, and I could only assume that Miss Bang was helping the professor to shift the rubble.

Bit by bit, the weight on my legs lessened as they peeled away the debris. One of them moved a piece directly on top of my ankle and I flexed my foot for a second before a hand landed atop my leg. "Please try not to move, my lord," Miss Bang called to me. "You may have injuries you don't realize. If you move you could do permanent damage."

"You can't just pull me out?" I asked.

"No, my lord, if we did, we might do irreparable harm!"

"Titania," Professor Crackle interrupted, "We can't just wait until rescue services arrive. Once we get him cleared, we have to move him, even if we hurt him in the process."

"What?" I yelped.

"I'm sorry, but it can't be helped. The only chance any of us have is to get out before the gas reaches the flames."

"You're right, Harmonious. Just try to keep calm, my lord. We'll have you out of there as soon as we can."

I could feel Miss Bang's hands pulling the debris out from around my legs as the professor continued to shift the larger pieces from the pile.

With a grunt, the professor sent another block tumbling from atop me. "Hold tight," he panted, "We'll have you out in a jiffy."

I felt the weight lifted from my other leg as they cleared the debris. They scooped away the clutter and I could feel a hand grasp each of my ankles.

"Hold on, my lord. We're going to try to pull you out," Miss Bang called out. "Are you ready?"

"Do I have a choice?" I replied.

"No," she answered, and the grip on my ankles tightened as they hauled on my legs. I slid across the rough surface, stone and wood digging into me as they pulled. I cried out as they wrenched my arm from the weight that held it trapped. My sleeve caught beneath the press, and I heard the cloth tear.

Something pressed hard against my leg, before shifting on the sliding debris. The slab above me suddenly pressed me into the floor like a vise, and I was stuck fast. My breath was pressed from my body with a shuddering gasp.

The professor called to me, "Are you all right, my boy?"

I could not draw a breath to answer him for the weight of rock now bearing down upon my chest. I wiggled my feet feebly to show that I was still clinging to life.

"Something's shifted and he's trapped. We've got to find a way to get this wall off of him." Miss Bang's voice was crisp and matter of fact. "Help me lift, Harmonious." I could hear them grunt and strain for all they were worth, but the section of wall did not budge.

"We need more leverage," she cried as they paused, gasping from their efforts. I heard one of them scramble over the detritus.

"I don't think we'll find anything strong enough down here," Professor Crackle said. "Everything is broken and shattered."

One of them scrambled back. "I might have something," Miss Bang said. I head the sound of something being dragged across the floor. "Take an end and tie it around that corner of the wall."

"Good thinking!" Professor Crackle cried. "Yes, toss it over that cross-support. A crude pulley! Excellent," he declared.

I strained to draw in a breath. My ribs felt like they were about to snap at any second as I lay pinned to the floor. My blood roared in my ears as my heart struggled to keep pumping. I heard a voice at a distance. "Grab his feet. When I pull, you must get him out. If I manage to raise it just a little, pull for all you're worth." I couldn't tell who was speaking. Hands grabbed my ankles once again.

I could faintly hear the sound of someone straining, and the clatter of stone shifting. The pressure on my ankles increased as someone tried to pull me from beneath the slab, but I remained wedged fast.

I heard a shuddering scream. At first, I thought it was my own, but

I still couldn't draw a breath. As the scream continued and rose in pitch, the shattered fragment of the wall shifted and tilted upwards, relieving the pressure on my chest. As the weight lifted, my legs were yanked again. This time I slid across the floor in response to the pull. My trapped arm came free, the sleeve of my jacket ripped clean off and left in the dust. My body was yanked over the broken floor and I emerged from beneath the section of wall as the professor dragged me free.

The dim firelight filled my light-starved eyes. It was feeble, but enough for me to see the blasted wreckage all around us. One of the stage ropes had been tied around a corner of the broken wall, and it stretched up and over a surviving cross-beam from one of the stage supports. Miss Bang clung to the free end of the cord, her muscles straining and her feet braced against one of the uprights.

I rolled away from the hovering masonry just as Miss Bang gave a final cry and released the line. The cable whipped through her fingers, and the block crashed to the floor raising a shower of dust and dirt as she fell backwards into the debris.

Chapter Four

An Unwelcome Deliverance

I lifted myself out of the rubble and the professor and I scrambled to see to Miss Bang. Her dress was the color of the stone, covered with dust except for a few streaks where she tried to brush it off.

"Are you injured, my dear?" Professor Crackle asked as he took one of her hands in his.

"Nothing of consequence, Harmonious," she said as she pushed herself up off the floor. "Our injuries can be dealt with later. We must be away at once."

We helped her to her feet, and I found my own knees somewhat rubbery as well.

Professor Crackle jumped up brushing the dust from his clothing. "Yes!" he cried, "We have no time. We must be gone! Hurry!" He urged us across the floor, away from the guttering fires.

We scrambled into the shadows, away from our only light source, moving over and around scattered chunks of rubble. Peering desperately into the darkness, I asked, "How will we get out? Won't the stairs have collapsed?"

"Perhaps not. If the stairwell was framed properly, it may still be intact. Let's try over here." The professor moved off to the left, into the shadow behind a partial wall canted slightly towards us at an angle. "Aha!" He reappeared. "This is a section of the upper wall. The stairs are back here. You'll have to feel your way. Hurry." He motioned for me to move ahead of him and I stepped into the black.

With one hand on the wall above me, I groped in front of myself with the other. As the professor reported, my hand encountered the treads of wooden stairs. Blind in the gloom, the firelight blocked by a bulwark of theatre curtains and half-formed walls, I climbed on all fours, trusting my hands to find the treads ahead of me. I moved rapidly, scrambling up the stairs with greater confidence as I went, but my progress was brought to a sudden halt about halfway up when my hand came down on empty air and I almost pitched over the edge.

"Professor, we have a problem!" I called.

"What is it?" His voice came from just behind me.

"The stairs have gone." I felt around on either side of the gap in front of me. Splintered wood scratched my hands until I encountered masonry on each side. "They seem to have broken completely away." I reached ahead of myself, but was unable to find any kind of handhold. "I don't think we're going to be able to go this way."

"Damnation! Very well, we have no choice but to retreat and discover another way out." We backed down the stairwell and into the wan light, which managed to leak past the edges of the curtains and other debris. The thick, dusty air made me cough again.

"Harmonious?" Miss Bang's voice called out from somewhere along the back wall of the theatre. I could barely make out her shape in the faint light. "I think I've found something."

The professor and I felt our way over to where she stood. Her hand was upon a small metal door set into the wall. It was short and appeared to be very heavy. After a minute I realized it was a hatch, such as those used on naval vessels and airships.

"Excellent, Titania! This may just be our way out!" He grasped the wheel set in the center of the hatch and gave it a twist, but the wheel hardly moved before it caught fast and stuck. The professor bent down to examine it, probing with his fingers. He exclaimed as he found something: a small hole in the door to one side of the wheel. "It is either locked, or jammed. Let me see what I can do."

He reached into his coat and pulled out a small tube, perhaps eight inches in length. In the dim illumination, I couldn't make out any details of the tube's construction or discern its purpose. He rummaged in his pockets again, and pulled out a small tuning fork, which he attached to the end of the tube.

"Let us hope this works." He struck the prongs against the masonry wall beside the door. A single, bright, clear note sounded from the vibrating metal. A half a beat later a chorus of similar notes rang out from the device. He pointed the rod at the hole in the door and twisted it in his hands. The pitch of the note shifted, and the accompanying tones converged on the main note. Our little corner of the basement seemed to become momentarily brighter as more dust filtered down on us from above and caught hints of firelight. I heard noises above us. Stone rattled as it shifted and fell. Wood squeaked and creaked. The vibrations of Crackle's device agitated the suspended debris into motion once more.

"Your gadget isn't going to bring anything down on us, is it, Professor?" I asked, but then a loud click sounded from the hatch, forestalling further inquiry.

"Yes!" the professor cried, and spun the wheel with one hand. He fumbled with the other, silencing the odd machine and shoving it into one of his outside coat pockets. He hauled against the wheel opening the thick door. "Inside!" he commanded.

Miss Bang stepped through the hatchway, her shoes clicking on the stone floor. She moved forward with a hand on each wall. I followed after. The air in the small tunnel was moist, but considerably fresher than in the basement behind us. The professor climbed in and slammed the portal closed, shutting off the little light we had.

"That should give us some protection," he said, his voice seeming eerily detached in the gloom. "Use your hands and feet to feel the way. Keep moving. There should be some sort of ladder before too far, I wager."

"Yes, Harmonius," came Miss Bang's voice from the inky black ahead of me. I heard faint sounds of her feeling her way along the tunnel.

"Where are we?" I asked, "And what was that thing you used?" I groped my way along the wall trailing behind the sound of Miss Bang's shoes against the stone.

"I call it 'The Harmonic Spanner,'" came the answer, pride thick in the professor's voice. "A very useful device, my boy. As to where we are, I suspect it is an old access tunnel for inspecting and working in the storm drains. The opera house was old enough to be connected to the drain system, although the door might be a more recent replacement."

I nodded, forgetting for the moment that he couldn't see the gesture. We turned a corner in the dark tunnel and caught sight of a thin shaft of brightness ahead.

"Harmonious, I may have found our way out," Miss Bang said.

We shuffled closer to the beam, which proved to be light seeping down through a small hole far above us. Dust floated down through the hole and caught and scattered the faint radiance into the tunnel. More debris from the opera house's demise.

Miss Bang stopped under the glimmer of light and searched along the wall. She discovered a small alcove with metal rungs set into the brick, and climbed up the rungs at the professor's urging, blocking out our tiny shaft of illumination.

I could hear her hand slap against something solid a few times, and she called down, "There is a cover. I think it is a manhole. I can't shift it. Can one of you come up and give me a hand?"

"Move to the left, Miss Bang. Let me see if I can climb up along the right." I found the rungs with my hands and shifted my grip to the side. I carefully made my way up the ladder, pressing against Miss Bang's soft curves as I moved alongside her in the confined space. I achieved my desire to be close to her, but there was no opportunity to appreciate the moment. With a thump and a mild curse, my head found the hard metal above us.

Holding on to the top rung with one hand, I pressed above me with the other, feeling the cold steel of a manhole cover. I pushed upwards, but was unable to convince the lid to move. "It is heavy," I said.

"It may be blocked." Miss Bang's voice was close to my ear. I could hear the worry in her voice.

"I can't tell. I don't know how much one of these things is supposed to weigh." The cold stone of the shaft pressed in on me from all sides, except for the one occupied by the warm softness of Miss Bang. "I think I have an idea." Her proximity was giving me other ideas, but I wisely didn't say anything.

I curled my body around my knees as I moved my feet up a few more rungs. I leaned into the stone behind me, pressing my head and shoulders up against the cold metal of the manhole cover. Like Atlas of Greek mythology, I braced my arms above me and took the weight onto my shoulders. I pushed upward and felt the metal of the cover give way above me. I put my right hand on the top rung of the ladder for better leverage and pushed again. With a grinding noise, the heavy metal disc slid upward and I shoved an edge of it over the cobblestones bordering the hole. A thin crescent of light shone onto us.

Miss Bang and I wriggled our fingers through the gap and gripped the edge of the manhole cover. Pushing the heavy lid to one side proved easier than lifting it. With the metal disc thrust out of our way, we looked up into a moonlit back alley bordering the opera house. One wall of the old building still stood defiantly, defining a side of the narrow lane, but it was roughly truncated a few feet above the cobbles. While most of the wall fell into the building, along with the roof, a few shattered bricks were scattered about the street.

I handed Miss Bang out ahead of me, then hauled myself out of the shaft. As I cleared the manhole, the professor pulled himself up the ladder. From somewhere he produced his battered top hat and perched it on his head, cocked over one ear. One side of the hat was crushed, but the two sets of mismatched goggles still clung to it, apparently untouched.

I held out a hand to pull the professor from the manhole. As he reached up to grasp it, he said, "We must get away from here, there is still a danger of..." but he never finished his sentence.

He was interrupted by a sudden pressure, which built to a quiet roar in an instant and transformed into the noise and light of the explosion of the gas filling the basement of the opera house.

Timber and stone flew high into the air, riding the shock wave. The night sky turned bright red as a ball of expanding flame leapt into the heavens over the ruins of the opera house. The professor shot from the tunnel below, cannoning into me and knocking the two of us to the dirty cobblestones. Heat blossomed above us as a second gout of flame shot from the tunnel we just vacated.

As the flares of burning gas spent themselves in the night sky and faded, shards of wood and stone rained down on us again, joined by shattered glass which moments ago formed the windows of the surrounding buildings. In the distance, I heard the ringing sound of other manholes crashing back to earth in the neighboring streets and byways.

We rolled to our feet and staggered out of the alley to the street fronting the opera house, or rather, the ruins of the opera house. The street was clogged with pedestrians, carriages, and panicking horses, each trying to move to avoid the other.

I was heartened to see the vast majority of people filling the street appeared to be patrons of the opera, survivors of the evening's disaster. They gathered in knots exclaiming to each other. Some attempted to treat the injured, or clear away from one frightened horse or another. A number of constables directed the crowd to move further from the burning building and clear a path for the fire brigade.

We took a moment to take stock of each other's injuries. Miss Bang and I each suffered a number of bruises and contusions, and she confirmed I had a shallow gash along my hairline. As she tried to clean the blood from my hair, a woman from the crowd seized one of the constables and gabbled at him in high, excited Bohemian while pointing in our direction. The constable summoned two of his fellows and the trio approached us with a purposeful stride. Their posture was deliberate and wary, as if they expected difficulty. The first constable stopped in front of us and addressed us in Bohemian as his companions moved to either side, flanking us.

"I'm sorry, I don't understand," I said, spreading my hands to indicate my peaceful intentions.

"He said," the professor supplied in a dry voice, "the three of us will have to come with him and his men."

As I blinked at the professor and tried to fathom his meaning, one of the guards grabbed my arms and secured them behind me with a set of manacles.

Chapter Five

An Encounter with the Constabulary

I roused from my slumber at the sound of the interrogation room door slamming. I raised my head from the table and looked blearily up at the officer who entered the room.

He was an older gentleman in plain clothes. Greying at the temples, he sported a thick, dark mustache. His brown eyes were deep-set and he looked almost as tired as I felt. I struggled to sit up as he took the seat across from me. He threw a folder down on the table, and produced a fountain pen from within his coat. Flipping open the folder, he removed a pad of paper, and shuffled through a handful of loose documents.

As I tried to move my manacled arms to a more comfortable position behind my back, I idly wondered what tactic the officer was going to try. In the hours since the constables brought me to the station and shut me away in an interrogation room, other officers tried cajoling and intimidation, but seemed unwilling to accept the answers I gave them. They obviously did not believe I was telling them the truth.

He kept his attention focused on the papers, making no sound as he flipped from page to page. His theatrics were clearly to demonstrate I was beneath his notice, him being an officer of the law and I the presumed criminal.

Perhaps these power games were effective on the type of person he usually dealt with, but after being used and abused by various noble upperclassmen, I was quite immune to such treatment. My family's standing among the peerage was low, so such treatment was commonplace. At times I even dealt with contempt from the commoners. Between my classmates and my professors, I witnessed just about every power play known to man.

I tried to sit back and wait for him to choose to acknowledge my presence, but was unable to find a comfortable position. After attempting a few positions and finding them all untenable, I leaned against the table and attempted to read from his folder to relieve my boredom.

I could decipher the letters easily enough despite the squat script the notes were written in, but the Bohemian language quickly defeated me, so I waited as the officer carefully reviewed his documents. Among the depositions were freshly developed photos of the destruction at the opera house, and one particularly unflattering image of myself, freshly pulled from the rubble. Many of the shots were blurry, but it was clear very little of the building remained standing. After a few minutes of studying, he returned to the first page of the portfolio.

"I understand you have been refusing to cooperate," he said at last, his English thick with a Bohemian accent.

"On the contrary," I replied, trying to maintain an even tone, "I have been doing my best to cooperate, but your officers have chosen not to believe my statements."

"You say this, but you have not even given us your real name," he said, and looked me in the face, measuring me with his eyes.

"Actually, I have given my real name to three of your officers. All of them were suitably appalled, for which I cannot blame them, although the third one struck me in what I consider to be a most unprofessional matter." My cheek still stung from the blow and I would not be surprised to discover a red handprint was still visible on my flesh. "I fear I could not convince them I have been telling the truth. Please forgive me if I do not hold out any hope you will find my story more believable than they did."

He sat back and considered me for a long moment. "Perhaps. Perhaps I will surprise you. Perhaps you will try me now."

"You wish me to tell you my name?"

"It would be a start." He sat and stared at me, unmoving except for his steepled fingers, which gently tapped one against the other.

"I don't suppose I could get you to give me your solemn promise not to strike me."

"I am not in the practice of striking prisoners." He leaned forward again, doing his best to look bored. His face remained impassive, but he picked up the pen and held it poised over the pad, ready to write down whatever name I gave him. I did not find it the least bit reassuring.

"Could you perhaps explain why I have been taken prisoner? I think it might encourage me to be more responsive to your questions."

"Let us not get ahead of ourselves. Your name, please." His face was relaxed. He appeared calm and composed, but there was an unspoken threat to his tone.

"You are sure you want to hear this?" I did not have a good feeling about how this interview was going.

"Yes. It is a simple thing to speak your name. Let us not delay any longer."

"Very well," I said, "You have been suitably warned. I hope you won't regret it."

I told him my name.

The color drained from his face, but otherwise he didn't move a muscle. I must admit being impressed by his composure, although he was thrice warned about the sort of answer he was going to encounter. As the shock wore off, I could see his cheeks heating, but he controlled his expression and managed to suppress an angry blush.

His brows furrowed and he said, "This is not a game, sir. Your joke is not funny." He practically spat the last two words.

I sighed. "I regret, officer, I am not joking. I am struggling with the legacy of an ancestor with a perverse hatred for polite society. His influence is responsible for my unfortunate name, and the consequent difficulties, which plague me to this day. I suggest you do not take my word for it. I recommend you confirm my identity with my uncle, Duke Randolph."

He picked up the pad and dropped it into the folder, closing it again. "I am sorry to see you are not taking this seriously." He stood to leave.

I spoke up. "I am taking this whole process quite seriously! My uncle is the duke. He must be wondering where I am. He was supposed to meet me at the opera. Just send a message to the castle, for heaven's sake! You've already taken my papers and my calling cards. They've all got my name on them. What more do I have to do?" I did not want to go through another round of pointless questioning.

"I am not about to send such an obscenity to the duke! Do you think me a fool to fall for such a trick?" He scowled at me, and I got the distinct feeling I would soon be struck again unless I could persuade him to listen to reason.

"Then send a message to the castle and ask for the name of the duke's nephew. See if they send an obscenity back. Or at least ask if they could send someone who knows the duke's nephew by sight. It would solve the whole problem. One of the duke's carriage men drove me to the opera. At the very least, he should be able to identify me. He knew I was there tonight. They must fear I am among the dead!"

The officer's expression softened as he pondered the idea. I believe it was the first time someone considered the possibility I might be telling the truth. He retrieved his folder from the table.

"We shall see," he said and swept out of the room again.

I leaned over the table, resting my head on its smooth surface, and silently invoked my name to curse my great-grandfather and his "social experiment," which made such a wreck of my life. My familiarity with the words left me feeling hollow. A distinct lack of satisfaction was all I had.

I do not know how long I slumbered hunched over the desk before the door opened again and the same plainclothes officer scurried into the interrogation room. He jabbered at me for a moment in Bohemian before realizing I could not understand a word of what he said. He stopped, swallowed, and then began again more slowly in his heavily accented English.

"I am so very sorry, my lord. We, we had no way of knowing..." he broke off again, but I picked up where he left off.

"That someone would have the poor taste to name their child such a vile string of obscenities?" I suggested, and sighed. "In this matter, I hold you blameless and put the entire fault upon my great-grandfather, who seemed determined to find new depths of poor taste." The officer produced a handful of keys and moved behind me, hastily removing the manacles from my wrists. I spoke to him over my shoulder as he did so. "I *have* run into this before. Rather a lot, actually."

I stiffly brought my right arm forward as the constable worked to remove the remaining manacle from my other wrist. My muscles protested as they flexed for the first time in hours.

The final binding freed, he rounded the table to face me once more. "I must offer my deepest apologies, Lord ..." His next words caught in his throat. Several different expressions struggled across the officer's face. I recognized that particular look. Usually it was an indication I was dealing with a person of quality, who was torn between opposing social niceties: the need to address me properly, and the need to avoid uttering the filth, which was my given name.

Despite the mistreatment I'd endured, I chose to rescue him before he suffered too much.

"Most people find it sufficient to simply address me as 'your lordship'. It avoids the difficulties of pronunciation," I offered.

"Thank you, your lordship. Most kind of you. The... the behavior of my officers and myself was... inexcusable. All I can offer in explanation is that this assassination attempt has got us..." He shut his mouth with a sudden clack of teeth, biting off the rest of his sentence, knowing he had already said too much.

I stared up at the man as I rubbed my sore wrists. "Assassination? You mean to say tonight's disaster was an assassination attempt? An entire building brought down to kill one person? Good God! Who was the target, man?"

He raised his hands, palms toward me in a defensive gesture. "I am sorry, my lord, I am afraid I cannot discuss an ongoing investigation, even with someone of your rank. I... I have already said more than I should."

I sighed. "Can you at least tell me why I was being held here? It has been hours and no one has even told me why my companions and I were detained."

"Yes. Certainly," he said and seated himself across the table from me. "I am Inspector Janecek. My officers detained you when a woman from the audience at the opera house identified the gentleman you were seen with as an individual who leapt upon stage and attempted to kill the performers just prior to the collapse of the building. You were taken into custody until the particulars of the report could be determined."

"That isn't what happened," I protested. "Something went wrong with the performers before the professor went to investigate." The image of steam pouring out of the singer's ruined face came to my mind. "Someone else did something to them well before the performance."

"These are the things we would like to determine. I need to take your statement, my lord. Would you pardon me for a moment while I gather my notes?"

"Very well. Could I get something to drink? It has been a bit of a long night."

"I will have someone bring you some water, sir, while I get my papers." He stood, bowed quickly, and stepped briskly through the door.

I leaned back in the chair for the first time since they brought me into the room. I would have preferred something stronger, but I supposed water would have to suffice.

A few minutes later a young officer in a uniform arrived with a tumbler and a pitcher of water. He placed them on the table in front of me with a few words of mumbled Bohemian and then bowed his way out of the room. I filled the tumbler and sipped from it, finding the water to be cool and refreshing. I drank more freely and finally cleared the dust from my throat.

Inspector Janecek returned with his folder in hand once more. He sat and meticulously laid the papers out in front of himself, placing each page precisely in its place. He concluded his ritual by placing his pen in his hand and poising it over the blank page, ready to take notes. "Now, Mister... ah, my lord. Um, how familiar are you with the gentleman you were accompanying when you were detained?"

"Professor Crackle?" I replied, surprised a bit by the angle of his inquiry. "I just met him this evening, when I arrived at my uncle's private box. He said he was an associate of my uncle. Apparently, Uncle Randolph was off on some business or other and offered them the use of the box for the evening."

"Were you aware this gentleman and his companion, a Miss Titania Bang, have been linked to a number of dangerous incidents throughout the European Protectorate?"

"I, um, no," I stammered, "As I said, I hadn't met them before tonight. To be honest, I hadn't even heard of them. You're saying they're some kind of international criminals?"

The inspector made a note, and sifted through the papers in front of him. "Their role in the incidents is... unclear. Their names have featured prominently in several reports, but I don't have any record of charges being filed against them." He looked up at me from under hooded brows. "But they do not appear to be the most savory of companions, my lord. My records say Professor Crackle was exiled from England back in..." He frowned at his papers, "This must be a misprint. In any case, my lord, the Eternal Empress saw fit to exile him. I thought it important you be warned."

"Thank you." I said, my head reeled from this latest revelation. "Pardon me, Inspector, did I understand you to say he's been exiled from the British Empire?" I could not imagine how my uncle would have associated with such a criminal.

He shook his head slowly. "No, my lord. He is free to travel in the Empire, but he is forbidden to set foot upon the island of Britain without the express permission of Her Eternal Majesty, Empress Victoria."

"Oh. Um. Ah... Thank you for the clarification, Inspector." I could not help but wonder what Professor Crackle did to so anger the Crown.

The inspector cleared his throat. "Let us start at the beginning, my lord. You said they were waiting for you when you arrived at the opera house?"

"Yes, Inspector." I related the events of the past evening from the moment I entered my uncle's box to the time we were taken into custody. The inspector seemed particularly interested in the behavior of the two soloists and the timing of the events leading to our presence on the stage.

I corrected him several times when he suggested Professor Crackle went down to the stage before the soloist's face began to slide off, and was in fact the cause of her transformation.

Having to repeat the details of the incident fixed them quite well in my mind, and I fear I may never be free of the image of the woman's collapsing face, or of the horrible keening noise she'd made. The very thought made me shudder.

At length Inspector Janecek ran out of questions and packed up his folder again. "Thank you for your cooperation, my lord. I regret the mistreatment my men and myself have done to you tonight. I do not believe we need to detain you any longer. If you will wait for a few minutes, I will see about having your personal property returned to you. I hope that if we should have any additional questions we will be able to contact you."

"I cannot imagine what more I could tell you, Inspector, but, if you need me, I should be in residence at the castle for a few more weeks. Unless my uncle decides the destruction of the opera house is somehow my fault."

The inspector fixed me with a curious look for a moment, prompting me to add, "A joke, Inspector, and a bad one at that. Please excuse me, I am tired and it has been a very long night."

"As you say, my lord. Let me see about your belongings." He exited the room, leaving me alone to consider my situation. Could my uncle's associates have something to do with the destruction of the opera house? Were they even truly associates of my uncle's, or was it all just a tale to gain my confidence?

I sighed and rubbed my forehead. My mind was fuzzy from exhaustion and I would be able to think more properly on it once I returned to the castle and got some rest. It would all make more sense when I could think straight again.

Another young officer appeared with a folio containing my papers and other personal items. I emptied the folio and confirmed all of my possessions were accounted for. In broken English he asked me to sign a piece of paper to indicate my receipt of the property. He averted his eyes as I signed my name to the document, and folded the sheet over to avoid having to look at the words directly.

I chuckled to myself as I noted the name written on the folio was "unnamed suspect" and someone amended it, writing the word "Lord" in front of it. I am sure my great-grandfather would have been quite amused.

The officer indicated someone would escort me out when I was done and left with the empty folio, leaving the door open for the first time. The sounds of the busy office drifted in through the opening. I put on my rings and returned my papers and my other accessories to my pockets. As I placed my pocket watch back into my vest, I glanced at the time. Six-seventeen in the morning. Or was it evening again? I know I drowsed a few times, but Heaven help me if I'd been there around the clock. Uncle would be livid!

I stood up stiffly and walked to the door. I imagine I looked a bit like a brawler, or someone dragged from the streets. Dust and dirt still clung to my suit. There were spots of blood on my shirt, and my starched collar was stained as well. At least they cleaned the cut on the side of my head. It wasn't deep, but as a scalp wound, it bled.

Finally, my ragamuffin appearance was noticed and one of the officers who originally interrogated me approached. "My lord, I pray you will forgive me. I, I..."

"I would be grateful," I interrupted, "if you could see me on my way. It has been a long day and I am very, very tired."

He swallowed nervously. "This way, my lord," he mumbled and directed me through the station and to the front door.

I strode down the steps of the building and looked about. Across the street was a large park. I looked up and down the street, but failed to recognize any landmarks. I turned back to the officer, only to discover he had quietly shut the door behind me. I was alone on the streets of Prague.

I leaned against the stair rail leading up to the building and wondered how easy it would to be to hail a cab at six-thirty in the morning outside of a police station in an unknown part of Prague. Especially while looking like I'd been dragged out of a demolition site. Which I suppose I had been.

Chapter Six

A Stroll through the Park

I tasted the irony on the morning air. The events of the previous evening had given me what I yearned for: a chance to be on my own out in the world. Doubly ironic, since I was on my own at last, but my fondest desire was to return to the familial bonds I found so confining before.

In some ways, my parents were more permissive than those of many of my peers. But, like all parents, they had certain expectations of how I should conduct myself, and the path I should take in life. And they were adamant that I would fulfill those expectations, regardless of my willingness to do so.

I found their idea of respectable life to be dreadfully boring. At least, I did until I got my first taste of real excitement. The previous night's events left me with a new appreciation of boredom. Mostly. I still found much to be desired about respectability.

I waited in the early morning light hoping for some sign of a cab, or better yet, a proper carriage from the castle to gather me back into the protecting arms of family. Or, if my family's arms proved less than protecting, to at least send me to the embrace of a large bathtub full of hot water, and an equally large snifter of brandy.

I considered the merits of just setting off in a random direction until I was able to find a cab for hire, or otherwise establish my location and find either some transport or accommodation, when the door of the police station slammed open and sounds of protest poured forth into the cold, quiet morning.

"The cheek, the unmitigated cheek of it all, to accuse me of being behind the assault on Paris! After all I did to try and keep the tower from being damaged! The marquis assured me he set the record straight on the matter! See if I trust a Frenchman again!"

Professor Crackle shot from the door of the station and stomped down the stairs to the street where I waited. Unable to contain his energy, he paced along the sidewalk. His battered top hat with the two pairs of goggles bobbled on top of his head as he stalked back and forth, but somehow managed to remain perched on top of his head.

Miss Bang trailed serenely behind him down the stairs, ignoring his tirade and smiling in my direction.

"My lord," she said, "Are you quite all right?" I remembered the words of the police inspector: the professor and his companion were linked to a number of dangerous events across the continent, but not enough evidence was available for charges to be pressed. Was it coincidence, or were they somehow involved? Despite some of my baser desires, for a moment I considered turning away and ignoring her words, but then I saw the genuine look of concern in her eyes.

"Yes, Miss Bang. I am fine, just a bit tired," I replied.

The sound of my voice summoned the professor's attention. He whirled to face me, saying, "Ah! My boy, how good of you to wait for us! This whole affair has been positively ludicrous! Keeping us locked up like criminals, instead of letting us examine the evidence and determine who is behind this horrible attack. This incident wasn't some accident! It was planned! A deliberate strike! Mark my words."

"I haven't been waiting long, Professor," I said, "They only released me a few minutes ago. I'm still trying to determine how I am to get home." I knew I should not have said as much, but I was finding it harder than usual to control my tongue. My fatigue, I suppose. And there was something about the professor, which, despite the accusations of international terrorism, engendered trust and confidence. Something I couldn't quite put my finger on.

"They held you? Imbeciles! Didn't you tell them who you were?" No sooner were the words out of his mouth than a concerned look crossed his face as he realized the consequences of his suggestion.

"Yes, actually," I replied dryly, "several times."

The professor's outrage was undeterred. "You see! This is the kind of ham-fisted incompetence I am talking about! To detain a noble without cause and then just turn him out on the street when they are done with him. Appalling! Come, allow us to see you safely home."

"You have transport nearby, Professor?" I asked, surprised at the invitation.

"Always, old chap! Let us move to the other side of the park and my vehicle will be by in no time. Surely it is the least I can do."

I hesitated, remembering again the words of Inspector Janecek. What did I really know of the man? What had he done to be exiled by the Eternal Empress? *Was he* somehow involved in the destruction of the opera house? Or was he the assassin's target? Those questions whirled around my head as I looked at the disheveled man. But then I saw something in his eyes and they all evaporated.

There was a certain bond between men and women who share adversity. The man I was questioning was willing to lay down his life in the ruins of the theatre. When I was trapped, he and Miss Bang's thought more of my life than their own. They risked death rather than leave me behind. I knew he was a man I could trust. Both him and Miss Bang. Whatever their game, they did not mean me harm.

"Very well, Professor. I accept."

We crossed the street and entered the park, Professor Crackle leading the way and continuing his rant on the foolishness and stupidity exhibited by the police. I could hardly fathom how he managed to summon so much energy after being up all night, and after having a building fall on us. It was clear from his diatribe the questioning occupied most of the evening and finally ended when he demanded they either file charges or release him.

Miss Bang and I plodded along behind him with considerably less energy. She reassured me her encounter with the Bohemian police was long and repetitive, but not otherwise noteworthy. Still, I noticed she seemed concerned about something, although apparently not the events the professor expounded upon. I glanced about, thinking perhaps she spied some ne'er-do-wells who had taken it into their minds to assault a trio of gentles despite being within sight of the local constabulary.

Then again, we were quite a sight. All of us still covered with dust and dirt, scraped and scorched. The professor with his beleaguered top hat, dented and hanging at an odd angle on his head as he strode ahead of us in a high dudgeon.

The park itself was most orderly and ordinary. We walked along a broad promenade lined with tall trees on either side. Statues honoring various notable Bohemians stood at irregular intervals along the path. I failed to see anything alarming. The only thing notable about the park was the fact we three were the only persons present. The early morning air was strangely quiet. Not even the birds were singing, although I could see a few of them foraging about in the grass.

"Harmonious," Miss Bang called out, her voice shaking slightly with nervousness.

The professor continued his monologue, apparently without noticing the interruption.

"Professor!" she called again, more urgently.

"... and do they remember I was the one who stopped the prelitt infestation of Rome? I even received thanks from His Holiness himself! Do they remember that? No! They just go on and on about the damage to the west side of the Basilica! I hadn't even *arrived* in Venice when those streets began sinking into the canals, but they dared to suggest I was responsible!"

"Harmonious, the birds!" Miss Bang shouted in the quiet morning air, breaking into Professor Crackle's tirade at last. He stopped and turned to face us, confusion written plainly upon his face.

"I beg your pardon?"

"The birds, Harmonious!" she replied.

We looked about ourselves. A number of small birds were hopping about in the grass on either side of the path. They looked like starlings to me, but I couldn't be sure because of the distance. They were cautiously moving towards us, perhaps hoping for some crusts of bread.

Professor Crackle looked back to Miss Bang. "What about them, my dear?"

"They're too regular." She looked distinctly worried, almost frightened.

"Regular?" he asked, then took another look at the birds surrounding us.

Miss Bang spoke again. "Look at them, Harmonious. They're all evenly spaced!" As she said it, I saw it too. The birds were not scattered about the park, but were laid out in even rows a precise distance apart from each other. Rows that slowly curved together to form a circle. As I watched, they hopped closer.

"Oh, dear," the professor said. "Let us not tarry here. Let us move along nice and easy." His tone was worried, although he affected a nonchalant manner.

We began walking again. The birds didn't take fright at our movement. Indeed, they continued to move closer to us, surrounding us in a tightening cordon.

"I do believe the situation calls for a demonstration of extreme celerity," Professor Crackle advised us.

"What?" I asked.

"Run!" he shouted, and we bolted, dashing down the promenade as the birds around us took flight. Under normal circumstances, I would have expected the creatures to scatter in all directions, moving away from us. Instead, they flew at us and we were pelted by their hard little bodies. Beaks and claws tore at our clothes and skin. Miss Bang flailed her arms about, deflecting them, and from somewhere she produced an elegant fan and used it to swat the avian attackers away with surprising accuracy, blocking their progress and propelling some of them into the ground.

We ran pell-mell down the pathway, and the professor pulled something from one of his vest pockets and jammed it into his mouth. He blew franticly through the small device, but I was unable to detect any sound emitting from it. The birds, however, reacted dramatically to his silent whistle. They whirled on the professor, redoubling their efforts to strike him, some of them changing course in mid-flight in order to hammer him with their tiny bodies. In less than a second, the entire flock was attacking Professor Crackle.

The sudden assault caused him to sputter, dropping the device, which bounced off the pavement and was instantly lost in the surrounding grass. As if a switch had been pulled, the birds resumed their previous behavior, no longer targeting just the professor, but attacking the three of us equally and with lesser intensity.

The professor skidded to a halt crying out a loud, "No!"

He flung himself down on his hands and knees and dug through the grass searching for the object. Miss Bang and I stopped before we ran into him. So intent was he on finding his lost knick-knack, he ceased paying attention to our avian attackers as they tore at his coat.

From the corner of my eye I caught a glimpse of one of the birds flying directly at the professor's face. On instinct, I reached out and caught the creature scarcely an inch in front of the professor's nose. The sudden proximity caught his attention.

As I wrapped my hand around the bird, it curled into a ball in my palm. It felt strangely cold in my hand, almost metallic. I barely registered the odd sensation when the bird turned its head back over its shoulder and sliced into my hand with its beak. Startled by the pain, I let go and it escaped over the professor's head.

"Grab it," he cried, "We need a sample!" He turned after the fleeing starling, but two more attacked him from behind, knocking him to the ground.

Miss Bang and I took position over the professor and attempted to fend off the attacking creatures. Their bodies were unusually hard and my bare hands stung from my attempts to intercept them, feeling as if I was fielding cricket balls instead of projectiles of flesh, feathers, and bone.

Each time we swatted one of them away, it simply spun around and came at us again, rebounding on us like rubber balls bouncing inside an invisible room.

"Knock them to the ground!" Miss Bang cried, spreading her fan and using it to strike the attacking starlings from the air, the strange little creatures bounced off of the pavement with a hollow, metallic sound.

I attempted to follow her lead, but had difficulty striking down from above as the birds continued to pummel us. I was sure we were going to be overwhelmed by our little attackers when I stepped forward while striking at a bird and my foot accidentally pinned another of the creatures, which Miss Bang knocked to the ground.

As my weight came down, crushing the small creature, the others abruptly broke and banked off, scattering in all directions. The sudden pause left us all gasping for breath. We stood dazed, trying to recover our wits while waiting for the birds to renew their attack. Instead, nothing happened. As far as we could tell they all flew off, leaving us battered and bruised but in possession of the park.

"Found it!" the professor cried, picking his odd brass device from the grass at the edge of the promenade. He blew on it to clear the dirt and clippings from it.

"Harmonious," Miss Bang said, claiming his attention. "Perhaps we should move away a bit before you try again. Just in case they are attracted by it."

"Yes, yes. That would be prudent," he agreed. "But first, could you be so kind as to lift your foot, my lord?" he said and squatted down next to my left foot. I looked down and realized he was looking at the foot that crushed one of the odd birds, causing its fellows to flee the scene. I raised my foot gently, but the creature remained attached to the bottom of my shoe, causing my stomach to flip alarmingly.

The professor removed an unusually large handkerchief from an inside pocket and gently gripped the creature's remains. With a slight pressure, he popped it off of my shoe and stood up, examining it closely. I realized the bird had not stuck to my shoe by virtue of its own vitreous humours, but instead had bent firmly around my foot and required some force to dislodge.

"Look at you!" cooed the professor as he stood. "Where did you come from? Aren't you the pretty one? Oh you poor thing..."

"We are attacked by Budgies of Doom and now you're making friends, Professor Crackle?" I craned my neck to try and see what he found so fascinating about the small form he tucked into his handkerchief.

"Don't you see?" he said smiling like a small child with a new toy. "It's a clockwork! It is a work of art! Someone built this incredible replica, no, not a replica. An automaton, correct down to the minutest detail..."

Miss Bang interrupted him, saying, "Harmonious, shouldn't we be moving along? You did promise to return his lordship home."

"Ah, yes, my apologies, my lord. Let us be going." He turned and continued along the path, leaving Miss Bang and I to follow along behind him, and seeming to all the world as if he was simply out for a morning stroll and none of us were attacked just moments earlier.

I sidled up to Miss Bang as we followed and asked, "Does this sort of thing happen often? Automata? Buildings collapsing? Attacks in the park? England seems quite dull in comparison." *And tremendously safer,* I thought.

"Oh, no. Not nearly as often as you'd think." She favored me with a slight smile and hurried after the professor, tucking her fan away as she went.

Shaking my head, I followed along in their wake, wondering exactly what I had gotten myself into.

Chapter Seven

A Visit to The Argos

On occasion, I've found myself unexpectedly without transportation and been forced to make my own way home. Usually, I made my way back on foot, but at times I've had to find more creative forms of conveyance. But not even the time I begged a ride on a dogcart prepared me for the lift the professor offered me.

The promenade of the park opened out onto a square. Early morning traffic had not yet begun, and the area was open and effectively deserted. It seemed oddly peaceful after the excitement of the past few minutes. Professor Crackle walked to the center of the square and once again put his odd device to his mouth. I looked around nervously as he blew into it, but there was no sign of our avian assailants returning.

After a few blasts, he pocketed the whistle-like device and declared, "That should do it. Now all we have to do is wait."

"Wait?" I asked. "What are we waiting for? Another attack by Killer Clockwork Budgies?"

"No, no, my boy! For our transport!" He smiled broadly. "Fear not, we shall be traveling in style."

"I'm not sure I want to continue if we are likely to be attacked again. I believe I have had quite enough of being a target for an evening."

"Well, that is the question, isn't it?" The professor took off his battered hat and examined it for a moment.

"I beg your pardon?" He was clearly implying something, but I could not fathom what it was.

The professor looked at me over his glasses. "We were attacked, yes. The question is which of us was the target, my lord."

I recoiled from the accusation. "What? Why would I be a target? Who would want to assassinate me?" The pace of the conversation was quickly getting away from me.

"Assassinate? Ooh, now there is an odd notion. I was considering how an attack against yourself could be used as leverage against your uncle. I think a kidnapping would be much more effective means of gaining influence over the duke and duchess." The professor considered me. "Whatever put the idea of assassination into your head?"

I hesitated. Did Professor Crackle just say he intended to kidnap me? I cleared my throat.

"The Inspector said the incident at the theatre was an assassination attempt. It seemed ludicrous to me to destroy an entire building to try to kill one man, but now, after this latest attack, I am not so sure."

"Interesting," said the professor. "I wonder what our good inspector is thinking..."

A dark shadow crept out over the square, blocking the early morning sunlight. I looked up to see a huge airship maneuvering above us. It seemed to blot out half the sky, but was still flying so far above us I could just barely make out the faintest hint of the engines.

"Are you ready, my lord?" Miss Bang inquired.

"*What* is that?" I asked, and winced inwardly as I heard my own voice crack with fear. "Is it another attack?" I glanced about, wondering where we could find cover from such a leviathan.

"No!" crowed the professor. "That is our transport!"

The professor peeled both sets of goggles from the ruins of his top hat and tossed the beleaguered head covering to one side. He strapped one pair upon his forehead and passed the remaining pair to me. "You'll be needing these."

Puzzled, I held them in my hand and looked up at the airship as it maneuvered into position above us. It reminded me of a Zeppelin, but the markings on the body of the ship were in clear block letters and not the gothic script the German manufacturer used. The Union Jack painted on the bow indicated it was of English construction and faded letters denoted a Dover registry.

I could not recall ever seeing an airship like it. It was of extraordinary breadth and seemed like a small city hanging in the sky. The registry number was stenciled down the side of the ship, but no name graced the hull on any surface I could see.

As I stood staring at the ship, something small detached itself from the bottom of the craft. It appeared at first to be a small, dark disc, which then flipped light, then dark, then light again. As the object fell out of the shadow of the airship, a sparkle of bright brass reflected from it as it tumbled. As I watched, I realized the tumbling object was falling directly on top of us! I started to back away, but hesitated when I saw the others simply stood and watched as it plunged earthward.

I was about to shout for them to get out of the way, when the object re-oriented itself and slowed its headlong plummet. As it closed with us, I caught sight of a thick cable connecting the object to the airship above.

The disc slowed to bump gently against the cobbles of the street, and I was finally able to resolve it as a large, circular deck with sturdy brass rails surrounding it. A brass tower stood in the center of the platform with handholds spaced about its circumference. A bizarre collection of springs ran around the top of the tower and joined it to a thick metal plate, where the cable to the ship was affixed. Pneumatic pistons hissed as they countered the springs and dampened the swing of the lift.

The professor and Miss Bang strode calmly towards the hovering structure, looking for all the world as if there was nothing remotely out of place in having a platform suddenly descend out of the sky.

"Come along, my lord," Miss Bang called out to me. "It's perfectly safe."

Professor Crackle lifted a brass bar and ushered Miss Bang onto the floating deck. She pulled a pair of goggles from her reticule and put them on, then gripped one of the handholds on the central tower.

"Step aboard. We'll have you home in no time!" the professor said as he beckoned. With trepidation, I approached the disc and reluctantly stepped onto it. The professor secured the brass gate behind me. "You'll want to wear the goggles, old chap. It can get a mite windy," he said as he pulled his own pair down over his eyes and moved to the central tower.

Feeling quite a fool, I placed the lenses on my head and slid them down over my eyes. What was I getting myself into?

"Hold on!" said the professor.

I reached out to grasp one of the brass handholds, while the professor reached inside the tower and tugged twice on a thin cord. The disc immediately shot into the air, and I nearly missed my purchase upon the brass grip. My knees buckled underneath me and I held on for dear life as the platform flew upwards, slewing in the crosswinds as it sped towards the airship.

The wind screamed about us as we rocketed skyward. I held onto the tower with both hands and closed my eyes, bracing myself for the inevitable crash into the bottom of the ship.

A few moments later, the wind ceased abruptly. All was quiet, and I no longer felt any motion. I opened one eye to find the platform nested inside a plain room paneled in a cheery oak. A second brass rail mirrored the one attached to the disc, and an elaborate winch was suspended from the ceiling. One wall featured a large glass window.

"Welcome to my home!" boomed Professor Crackle as he opened the gate and held it for Miss Bang to exit. Still clutching the brass tower, I tried to pull my legs beneath me. After two attempts, I managed to rise to my feet.

The man on the other side of the window did not make me feel welcome. He wore the dark livery of a butler, but with a primitive touch: the striped pelt of a wild beast draped over one shoulder and tucked into his belt. His crisp white shirt and starched collar shone out between his dark skin and the black fabric of his coat. His fierce eyes swept over me, and a spike of fear held me rooted to the spot. Those dark, emotionless eyes continued on to the professor and Miss Bang, and a sigh of relief escaped my lips.

"I hope you didn't mind the lift, my lord," Miss Bang said. "We always find it quite invigorating."

"Invigorating," I stuttered, "I, um, I suppose you could say that."

I stepped off the platform with shaky legs. The man in the adjoining room opened a door set next to the window and entered, his movements smooth, flowing, and graceful like a panther. In addition to the fur over his shoulder he wore a kilt made from the skin of a similar creature. He exuded a strange air of civilized and savage mixed, of menace held in check.

It was my first time on an airship, and it was nothing like I was given to expect. The deck was reassuringly firm beneath my feet, and the wide room showed no signs of access to the outside, aside from the lift. Even the adjoining room appeared to be free of the portholes, girders, and ladders I expected to find on an airship. It reminded me of the mudroom of my maternal grandfather's country estates.

The professor spoke to the half wild man, "Manqoba, this is Duke Reggie's nephew. We will be giving him a ride over to the palace, but we have all had a *very* exhausting night. Would you be so kind as to show him to quarters? And see if we have some clothes that might fit him. We certainly cannot return the duke's nephew looking like we've mistreated him, can we?" He turned to me and gestured to the looming servant. "My lord, allow me to introduce Manqoba, my butler. Rest assured, he will take the finest care of you."

"Certainly, sir. If you will follow me, your lordship?" The dark skinned man spoke with a deep voice, which rumbled in his chest, as he gave me a sweeping gaze from head to foot. He gestured towards the door with one arm, and I dithered for a moment, knees begging to run the other way.

Turning to my host, I asked, "This is your home, Professor?"

"Yes, I live, work, and travel aboard this ship. I find it saves a lot of valuable time. She is my pride and joy. The ship..."

"*The Argos,*" interjected Miss Bang.

"The ship..." the professor corrected, but Miss Bang interrupted again, completing his sentence with, "... is called *The Argos.*"

The professor began a third time, "The ship, which Miss Bang insists on calling '*The Argos*', has been my faithful conveyance for many years now.

But we have time enough for all that later. You are tired. Get some rest, we will be at the castle soon enough."

Despite my misgivings, I followed the hulking butler through the observation room and into a comfortably appointed lounge with angled windows along one side, providing an excellent view down into the city. The lounge was laid out like a sitting room, with wallpaper and a wooden rail around the edge of the room at chair height, excepting, of course, the one windowed wall. From there he led me out into a wide hallway, up a flight of stairs, and into a corridor lined with bright gaslights.

Manqoba opened one of several doors along the hallway and motioned me within. I paused for a moment and was startled when Miss Bang spoke from just behind me. I had not realized she followed us.

"I am just two doors down, my lord," she said. "Should you need assistance with anything, feel free to call." She continued on down the hallway and entered her room on the opposite side of the corridor.

I entered the indicated room, and the butler silently followed as my larger than life shadow. The room was richly furnished, easily the equal to the finest estate I ever visited. The pristine furniture appeared to be antique, or else excellent reproductions, and the room was scrupulously clean. A large canopy bed sat off on the left side of the room, with a conversation suite arrayed to the right. Shuttered windows on the wall opposite the door looked down at the city below. The butler flowed past me without a sound and indicated one of two doors set in the wall just beyond the bed.

"You will find the lavatory through here, my lord. Shall I run a bath for you?" he rumbled.

"Ah, no. No, thank you. I believe I can manage."

The man nodded and retreated to the door as I sat heavily on the side of the bed.

He turned and added, "I will return in a few minutes with fresh clothing, sir. Will there be anything else you require before I go?"

"No. No, I don't think so. Thank you."

The butler silently disappeared, securing the door behind him. I confess I felt a strange sense of relief at his going. Being in the same room as Manqoba felt like being in the company of a live tiger. There was nothing in his manner or appearance to account for the feeling, but I still could not shake it.

The closest I ever came to feeling that way was old Professor Kirkpatrick, an octogenarian Scot who was the bane of my existence for my entire first form at university. The two men were completely unalike, with the exception of the aura of danger each wore like an invisible cloak. I had the distinct feeling that Manqoba could break me like a dry twig if he so chose.

Finally given a moment on my own, the weight of my exhaustion hit me like a hammer and I sprawled back upon the bed. I think I would have dropped right off to sleep at that moment, were it not for the bruises, which covered my back and shoulders. The weight of my body as I lay on the bed prodded my injuries and set them screaming again. I rolled my eyes, heaved over onto my side, and dragged myself back upright.

I stripped away my jacket and kicked off my shoes before stumbling into the washroom. The floor was marble, but it was warm to my feet. I wondered at the weight and expense of such furnishings until I remembered how monstrously large *The Argos* was. The gas reserves must be enormous!

A large claw-foot tub sat upon a dais across from a basin, a water closet, and a bidet. A small cabinet was mounted into the wall to one side of the dais. I opened it and found it was stocked with thick towels, soaps, a shaving brush and a razor. I closed the door and looked at myself in the mirror above the basin.

I looked like someone dragged me through the sewers. I couldn't keep myself from laughing out loud at the thought. Actually, I looked like a building was dropped on me, I was dug out from the rubble, ran through a sewer, was blown up, and then attacked by Killer Clockwork Budgies.

The bath suddenly sounded very inviting.

I twisted the knobs above the tub. They turned smoothly and easily with nary the squeak or groan of lesser plumbing. The only sound was the soft gurgle of fluid as it gushed forth into the tub. The hot water took almost no time at all to pour steaming from the tap, making me all the more eager to immerse myself in its warm embrace. Stepping back into the bedroom, I stripped off the rest of my tattered clothing, dropping it on the bed. I returned to the bath and gratefully dipped my body into the steamy water.

I winced as the first shock of immersion made my injuries protest anew. But after a moment to adjust, they quieted down again and I felt the heat of the water as it splashed over my body. A sigh escaped my lips as the warmth slowly penetrated my aching limbs and little by little the pain began to blur and subside. My muscles unknotted as I sat and soaked. I could feel the tension bleeding out of my frame and into the delightful water. Leaning back in the tub, I closed my eyes and let the trials of the last few hours slip from my mind.

Chapter Eight

An Uncomfortable Question

There was something about a tub of warm water that brought about a sense of peace and well-being. Perhaps it was the symbolic return to the womb, or the feeling of weightlessness. All I knew was as I surrendered myself to the bath and let the warmth penetrate my flesh, I was overcome with a sense of lightness and thoughts fell from my mind, leaving me with a profound feeling of tranquility and contentment.

In short, I fell asleep.

I returned to consciousness a considerable time later. I didn't remember shutting the water off, but the tub did not overflow. The bath cooled as I slept. I dunked my head to wake more fully and hastily washed in the tepid fluid instead of running a fresh bath. Surely by now we had arrived at the castle and the others were waiting impatiently for me to emerge. While my hosts might not be willing to intrude upon a guest, I was half surprised Uncle Randolph hadn't seen fit to send someone to retrieve his errant nephew.

As I toweled off, I noted the room was lit by an ingenious combination of gaslights above the mirror and a glowing glass trim mounted into the wall. The light from the trim had an odd quality to it, and I could not fathom how the trick was done. Perhaps it was similar to the deck prisms naval ships used to feed sunlight down into the lower decks? After a few moments of wondering, I gave up the puzzle and scolded myself for pointless woolgathering.

I discovered a dressing gown hung on the back of the bathroom door, which I did not remember being there before. Wrapping the robe about myself, I exited the lavatory. My clothing was gone from the bed and a new suit hung on a valet standing next to a privacy screen. On top of the vanity the contents of my pockets were neatly laid out so I was easily able to account for my possessions. My shoes likewise were missing from where I kicked them, but were nowhere to be seen. In their place, a pair of stylish boots, which appeared to be in my size, stood at attention at the foot of the bed.

I crossed to the valet and inspected the outfit. It was of good quality and if it was not new, it was well cared for. It was not a stylish cut, but it was much better than I had a right to expect. After the events of the previous night, I would have been happy for a mismatched set of laborer's clothes, so I was doubly grateful for the loan of a tasteful ensemble.

More than satisfied with the clothing supplied for me, I dressed quickly and made myself presentable. A set of brushes was thoughtfully left on the dressing table during my bath and I snatched them up and tried to tame my hair into some sense of order.

Everything fit well, the butler apparently having an excellent eye for sizes. The boots were a little tight, but appeared to be new and never worn, which suited me rather well. I have always felt there was something unnerving about wearing another man's boots.

I checked my attire one final time in the full-length mirror, and, finding myself in a greatly improved state, I declared my toilet complete and exited the room. Seeing no sign of other activity in the corridor, I moved down the hallway towards the door Miss Bang indicated was hers.

The thick carpet on the floor absorbed the sound of my footfalls as I approached the room. The door in question was slightly ajar and I could hear a conversation within. I paused outside and was about to knock when the voices resolved into distinct words and I waited for a break in the discussion before knocking.

"He rescued you from the ruins? That is so *romantic*, Tanya! He risked his life to come back for you!" an unfamiliar female voice squealed.

"Don't be silly, Tinka. We were all caught in the collapse. Harmonious simply recovered faster. It took the two of us to dig out the duke's nephew. We were very lucky." The second voice I recognized as Miss Bang's, but she sounded much more relaxed. She was clearly speaking to someone with whom she shared her deepest confidences.

I perceived I was inadvertently eavesdropping on a very private conversation, and started to turn to leave when the other woman continued.

"That other bloke was lucky that you and the professor were about. You probably should have hoofed it as soon as you got up, but, you know the professor! He's a tough old bird! He can take just about everything!"

"He isn't quite immortal, Tinka. I worry that one of these days he will run into something that even his thick skin can't deal with." Miss Bang sighed, "Much as I love him, Harmonious will never accept me until a cure is found for his condition, nor until the Empress lifts his exile. He is a very proud man, you know. He cannot bring himself to let another share in what he considers his dishonor, not again. His heart was broken that way once before, and I would not put him through it again, even if it means I must break my own heart for his sake."

"Maybe I should just tell him for you, Tanya..." the other voice wheedled.

"Tinka!"

"Oh, I'm just teasing you. I wouldn't do that to you!"

"Just as well."

"Besides, what about your new young friend? He's so good looking! He's positively dreamy!"

"Tinka! Have you been spying on our guest?" scolded Miss Bang.

"I just sneaked a little peek as he was coming on board. It's not like I went into his room or anything." The voice sounded like a teenage girl. "Although that might not be a bad idea!"

"Tinka! Tinka, don't you dare!"

The door in front of me suddenly swept open and I was staring into the blue eyes of a tanned young woman with strawberry blonde hair swept back into a loose tail behind her head.

"I, I, uh..." I sputtered, and dropped my eyes from her face in embarrassment at being caught listening outside the door.

My eyes next lit upon her breasts and I stepped back in sudden surprise. Instead of a single pair of breasts, two pairs blossomed from the young woman's chest, a larger pair placed above a smaller and each bound into her dirty white shirt by a leather harness, which cupped and supported them and was as stained and worn as her leather pants. I threw myself across the passage in horror. A second set of shoulders budded from her rib cage, and an extra set of arms sprouted from those shoulders. The sight so unsettled me I blurted out, "Oh, my dear god!"

The young woman cried wordlessly, turned, and fled down the corridor, disappearing around a corner in an instant, leaving only the sounds of her sobbing in her wake. I leaned against the far wall babbling incoherently as Miss Bang emerged from the door of her room.

"What was that?" I cried out, all pretense of composure banished by my shock at the sight of the deformed young woman.

"Who," replied Miss Bang, her tone as cold as ice. Her demeanor transformed the pale blue day dress she wore into a suit of chill armor. "She is a 'who', not a 'what'. In particular, she is Professor Crackle's daughter and my best friend, so I shall thank you to keep a civil tongue in your head, sir."

"His daughter? How...?" I could see by the expression on Miss Bang's face I was only digging myself in deeper. I held up my hands in a gesture of surrender. "Please, please! Too many shocks, too fast. I cannot take it all in. Please, give me just a second."

Her face relaxed marginally, but I was still on dangerous ground. I tried to break the confusing thoughts bouncing about in my head down into individual ideas.

I composed myself and asked in an even tone, "I don't understand. How can she be his daughter? He's not nearly old enough."

Miss Bang replied matter-of-factly, "Professor Crackle is considerably older than he appears. While he is quite old enough to be Tinka's father, as it happens, she is adopted. We believe her parents were missionaries who died while ministering to some of the more remote tribes of Africa. Harmonious discovered her running wild in the jungle and took her in when she was about six years old."

"And her..." Words failed me and I gestured to my own chest and arms in my struggle to find a way to ask the question.

Miss Bang replied to my unasked query, her tone still dry, but not as cold, "Tinka is a kalinid. She has an extremely rare form of polymelia known as Kali's syndrome. It is a very rare genetic trait, which causes additional limbs to form in the womb. It is similar to chimera or conjoined twins, although with polymelia it is one individual with additional appendages, not siblings whose bodies have grown together. In most cases, the appendages are not fully formed, but with Kali's syndrome, each limb is whole and healthy."

"Is there no treatment?" I asked.

She looked at me archly, and the chill crept back into her voice. "Treatment is hardly necessary. Would you be willing to give up a perfectly good arm or leg, simply because those around you lack it?"

I felt my cheeks flush with embarrassment. "No, no, I take your point, Miss Bang. All I can say in my defense is I was not aware of such..." I stopped myself before I could use the word "deformity". "Of such a condition," I concluded. "I had no desire to upset you or your... friend."

"Tinka is very self-conscious about her appearance. I should think the proper thing for you to do is to apologize for your behavior." One eyebrow lifted as Miss Bang regarded me, and I got the distinct feeling I would be in grave peril to disregard her advice.

"You are quite right. I shall endeavor to do so at the first opportunity. But I do not believe now would be the ideal time to attempt such an apology."

"True," she replied in a dry tone.

I turned away from Miss Bang, looking for some escape from my embarrassment, but she recaptured my attention once again.

"My lord, a question," she said.

I turned back to her, feeling the flush upon my face again. "I am at your service, Miss."

"It is perhaps my turn to be impertinent, but the mystery of it keeps nagging at me. When your uncle mentioned you, he only referred to you as 'my nephew'. He never mentioned you by name. What is your name, my lord? And why all the mystery concerning it?"

My throat became quite dry, and I cursed my great-grandfather once again. "My name..." I paused again, trying to find a phrasing that would not further my embarrassment. "Well..."

"Yes?" Her tone indicated she was quite seriously interested.

"Suffice it to say," I proposed, "my name could be considered a most impractical joke from one of my ancestors. My great-grandfather, in fact. Through his influence, both my father and myself were saddled with names that are, frankly, not fit for polite society. Unfortunately, he also added a clause to his will stating that should we attempt to have our names changed, or adopt a more socially acceptable pseudonym, we will each forfeit our inheritance. My great-grandfather was a bitter, bitter man, but an excellent lawyer. My father has been trying for most of my life to get the will broken. So far without success."

"I am not sure I understand," she said.

"When my father was born, my great-grandfather invoked an obscure right as head of the line to name the child. He then christened my father with a collection of curse words as his name. Great-Grandfather apparently felt the forms of social politeness were an elaborate deception and sought to make my father a weapon against polite society. Or it may have just been an expression of his grief at the recent deaths of his own wife and son, the son being my grandfather. By the time anyone sought to object, the deed was done. At the very least it kept father from being announced at court."

"Your great-grandfather does sound like a very troubled man, but we were speaking of your name, not your father's."

I sighed. "When I was born, the old man invoked the right again, over my mother's very loud objections. Her family tried to support her, but in the end they gave in, when Great-Grandfather threatened to disinherit my father and me. It seems my father's name failed to elicit the response he desired. After taking many years to think at great length upon the subject, he crafted a name of surpassing obscenity for myself. I have noticed it has quite an unpleasant effect upon people who are unprepared for it. I would not inflict it upon you unless you are quite sure you are braced for the shock."

"If you cannot tell me your name, then what am I to call you?" Miss Bang eyed me skeptically.

"If you insist upon knowing it, I can give you one of my calling cards if you like. But I doubt you will be comfortable speaking any part of it. As I said, it is not fit for company. As to what you may call me, most people settle on simply addressing me as 'my lord'."

"Really?" She did not sound convinced.

"Perhaps this is a matter where we might consult the professor?" I suggested, hoping to change the subject. "Surely he has waited over long for me to emerge from my cabin."

"Very well," she said and stepped out of her room, closing the door behind her. "At the very least, I should inform him you have refreshed yourself and are ready to continue."

"That would be ideal," I agreed.

Chapter Nine

The Professor's Laboratory

To say my name has been an embarrassment to me all my life would be putting it mildly.

It brought shame and distress to my parents and myself, but it also spawned other humiliations more numerous than I care to mention, starting from the day I discovered that my name was not "Son", and leading up to the scene with the professor's daughter in the corridor.

Normally, I wished for the ground to open up and swallow me whole. In this instance, it would prove sufficient for the deck to simply give way beneath me and drop me to the pavement below.

I sincerely hoped that Professor Crackle would find some way to deflect Miss Bang's curiosity, at least until I could leave the ship and deal with whatever punishment Uncle Randolph was sure to mete out for the disastrous evening at the opera. My only hope was someone else would reveal my name to her, if she continued to pursue this curiosity.

Preferably after I had departed the country.

Miss Bang led me up a flight of stairs and down another long hallway. I expected her to take me to the bridge of the airship, and was unprepared when our destination proved to be a large laboratory.

The room looked as if it was lifted whole from a university. Workbenches were arranged in orderly rows, each apparently dedicated to a different scientific study.

Along one wall was a table supporting a large and intricate assortment of glass pipets, flasks, and other unidentifiable bits connected in a vast and confusing array. Burners were arranged beneath several boiling flasks, and a brown liquid, dripped into an equal number of insulated bottles on the opposite end of the table. The fluid gave off a rich, heady aroma, which managed to be woody, nutty, and pungently roasty at the same time.

Another table contained a microscope and a variety of weights, scales, and tools for handling mineral samples.

At the far end of the room stood several large pieces of equipment bearing the Holyfield Industries gear and star logo. Each of these was festooned with the thick cables and massive switches, which marked electrical experiments.

Another bench resembled a machinist's workstation, with a number of belt driven devices for cutting, boring, and shaping metal.

As we entered, we found Professor Crackle, still in his attire from the night before, working at a table littered with cogs, springs, and all manner of small tools.

"Harmonious," Miss Bang called as we entered.

The professor did not appear to notice our approach. Indeed, he seemed to be intently studying something through a jeweler's loupe lodged in his right eye. He muttered something to himself as he did so, but I was unable to make out his words.

"Harmonious," Miss Bang repeated more forcefully as she laid a hand upon his shoulder, "we need to speak with you about a matter..."

"I know this hand! I know I do. I just can't remember where I've seen it before," the professor interrupted, turning to Miss Bang with the loupe still firmly affixed to his eye. "But I know I've seen this work before! It is exquisite! How could I have met someone who could produce work of such quality," he gestured with what appeared to be a wing from the bird I crushed in the park, "and not remember who it was?"

"Harmonious, I need to ask you about our guest," she said gesturing to me where I stood near the door marveling at the perplexing array of equipment in the laboratory. "He says..." she started, but with his attention directed towards me, Professor Crackle charged over and regarded me through the loupe.

"How could I forget seeing work of this quality? I know the maker, but I just can't remember the name. Have you ever seen such work? Look at it, look at it!" He shoved the detached wing at me, and I recoiled as the metal appendage flapped in my face. "It is a masterwork! Each feather is individually modeled and attached. The articulation is perfect! The attention to detail..." I tried to look at the proffered wing, but the professor kept gesturing with it and manipulating the wing as he talked, making it impossible to focus on any portion of it.

"Professor!" Miss Bang came close to shouting, "about our guest!"

He fluttered his hand over his shoulder. "Let him rest, let him rest. He's had a very trying evening. I'm sure he must be exhausted." The professor continued to fiddle with the detached wing.

"He's right here, Harmonious!"

He whirled around in a circle. "He is? Where?"

"Right there, Harmonious," she said pointing at me once again.

"Oh?" He looked at me again through the loupe. "Oh?" He opened his left eye and regarded me again. "Oh! My boy, are you feeling better now? I know I promised to return you promptly to your uncle, but you were so tired, I figured it wouldn't hurt any to let you get some rest. And I've made such amazing discoveries! It is a pity our only sample is so damaged, I would have loved to..."

"Harmonious, will you pay attention?!?" Miss Bang appeared to be on the verge of losing her temper.

"What is it now?" he asked. "Can't you see I'm working?"

"Harmonious, do you know our guest's name?"

He looked from Miss Bang to myself and back. "What? Yes, yes, of course I know what his name is. Don't be silly."

Miss Bang carefully composed her expression before continuing. When she spoke, her voice was smoothly courteous, as if she were simply making polite conversation at a social gathering. The overall effect sent a chill down my spine. "Harmonious, would you please introduce me to our guest?"

He looked at her, clearly confused, and I did my level best to keep from laughing at the expression on his face. "But you've met. He's been with us all evening."

Her tone was utterly calm, and she spoke with a measured precision indicating the listener better satisfy her or he would be in an immense amount of trouble. "Harmonious, would you be so kind as to tell me our guest's name?"

"Why, certainly. His name is..." and he stopped, jaw frozen and a look of horror contorting his features. I could almost hear the click as the pieces came together in the professor's mind. The sudden realization of the name my great-grandfather bestowed upon me appeared to have left him momentarily unable to speak. His eyes opened wide in shock, and the loupe tumbled from his face. I dove forward and was able to grab it before it hit the floor.

I straightened and handed the loupe back to the professor. "I did try to explain to Miss Bang my name isn't exactly fit for proper society. I fear she didn't believe me."

"Ah. Well, I am afraid that... our young friend is... um. That is... he is quite correct about the, ah, impropriety of his given name. It would be... terribly unseemly for me to utter such language..."

"You're serious!" Miss Bang's brow was creased in ire. The hint of fire blazed behind her eyes.

He blinked at her. "Of course, I'm serious. Such a joke would be in very bad taste!"

"I don't believe anyone ever accused my great-grandfather of having good taste," I commented ruefully.

The professor turned to me. "Your great-grandfather was actually quite a thoughtful fellow in his youth. He did throw the most excellent parties. I never did find out what made him such a misanthrope as he got older. I'd often wondered... Wait! Wait, I was going to tell you something. Something I'd just discovered." He looked down at the wing in his hand. "Yes! That was it! You remember the birds, the clockwork birds?"

I nodded. "Yes, Professor. It *was* just earlier this morning." I wondered if it was still morning.

Professor Crackle nodded vigorously. "Yes, they're a perfect recreation of the living creature. Or at least as best as I can tell, given the damage the sample sustained. If only I could examine an intact specimen."

Miss Bang spoke up. "You're drifting again, Harmonious."

"No, no, no, no! This is important. Did you get a good look at the singers? The male and female leads?"

"At the opera?" I asked. I wasn't quite sure where he was leading.

"Yes! Did you get a good look at them?" He seemed very agitated as he leaned toward me for my answer.

"Well, Professor, I am afraid I wasn't really concentrating on them for most of the performance. And when things livened up at the end, my attention was, well... on other things."

"And you, Titania?" He whirled to face Miss Bang.

"Other than the final song, they seemed quite capable, although somewhat uninspired performers." She paused in thought for a moment, touching one finger to her lips. "I'm not sure how to describe the final performance."

"Drat. I hoped one of you got a better look. Now we shall have to find what is left of them." The professor moved back to his workbench and put down the wing and his loupe.

"You want to go find their bodies, Professor? Isn't that a task better left to the police?" I did not fancy the idea of sifting through the rubble for pieces of the dead performers.

He turned to me. "Their remains, yes. But their bodies, I think not." He lifted the wing again and shook it to illustrate his point. "I think they were clockwork."

"A clockwork man? How is that possible?" I looked to Miss Bang, but she seemed fascinated by the idea.

"But such intricate detail, Harmonious... and such a complex series of actions to perform upon the stage. They were actually singing. It wasn't a phonograph recording. Even with the latest equipment, one can tell the difference. I've never heard of an automaton that could truly sing."

"Yes!" The professor looked like a child who had been promised a new pony. "Exactly! Such perfect duplication of the living form! When I went down on the stage and examined the woman, she looked otherwise normal except for the side of her face. The flesh sagged under a weight. I think a piece detached from the underlying support structure and dragged it out of shape. I believe the same person who made these birds constructed the opera singers as well. But I need more evidence. We need to find what is left of those performers."

"So, we're going back to the opera house?" Miss Bang asked.

"Yes! Well, no! We're already there. I'm sorry about the little detour, my boy, but I'm certain your uncle is going to want to see whatever evidence we can find."

"Surely he will be worried about my disappearance? Perhaps it would be best to just drop me off first and I can explain your theory to Uncle Randolph?" Much as I would like to avoid his wrath, putting off seeing my uncle could only make things worse.

"After losing a major landmark?" Professor Crackle asked. "Don't be ridiculous! He may be worried, but he will have hardly a moment to think on it. No, trust me, even if you went back now you wouldn't be able to get in to see him. But if we can find something to prove it wasn't an accident, we'll be able to get right in to see the duke."

"And the police, Professor?" I asked, wondering what Inspector Janecek would think about the professor's clockwork people theory.

"Yes, we must get there before they do! The last thing we need is for them to tromp all over everything and destroy the evidence we need." He grabbed a pair of goggles off of a bench and strode through the door. "Come along!"

"But, but that's not what I meant!" I sputtered and hurried to catch up to Miss Bang as she swept out of the room in the professor's wake.

Chapter Ten

The Fall of the Opera house of Prague

We followed the professor down two decks and back to the lounge where we first arrived on *The Argos*. Instead of heading directly to the descent platform, the professor detoured to the lounge's large windows and looked down at the city. I stood next to him and got my first sight of Prague from above.

The city was laid out in repeating patterns below us. From the color of the materials, the size of the courtyards, and style of the construction, one could easily trace the different cycles of the development. Prague glimmered like a jewel in the morning light. The day advanced since we left the police station and traffic thronged through the streets. Horse driven carts, steam driven jitneys, and a few heavy trucks with diesel engines fought their way back and forth across the roads. Each was part of the life's blood of the city, maintaining the flow of people and goods.

Below us, that precious flow was disrupted. Streets and alleys were blocked by police lines, bright linen banners strung from lamppost to lamppost to discourage foot traffic, and barriers set up to carve out space for a collection of police vehicles.

The fire brigade apparently came and went, for there was no longer any indication of fire, or even smoke. In the center of all the activity, where once the proud and stately opera house stood, a shell remained, formed by the few exterior walls that refused to fall. The roof collapsed into the foundations of the building, leaving a broken scar on the face of the city.

The professor surveyed the scene for a minute or two, muttering comments about suitable locations I couldn't hear clearly. Finally he said, "Yes, that should do nicely!" Turning from the window, he strode for the door against the far wall, calling over his shoulder, "Make yourselves comfortable. We're going to have to maneuver for a bit before we can go down."

"You're going to land the ship, Professor?" I asked. "Where?"

"The ship? Oh, no. Goodness me, that would be a huge waste of time, my boy. No, just us," he said and vanished through the door.

Miss Bang directed me to one of the divans with a gesture and seated herself in a nearby slipper chair. "Landing a ship this size would involve the effort of the entire crew and a fair bit of coordination with local authorities. It is much simpler to hold *The Argos* stationary above a point and drop the landing platform. About the only time we ever truly land is when we are taking on heavy equipment or large amounts of supplies." After a moment, she added, "or making structural repairs."

Remembering the rather terrifying ascent, I inquired, "And the whole process is quite safe?"

"Of course! Just keep a firm grip on the safety bars and you'll be right as rain. You did bring your goggles with you, yes?"

"Um, no, actually. I didn't realize they would be needed so soon. I'm afraid I left them in the room." I started to rise. "Shall I go and fetch them?"

"Oh, no. That won't be necessary." She waved me back into my seat and continued her explanation as I settled myself. "We find goggles are so generally useful we usually keep them with us at all times. But don't worry, there are always a few extra pairs in the observation booth."

I became aware of the hum of engines in the background when they abruptly ceased and I realized it was the first time since I came aboard the sound was not present. Manqoba appeared beside us as if by magic and bowed. "Sir, Miss, I believe the professor is ready to depart."

"Yes, Manqoba, thank you. Would you be so good as to provide a pair of goggles for our guest? He seems to have forgotten his in his room."

"Certainly, Miss." He snaked a hand into his jacket and withdrew a set of the protective eyewear from an inside pocket and presented them to me. "I do hope these will serve you well, sir."

I thanked Manqoba as I accepted the lenses and we proceeded into the next room. The professor's face was pressed up against a tube, which extended up from the floor. His hands were making minute adjustments to a series of levers mounted on the side of the device. He pronounced his efforts to be perfect, and then looked up at Miss Bang and myself.

"Ready to go? Hopefully it won't take too long to find what we need. I don't think we'll need to recover an intact specimen. A large enough piece to show the construction should be sufficient for our purposes." He ushered us towards the door to the landing platform and its brass railings.

"Won't this be dangerous, Professor?" I remembered the terror of our late night escape from the wreckage below, and part of me could not believe he intended to go back into the same environment.

"Well, there is some risk. Parts of the building may still be unstable, but most of the danger is past. The fire brigade will have the gas shut off, or they never would have gotten the fire under control. As long as the police don't bother us again we should be in and out of there in no time."

Miss Bang seemed perfectly at ease as she strode onto the suspended deck, donned her goggles, and made sure the hat she retrieved from a cupboard in the control room was well secured upon her head. The professor likewise pulled his lenses over his eyes and took his place next to the central tower.

"P-perhaps I should stay here?" I ventured. "Surely I would only get in the way."

"Nonsense! We could use another pair of eyes. Don't fret a moment about it. We'll keep you quite safe." A huge smile split his face.

Unsure of the wisdom of my actions, I let myself drift forward inside the brass railing, slipped the eyewear into place over my head, and grasped a handhold on the tower.

I turned to the professor to ask another question, but before I could speak he nodded to Manqoba in the control room. The butler threw a large switch and lightning crackled through the apparatus above our heads. I nearly fell over when I tried to step away from it as I discovered my feet were rooted to the spot. I gripped the tower to steady myself, and it was at that point the floor dropped out from under me.

To be perfectly honest, the floor and I did not part ways. Indeed, we were just shy of being riveted together. The entire platform fell away from *The Argos*. My stomach lurched as we dropped into the open air and plummeted towards the ground. The wind whipped around me as the swinging disc tumbled from the sky, pitching first one way, then the other, but never going completely over as it descended from its mooring on the underside of *The Argos*.

Despite the feeling I was due to be flung off into space at any moment, my feet remained fixed to the deck. I established a death grip with my left hand upon the brass handhold, but was unable to contort my body in any fashion to would allow my right hand to likewise make contact with one of the grips.

My companions held lightly onto their single handholds and even enjoyed the sights as we plunged towards the pavement below. The wind roared around us, causing the professor's jacket to flutter madly behind and above him as we plummeted. Oddly enough, while Miss Bang's skirts flipped around her legs in a similar fashion, the hem of her dress clung to the floor of the platform as if nailed down around her feet.

The city rose to meet us with alarming speed, the spires and rooftops seeming to stab up at us in our descent. I was convinced the mechanism failed completely, and instead of lowering us gently to the ground, was dropping us to a sudden and painful death, when the floor abruptly leveled and ceased pitching about. The horizon steadied itself and we plunged into the space between two buildings, their ancient stone facades rushing by us with great speed. I was sure we were to be smashed to pieces against the walls, or splattered against the streets below, when I realized we were rapidly shedding velocity along with our altitude. In another moment, we hung motionless scant inches above the cobblestones of a wide alley. The cable stretched taught above us, tracing a gentle arc upward to *The Argos*, floating serenely in the sky.

"See," said the professor, "perfectly safe."

He went to step off the floating dais, but found his feet remained fixed in place. "Interesting. I must have accidentally overcharged the capacitors."

"C-c-capacitors?" I stammered, still pulling my wits together after our meteoric descent.

"Yes, my boy. Capacitors to power the electromagnets built into the debarkation platform. Without them, you'd fly off into space halfway down from the ship."

"Ma-magnets?" I repeated.

"Yes," Miss Bang answered this time. "There are a series of metal plates built into the soles of your shoes. They are each small enough to keep from impairing the flexibility of your footwear, but taken together they provide something for the electromagnets to attract."

The professor nodded. "Every now and then I miss my calculations and leave in a little too much of a charge. It should let go in a moment or two." He moved his legs again, trying to shift his feet. On his third attempt, he was able to lift his foot from the deck and cross to the edge.

I tried to move and found my feet were no longer welded to the floorboards. I followed the professor to the edge on shaky feet and stopped to hand Miss Bang down to the surface of the alleyway.

"Professor, where are we?" Once again, I was lost in the back streets of Prague.

"We're only a few blocks from the opera house, or at least what is left of it. I put us far enough away to get down without attracting attention."

I looked up at the underside of *The Argos* and the thick cable snaking down from it to the nearby platform. It hovered with eerie stillness.

"You don't think someone will notice that?" I asked pointing to the airship.

"People don't look up in the city! You'd be surprised at what people won't notice right under their noses. We'll be fine. Come along!" He strode boldly out of the alley as if he didn't already look like a dustman who pilfered one of his employer's old coats.

Oddly, as Miss Bang and I followed the professor, I noticed he really didn't draw any unusual attention. Even with the lenses of his goggles perched upon his forehead, no one seemed to give him a second glance. I began to wonder if the people of Prague had seen a bit too much in their time.

We attempted to re-enter the opera house from a couple of different directions, but each time we were thwarted by the police cordon, which warned us off for our own protection. Apparently a number of sightseers, or perhaps looters, previously attempted to gain access to the ruins and the police threw up a particularly tight security screen to keep them out.

The professor, however, remained undaunted. He was convinced the evidence he needed to prove his case was there among the rubble. We were on our third attempt, trying to retrace our steps from the previous night and follow the storm sewer access tunnels back to the basement. We approached the alley where we escaped from the opera house the night before, but were stopped at the far end by another police officer manning a blockade at the mouth of the alley. Before Professor Crackle could try to persuade him to let us pass, the ground began to shake and buckle as if some creature was burrowing up through the cobbles underneath us. We staggered and clung to each other in a bid to keep our feet. Around us, flowerpots, pieces of brick, and other small items fortunate enough to survive the previous night's excitement crashed to the street.

"Is it an earthquake?" I cried. Miss Bang shook her head, indicating it was not.

I looked down the alley, at the ragged wall which remained of the majestic opera house, when, without further preamble, the wall simply dropped away. It did not crumble, nor did it fall in on the ruins, or fall outwards in pieces. The remnants of the opera house, jagged as they were, simply fell. The entire building, its foundations, even the grand staircase leading up to its main doors, dropped evenly, straight down into the earth. We rushed past the dazed constable and stopped at the edge of the pit.

By the light of day, under the watchful eyes of Prague's finest, the opera house was stolen.

"Damn," said the professor.

Chapter Eleven

A Trip to Castle Prague

The shock of the opera house's sudden disappearance sufficiently unnerved the constable to permit us to escape the premises without further questioning. We retreated to the alley where the debarkation platform awaited. Despite the fact it dangled on a cable at least a thousand feet long, it remained almost unnaturally still.

I returned the goggles to my eyes and handed Miss Bang on deck once again. As I took my position for the ascent, I noted my colleagues' casual positions and attempted to mimic them. This proved to be a wise choice, as I was better prepared for the rapid acceleration, which followed once Professor Crackle signaled *The Argos* to retrieve us. My previous ascent felt like I was catapulted into space with no surety of a safe landing. The second experience was more like taking flight.

It was powerful, but controlled, as well. A purposeful evacuation to a place of refuge. As we shot above the tops of the trees and buildings, the city unfurled itself around us. For the first time I began to understand why my companions were so enamored of their mode of travel. It leant a perspective most earth-bound men never got the chance to appreciate.

As we exited the lift and headed for the debarkation lounge, a worried expression crossed the professor's face. "This is very inconvenient. I hoped to gather additional evidence of my suspicions to present before Reggie, but I'm afraid that won't be possible now." The professor turned to me. "We must see about returning you to your family, old chap. I hope they are not too worried about you."

"I am sure Uncle Randolph will thank you for your care, Professor. If you don't mind my asking, from whence do you know my uncle?"

We followed the professor into the hallway and up a flight of stairs to a long corridor. "It was many years ago. Back in my university days. Your uncle was one of my most promising students. I always felt he could have applied himself a bit more."

"Your student, Professor? But, surely Uncle hasn't been in a classroom for years. Decades. And he is considerably older than you. How could he be your student?"

Miss Bang chimed in, a hint of humor in her voice, "I did mention the professor is a bit older than he looks."

"As our dear Miss Bang says, I do manage to carry my years somewhat better than most. Rest assured I am considerably older than your uncle, despite my youthful demeanor. He was my student back when I was teaching applied physics in Dusseldorf. I believe he could have quite a career as a scientist, had the lure of politics not pulled him away." He made a curt gesture as he trotted up another flight of steps, sweeping the subject aside. "But let us save such reminiscences for another time. Now, we must go to the castle."

We strode down another long hallway and entered a door at the very end of the hall. The door opened to the command center of the ship. A brace of crewmen manned their stations, monitoring assorted dials and indicators and standing ready to attend their equipment. A young officer to one side of the bridge kept up a litany of meteorological information, mostly wind speed and direction changes, with little pause. Others listened to the information and made small adjustments to their apparatus in response. Some of them used acoustic tubes to pass orders to other parts of the ship in a measured cadence of call and response. While the layout was completely unfamiliar to me, I got the impression of a tight, well run ship.

The bridge was dominated by a large wheel in dark mahogany with brass fittings and leather wrappings on the handholds. The wheel was mounted at the end of a raised deck extending from the rear of the chamber, giving it a commanding view of the other stations and the large windows, which arced across the front of the room. The arrangement provided an excellent view of the city and sky to whomever was manning the wheel. I realized the bridge was at the very front of *The Argos*, finally providing me with a point of reference with which to understand the layout of the ship.

An older man stood at the ship's wheel, although it appeared to be secured at the moment. The professor jogged up a few steps to stand next to the helmsman, but addressed his words to another man who was almost lost in the shadows at the back of the bridge. This worthy was a tall, bearded man with a heavy bearing, but clearly his most remarkable feature was the fact both of his legs were mechanical replacements. A clockwork ticking came from inside each brass leg, providing a measured rhythm to the scene. By the bars on his coat, I surmised he was the vessel's captain, which was confirmed when the professor spoke to him a moment later.

"Captain Peerless, we need to make way to the castle and return our guest. Please let me know as soon as we arrive."

The Captain nodded, but gave a caution in a rough, gravelly voice, "With all that has been happening in the last few hours, I doubt they'll be very happy to see us parked over their heads, sir."

"I understand, Captain. I will accept full responsibility as owner, but I don't think they will shoot at us. If they do, I expect you will do what you must to protect the ship." The professor looked grim, but determined.

"As long as we understand each other, sir." The captain nodded to the professor. "All hands! Prepare to come about! Riggers to stations!"

The bridge exploded in a frenzy of activity as the crewmen jumped to carry out the captain's orders. The ship rang with a series of notes played on steam whistles. Men repeated orders down acoustic tubes. The professor turned and came back to us where we stood just inside the entry to the room. He ushered us back into the hallway and closed the door on the frenetic activity of the bridge.

"Shooting at us, Professor?" I asked, and swallowed to try and keep the nervousness from my voice. "Is there really a chance of that?"

"It has happened on occasion. Especially when strange things have occurred and people are unsure whom they can trust. But, I *have* recently spoken to your uncle, so it shouldn't be a problem, unless someone acts precipitously. Besides, he should be glad to have our assistance on this matter. It is not the kind of thing the police, for all their bravery, are truly equipped to deal with."

"If they *do* shoot at us?" I wasn't as optimistic as the professor. Unused to being fired upon in any capacity, I was not about to be sanguine about it.

"Have no worries. This is a stout ship. She has taken a few hits from pirates and the like, but she's always seen us through."

"But, Professor, if the balloon is ruptured?" I was not thrilled at the prospect of riding down into the city on the last gasps of a flaming airship. I really wanted some surety such an eventuality was not going to happen.

The professor looked confused. "Balloon?"

Miss Bang opened a door from the hallway into what appeared to be another sitting room. She guided us in to allow us to continue our conversation without clogging the hallways.

"*The Argos* doesn't actually have a balloon in the sense some airships do, my lord. Or rather, it has several, but they are all well protected inside the airframe."

The professor nodded and gestured for me to sit.

"Ah, now I see the problem. Yes, while the outside of the ship may look like a large balloon, it is actually the airframe. It is quite sturdy and well armored. The gas providing us with lift is contained within several chambers inside the airframe. The shape of the outer hull is to allow the air to move smoothly over the ship. We actually have a considerable amount of space up there. Would you care to see it?"

"Not right now, thank you," I answered as I slid onto a settee facing him. "So if the ship did take a hit, we wouldn't crash?"

"Oh, no! Not from a single shot. It would take much more than a single hit to bring down this vessel. And we have an excellent crew of riggers to repair any damage."

My fears were somewhat dispelled, but my confusion remained unabated. "Riggers, Professor? *The Argos* isn't a sailing ship."

"A nickname for the air crew who work on and around the airframe.

Mechanics and engineers, really. That part of the ship is such a large space, and much of it is open, so the crew has taken to using an arrangement of ropes and pulleys to get around rapidly. For lack of a better term, it became known as the rigging, and they took the name Riggers." He leaned back into his armchair. "Quite simple, really.

"They are quite an interesting crew, too," he added. "You must meet Tinka. She is the head of the riggers, and quite a remarkable girl, in her own right. She has a first rate mind, even if she does prefer to clamber about the ship all day."

I could feel the heat rise in my face as Miss Bang informed the professor Tinka and I were already acquainted. "I'm sorry, Professor," I said, "I hadn't known about her... medical condition..." I began, but he interrupted me before I could utter another word.

"Yes, isn't it a fascinating adaptation? Did you know the tribe who raised her after her parents died is completely arboreal? They live entirely in the trees. Some of them spend their whole lives without ever setting foot on the ground. Apparently, where most societies would consider a child born with a condition like hers as deformed, they believed it to be a blessing from their gods and such children were revered. Had their people not been attacked..."

"Professor." I interrupted him, a quaver in my voice. "I'm afraid I didn't make a very good impression upon her."

"Nonsense. I'm sure she'll warm to you as she gets to know you! I feel as if we are already fast friends."

"Professor, I mean I am afraid my behavior... my reaction..." I sighed. "I fear I offended her."

"Oh."

"Rather severely," Miss Bang added dryly.

"Oh, dear."

"I feel absolutely terrible about it, but I fear the wound may be irreparable and... And I don't think it would be the best of ideas to bring the two of us together right now." I felt abysmal, and I wished the settee would swallow me whole. I knew firsthand what it was like to be an outcast through no fault of one's own. I wouldn't wish that feeling on anyone.

Professor Crackle sighed. "I do not envy you your next encounter with Tinka. For all her many admirable attributes, I'm afraid my daughter does have a bit of a temper. As the Chinese philosopher might say, you do live an interesting life, my boy." He leaned forward and patted my knee, paternally.

Before I could answer, a sequence of whistles came from a hitherto unnoticed series of pipes set into one corner of the room.

The professor jumped up. "Ah, we've arrived!" He looked down at me. "Let us return you to your uncle and see what he has to say about this business with the opera."

I rose and followed them with a sense of dread, remembering Uncle Randolph's directives regarding acting in a matter befitting my station. It seemed unlikely that he would consider insulting my host's adopted daughter as suitable behavior, no matter how forgiving my host might be. I feared I would soon be under guard for the remainder of my stay.

In my particular state of mind, the sudden drop from *The Argos* was almost a relief. For a few moments I was able to savor the idea I would soon be smashed to pieces on the stones of the courtyard below, and thus be spared the wrath of my uncle, and the disapproval of the rest of my family. And all the new restrictions on my freedom that were sure to come with their censure. It then occurred to me, for the second time in a single day I was bodily dropped from the bottom of an airship. Surely if I could survive that, I could survive anything. The thought helped buoy up my spirits.

As we came to rest just above the surface of the courtyard, troops poured out of the castle all around us. They quickly formed up ranks surrounding the platform, their rifles raised and pointing in our direction. The air was filled with the sounds of their shouts, and with the pronounced hum of their lightning rifles.

I raised my hands slowly over my head. "Professor," I whispered, "Those aren't Bohemian troops! They're the Imperial Guard!"

"Indeed they are," he answered as he raised his hands over his head as well.

Chapter Twelve

A Royal Visitor

We were escorted from the embarkation platform under the watchful eyes of the Guardsmen and taken into the castle. As soon as the soldiers cleared us from the deck, *The Argos* retrieved the lift and moved away from the castle. Apparently Captain Peerless decided to avoid making the ship into another target. I couldn't blame him. No one in his right mind would challenge a British soldier holding a lightning rifle.

Once inside the walls, we were searched and a number of odd devices were removed from the professor's pockets. The process seemed to take an extraordinary amount of time, as the professor had a rather large number of pockets sewn into his garments. The guards were very thorough about their work.

Once it was deemed any potentially harmful possessions were removed from our persons, we were led into my uncle's study and a squad of guardsmen distributed themselves about the room to ensure we didn't get up to any mischief. We sat nervously, waiting for someone to arrive to tell us what transpired.

I expected a certain amount of alarm, given the destruction of the

Opera House, but something much more dire must have been in the offing if the Imperial Guard were present.

When I attempted to ask a guard what happened, he informed me, "The prisoners will not speak unless spoken to!" and they all raised their rifles in a most threatening manner.

In those close quarters the rifles in question were simple carbines. One man in the squad was still carrying a lightning rifle, although it was not powered up. When I attempted to speak to the professor, the guard repeated the command, so we resigned ourselves to sitting in silence.

Miss Bang composed herself and waited with an air of calm patience, which I envied. She studied each of the men in our guard detail, and I believe she started to read the titles of the books on my uncle's shelves.

In contrast, Professor Crackle fidgeted like a five year old. He played with his hands, reached into his empty pockets, raked his fingers through his hair, and squirmed in his seat. Several times he reached for one of the knickknacks on the table in front of him, only to subside as the guardsmen raised their weapons towards him.

I tried to relax, but I couldn't keep myself from worrying what my uncle's reaction would be to my disappearance the night before. The presence of the Imperial Guard meant things were very serious indeed. Bohemia was protected by the Empire, but not officially a part of it. If the Eternal Empress decided they were no longer capable of managing their own affairs, the Empire might annex the country. If that happened, it would not go well with Uncle Randolph or Aunt Katerina. Most of their lands would be forfeit to the Crown, and they'd lose rank in noble circles. As bad as I thought my position was, it looked like a disaster for my aunt and uncle. One that my parents would no doubt hold me responsible for.

After about an hour, a man in a beautifully tailored, brown suit walked into the room studying a handful of papers. The Guardsmen snapped to attention as soon as he entered. He proceeded at a sedate pace, taking his time in a clear show of status and power. He crossed behind the desk and laid his papers out in three neat piles before sitting down in Uncle Randolph's chair and studying each of us in turn.

I thought he seemed familiar when he entered the room, and when he sat I recognized the man, and suddenly understood some of what was happening. I shot to my feet, and the professor rose slowly to his feet in my wake. Miss Bang looked at the two of us, and then rose as well.

His Royal Highness, George, Prince of Wales and heir to the Eternal Throne, leaned back in the overstuffed desk chair and calmly asked, "Which one of you would care to explain how you became involved in the attempt upon my life?"

A stunned silence filled the room for several seconds. Then the professor cleared his throat and spoke.

"I'm sorry, sir, I don't mean to appear to be rude or impertinent, especially since you seem to be a man of consequence. But, if you don't mind the question, who exactly are you?"

The question clearly provoked the prince's curiosity. Unfortunately, it also inflamed my own incredulity. I could not stop myself from blurting out, "Who is he? How can you not recognize the most well-known man in the Empire? How do you not know the Prince of Wales?"

The prince held up two fingers in my direction, and I managed to stem the flow of words. His highness returned his gaze to the professor.

"Your compatriot asks a good question." The silence hung for a moment, leaving unspoken the prince's order to answer my question, since it had been asked.

The professor nodded. "I am familiar with the Prince of Wales. I've met him on a number of occasions. I found him to be quite charming, but Prince James is clearly not you, sir."

The prince smiled and picked up one of the papers. "Yes. Harmonious Crackle. Father told me about you. He mentioned you tend to show up at the most awkward of moments. My father abdicated the title of Prince of Wales to me some fourteen years ago. Are you saying you were unaware of this fact?"

The professor looked thoughtful. "James abdicated? Hm. He never did seem to think he was cut out for the office. I do travel quite a bit. Sometimes I miss a bit of news between here and there. I believe I was spending a good deal of time in some of the remote parts of Africa back then. I hope your father is doing well."

"Let us say he is happier now weeding gardens than he ever was at weeding out intrigues. As for you, what is your business in Prague?" The prince's tone started out jovial, but became deadly serious.

"Simply visiting one of my old students, Your Royal Highness. I heard word of some interesting scientific developments by some of my colleagues in Asia, and Prague was conveniently along the way, and had the benefit of housing an old friend. Miss Bang and I merely dropped in to visit old Reggie when events unfolded in the most extraordinary manner."

"So you just 'happened along'?" The prince looked skeptical.

"Yes, Your Highness."

The prince's expression remained dubious, but he said nothing as he put down the paper in his hand and picked up another page from the stack next to it. "Miss... Bang, is it?"

"Titania Bang at your service, Your Royal Highness." She curtseyed in a single, smoothly flowing motion.

"Do you have anything to add to your employer's statement?"

"Colleague, Your Highness."

"I beg your pardon?" The prince's expression showed no trace of begging.

"Professor Crackle is not my employer, Your Highness. We are colleagues doing scientific research in the field."

"I see. And what is the subject of your research?"

"Analysis of paranormal phenomena."

"Para-what?"

"We investigate the strange and unusual, Your Highness."

"I see." He made a note to one of the documents. "Do you have anything to add to Professor Crackle's version of events?"

"No, Your Highness."

The prince sighed and turned to the third set of papers displayed before him. And to myself. "You. What is your association with these two?"

"I, I, I..." I stammered, then paused to regain control over my faculty of speech. "I'm sorry, Your Royal Highness. I just met Professor Crackle and Miss Bang this past evening at the opera. I am afraid I barely know them." It felt as if I had just denounced them, but it was the truth. I did not know them well enough to vouch for them, or they for me.

"You took off with someone you'd just met at the opera?" His voice was awash with distaste. "Is this the kind of behavior we can expect from you?"

"No, sir, er, Your Highness. I mean, um, it wasn't like that!"

"So you *did* know them before hand?"

"No, sir. I met them at the opera house, but before it fell in. When the disaster struck we needed each other's help to escape alive. And then the police took us, but then they let us go. And then the opera house disappeared." My explanation deteriorated into a disorganized jumble. I tried to order my thoughts, but each phrase from my mouth sounded like gibberish.

"Why were you at the opera?" The prince's question cut through the confusion in my mind and allowed me to form a coherent statement.

"My uncle insisted. He is trying to introduce me to the culture of Prague." I remembered my manners and added, "Sir."

"So he sent you to the opera alone?" The prince sounded skeptical.

"Ah, no, sir. Uncle Randolph was supposed to meet me at the opera house, but when I arrived at the box I found Professor Crackle and Miss Bang instead."

"I see. And what reason did they give you for being in Duke Randolph's box?"

"The professor said they were there at Uncle Randolph's invitation. They were his guests, Your Highness."

"And you believed him?" The prince's voice was incredulous.

"I had no reason not to. If you'll pardon me, sir, I'm sure Uncle Randolph could straighten the whole thing out in a trice. Surely he can confirm all of this."

"Sadly, he cannot. Duke Randolph is dead."

Chapter Thirteen

The Fallen Duke

"Dead?" I couldn't believe my ears.

The prince's eyes were unflinching as he repeated the word. "Dead. Duke Randolph was killed when the roof of the opera house collapsed." I was dimly aware of Miss Bang sagging back onto the divan. I remained still; my mind trying to process the news.

"But... but, he wasn't there!" My mind struggled to make sense of the situation.

The prince spoke in a level voice. "Duke Randolph was not in his box at the opera last night, but he was there. He was attending me in the royal box. When the performance deviated from the planned schedule, he assisted my guard in evacuating my person from the building. He then went back to help remove the remaining patrons. He was caught inside when the building collapsed. Eyewitness reports from some of the survivors indicate he was killed instantly. He died a hero."

I knew I should have held my tongue, but I needed to ask one more question. "Do we know who was responsible, sir? Do we know who killed my uncle?"

"No, we do not. If we had that information we would be taking much stronger action already." I got the impression the prince fervently desired to take stronger action.

I felt numb. Dead? I'd gotten so worked up wondering what he might do to me, and suddenly he was dead. I was afraid of Uncle Randolph, but I didn't want him to die.

The prince continued on. "Unfortunately, at this point, we have no clues. All the evidence pertaining to the attack was destroyed with the opera house."

The professor spoke up, "With respect, Your Highness, that isn't exactly true."

He fixed the professor with an angry stare. "Of what evidence do you speak, Crackle?"

"Part of the reason I came here today, aside from returning his lordship to his family, was to discuss with the duke what I saw at the opera house, and the subsequent attack upon our persons as we were leaving police custody. Your Highness, I believe the two performers who brought down the house last night were not human, but exquisite clockwork facsimiles. Prior to our arrival, we attempted to acquire additional physical evidence to support my suspicions, but unfortunately the remains of the building were swallowed into the earth, along with any evidence we might have acquired."

The prince looked skeptical. "Clockwork people? Good enough to pass for human, able to perform upon the stage in front of hundreds of witnesses? Surely you're joking. And you just said the evidence you were looking for was destroyed. I need more than unsupported theories."

"Of course, sir. I was coming to that. When my companions and I left the custody of the police this morning, we were attacked by a flight of mechanical birds employed by some unknown party."

"Mechanical birds?" The professor's words did not seem to be swaying the prince.

"Killer Clockwork Budgies, Your Highness." I volunteered.

"They weren't budgies, my lord." Miss Bang added.

"As our young friend so colorfully put it, Your Highness, these birds were clockwork, and made of metal. They were of such exacting detail they could only be told from natural birds upon close examination."

"Or by their behavior, Your Highness," Miss Bang said.

The prince turned his attention to Miss Bang. "Their behavior? How so?"

Miss Bang stood to address the prince. "Yes, Your Highness. Birds will tend to cluster together for mutual protection. At most they will scatter randomly as they search for food. These birds were distributed about the park at very regular intervals and, until they attacked us, they kept a very regular spacing. Of course, the attack itself was very unusual behavior for a flock of birds."

"Your case improves, but I am still waiting for your evidence to come to light."

The professor continued, "Your Highness, we were able to collect one of these mechanical birds during the attack. I have been examining the device to try to determine its origins. It is the work of a master craftsman. It is clockwork, and more than clockwork."

"More than clockwork? Now what are you on about, Crackle?"

"Yes, Your Highness. More than just clockwork. An entirely new technology. Like nothing I have ever seen before. Amazingly small engines, and some sort of control interface the size of my thumb, which seems to have capabilities to rival the most complex Babbage Engines I have ever seen."

The prince scoffed. "A Babbage Engine the size of a thumbnail? Impossible. The Empire employs several such engines, and they occupy warehouses of space."

"Your Highness, I find it hard to believe there could be two such craftsmen acting independently. I think the attack at the opera house and the attack upon our persons were linked. The same culprit must be responsible for both."

The prince steepled his fingers together in front of him. "I should like to see this new technology you say you have found. Where is this mechanical marvel, now?"

"In my laboratory, sir, aboard my ship."

"A ship which is conveniently absent."

"My captain took what action he believed to be prudent when we were taken into custody, Your Highness. He cannot be faulted for taking appropriate care of my vessel. Especially when we had no idea you or your men would be here. I am sure we can summon the ship and then I should be quite happy to show you what we have discovered." The professor seemed positively eager to have the chance to give the prince a tour.

"No. I don't know what part you may have in this incident, Crackle. I will remain here, and so shall you." The prince considered for a moment. "You." He pointed a finger at me. "You will go aboard Crackle's airship and retrieve the device."

"I will do my best, Your Highness, but I am afraid I don't really know my way around." I tried desperately to remember the path to the professor's laboratory. I was there only scant hours ago, but I couldn't recall the way.

"If I may, Your Highness?" Miss Bang spoke up, "I am familiar with the professor's laboratory and his methods. I can easily retrieve the pieces and package them for safe transport."

"Very well. Sergeant," The prince raised a beckoning finger to one of the guards who lurked behind us. The soldier stepped a pace forward, clicking his heels on the polished floor. "Take Miss Bang and two men. Find a large space away from the castle grounds. A field. Have her summon the ship there. Retrieve the specimen from the laboratory. Brook no interference from the crew. If they resist, use whatever force is necessary."

"Yes, My Prince!" The man's voice was crisp and you could hear the capitals as he spoke. He turned to Miss Bang and bowed slightly. "If you will come with me, Miss?" His tone left no doubt she would come with him.

Miss Bang turned toward the professor. He spread his empty hands in front of himself and addressed the prince. "Your Highness, your men took my signaling device from me when we entered. A small device. Much like a whistle in appearance. Miss Bang will need to use it to summon the ship."

The prince nodded. "Sergeant, you will permit Miss Bang to retrieve the object, and nothing else from the confiscated effects."

"Yes, My Prince!"

"Thank you, Your Highness." Miss Bang curtsied, then turned towards the guardsman and said, "If you would be so good as to show me the way, Sergeant?" He gestured with one crimson uniformed arm and they turned together and exited the study, looking more like a lady and her escort than a guard and his prisoner.

"As for you gentlemen," the prince added after the door shut behind Miss Bang and her escort. "I am still unsure as to what to make of you. Your reputation is dubious at best," he said indicating the professor, "and your family," the prince continued with a curt gesture in my direction, "has dabbled overmuch at radical social reformation for the Crown's liking. The two of you may be cooperating with me for the moment, but you are still both suspect."

It was clear things would not go well for us as long as we remained under suspicion.

He continued before I could muster a defense for my family, apart from my great-grandfather, "Unfortunately, I don't yet have cause to question your actions thus far," his voice lowered ominously, "nor to clear you of suspicion in these matters. If you *are* a part of this villainy, I *will* uncover it."

The professor nodded. "We will do whatever we can to aid your investigations, Your Highness. I assure you we want the truth in this matter as much as you do. Don't we, old chap?"

"Ah, certainly, Professor," I agreed through my nervousness. "Whatever I can do to cooperate, Your Highness."

"That remains to be seen." The prince stood. "You will stay in the study to await Miss Bang's return. For now, you may consider yourselves to be at the Crown's discretion. Am I clear?"

"Yes, Your Highness," we replied together.

The prince gathered up his papers and walked to the door. He paused at the threshold and spoke to a guardsman outside loud enough we could hear. "Major Lawrence, let them have some refreshment if they want, but keep them here until I return."

His orders delivered, the prince left. The Guardsmen relaxed from their attention stance, but kept their positions, a living wall of red wool and glittering braid eyeing us warily. The message was clear: we were being given some room to breathe, but we were still being watched.

I moved closer to the professor. "What are we going to do?"

For a change, the Guardsmen did not command us to silence.

"Whatever we can to solve this mystery. What else can we do? Someone is threatening the Crown Prince, and we must do all in our power to protect him."

I rolled my eyes. "That's not what I meant. He thinks we are involved! That we are somehow part of a plot. What are we going to do about that?"

The professor smiled at me. "I know, but the same answer suffices. You cannot allay another's suspicions by denying them. Indeed, you cannot allay another's suspicions at all. If they choose to suspect you, then no amount of argument will set them from their course. All we can do as upstanding gentlemen is continue to conduct our business in an honorable fashion. Let those who claim we are false prove their cases. If we have acted with honor, they will have nothing to hold against us, and our own actions will be our defense."

I sighed and ran through our conversation with the prince in my head. "Professor?"

"Yes, my boy?" he asked.

"When you were telling the Crown Prince about the Clockwork Budgies, you mentioned a Babbage engine. What is a Babbage engine?"

"Ah!" The professor drew himself up as if he were addressing a lecture hall. "A Babbage engine is a computational device devised by Charles Babbage many decades ago. It is an array of gears and cams, which permits a machine to make logical decisions based on the input it receives. Of course, the more complex the inputs the device must process, the larger and more complex the engine must be. That was what struck me about the mechanical bird I examined. It executed very complex behavior, but did not appear to have any sort of control mechanism. In the place where such mechanisms should have been, I found flat grey slabs of some material with minute wires sprouting all around the edges. Those *must* be control mechanisms, but their design is completely foreign to me. Whoever is responsible for these events has developed an entirely new technology. These tiny grey bricks he uses *must* be his equivalent of a Babbage engine."

"Oh," I said, sorry I asked. I changed the subject before he could resume the lecture. "What can we *do*, Professor? We're shut up in *here* and all the action is out *there*!"

"Our bodies may be caged, but our minds are free!" A gleam entered his eye. "We can still think and deduce. So, what do we know now we didn't know before?"

I considered a moment, mentally cataloging everything we learned in the past twenty-four hours before the simple, obvious answer hit me. "We know who the target is! The Crown Prince. Someone is trying to kill him."

The professor nodded. "Exactly. The motive may not be entirely clear, but for the time being we can assume the attempt is based upon Prince George's office and not upon any quarrel someone might have with him personally. Monarchs and their families have always been targets for those with political ambition. But the Empress? She is a particularly difficult target."

"You think someone would make an attempt on Her Eternal Majesty? It would be madness!"

"The world is full of madmen, my boy. I fear she has already survived more assassination attempts than any other monarch in history. Given the fact she is Eternal, she will most likely survive many more. Which might convince someone to try to influence the Empress through her family. They are much more vulnerable, if only because they are mortal."

"I don't understand, Professor. If someone were targeting the prince to make a point to Her Eternal Majesty, why would they try to kill him by collapsing the building? It would seem like an accident, not a political killing. If they wanted to cause confusion, wouldn't they be more likely to fill the basement with black powder and blow the building sky high?"

"An excellent point! You are quite right. The method must have some meaning. Perhaps a signature?" The professor walked back and forth for a moment under the watchful eyes of the guardsmen. "I can think of two possibilities. Either the method has significance to the killer, or collapsing the building was not the intended method, but a device for covering up a failed attempt."

"Dropping the roof was a failed attempt?"

"Quite possibly. Consider." He raised a finger in front of his face and punctuated his statement with a jab in the air. "When we attempted to gather evidence at the opera house, what happened?"

"It fell into a pit!"

"It was made to fall into a hole someone created. Not a natural sinkhole. It was a deliberate attempt on some party's behalf to destroy the evidence. But if one possessed the power to drop an entire building into the earth in the first place, why not do that?"

"I don't know. If someone was trying to make a big show of power, wouldn't it be more impressive?"

"Not necessarily. It usually isn't a good idea to bring out your most powerful weapons in a conflict. Doing so gives an opponent time to counter them. It is usually much more effective to use a less destructive, but more precise weapon."

"So if our killer pulled out his tunneler, or whatever, it is because something else already failed?"

"Yes! And if he needed to collapse the building..."

"It was because some other weapon failed! Something designed to take out just the desired target?"

"I think so. I think the female soloist was an assassination weapon, which failed just as it was supposed to take out its target. The male contained a failsafe device designed to bring the building down to cover it all up."

"But why use clockwork opera singers, Professor?"

"Access? If you want to get to the cream of society, you either have to breach their internal security, or you have to be able to go where they are without raising suspicion. Performing clockworks have been known for centuries, although in the past they have always been obvious machines. A performance would be a set series of actions. All one has to do is put the clockwork into the correct position and start it in motion."

"But you would also have to know where the target was, Professor. No one even knew the prince was in the city, how could someone know where in the audience he would be sitting? And how would they know far enough in advance to place a device to kill someone in a particular spot?"

The professor whirled to face me. "Yes! Precisely! You're picking this up very quickly. Our killer needed advance notice the prince was going to be at the opera in order to place his mechanical assassins, and some method of aiming at the target. The killer needed to be in the building, to control his assassins, or have some other method of placing his shot."

"Any gunman can take a shot at someone from back stage, Professor.

If he was in the opera house, why bother building the mechanicals? A rifle and the right vantage point would have been sufficient. Perhaps not so flashy, but no less lethal." I shook my head. "This is giving me a headache. We think someone created these mechanicals in order to kill the Crown Prince, but just about any other method would have been simpler and more effective. Why go to all the trouble?"

"Very good questions, my boy. You would make an excellent student. Perhaps... perhaps there is something important about the method? The problem is, since the attempt failed, we don't know exactly what the method was." The professor resumed his pacing. I took my seat again, holding my head.

After a minute, the professor stopped again. "Let's take stock of what we do know."

"Very well, Professor."

"We've been working backwards from the latest attack, but it was the first attack we cannot place. So we need to work forward from there."

"Are we still working under the idea the Crown Prince was the assassin's target?"

"For the moment. Although we may have to revise that idea if we find another explanation fits better. So what did we notice first?"

"Well, Professor, the first thing I noticed was when the woman's face..." I gestured with my hand, indicating the side of my face sliding downward, "and then she made that awful keening noise."

"Yes. I suspect she dislodged part of her voice box during the performance and was unable to sing. Unfortunately we may never know. Then what?"

"Then you jumped down on the stage to look at the woman and the side of her face practically fell off. And the mist came pouring out of her mouth."

"Steam," the professor corrected. "Quite possibly steam pushed through a series of pipes designed to mimic the human voice. Much like the signaling pipes we use aboard my airship."

"That was when the man went down on his hands and knees and sang really low. Then the building began to shake."

He nodded. "And brought the house down."

"I still don't understand how it was done, Professor. How could someone collapse the building?"

"Harmonic resonance. Generate a tone at the correct harmonic frequency and the building will literally shake itself apart. The longer the tone is maintained, the more violent the vibrations become. Normally it would be practically impossible to find the proper harmonic resonance for an entire building, but with an opera house..." he stopped short and snapped his fingers. "Of course! How could I be so blind?"

"What, Professor?"

"Acoustics! The one reason it would be easier to level an opera house than any other building. The building is designed to channel and focus sound. It has, er, had excellent acoustics. And there is one place in any opera house with the best acoustics. A place where the sound from the stage is specifically focused."

"The Royal Box?" The implications chilled me.

"Precisely. The one place where a weapon of focused sound waves would be at its greatest effectiveness."

"You wouldn't even need to aim it, because the prince would automatically be given the best seat in the house. He'd be a sitting duck."

"Quite literally."

"But wouldn't such a weapon also affect the rest of the audience, Professor? Wouldn't it be just as bad as explosives?"

"Not necessarily. I've never heard of anyone developing such a weapon, although I would not be surprised to find out someone from the royal laboratories has tried such a thing to add 'thunder' alongside the Imperial Forces' lightning guns. Theoretically, some persons might be more susceptible than others and might suffer deleterious effects despite being away from the epicenter."

"Then it sounds like we've come up with an interesting idea which isn't very effective as an assassination tool. It just doesn't fit together, Professor."

"There, I think you are wrong," he said as he crossed to me and sat down. "Other experiments indicate the proper frequencies may induce a pliable state in a subject. The intent may not have been to kill the prince, but to make him... suggestible."

"Suggestible? Professor, are you intimating our attacker may be trying to use some form of musical mind control? To take over the mind of the

Crown Prince?"

He laughed out loud. "My boy, you have such a way with words. You should take up writing. But to answer your question, I do think we may be dealing with someone trying to use some form of mind control to influence Prince George. It might explain many things."

"I'm afraid you've lost me again, Professor."

"Our attacker must have information on the prince's whereabouts. That's very closely guarded information. To get such information, someone would have to betray a trust, or be under some kind of mesmeric influence. His highness' staff is comprised of the most loyal men and women to be found in the Empire. For one of them to betray a trust at this level would almost certainly require some kind of overriding influence."

I looked at the guards, who watched and listened as our conversation unfolded. They all looked quite capable, and lethal. I did not want to entertain the thought of one of those men breaking their oath to serve the Empire.

I hoped Miss Bang would return soon. And safely. Prague had proven to be full of perils.

Chapter Fourteen

A Tale of Two Scientists

*I*t was some two and a half hours later, after we succumbed to the needs of the body and requested the luncheon promised in the prince's orders, when Miss Bang finally returned. We were quite happy to see her again, but surprised when she appeared without the mechanical bird.

"I had no problems retrieving the pieces, Harmonious," Miss Bang explained after we sat her down and plied her with her own servings of mushroom soup, roast pork, dumplings, and sauerkraut. "The crew was completely cooperative, although the captain wasn't very happy about having the Imperial Guard on his ship 'uninvited'.

"As soon as my escort and I returned to the castle, we were taken off to another wing. Prince George's scientific advisors examined the parts we recovered. I don't know how helpful they are going to be, Harmonious. They were very appreciative of the craftsmanship, and they marveled at the careful replication of the natural movements, but when I tried to point out the new components you found, the ones with all the little wires and odd pieces, they dismissed them as decorative embellishment."

"What?" The professor looked incensed.

"I believe his exact words were, 'It is obviously nothing more than exaggerated ornamentation. The piece obviously has no mechanical function and contributes nothing to the workings of the automaton.' They wouldn't even look at the tiny engines you found." Miss Bang looked down at her hands, then up into the professor's eyes. "I'm sorry, Harmonious, I'm afraid I failed to present your case very well."

The professor reached over and patted her hand. "Nonsense, Titania, nonsense. You did the best you could. You can't be held responsible for the prince's scientists' refusal to acknowledge facts laid plainly in front of their faces. We can only hope the prince himself has more than a passing interest in science."

"I beg your pardon, Professor," I said, "I'm afraid I don't understand the significance of all this. Don't most craftsmen add decorative elements to their creations?"

"Most do, my boy. But the particular pieces we are referring to were all installed inside the device. Completely sealed inside. These birds are built like clockworks, but there is no winding, no spring. Instead I found these odd little components, very tiny engines wrapped in copper wire, and a large chunk of lead, or some other heavy metal with two wires coming from it. They also aren't particularly pleasing to the eye. In any case, given the parts could not be seen, and they were installed in just the locations necessary to actuate the tiny engines inside the bird, and there was no other apparatus to engage any of the joints, they could hardly be considered decorative. I think they are electrical in nature, but I've never seen any electrical components built on a scale so delicate."

"Electrical, Harmonious?" Miss Bang seemed intrigued. "In something so small?"

"Indeed, if my guess is correct, each of these birds operates using electrical power on an incredibly tiny scale."

"I'm afraid you've lost me again, Professor," I confessed. "This is a different kind of physics than what I studied at University."

"I'm sorry, I forget you're not a scientist by trade. Practically all of our work with electricity involves the generation of high voltage power. It depends on unleashing a bolt of lightning of a pre-determined power. Electricity is very useful, but the power generation requirements are enormous, and the generators themselves are quite sizable.

"This technology goes beyond all that. Unless I have missed my guess, someone has been experimenting with micro-electricity, extremely small amounts of electrical current. It is an otherwise unexplored realm. There is no telling what far reaching effects such a technology could have."

Miss Bang took pity upon me and further explained the situation. "Do you remember the equipment which took up one end of the professor's laboratory, my lord?" I nodded. "That equipment is conventional for electrical work. At that, it is considered a small, portable workstation. The power levels are still quite considerable, and if the cables and connections were not made so thick they would melt through instantly with the heat generated by the lightning."

"Precisely," said the professor, "but these new components use cables which are gossamer thin in comparison. Instead of a three-inch cable, these use wires scarcely thicker than a hair. Either our mystery inventor has discovered a new material, which can conduct electrical power without melting, or he's made a breakthrough in using small amounts of power. Hair thin wires, relays smaller than a pea! I can't begin to imagine! It is an entirely new realm. And he must have been working on it for years to develop it to this level of sophistication! We are definitely up against a mind of the first order!"

"So how do we fight it, Professor?" I asked.

"I don't know, my boy. I don't know."

Then, almost as punctuation to the professor's statement, we heard an explosion in the distance. The noise brought the three of us to our feet, and our watchdogs sprang to life as well. They leveled their weapons at each of us and barked out orders, demanding we re-take our seats. We slowly sat back down, keeping our hands up where they could easily be seen. An officer entered the room. At least I took him to be an officer, judging by the sword he wore at his waist and the silver gorget around his neck. That piece of insignia still looked odd to my eyes, having only just come back into fashion in the last year. He assured himself we were still well secured and under his compatriot's control. He instructed the guards to hold us there, and then swept back out the door of the study.

Miss Bang was the first to break the silence. "What is it, Professor? What could have happened?" she asked in a whisper.

"I don't know, my dear. It sounded like an explosion, but I can't say where it occurred or what could have caused it." The professor spoke in calm, even tones. He considered for a few moments. "When they brought you back to us, what were the prince's pet scientists doing? Were they still examining the pieces you brought them?"

"Yes, Harmonious."

"Did you give them my notes on the disassembly?" he asked.

"No," She replied dryly, "I didn't see any notes. I wasn't sure you'd taken any, since you started working on it without me. You do have a habit of working without notes unless I am there to take them for you."

"I do? Oh, perhaps I do."

My arms were aching from the effort to appear harmless for the guards. "What difference would the notes make, Professor?"

"You have to understand how scientists think. If they have documentation, they will study it for clues while examining the artifact. But lacking any kind of documentation, their options are more limited. Give them something put together, and they will take it apart. Give them something in pieces..."

"And they'll put it back together?"

"Exactly! Just to see if they understand how it was built."

"But the bird was broken. You said so yourself."

"Yes, well," the professor looked somewhat sheepish, "give them something broken..."

"And they will try to fix it," Miss Bang concluded.

"Quite."

I was alarmed. "You mean those clockwork budgies were rigged to explode?" The vision of one of those avian grenades going off as I stepped upon it filled me with horror.

Miss Bang arched an eyebrow at me. "My lord, I keep telling you they are not budgies. They're much closer to starlings."

The professor looked grim. "One possibility is the birds were designed to explode. There wasn't anything I could recognize as part of an explosive, but I wouldn't rule it out entirely. Another possibility is through their own incompetence, the prince's tinkerers managed to combine the pieces with disastrous results. At this point, we won't know what happened unless someone sends word. But I have the feeling it will not go well for us in any event."

"What is the meaning of this?" Prince George demanded as he stormed into the room. His previously cool composure was gone. His face flushed with anger, and he seemed mere moments away from doing something extremely rash. More of the Imperial Guard poured in through the door in his wake.

One Guardsmen did not carry a rifle. This was the officer who looked in on us after the explosion. He pleaded with the prince as he entered, "Please, My Prince, allow me to interrogate these three. Don't expose yourself to more danger!"

"Enough!" He silenced the officer's protests with a gesture. "I will not cower before any man." He turned back to us. "As for you, first you try to kill me at the opera house, now you try to blow me up here! Are you working for someone, or is this attack your own twisted idea?"

"Your Highness, we had nothing to do with either incident!" the professor protested. "Our presence at each location has been purely coincidental."

"You brought explosives into this castle!" The prince stabbed an accusing finger at the professor.

Miss Bang spoke up. "Please, Your Highness, we had no idea the samples possessed any explosive properties at all. If we knew there was the potential for danger we would never have brought them anywhere near without giving some kind of warning. We have no reason to wish you any harm, sir!"

The prince turned towards me and thrust his finger at my face, forcing me backwards. "Did you hire them? Is it some warped attempt to seek revenge for being banned from spreading your filth at court?"

"Dear God, no!" I blurted out. "I, I, ab, ah... Your Highness, no! I mean. I would never try to harm you, I swear! I have no quarrel with the court, Your Highness! I swear to you my only complaint in life is with my great-grandfather, and he is now beyond all mortal reach. I only wish to live a normal life. I have no ambitions, political or otherwise."

Professor Crackle interceded. "We wish to be of service to the Empire, Your Highness. Truly! We didn't cause the explosion."

"I'm afraid he is right, My Prince." The new voice came from a man in a soot-stained lab coat who appeared leaning against the doorway. His left arm was in a sling, and bandages covered most of the left side of his face. His speech was slightly slurred and carried a hint of a French accent. He stepped slowly and painfully into the room. "They could not have caused it. I'm afraid that honor goes to Doctor Ricks. He was examining one of the larger pieces. It appeared to be made of lead. He put it down on a metal plate and it sparked. I don't know how. It was like a discharge of current from nowhere. The piece ruptured, spraying acid over both of us, and then exploded. It was an accident, Your Highness. A tragic accident. There was no way we could have known what would happen. We never imagined anything so small could pack so much power."

"And Doctor Ricks, he agrees with your assessment?" The prince did not seem convinced.

"Your Highness, Doctor Ricks... is dead." The man hung his head.

"Thank you, Doctor Roche. I appreciate your candor. Go and rest."

"Yes, Your Highness." Doctor Roche turned and left the study, his pace slow and weary.

The prince seemed suddenly subdued. Gathering his composure around him again like a cloak, he turned back to the rest of us. "It appears my temper has gotten the better of me in this instance. I owe you all an apology."

The professor dismissed his statement with a wave of his hand. "Not at all, Your Highness, we were all caught by surprise. A very understandable reaction. Think nothing more of it."

"No. No, I allowed myself to overreact. I should know better. I should have waited for the Major's report, and interviewed Doctor Roche before making any accusations. This business has me on edge. I am unused to being a target."

"I should hope you never become used to it, Your Highness." Miss Bang said quietly.

The prince nodded. "I appreciate the sentiment, miss, though I fear it may not be my lot in life." He regarded the professor. "Not unless I choose to follow my father into retirement and put politics behind me."

"There are other careers, Your Highness," the professor ventured.

"Perhaps. But even an Empire with an Eternal Empress must secure the succession. I know my part to play, even if it is likely my children and I will never get the chance to play it." He sighed. "I have wronged you. I must make amends."

Prince George turned and strode behind my uncle's desk. "But these matters are not disposed of so simply. I accept you are not responsible for this most recent incident, but there still remains the matter of the opera house. It seems, Crackle, the evidence which might have cleared you has been destroyed." He sat heavily. "Unless you have something else to offer to prove your innocence, I am afraid I will have no choice but to hold the three of you until the investigation is over."

"Your Highness, surely the case against us is purely circumstantial?" The professor held out a beseeching hand. "It would just as easily apply to any of the other survivors of the opera house disaster. Will you be detaining those persons as well?"

"Clever, Crackle." The prince grinned at us. "But you forget your own scientific reputation, and the swath of destruction you have carved across Europe. If it comes to light someone else at the opera has a similar background of leaving craters in their wake, rest assured they, too will be detained."

"Begging your pardon, Your Highness," I ventured, "but surely I have no such reputation. I've barely completed university, and I've had no chance to do anything."

The prince's face betrayed no emotion as he considered me. "Had you not become entangled with Crackle, that argument might have held sway. But the fact is you are now one of his associates and as such must share in his suspicion."

The professor and I looked at each other. We knew we were innocent, but what could we say to sway the prince?

Miss Bang's quiet voice broke the silence. "If I might make an observation, Your Highness? With the loss of your scientific advisors to death and injury, you're in a position where you lack the qualified personnel to properly investigate these incidents. Yes?"

Prince George nodded. "True enough, miss, but I don't see why that would alter my decision to hold you pending the results of the investigation."

Miss Bang inclined her head. "An investigation without investigators, Your Highness? It would take a very long time. However, Professor Crackle and myself have been instrumental in a number of investigations. As you have already pointed out, the professor has the appropriate background to understand the forces involved here and seek out the culprit. Surely it would be prudent to enlist our aid in finding the person responsible."

"Very prettily put, Miss Bang, but I still require proof neither you nor Crackle is the person in question. If you are the authors of this disaster, you certainly wouldn't implicate yourselves. Why should I trust you?"

"No reason at all, Your Highness," she said before gesturing towards me. "Fortunately, his lordship is available to accompany us and ensure we take no action to pose a danger to yourself."

The prince leaned back in the chair. "But it would require me to trust him, and as I've just said, he's already under suspicion due to his association with you. What assurance do I have he is not a co-conspirator?"

"When would we have time to conspire, Your Highness? Professor Crackle and myself only arrived in Prague yesterday, and we met His Lordship for the first time last night. And surely, even if he was implicated..."

"I say!" I protested.

Miss Bang continued on as if I had not spoken, "He would not have risked the life of his own uncle in order to strike at your person."

The prince rubbed his chin thoughtfully. After a long moment he spoke. "Almost you convince me. Almost."

"Then, consider, Your Highness, none of us knew you were in Prague until you walked into this very room earlier today. Obviously, you are traveling in secret, so how would any of us have the time to prepare such an elaborate attempt on your life?" Miss Bang stood facing the prince; her arms held out as if presenting her argument and waited for Prince George's answer.

The prince's face remained impassive as he considered Miss Bang's words. Silence descended upon the room, broken only by the ticking of a clock.

"That is an excellent point, Miss Bang. But it doesn't rule out an attack of opportunity," The prince leaned forward across the desk. "Someone with resources in Prague might take advantage of my presence in the city to stage an attack."

She nodded. "Yes, sir, but who, aside from your staff, would have that information?" She leaned her head to one side.

"Duke Randolph knew. Perhaps his staff was compromised. That still doesn't give me reason to trust any of you." He pointed a finger at me. "He has access to the Duke's staff. He could have told you I was in town, allowing you to use resources you already had in place."

"Or, more likely, Your Highness, the information could have been leaked to someone already in Prague with an established base of operations. As Professor Crackle and I have stated, we only arrived in the city yesterday morning. *The Argos* is large enough to be remarkable. We can verify our last port of call, and I'm sure you can find witnesses to establish our arrival."

The prince raised a hand. "Enough. You're correct. I can't connect you to the attack." He sat back in the chair. "But that doesn't give me reason to trust you."

Miss Bang smiled. "And there is the beauty of my proposal, Your Highness. You don't have to trust any of us. You only have to trust that we are not conspiring together against you. The only way any of us can clear ourselves is to help you find those responsible."

"And what would stop you from trying to escape in the course of your so-called 'investigation'?" The professor bridled at the insinuation, but before he could say anything, Miss Bang continued.

"Seal the city, sir. You'll have to do that anyway until you can prove we are responsible. Even if we tried to leave in *The Argos*, which we would not, you have ample firepower at your disposal to bring the ship down."

I started to protest, but the professor quickly shushed me.

The prince stared at us, considering. I found my breath caught in my throat, as we awaited his verdict.

When he moved at last, he addressed the guardsmen. "Stand down, gentlemen. The professor and his companions are no longer under suspicion. They are free to go."

The guardsmen lowered their weapons and we put our arms down.

My muscles burned from the sustained effort of keeping them raised. I rubbed at my arms to soothe the ache.

The officer waved the extra Guardsmen out of the room, and then followed them out. We were alone with Prince George and only a pair of guards flanking the inside of the door.

The professor leaned forward. "Thank you, Your Highness, I believe we can be of significant help in tracking down whoever is making attempts upon your life."

"Professor, I will be satisfied if you can keep the property damage to a minimum. I think Prague has suffered enough. If I deem it has suffered too much, rest assured I will place you back under arrest. By whatever means necessary."

"Yes, Your Highness. We will do what we can."

Prince George looked at me. "Do you understand the charge I am placing upon you, boy? Are you capable of living up to it?"

"Are you sure I couldn't be more use to you here, at the Castle, Your Highness? I hardly know anything about Prague, and I'm no criminalist."

The prince's hand flashed up to stop me. "Enough. If you wish to stay here, I can have the three of you placed in cells. Or you can be my eyes and ears and make sure that these two," he pointed to Professor Crackle and Miss Bang, "do their utmost to investigate this attack. Your choice."

I swallowed the lump in my throat. "I will do my best, Your Highness. I will do what I can to help the professor with his investigations."

Prince George gave me a measuring gaze for several moments. "Very well. I wish you luck in your hunt."

I turned to the professor. "It would seem I'll be accompanying you for a bit longer."

"I'm quite happy to have you along! Let us do what we can to run the killer to ground, eh? For Reggie."

"Yes, Professor."

Miss Bang smiled, but she said nothing.

"Let us take up no more of the Prince's valuable time. By your leave, Your Highness." The professor stood and bowed to Prince George.

The prince nodded. "You may go. Ask my Guardsmen to arrange transportation back to where Miss Bang rendezvoused with your ship."

Miss Bang curtsied. I rose, bowed to the prince, and we took our leave. The professor spoke to one of the guards, who quickly arranged for a carriage to take us to the field where *The Argos* remained tethered.

As we rode, Miss Bang turned to me and asked. "I know I got you into this, my lord, but are you sure about coming along?"

I sighed. "Yes, Miss Bang. Quite sure. Much as I might prefer to stay behind, my presence is the price of your freedom, as well as my own." I looked at her. "And you were right. You and the professor are the best chance of finding this madman before he strikes again."

"There is likely to be a certain amount of danger, my lord. And you do realize if you come aboard, eventually you will have to deal with Tinka?" she asked.

I bowed my head. I hadn't considered that facet when I spoke in front of the prince, but I discovered there was no surprise to the revelation. I raised my head to meet her gaze. "Yes, Miss Bang. I do. I owe your friend an apology, and putting the task off will not make it any easier."

"Well, I wish you luck," the professor said. "Past experience has shown the courts are rather more forgiving than Tinka."

"I'm sure if she will just give me a chance to make amends, I can convince her of my sincerity, Professor."

Miss Bang looked at me again. "I think you may be forgetting something. Tinka is the head of the rigging crew. They are rather fiercely loyal to her."

"Emphasis on the word fierce, I'm afraid," the professor added.

Not for the last time, I wondered if I really knew what I was getting myself into.

Chapter Fifteen

A View from Above

From above, Prague spread out like a tapestry draped over the rolling hills. The river snaked its way through the middle of the city, spanned by bridges, and framed on each side by ports, fortifications, and warehouses. The streets climbed up from the river to the hills and changed from businesses, to government buildings, to townhouses of the Bohemian aristocracy.

East, across the river from Prague Castle, in the midst of one of these powerful neighborhoods, a dark hole defined the former location of the Prague Opera House. The three of us looked down at the city from the balcony of the forward lounge situated below *The Argos*' bridge. Goggles once again sat over our eyes to protect them from the wind.

"So, Professor, where do we start?" I asked as I looked over the city trying to spot the park where we were attacked as we left the police station.

"I have been thinking about that." The professor leaned onto the rail of the balcony and gestured to the city below. "Our opponent must have a base of operations somewhere nearby. I cannot begin to fathom what capabilities might have been built into these mechanical assassins with the new technology he has devised. Any chance of that was destroyed in the explosion. But I don't think our culprit was present at the opera house. Too much of a chance of discovery, or of being caught in his own failsafe. I think it is possible he may have built some sort of communicator into the mechanicals to allow him to control them remotely. Given the low levels of power he has been using, I don't think the signal could propagate far. So, the base has to be somewhere nearby."

"While that may be true, Harmonious, he also undermined the opera house to prevent further investigation of the ruins. To do so, he would have to dig underneath the site and excavate a considerable amount of earth. Shouldn't there be a tunnel from the opera house to his base?" Miss Bang asked.

"If that is true, wouldn't it be easier to just follow the tunnel?" I added.

"There should be a tunnel, but part of the problem is how deep is it? If the tunnel is below the water table, water will have started seeping into it as soon as the tunnel was hollowed out. If it is far enough below the water table, it may already be entirely flooded. The tunnel may not be exactly stable. Without a tunneling machine of our own, it would be dangerous in the extreme to attempt to traverse it. Yes, it is a possible lead, but I don't think we can follow it quite yet."

"Then how do we find the base, Professor?" I wasn't quite sure where he was going with his line of reasoning.

"Assuming our killer is still using the clockwork birds, or has other mechanical assassins, there should be signals emitting from both his mechanical surrogates and the base where he controls them. If I can fashion a directional detector, we should be able to sweep the city and locate him." He illustrated by passing his arm over the buildings below.

Miss Bang frowned. "Wouldn't it require our perpetrator to make another attempt on the life of the prince, Professor?"

"Not necessarily. It would require him to be transmitting while we are using the detector." He turned to the doors and we followed him back into the lounge as he explained. "Were I in his place, I would be tempted to test my technology, given the recent failures. Unfortunately, I have been up against opponents of this sort before. They are not generally the type to review their findings." The professor frowned as he secured the door behind us, shutting out the sound of the wind. By comparison, the lounge seemed almost unnaturally quiet. "It means if we do detect him, it is quite likely he will be in the midst of another attempt. And equally unfortunate, we will not be able to warn the prince."

"We won't?" I asked.

"No, my boy. Someone inside the prince's entourage must have betrayed his location to our assassin, and done so early enough for him to establish a base in Prague. Given the methods used thus far, I find it highly unlikely someone was just waiting for an event such as the prince's visit to terrorize the city.

"If we inform the prince, there is a possibility the spy will find out what we are up to, even if the informant is a hapless victim under sonic suggestion."

"You mean the musical mind control, Professor?" As I turned into the lounge, I was pleased to discover an informal buffet was laid out while we were occupied looking over the city. The professor motioned for Miss Bang to precede us.

"Musical mind control?" Her expression was puzzled as she picked up a plate from the stack on the table.

"A theory we came up with while you were off running your errand for the prince, my dear. I think it is possible the attack at the opera house wasn't an attempt to kill the prince, but to render him suggestible by the application of a sonic conditioning device."

"Good heavens!"

"Exactly. It would not do to have the second most powerful person in the Empire under the influence of a madman."

"So we need to find the madman first," I said as I filled my own plate with food from the buffet, "and make sure we don't fall under the sway of his mind control device."

The professor regarded me through the lenses of his glasses. "Yes. Quite. In any event, I thought we could all use a bit of a snack while we consider how to proceed."

We settled ourselves at a dining table with our selections.

"My compliments to your chef, Professor," I said. "I have endured formal dinners which failed to serve entrees as tasty as this little 'snack' of yours.

I would not invite the Crown Prince to dinner unless you're prepared for him to try and steal your chef away from you."

"Others have tried, my friend. I do my best by my crew and they stick with me, by and large."

"You are too modest, Harmonious," Miss Bang said. "You've created a family here. For most of us, you've provided a home when we didn't have any other place to turn. I doubt any of us would leave."

I glanced at her, "Surely you have family, Miss Bang."

"My parents were researchers, my lord. I was at boarding school while they went into the field. They were exploring the interior of Africa, cataloging flora, and trying to identify new medicines. Instead, they discovered a new disease."

Professor Crackle leaned over and patted her hand. "Their work did lead to a cure, even if it wasn't soon enough to save their lives. Their contributions to science will be remembered."

She looked at him and nodded. "Yes, Harmonious. They will be remembered." She turned back to me. "But their deaths left debts. I did have some inheritance, but once those debts were paid, I lacked any other means of support, and no family to which I could turn. The professor was good enough to offer me the opportunity to help him with his research, and I have learned more in the field with him than I would have learned in a dozen years in university. I think my parents would be pleased."

"Let us hope," said the professor, "they would also be pleased with our latest efforts."

"You spoke of building a detector, Harmonious? Do you have some insight into the method used to control the mechanicals?"

Professor Crackle put down his wine glass. "I think so. I believe our opponent may be using some kind of aetheric transmitter to control the devices."

"Aetheric, Professor? I'm not familiar with that term," I asked as I took another forkful of an excellent chicken cordon bleu.

"I'd be happy to explain, my friend. The aether is a medium that exists alongside everything else we see in the physical world. It is a perfectly elastic continuum, which is responsible for a number of physical phenomenon, such as the propagation of light, and the influence of gravity."

My brows knit together. "I seem to remember something about that in my early science classes. Wasn't it all disproven years ago?"

"No, not exactly. A number of new theories were advanced to explain how light and gravity interact with the physical world and don't require the presence of the aether. Many of these theories have found widespread acceptance, but there is no conclusive proof one way or the other. As a result, most researchers have abandoned aether theory."

"If it is just a theory, how can it be used to control these machines?"

The professor chuckled. "In science, we call something a 'theory' when it hasn't been conclusively proven, but it still fits all the known facts. That doesn't mean we can't apply that theory. A number of scientists have continued studying aether theory, and have developed several practical applications of it."

"But, if there are practical applications, doesn't that prove the theory?"

Miss Bang shook her head. "No, my lord, it supports the theory, but there may be other explanations for the same phenomenon. An unproven theory may lead to several discoveries that suggest a new theory that fits the facts better. In science, we keep revising theories to fit the available facts."

"Oh."

The professor gestured with his fork. "So, as I was saying, I believe someone has found an application which allows them to propagate signals through the aether to monitor and control these devices."

"I see. And you can build a device to detect these signals?"

He nodded vigorously. "I'm sure I can. It should only take a few hours."

Miss Bang looked doubtful. "Harmonious, what makes you so sure this person is using some form of aetheric signaling?"

"It's such an effective solution, my dear. The elasticity of the aether will allow the signal to propagate with minimal distortion, and the nature of the medium will permit it to penetrate walls. It really is the perfect solution."

"I'm sure it seems that way from a purely scientific perspective, but I believe you're over complicating things again, Harmonious. Let us consider some of the practical factors." She ticked off her points on her fingers. "As you said, aetheric study has fallen out of favor with most of the scientific community. Even among those who perform aetheric experiments, components are expensive or otherwise difficult to come by. And most importantly, how many disciplines are we expecting this person to have mastered? To do all of these things our opponent would need to be a master craftsman, an expert at sonic applications, have done an intense study of the natural arts in order to create lifelike automatons, and now must be an expert at aetheric science on top of developing another completely new technology?" She spread her hands. "I think that is asking a bit too much, don't you?"

"Couldn't a group of people with expertise in different disciplines be working together?" I asked.

The professor tapped his lip as he considered. "Unlikely. Partnerships do form from time to time, but even in the purely academic world they don't tend to last long. Egos get in the way. More so with anyone of a nefarious bent. Such persons don't cooperate well."

"So, a team up of a master craftsman, a sound expert, and an aetheric engineer..."

The Professor shook his head. "Not likely at all, I'm afraid."

"Which means we need to ask ourselves are there any other methods for sending signals we need to consider?" Miss Bang looked pointedly at the professor.

He rubbed his chin absently. "Well, light is effective for signaling over a distance, but it would be somewhat obvious. Unless, of course, one used a non-visible spectrum of light. But light wouldn't be able to penetrate the building. Well, unless it was reflected through a suitable conduit. No, no, that wouldn't work." He scrubbed at the air with both hands. "Even with the wonders we've seen thus far, I don't think anyone could make a sensor and an emitter small enough to fit into a human automaton, much less one of the birds. Not and have it look like a real living creature." He shook his head. "Couldn't be done."

"Well, if not light, then what?" I asked. "There must be something. I mean, how were you and Miss Bang able to summon *The Argos* to pick us up?"

"That? That is a simple enough trick." He produced a small device from a vest pocket. "This is an ultrasonic whistle. When blown it emits a specific frequency in a high band. Sound at such frequency can propagate for miles. Upstairs in the bridge is a tracker which orients on the signal and..." the professor stopped in mid-sentence. He moved forward and perched on the edge of his seat. "Of course! I've been so stupid! And it all fits!"

"Took you long enough." Miss Bang murmured.

He slapped his knee. "Our mystery man tried to use sonic manipulation to make the prince suggestible. When it failed, he used a harmonic resonance to shake the opera house down around our ears. He tunneled underneath the opera house and collapsed it, which can be done using intense sound waves to pulverize the soil. It makes sense he would also use sound to control his remote devices."

"Does it help us find our killer, Professor?" I asked. "Are there many people in Prague with this kind of expertise with sound waves?"

"People we know are currently in Prague? Let me see, my boy, it would cut the field down to just... oh." His thoughtful look was suddenly replaced by a dread realization.

Miss Bang leaned forward. "Is there a problem, Harmonious?"

He sighed. "Of the scientists known to be in the city currently, there is only one person with the necessary expertise to use sound in this manner. Me."

Chapter Sixteen

The Sounds of Prague

"Obviously, I am not behind the attack."

"It may sound predictable, Professor, but I am glad to hear you say that." I replied.

He laughed. "I am glad you can keep your humor about you, my boy. I suspect humor will be in short supply in the coming days. Especially if we have further encounters with the police. I suspect it is only a matter of time before they come to the same conclusion, and once the field is narrowed to a single suspect, I doubt they will entertain the idea of looking for another one."

"What can we do, Harmonious?" Miss Bang asked.

"We can keep after our unknown assassin, and hope we can uncover enough evidence to convince even the police of his guilt. Preferably, before he claims more victims." The professor stood. "But for now, I think we should all get some rest. We've had a very long night, and a long day, and not nearly enough rest. We can consider our situation anew in the morning. I'm sure things will seem much clearer when we consider them with well rested minds."

It seemed an excellent idea to me, especially when I considered that while I was afforded the chance to nap from time to time, the professor had not slept since before the opera.

Miss Bang and I took our leave of the professor and she was kind enough to escort me back to my room.

"I am sorry for being such a burden, Miss Bang, but I'm afraid the scale of *The Argos* continues to surprise me."

"I understand. Since you will be staying with us for a while longer, I'll ask Manqoba to provide you with a map of some of the more common areas on the ship. You can use it to find your way around."

"I should be most grateful for that."

"Then I shall bid you good night, sir, and I shall see you at breakfast in the morning."

"Good night, Miss Bang."

I watched as she turned and walked down the hall to her own room. I was reminded of my first impulses when I met her. I still admired her as a beautiful woman, but after getting to know her, I realized her beauty was more than skin deep.

Once she went inside, I entered my own quarters and discovered the mysterious butler continued to work on my behalf. Pajamas in my size were laid out upon the bed and my suit, cleaned and repaired as well as possible, hung from the open door of the wardrobe. The outfit had been made whole again, but it still bore the scars of the previous night's events. The holes and scratches were neatly mended. Even the missing arms on both the jacket and shirt had been replaced with new ones that almost perfectly matched the original fabric. It was a masterful attempt at a repair, but there were too many individual tears and punctures to go unnoticed. While my garments would adequately cover me for modesty's sake, their mistreatment at the opera house would always leave them looking shabby. But Manqoba foresaw my need, for hanging on the valet was a full suite of evening wear, including white and black ties and matching waistcoats and dress boots similar to the daywear boots I wore.

When I looked inside the wardrobe, I found it was also stocked with an assortment of gentleman's clothes of proper style for a variety of occasions. It would seem no matter what my plans were, the good butler believed we were intended to become shipmates for some time to come. I knew when I eventually left *The Argos*, I would dearly miss that sort of care and attention to detail. If all of the ship's crew took their duties as seriously as Manqoba, I could understand how strong a feeling of family could grow up around *The Argos*.

I resolved to thank him for his care in the morning, and prepared myself for bed. I thought the events of the past day would keep my head abuzz for hours to come, but as soon as I blew out the last light and let my head hit the pillow, I was fast asleep.

I awoke the next morning with a feeling of rest and comfort I'd not known for many years. The sunlight on the windows told me it was still early in the morning, and the ship faced to give my room an eastern exposure. I rose to discover several pages deposited on my dresser. Examination revealed these to be diagrams of the lower decks, including a detailed route from my room to the main dining room on the floor above.

I bathed and made myself presentable, tucked the pages into an interior pocket of my coat, exited my cabin, and made my way to the dining room.

While the diagrams indicated *The Argos* was equipped with a grand dining room suitable for formal dinner affairs, this was a smaller, more intimate room capable of seating up to a dozen. Upon entering, I discovered the table was only set for four. At one place setting, it was clear someone had previously dined and departed. Sitting next to that place was Miss Bang.

"Good morning, my lord," she greeted me as I entered, "I trust you slept well?"

"Surprisingly so, Miss Bang," I said. "I hope I am not too late. Has the professor already eaten?"

She looked at the setting next to her, and back to me. "No, I'm afraid our fourth was Tinka. She... chose to dine early today and be about her work."

I frowned. "I hope my presence will not prove disruptive to the professor's household."

"I am afraid she is very sensitive about her appearance. It may take her some time before she is willing to give you an opportunity to apologize."

I took a place at the table across from Miss Bang. "I don't suppose I can persuade you to present my case for me?"

Her dark eyes flashed. "In this, you are on your own."

"I... understand. Thank you for your candor, Miss Bang."

Her next words were cut short as the professor walked into the room. "Good morning, my friends! What a beautiful day we have in store for us!"

"Indeed, Harmonious," she smiled at him and seemed to shine with an inner light. "I trust you slept well?"

"Exceedingly well! I am brimming with ideas! All thanks to you, old boy," he said as he swept the lids from the dishes in front of us and served up portions of eggs, sausages, and roasted potatoes onto each of our plates.

"Me, Professor? But what have I done?"

"You reminded me there was another way to exchange signals over a distance! All we have to do is find out what frequency of sound is being used to 'shout' across the city and we shall be able to find our adversary. And I have just the equipment to make it possible."

"I am flattered, Professor, but all I did was ask a question." I opened my hands before me in a gesture of helplessness.

"Harmonious, if our quarry is not actively using the equipment, how will we find anything? He still has to be sending a signal in order for you to track it."

"Ah, but that is where my new method will be much better! We aren't going to wait for a signal to be sent. You will see. Right after breakfast. Now, eat up, my friends!"

The professor led us to a special laboratory in the stern of the ship. It wasn't just a single room, but a series of rooms and chambers connected by a peculiar arrangement of apertures and baffles.

"Professor," I asked, "what is this place?"

"I'm so glad you asked. This is an acoustic suite. It is designed to allow one to work with sound in a variety of different ways," he explained as we walked into the heart of the suite. The room fairly bristled with an assortment of levers, pulleys, chains and other devices. He talked continuously as he moved about pulling levers and engaging different types of equipment.

"Instead of searching for what we think might be there, we are going to listen to everything, and eliminate the resonances we can identify. Then if there are any noises we can't account for, we'll be able to isolate them. And I just happen to have the right equipment!" With a flourish, the professor threw a large lever and the room was filled with a tremendous clamor.

My hands flew to my ears to try to protect them from the racket.

"Hark, my friends!" the professor shouted over the din, "the sounds of Prague!"

Miss Bang, her hands also covering her ears, crossed to a cabinet on one side of the room.

"How is this possible, Professor?" I yelled, trying to be heard over the din.

He showed no sign of being discomfited by the pandemonium filling the room. "Normally, I use these rooms to try and cancel out external noise so I can perform my experiments in relative isolation. Now, instead, I'm processing the external vibrations through a series of chambers to amplify the volume of the individual sources."

"How can we pick out an individual sound in all this racket, Professor?"

"Simplicity, itself! Once I isolate a particular set of vibrations, I can identify those frequencies and invert the wave form, thus canceling the signal."

"You're talking about magic, Professor!"

"Nonsense! There's no such thing as magic. This is acoustic science! Mankind has been studying sound for centuries! Great minds like DaVinci, Boyle, Mersenne, Newton, Bernoulli!"

"Professor, I have no idea what you are talking about!"

He laughed. "Just listen and learn, my boy! Listen and learn!"

Miss Bang appeared at my elbow and handed me what appeared to be a pair of earmuffs. She wore a similar pair over her own ears. I put on the offered ear coverings and sighed with relief as the ruckus abruptly stopped. I could still hear the professor cheerfully going about his work, but the assault of the city's noise was reduced to a dull background roar.

The professor refused the offered ear protection, and continued spinning dials and shifting levers. Working with several large machines, he systematically isolated and canceled out the sounds of an army of marching feet, a stampede of hooves on cobblestones, a crowd of voices, and dozens of other individual noises over the next few hours.

I never appreciated the variety of activity that goes on in a city before. Once the professor eliminated the everyday sounds of people, we could hear a variety of different steam engines, diesel jitneys, factory machines, furnaces, ships, and even the engines of other airships. Other noises were curious and somewhat more intriguing, but the professor eliminated them before I could accurately identify them.

The professor applied himself with a will, his hands flying back and forth as he focused in on each sound, identified it, amplified it, and negated it. Miss Bang and I tried to assist the process, but the professor relied upon his own hearing. I found the process fascinating, although much of it was incomprehensible to me. After several hours of work, the room went silent. I removed the ear covers, but couldn't detect so much as a whisper.

"Has something gone wrong, Professor?" My own voice seemed oddly muffled to my ears.

"Hmmm? Oh, no, my boy. We've eliminated all the ordinary noises to make it easier to find the signal we are searching for. But it won't be in the normal range of hearing, or people would have noticed it all along."

"If we can't hear it, how can we find it?"

Miss Bang supplied the answer. "The same way we are able to tune the professor's whistle. In addition to being able to negate a particular vibration, we can use this equipment to shift the frequency of a signal. Think of it as being able to bend a sound down into a range where it can be heard."

"Precisely! We've cleared up all the other noise, now it will be easier to shift the ultrasonic down where it becomes audible. Like so!" The professor grabbed two large levers and slowly brought them down. As he did so, the room was filled with a high-pitched pulsing noise, which hurt my ears. I hastily replaced my ear covers.

"Is that our signal, Professor?"

"No, it isn't. Unless I miss my guess, we are hearing an ultrasonic drill at work. It would seem someone is digging a tunnel beneath the city."

"Another tunnel? But why?"

"I presume as part of another attempt on the prince's life. The prince knows someone is after him. He is going to stay in areas he knows are secure until he is ready to leave the city. In this case..."

"That means the castle," I finished for him.

"Exactly." The professor nodded

"We've got to warn them!" I started for the door, but then remembered I was on an airship high above the city. I couldn't just run out to the castle and ask to talk to the prince.

"We can't do that. There is still the chance there is an informant among the prince's staff. No, our best chance to save him lies in tracking this tunnel to its source. If we can find the base, we can put a stop to these attempts."

"How much time do we have, Professor?"

"I don't know, so we'd best not waste any more of it." The professor consulted a series of gauges, calling off numbers, which Miss Bang dutifully recorded. At last he finally shut down his equipment and we sped through the corridors of the ship to the bridge.

Chapter Seventeen

A Culprit Is Named

"Good afternoon, Captain," the professor said as Captain Peerless lumbered onto the bridge through a door behind the chart table. A napkin tucked into the captain's collar, and the stains apparent on the cloth, indicated the professor's call interrupted the course of the captain's luncheon. "I believe we are going to want to do some maneuvering soon. I need to make some adjustments to the locator first."

The captain's mechanical feet clanged on the deck as he approached the ships wheel. "Are we expecting a departure, sir?"

"Not exactly, Captain. We're not leaving the city, but we're going to be moving around above it. Looking for a needle in a haystack."

"More like a needle buried under a haystack," I quipped, my voice carrying clearly across the suddenly silent bridge as the crew halted their activity and waited for orders. I felt heat rise to my cheeks as my unexpectedly audible comment drew looks from the crew.

The professor gestured to a crewmen, a dusky-skinned young man with dark curly hair, who proceeded to remove several panels from a device to one side of the bridge. The professor moved over to the machine and soon buried himself head and shoulders into the chassis, muttering as he tinkered within and occasionally flinging an arm backwards to be handed another tool by the dark-skinned rating.

After a dozen minutes or so, a bell inside the apparatus began ringing. The captain came over to observe the professor's work. "If you are on board, sir, what are we tracking?"

Professor Crackle removed himself from the apparatus. "Someone is doing a little unauthorized digging, Captain, and we intend to determine where they are and stop them."

Captain Peerless looked at him for a moment, a question poised upon his lips, but he grimaced instead of speaking the thought. He turned to the crew and called for maneuvering stations. The bell in the professor's device continued ringing as the curly haired crewman replaced the sides of the instrument and began calling off bearings in oddly accented English, reading from the meters set into the top of the machine. The captain barked out commands and the bridge became a flurry of activity.

The Argos made a stately progression across the river and floated over the spires and buildings of the New Town. The ship angled back and forth over the town, slowly homing in on the location of the drilling sounds as indicated by the tracking machine.

"Professor," I said, "I have been thinking..."

"Always a good practice!" he quipped.

"Harmonious," Miss Bang chided, "let him speak."

"I'm sorry. I'm sorry. You were saying?"

"You said you were the only person we know to be in Prague with the necessary skills with sound to do all these things."

"Yes."

"Well, I don't imagine there are a lot of people who have the necessary skills to use sound in all these different ways, not in the whole world."

"You are correct there. Aside from myself, there are perhaps a handful of individuals who have the necessary understanding of the properties of sound."

"I thought as much. You also said that our culprit needed to be a master craftsman to make the clockwork birds, and have studied natural science in order to make them so well."

"Yes, that is right."

Miss Bang gasped. She looked stricken, and for the first time, scared.

"Titania, are you all right?" The professor reached out a hand to steady her.

"Think, Harmonious, how many people in the world can boast a mastery of sound, the mechanical skill and natural knowledge to create a flawless clockwork performer, and also possess the ability to develop a completely new technology using small amounts of electricity."

The two of them stared at each other for a long moment, the professor's face slowly going slack as realization dawned on him.

Dread haunted his voice when he spoke at last. "He does have the necessary skills. And if anyone could have developed an entirely new technology in secret, it is him."

"Who, Professor?" I asked.

"One of the most brilliant and ruthless minds I've ever encountered. And the most wanted criminal in the entire British Empire. Quite possibly the most dangerous man alive."

Miss Bang spoke in a whisper, "Lord Scaleslea."

The professor looked grim. "It may not be him, but we cannot discount the possibility."

"I'm sorry, Professor," I said, "Who is Lord Scaleslea?"

"He's been on the run for years now, my boy. Well, 'on the run' doesn't describe it properly. He moves about, going from crime to crime and eluding the authorities at every turn. I'm actually not surprised you haven't heard of him. I suspected for a while now tales of his exploits have been suppressed to prevent a general panic. It is my task to do what I can to bring him to justice. If it is him, we could have a great opportunity to apprehend him, but it makes our position much more dangerous."

"He's that bad, is he, Professor?"

"Yes. There is the possibility it might be some other villain, but if we are up against Lord Scaleslea, we are all at risk."

"Aren't we at risk anyway, Professor? We are dealing with someone who is willing to destroy a theatre full of patrons in order to cover up a mistake. I can't see how much more ruthless Scaleslea could be."

The professor shook his head. "It isn't a matter of ruthlessness, but of capability."

Miss Bang picked up from there. "Lord Scaleslea is a genius, by any scale you choose to measure, and very efficient and effective, but he completely lacks empathy. He sees only his own goals. The rest of us are simply pawns to be played, or obstacles to be crushed.

"Other men may be as willing to shed blood, my lord, but Lord Scaleslea is incredibly cunning. His plans are both subtle and intricate, and for nearly every possibility, he has a contingency. It is what makes him so dangerous."

The professor nodded. "Indeed. I daresay your family has suffered enough loss already, my friend. I think it really would be best for you to stay at the castle until the danger has passed."

Miss Bang added, "It would be the wise choice."

I looked at her. She was still stunning, but she seemed sad and resolute. I asked her, "Will you be coming to the castle with me, Miss Bang?"

She blinked in surprise, and replied, "No, my lord, my place is with the professor."

I looked Professor Crackle in the eye. "You're forgetting one thing. No, two. The castle is itself a target. If I were to wait there, I would be helpless should you not be able to prevent the next attack. And I'm supposed to be the eyes and ears of Prince George, making sure you're not the attacker but are instead hot on his trail. If I were to return to the prince, he would have the two of you seized as well. Then no one would be free to stop this Lord Scaleslea. If I cannot avoid the danger, which it appears I cannot, I would much rather take the fight to the enemy. I am with you, Professor."

"You're certain? I'm sure I could come to some accommodation with his highness."

"Positive. Besides, if Scaleslea is truly this dangerous, you'll need every hand you can get. At the very least, I can keep the prince's men off of your back."

The professor's face split with a wide grin. "Glad to have you aboard."

"Sir, I think we've located it," a blonde crewmen with a Scandinavian accent called from the navigation table at the rear of the bridge.

The professor turned and bounded up to join the captain and the crewman at the chart-strewn table. Miss Bang and I quickly followed. A map of Prague was spread out over the top of the table with a number of pencil marks indicating various locations.

The crewman explained the marks. "We first located the signal in this area," he said pointing to a cross with a circle around it, "but when we came around for a second pass to verify the location, it moved. I plotted the positions on the subsequent passes. Whatever the source of the signal, it is moving in a definite direction." He placed a straight edge through the pencil marks and drew an arrow over the map. The arrow pointed directly to Prague Castle.

"I was afraid of that. It seems subtlety is no longer being employed." The professor put his finger on the paper and traced the arrow back in the opposite direction. He continued until his finger traced over a large park. The topography indicated it was a high point in the surrounding areas. "Oh, dear. It would be just like him."

"Harmonious?" Miss Bang asked. "What is it?"

He sighed. "Vitkov Hill. It was the site of a battle of great importance to the Bohemian people. The hill and the park around it are part of a national memorial. It would be just like him to build his base there to make a mockery of them, and to use their own national pride to protect his base from discovery." He tapped the map a few times. "I don't think we'll be able to approach his base from above as I originally planned. We're going to have to take a more dangerous approach."

"What did you have in mind?" I asked.

He moved his hand and tapped another spot near Wenceslas Square. Right where the opera house used to be. "It seems we're going to have to approach from below."

"Through the tunnel used to collapse the opera house?"

"Yes, my boy. Providing it hasn't already collapsed in on itself, the tunnel would seem to be our best method of approach. If we attempt to enter through the Vitkov Hill memorial, we will potentially be facing Bohemian patriots trying to defend their nation's honor and unwittingly fighting alongside Scaleslea's minions. Even if we can manage to slip by them, there is no guarantee we can access the base from the memorial. It is possible the only entries are via lateral tunnels in the surrounding neighborhoods. While we might be able to track those down, we won't be able to do so until after Scaleslea has a chance to undermine the castle. I don't want to be party to the city losing another major landmark. Not while we have a chance of stopping it. This tunnel," he tapped the map again, "is the only one whose location we have positively identified. It is our best way in."

"Do we really have a chance of stopping it, Harmonious?" For the first time, Miss Bang showed doubt. "Can we get there in time?"

"I hope so. If the two tunnels connect with each other short of the base, there is the possibility we can sabotage the tunneling machines before they can get to the castle. Otherwise, we'll have to try to sneak into the base and find a way to disable the tunneling devices at their source."

"Is there any chance they might be manned, Professor?" I asked.

"Possibly, but it would surprise me if he put much power in the hands of another. I can't see Lord Scaleslea doing so unless he believed he controlled his operatives completely. Then again, if he has developed a form of sonic mind control, he may just believe he can."

"What is next?"

"Unfortunately, if we're going to take him by surprise, we'll need to approach under cover of darkness. Fortunately, it does give us some time to prepare. We'll need to gather some special equipment before dark. I'm afraid we have our work cut out for us."

Chapter Eighteen

An Encounter With The Riggers

The previously empty hallways of *The Argos* thronged with crewmen heading back and forth laden with equipment. These men, unlike the bridge crew, didn't have any particular uniform, except the fact they were universally clad in leather and canvas, and carried a variety of tools and cables strapped about their persons.

I attempted to keep out of the way of these men as they went about their work, but it soon became obvious that was not to be allowed. No matter how I dodged or tried to evade them, one or the other would detour to smash me against the wall with the burdens they carried, tread on my feet, as they passed, or deliver a strike away from the eyes of other crew. It seemed I had met the Riggers.

I took another elbow in the ribs and a growled, "Wotch where y'er goin', toff!" as I attempted to slip into the debarkation lounge.

I quickly grew tired of cheap shots and growled curses from men who went out of their way to trap and corner me as they moved gear into place for the coming late night raid. I could feel my anger rising, but maintained my control as best I could. It was not the first time I encountered hazing. I hoped I had left such games behind with the idiots at university.

Unfortunately, Tinka's Riggers seemed to be cut from the same cloth. They were trying to provoke me, and if I responded, I would quickly find myself outnumbered. A physical confrontation was out of the question. I had to find another way to deal with them.

The windows in the lounge showed the last light of day as a breathtaking sunset spread itself across the sky. The colors unfurled across the vault of heaven were almost enough to make one forget the sinister acts being carried out under the surface of the city. Almost.

I moved to the control room, but a man stepped in my way. He was a large, muscular brute with a long scar down the left side of his face. He was dressed entirely in well-worn leather and smelled of sweat, cowhide, and faintly of beer.

"Where do you think you're going, eh? We got real men 'ere doin' important work. Hard work. Nothin' here for the likes of limp wristed sissies like you. Why don't you push off before you get hurt?"

I felt my face flush as my anger rose again. I had my fill of such treatment at university, and I knew that if it continued, it would only escalate further. It was clear I couldn't shift him by force of arms, so against my better judgment, I tried to reason with him.

"Look, I know I offended your chief, but I intend to make amends for it. If she would talk to me, I'd be happy to apologize. But right now, we're all trying to save innocent lives down in the city. Could you kindly let me do my part now and beat me to a pulp later?"

Spoiling for a fight, the rigger smiled and leaned in to me. Breathing at me with the sour smell of chewing tobacco on his breath, he said, "Oooh! Ain't you somethin'! Gonna save the whole city all by your lonesome, are you?" He poked me in the chest. "Nah! Not a cream puff like you. Who the hell do you think you are, little man?"

His attitude pushed me over the edge. I snapped. With gusto, I told him.

Two other workmen within earshot dropped their loads with a clatter, and from the sound of it, one of the loads broke. I kept my eyes fixed on the rigger in front of me. The smile dropped from his face and he blinked stupidly, twice, looking as if he'd been struck between the eyes with a cricket bat. He then stood up straight and considered me for a moment, his mouth half open as if it froze before he could deliver a response. Different expressions tried to form on his face, but never quite made it to completion.

At last, some part of his brain surrendered to the absurdity of it all and he burst out laughing in a loud, deep guffaw. The tones of menace were gone from his voice and he doubled over laughing. After a moment, he straightened and said, "You got me, guv'ner. I've heard some doozies in my time, but I ain't never heard no one who could curse like that. I can't believe you actually said..." He stopped mid-sentence and actually blushed, unable to say aloud even a part of my name. "Um, what you said. If'n you can say all that with a straight face, the Chief is gonna have to handle you 'erself. I'm out of this fight. Ha!" With the last he moved past me and smacked me on the back with the flat of one of his huge, meaty hands. The impact sent me stumbling forward into the control room.

I straightened up and assured myself my back was undamaged. I couldn't believe it had worked. I had blurted out my name in anger without thinking about the response it would provoke. I didn't expect the man to back off. Perhaps my great-grandfather actually had something in mind.

I shook my head to clear it, and glanced about the control room. The professor was conferring with one of the flight crew about some piece of business, when he looked up and saw me.

"Ah! Just in time. We've got our supplies ready and the ship will be over the site of the opera house in just a few minutes. Do go through and help Miss Bang, would you?" The professor turned back to the airman without even waiting for an answer.

I went through into the debarkation room and found a rather large and confusing mess. After a moment's puzzling I realized the odd sight was partially due to the fact two large cockleshell boats were up-ended and secured between the brass rail and the central tower of the debarkation platform. The rest of the room was littered with a variety of equipment, which plainly wouldn't fit on the lift. Among the refuse were two other boats of different sizes, what appeared to be a semi-portable steam engine, and a number of gadgets the engine presumably was meant to power.

Miss Bang stood on the platform dressed in a pair of sturdy trousers and a dark canvas jacket. I was at first surprised at her attire, but I conceded it was very practical. I similarly wore a pair of heavy wool trousers tucked into calf-high boots, a dark shirt, and a black double-breasted coat in a thick cotton fabric.

She was attempting to wrangle a bag full of odd-looking tubes into place next to the central tower. The boats complicated her efforts, and the fact the tower was already festooned with an assortment of ropes, grapples, and even a brace of harpoon guns. I made my way through the discarded cables, belts, and assorted equipment and went to help her.

"Oh, thank you, my lord," she said as I wrestled the bag into place and held it while she secured it to the tower.

"Do we have enough stuff?" I asked.

"Not nearly," she replied. "This is the only platform with a sufficiently long enough cable for our needs, and it just isn't big enough to take everything. We've pared things down to the barest essentials. Speaking of which, what would you prefer to carry, an axe, or a machete?"

"Are we expecting to find forests and jungles?"

"No, but if the professor can't figure out how to disable the device, we may need to use brute force to stop it. Most of our more effective equipment requires the engine, and there just isn't room. So it is down to the axe or the machete."

I pondered the issue for a moment and said, "I'll take the machete. If we run into opposition, I can always use it as a sword."

She stood up as she finished securing the pack. "A good thought. Do you carry a knife?"

"No, I'm afraid not."

"Then let me get you one. We'll need to offload the equipment quickly when the platform arrives at the bottom of the shaft." She turned and stepped lightly off the platform to dig about in a stack of assorted weapons.

"Where did all this stuff come from?" I asked as I looked around at the piles of discarded equipment. "It looks like a rummage sale in here."

Miss Bang answered without turning around from her search. "We have extensive storerooms, my lord. Honestly, you haven't seen much of the ship; you've only been on the lower decks where most of the living quarters are. Much of the storage is up inside the main fuselage."

"How can the ship even fly with so much weight on board, Miss Bang?

Shouldn't it all come crashing down?"

"It is actually very carefully balanced. The only reason we can lift this much is because the professor built *The Argos* on such a grand scale. She is one of the largest airships ever created. I believe only the Royal Air Force Air Fortresses have a larger lift capacity, but they need that in order to land and refuel the squadrons."

"You're having me on, Miss Bang! *The Argos* can't be that big!"

"It is, my lord, but as a general rule, we fly very high in order to give the impression of a smaller ship. Ah, here we are!"

She stood up with a weapon in each hand and returned to where I stood. The machete in her right hand was attached to a belt, while the knife's scabbard sported an empty belt loop. I took the belt and machete from Miss Bang and un-buckled it. She slid the knife onto the belt and I belted it over top of my coat and adjusted it until a blade sat on each hip. "I feel like I'm on safari or something."

Miss Bang smiled. "Or something."

"You sound as if you've done this before."

"I believe this is the first time I've gone spelunking in collapsing caves underneath a city, but we have had a few adventures in the past." Her eyes shone.

"So I have been led to understand. I also take it not everyone is happy with your adventures." I remembered the inspector's warnings.

"It is somewhat unavoidable, my lord. Some people will never be happy with the way events unfold, even if they are ultimately in their own favor."

"If we're going to be exploring caves, why are we bringing boats?"

"The shaft the opera house fell into is very deep. It is below the level of the river, and the local water table, so moisture from the surrounding soil will be pushed out into the hole. In addition, a number of water and sewer lines were broken by the collapse. The water lines may have been shut off by now, but they will also deposit their contents into the shaft. We're not sure, but we wanted to be prepared in case the shaft has already flooded and there is no solid ground to set down on."

The professor came into the room, a bounce in his step. "Are we all ready to go? We'll be over the pit momentarily." He was also attired in dark clothing, with a new top hat balanced on his head, complete with two sets of goggles.

"I think we have everything packed we can reasonably take with us, Harmonious," Miss Bang said as she took her place next to the tower. "We are going to be somewhat loaded down with cables as it is."

"Good, good!" he replied cheerily.

"Excuse me, Professor, you're going to wear a top hat to go exploring caves?"

"Of course! It's my favorite kind of hat." He grinned broadly at me. I looked to Miss Bang, but she appeared to be hiding a smile of her own behind her hand.

"So, how many of your men are we taking with us, Professor?" I maneuvered myself into place under one of the boats.

He jumped up onto the platform and squeezed in next to us by the tower. "None, my boy. We need to be able to move quickly. If we take a large number of men it will slow us down and make us more likely to be noticed. This is to be a surgical strike!" He reached out to the tower and grabbed a handhold. "Hang on!"

Sparks flew from the apparatus above the platform and we dropped into the night. I reached out and grabbed onto one of the cables wrapped around the spars of the brass tower. My feet remained locked in their positions, so I righted myself as much as one could with the platform pitching and swinging as it plummeted through the night.

We could see the lights of Prague spread out around us. Gaslights lit the streets, and candlelight and firelight illuminated the rooms of the houses and buildings of the city. Full night enveloped the city. We dropped towards a patch of darkness far below us. I fumbled in a pocket and managed to extricate a pair of goggles and slip them on one-handed. Once positioned over my eyes, the lenses blocked the wind and I found it easier to make out details as we fell.

The grey shapes of buildings leapt towards us as we hurtled into the black spot where the opera house once stood. The surrounding buildings became a momentary grey blur as we flashed past them and plunged into darkness. We continued falling, the world above defined by a shrinking rectangle of starlight.

For a moment my heart raced as I remembered Miss Bang's comment about the hole filling up with water from the river and the surrounding soil. Were we going to plunge into the water? How could they determine how much cable to let out to put us at the surface? What about the rubble of the opera house? My mind filled with the image of us slamming into remnants of the building sticking up like jagged towers above the water level. I closed my eyes, but realized it made no difference in the dark.

Chapter Nineteen

A Cruise Beneath The Streets

"That was bracing, eh! Very well, let us shed a little light upon the subject."

As the professor spoke, I realized I no longer felt the wind tugging on my clothes and hair. We had arrived... somewhere. The darkness was impenetrable, but I could hear water falling all around me at a distance, and a faint rustle of clothing nearby.

Miss Bang's voice came out of the gloom. "My lord, could you pull one of those tubes out of the bag you helped me stow?"

"I believe so," I replied. Wresting my hand from its grip on the tower, I groped around for the bag Miss Bang spoke of. It was still secured, but the top flap appeared to have come loose during our descent. My hand landed on the odd collection of cylinders inside. I grabbed the end of one and slid it out as carefully as I could without the benefit of sight. The ends felt cold, like metal, but the sides were slick, with a glassy texture. After a moment the tube came free. "I've got it. Now what?"

"Grab each of the brass ends, my lord. Twist them in opposite directions until they stop turning." Miss Bang's tone was calm, but her disembodied voice in the dark unnerved me.

The cylinder was about two feet long. I put a hand on each end and twisted one way, and then the other before the metal end caps moved. It rotated about a quarter of a turn before it stopped again. "Nothing seems to be happening."

"Press the ends towards each other."

I pushed my hands together and the tube shortened by a few inches. I heard the faint cracking of glass and felt an odd grinding as I pressed and the cylinder came alive with a bright green light that spread from my left hand. I stared dumfounded at the device until the professor took it from my hands.

"I believe we will need more than one," he said.

"How is...?" I stopped myself mid-question. How many times had I asked the same question? Perhaps it was time I accepted the impossible in the presence of Professor Crackle and Miss Bang.

"Chemical luminescence, my boy. There is an ongoing chemical reaction in the glow tube producing light as the reaction continues. It will provide light for about twenty to twenty five minutes."

In the eerie green light, Miss Bang leaned forward and slipped another of the cylinders from the bag. With a practiced hand she activated it before continuing her explanation.

"The crunch is a small glass capsule being broken. The capsule is full of a catalyst, which triggers the chemical reaction. Of course, once it starts, we can't stop it. If you could be kind enough to start cutting away the tie-downs on the boat, my lord?"

I looked at our surroundings as the glow pushed back the shadows. The platform hovered stock still about a foot over a lake, which vanished into the darkness. I could hear water falling into the lake in various places, creating ripples and echoes off the walls of the shaft. In the green light there was no sign of the shaft walls or of other solid ground.

I drew my knife, ducked under one of the boats and began working my way around the edges, cutting through each of the straps. When I sliced through the last of the ties, I pushed upwards against the bottom of the boat and was surprised to find it light enough to easily pick up and lever out over the brass rail of the platform.

"No, my lord!" Miss Bang shouted, but it was too late. I pushed the boat out and over the edge. The disc of the cockleshell boat slapped down against the water with a wet splat, sending dirty water in all directions. She rushed to the rail, ducking under it and holding on with her left hand while stretching with her right to grab the gunwale of the boat. Her hand missed by inches, and the boat slowly drifted farther from her fingers as she sought a purchase. The light flickered as the shining tube she hastily set down slid between two piles of equipment.

"Enough, Titania! Don't fall in. We can make do with the one boat." The professor took her arm and pulled her back onto the platform.

"I'm sorry," I said. "I wasn't thinking. I didn't realize it was going to drift away so fast." The boat disappeared into the darkness, quickly sliding past our small globe of illumination.

Professor Crackle dismissed my apology with the wave of a hand. "Think nothing of it. We've actually learned something. The boat didn't just drift off; a current swept it away. This means there is an outlet to the shaft, most likely the tunnel we're looking for. As long as the water isn't flowing in faster than the outlet is draining it out, we'll be fine."

"And if the water is flowing in faster?"

Miss Bang answered for him. "Then we'll be very lucky if the tunnel isn't already covered by water. If we can get into the tunnel, we'll have to move quickly to get to the end of it before it floods."

We continued untying equipment from the debarkation platform. When we freed the second boat, Miss Bang made us wait a moment while she attached a rope to an eyelet on the gunwale. When the professor and I pushed the boat off into the water, she used the rope to reel the small circular ship back in and tie it off on the rail of the platform.

I climbed over the rail and gingerly boarded the cockleshell. The wide, flat boat felt unstable under my feet, so I hunkered down as best I could. Miss Bang handed out the rest of the equipment as the professor freed it from the central tower: climbing ropes, pitons and hammers, and what appeared to be crossbows loaded with harpoons. She handed me one of the glowing tubes and directed me to a fitting behind a seat where I mounted the tube in an upright, standing position. We manhandled the case of glow tubes into the boat but I struggled to find space to stow them.

"We're running out of room, Harmonious," she said.

He looked over our progress. "So it seems. Go ahead and board. I think we can squeeze in a few of these cables." He removed several more climbing ropes, draping them over his shoulders.

Miss Bang came and knelt at the edge of the platform and stretched her hand out to me. I took her hand and helped her move to the center of the boat. She settled down onto the seat, and began to unship a pair of oars clamped to the inside of the vessel.

"Professor?" I asked.

"One second. Here, take this," he said and handed me one of the coils of rope from his shoulders. I took it and passed it over my head, wearing it like a bandoleer. He then handed me the other glow tube, which I passed on to Miss Bang. She put one free oar aside and affixed the tube in another bracket. The professor grabbed up a small package from inside a box attached to the tower and then joined us in the cockleshell.

As we settled into our places the ship seemed to teeter alarmingly. While the wide shell of the boat could seemingly accommodate more equipment, the shallow draft of the vessel left me feeling we were close to sinking with each movement.

Miss Bang instructed me to pull on the loose end of the rope, which held our boat secured to the platform. I pulled, and the cable slipped free and we drifted away.

"Excellent!" said the professor, and he opened the package he carried. From inside, he pulled a small revolver, which he loaded with a single shell and fired into the air. The shot burst into a bright reddish flare that streaked upwards and bounced off of the walls of the shaft before arcing back down to extinguish itself in the waters below. As I followed the movement of the flare, I realized the platform was no longer visible. The flare was a signal to *The Argos* to retrieve it.

The professor returned the small gun to its container and shoved the entire package into a pocket of his jacket.

"*The Argos* won't be waiting for us, Professor?"

"I'm afraid not. I had to leave the tracker set to follow the drilling machine. If we fail in our task, Captain Peerless has the task of warning the castle of the danger if the drill gets too close."

"I see."

"Harmonious," Miss Bang said with a note of alarm in her voice. "We seem to be moving rather quickly."

"Indeed, so it would appear," he replied. "It would imply a rather deep shaft nearby." The faint roar of rushing water was growing noticeably louder with each passing second. "I suggest everyone hold on!" he cried as the shaft wall came into view in the green light cast by the glow tubes.

A wide, low arch of earth opened above the surface of the water, a dark maw in the sickly brown face of the muddy soil. As low as the arch seemed to be, it was well over six feet in height and twice that in width, much larger than our little boat. The current swept us towards the opening and was already too strong to row against. There was no fighting it: we were going through.

The rush of the current grew deafening as we approached the maw, the surface of the water dipped down in the middle as it swept into the space beyond. Holding on for dear life, we hurtled, screaming, into the void. We dropped several feet, as we shot over the fall and into a long, low tunnel dimly visible in the ghastly light of the glow tubes. We managed to remain upright despite our sudden descent and were floating smoothly along away from the falls.

"Was that it?" I asked, surprised we seemed to have so quickly escaped the danger.

The professor shook his head. "No, the worst part is still ahead. We are moving quite fast. You just can't tell because the walls are regular. There is still a much bigger drop off somewhere up ahead. All of this water must be going somewhere. It may be a sinkhole or another shaft driven to prevent pursuit through the tunnels. We did bring the crossbows, yes?"

We scrabbled through the scrambled equipment on the floor of the boat and came up with two crossbows loaded with small harpoons. Each missile featured a small ring attached near its head. The professor and I went to work attaching the end of a cable to each ring and making sure it was secure.

"Harmonious, your lordship, quickly!" Miss Bang pointed ahead of us, where we heard the roar of falling water. The professor raised his crossbow and fired the shaft into the side of the tunnel wall. The rope leapt after the projectile and rapidly streamed away from us as we were pulled along with the current. The professor dropped his crossbow, which bounced over the side, and lunged for the rope. He caught the end, but it slipped from his hands as we swept closer to the unseen falls.

"Crossbow! Crossbow!" the professor cried, and I tossed him the crossbow in my hands. As he caught it and took aim, I pulled up the other end of the cable and flipped it around the seat of the boat. As I made a hasty knot and pulled it tight, the professor fired and the rope streamed out after the harpoon. Miss Bang ducked under the cable to keep from being swept out of the boat as the rope went tight.

"Hang on!" I cried as the boat came to a sudden, jerking stop at the end of the line.

I was anchored by my grip on the seat and the cable, but Miss Bang and the professor slid across the floor of the boat. Miss Bang managed to brace herself, having kept her weight low to the deck. The professor wasn't in as good a position. He pitched backwards and dropped the second crossbow, which fell overboard and was lost to the current. He managed to hook one hand into the boat, but his legs swung off the side and into the water, and he was hard-pressed to keep his hold on the ship.

A wave of water crested over the gunwale and momentarily swamped our tiny vessel, washing away loose equipment as it went. The professor sputtered as the craft bobbed back up, but he was still hanging off the gunwale and the current pulled at him, trying to drag him bodily away from us.

"Harmonious!" Miss Bang cried. She started to move towards him to help him back aboard the boat.

"No, not yet!" I yelled, "Brace for impact!" was all I could think to say as the tethering cable, which kept us from being swept away in the current, drove us towards the low earthen wall of the tunnel.

I ducked and grabbed hold of Miss Bang's shoulder as she stretched out and seized the professor's wrist. The boat slammed into the packed earth wall of the tunnel and broke through into another space sending clods of dirt in all directions. One of the glow tubes smacked into the low roof of the tunnel and shattered, splattering glowing chemicals and shards of glass into the boat. I also heard a crack as the rope tightened on the seat of the boat and the wood began to splinter.

What little equipment we kept from being washed away went tumbling along the boat and rolled off into the water, excepting only a handful of items under our bodies.

Miss Bang hauled on the professor's arms and dragged him aboard the small, pitching craft. The current bounced us repeatedly into the side of the wide, low tunnel. The roaring noise of more falls could be heard just beyond the light of our remaining glow tube.

"Grab the tubes," the professor cried, "We can't afford to lose those!"

The bag containing our light sources slid next to him at the tail end of the boat and somehow managed to keep from tipping over into the water. I crawled to the rear of the craft and slipped my hand through the strap of the bag, hauling it back into the center.

"Good, good," the professor said as he took stock of our situation. "We can't stay here, and we can't go back." He pointed to the muddy hole in the wall the boat bounced up against. "We have to go into the breach. Hopefully it is the tunnel we are seeking. My lord, can you carry the light tubes? Let Miss Bang take your rope."

In the low space of the tunnel, I slid the coil of rope from my shoulders and handed it to Miss Bang, who draped it over her own. I pulled another tube from the bag and handed it to the professor before hefting the bag of tubes onto my back and passing the strap over my shoulder. I said, "We'll need more light in there."

"Good thinking," The professor deftly activated the light tube as he replied. He handed the activated cylinder to Miss Bang. "Titania, you go first, and we'll pass you what equipment we have left."

"Yes, Harmonious," she said, taking the glowing rod. She turned and crawled to the edge of the boat as it bumped up against the rough hole in the wall. She slid the light ahead of her and called back to us. "It opens out into another tunnel. The walls are smooth, so it must have been dug out." She thrust herself into the space beyond, becoming smeared with mud from the wet walls and floor.

The professor slid up to the opening and began to hand ropes, grapples, and a few other small items through the gap to Miss Bang. The seat beneath me cracked again, and the boat lurched as the cable ate into the broken seat which held us against the pull of the current. "It's not going to hold much longer, Professor! I don't think we can wait!"

"You're right. Come along while we can!" He crawled to the gap into the new tunnel. I scrabbled after him, but the boat lurched again as another section of the seat broke away. The two of us held on as the boat swung briefly out and back, and then the professor scrambled through the rift with Miss Bang's help.

I crawled the rest of the way across the boat, my weight causing water to spray over the edge of the small vessel and pool in its center. As I attempted to push myself into the next tunnel, the pack of tubes on my back bumped up against the roof of the passage and pushed the boat farther away from the tiny breach.

"Damn! I'm going to have to hand the tubes through first. I'm too bulky like this." The boat swung away in the current and would be swinging back to slam into the wall momentarily. I shifted the pack from my back, held onto it with one hand and grabbed onto an interior support of the boat with the other. The professor's face and arm appeared in the gap, backlit by Miss Bang's glow tube.

"Quickly, I don't think it is going to hold -" His comment was cut off sharply as the last of the seat broke and the boat was swept away with the current.

The professor's hand shot out and he caught the end of the pack's carry strap. The pack, anchored by the professor, dragged me out of the boat and into the rushing water. The icy water made me gasp and sputter and pulled me in two directions for a second before I released my hold on the craft.

The current flung the small boat away and it disappeared into the roar of the darkness in an instant. I tried to pull myself up out of the rushing water by the strap of the pack, but in doing so I dislodged several of the tubes, which slid from the pack and struck me about the face as I held on for dear life. One of the tubes shattered the lens on my left goggle, flooding my eye with cold water. I felt the sting of glass shards as they dug into my cheek.

The chilly waters leeched the strength from my limbs as I dangled in the stream. I no longer had the energy to try and pull myself against the current. It was all I could do to maintain my grip on the bobbing pack.

The thin strap of canvas and leather was all that stood between myself and certain death.

The tubes contained in the pack would make the difference between my companions being able to survive and stop whomever killed my uncle, and an ignoble death lost in tunnels beneath the city. They also represented the only chance to prevent the next attack on Prince George and his men. If Professor Crackle and Miss Bang lost the pack, all would be lost. I couldn't hold on any longer, all I needed to do was to let go and give them all a chance to survive.

As I tried to coax my frozen hand to open, my chest struck the wall of the raging river. The professor and Miss Bang continued their attempts to pull me through the crumbling opening. They dragged me halfway up onto the soft mud, the icy current still claiming my legs. I released my grip on the strap, but before the flow could snatch me away, strong hands gripped my arms and hauled me up and over, rolling me away from the chilling hold of the water. I weakly opened my eyes and looked into Miss Bang's face, mere inches from my own and smeared with mud.

"I am so glad you could make it, my lord," she said, and then all went dark as I collapsed.

Chapter Twenty

To Kill a Drill

I emerged shivering from a nightmare of drowning half frozen in a block of ice as it sank to the bottom of an endless lake. Gasping, I regained consciousness to find the professor looming over me, examining the small cuts around my left eye. He held a glowing tube close over my face with one hand. He smiled as I blinked up at him.

"Good! Glad to have you with us. Gave us quite a scare let me tell you. You have a few small cuts around your eye, but there is no sign of damage to the eye itself. As long as they don't start bleeding again you should be all right. The cold water has mostly taken care of them. I wish I could give you some time to rest after the dunking you took, but I'm afraid we must be going. Come!" With the last word he stood up and held out a slightly dirty hand to me. I took his hand and let him help me to my feet.

"It seems I owe you my life again. Both of you."

"Nonsense, my boy. You saved our lives as well. Without you, we could well have been swept away, or lost the glow tubes. Think no more about it. We still have a lot to do."

We were wet and covered in mud. The tunnel we stood in was ankle deep with a fine layer of pulverized soil, which, when combined with water, instantly became a sticky muck. Our dark clothing was rapidly turning light as the silt worked its way into the fibers. In the green light of the glow tubes, it was impossible to tell the true color, but we were a motley looking lot.

Miss Bang approached from farther down the tunnel with another glow tube in hand. Professor Crackle handed me what was left of my goggles.

"At least you've got protection for one eye. I'm afraid I lost my goggles with the other equipment."

Miss Bang stood before us and said, "I believe I've been able to figure out which way is which. Back that way," she pointed behind her with the glowing tube, "there is a branch in the tunnel and the sound of rushing water. I believe it should lead to the base, but it may be somewhat difficult to make it back to the main tunnel. The level of the floor drops quickly where it branches, so it may lead into the shaft taking all the water. But there are two hoses across the gap." She pointed to a pair of thick hoses buried in the wet sludge on the floor of the tunnel.

One appeared to be covered in thick, heavy insulation. The other was of greater diameter, but was not thickly insulated and appeared to be held open by a coil of wire set into the inside of the hose. Both appeared to be under considerable pressure.

"The hoses go that way," she said, pointing in the other direction down the tunnel, "and there is a vibration in the floor, so I believe this is where the drill head lies. The question," she looked at the professor, "is which way do we want to go?"

"Do we need to go anywhere?" I asked. "If I cut through these pipes, won't it stop the drill head?"

Professor Crackle shook his head. "Not necessarily. And we may need the weight of the drilling machine to anchor the ends of the hoses in order to cross the hole that Titania described. We cannot go back the way we came. No, I think we need to visit the drill head first."

We gathered up the few pieces of equipment rescued from the boat. I shouldered the pack of glow tubes once again, and set out after the professor and Miss Bang as they made their way down the tunnel.

I expected the tunnel to be a long, featureless tube, and to be able to see from end to end. While the walls were generally smooth and roughly twenty feet in diameter, they were not featureless. There were occasional rock outcroppings and other obstacles where the drill diverted around some geological structures too tough to force through. Thus the tunnel tended to twist and turn and shift in odd ways.

As we moved away from the point where we broke into the passage, the mud on the floor quickly gave way to a thick layer of dust, or pulverized soil, which slid and drifted into the center of the bore. Despite being underground, there seemed to be a faint breeze as air moved towards us from where we hoped to find the drill head. The breeze helped to dry me off, but it also made me shiver as bad as the icy water from the underground river. I struggled to warm my tired muscles through exertion as I hurried behind the professor.

We could tell as we neared the drill head. The dust hovered above the floor, agitated by vibrations in the soil. It caused the mismatched tubing, which we followed, to disappear into the floor, and the footprints we left in the soft ground quickly erased themselves due to the excitation.

The professor stopped us. "We lost our ear protection with the boat, unfortunately. The drill head seems to be using ultrasonics, which are beyond the range of hearing, but are capable of doing some significant damage. We are going to have to improvise before we go much further."

"What kind of protection are you thinking of, Professor?" I asked.

"Offhand I'd suggest plugging our ears with cotton, but the medical kit also went with the boat."

Miss Bang gestured to the professor, "Do you still have your handkerchief, Harmonious?"

"I believe so." He reached into his coat pocket and removed a huge white handkerchief, which looked more like a small tablecloth.

"My lord, did you retain your knife?" she added. I checked, and found the snap on the sheath held it fast despite my tumble into the water. I unsnapped the knife and drew the blade. It shone a bit in the pale green light.

"Good," said Miss Bang, "If we cut strips off of the handkerchief, we should be able to roll them up and use them to stopper our ears. Will that suffice, Harmonious?"

"Good thinking! It won't be perfect, but it should help considerably to preserve our hearing."

I handed my knife to Miss Bang and she proceeded to cut strips off of the handkerchief. We cut the rolled strips off at a size to allow them to fit in our ears without falling out. In the end the professor gathered the remnants of his handkerchief and stuffed them back into his pocket, and we continued on with our hearing muffled by the rolled pieces of cloth.

As we continued down the tunnel towards the drill head, the vibrations grew, causing the dust to dance higher off the floor. Despite the plugs in our ears, other sounds came to us. While the drill used ultrasonic vibrations to pulverize the soil, its other functions appeared to utilize more conventional means. As we approached the drill head, the clank of machinery and whirr of fans quickly drowned out all other sounds. It was no longer possible for us to communicate with each other, even by shouting.

The professor stopped to tie the remnant of his handkerchief over his face, only possible because it was so large originally. Miss Bang and I donned our goggles; mine only protecting a single eye. She tied a scarf over her face and we moved onward.

The air became thick with dust as the drill unit finally came into sight. The professor squinted through the haze. I could feel my body quiver with the thrum of the vibrations, both audible and otherwise. Or perhaps it was the shivering as the water soaked into my clothing continued to evaporate, chilling me further. Miss Bang was likewise holding her arms close to her body. The professor seemed unaffected by his dunking, although all of us walked with heavy feet as the dust stuck to our wet boots and trouser legs, creating a thick, gummy layer of muck at the end of each leg.

The professor gestured as he approached the drill head. I couldn't hear him, but judging by the way he moved, he seemed enthused and excited by the construction of the drill. The device itself sprouted a number of mechanical arms, which stretched out from the central body. Wires ran up and down each limb in thick bundles. The wires terminated at a large round casing. The two hoses we followed ran up to a pair of large spools mounted high on the back of the machine. The heavily insulated tube emerged on the right side of one spool and connected to something the approximate size and shape of a small barrel.

High-pressure steam poured from a vent on the opposite side of the structure, raising the temperature of the air surrounding us, for which I was somewhat grateful. Drops of water fell from the end of the vent to be lost in the dust on the floor. The other tube emerged from the left side of the other spool and mated with a curved brass fitting connected to the bottom of the drill. A large cylinder was attached to the side of the fitting, and it appeared to contain a powerful fan. The intake for the fan was fitted to a pipe and acted like a snorkel, pulling air through a large filter at the top of the device, well away from the floor.

The professor ducked under the paired spools and examined the back of the drill by the light of his glow tube. He motioned for me to join him, then handed me the glowing cylinder. With both hands freed, he searched the edges of the flat panels, which sealed the back of the device. His fingers found a series of toggles at the corners of each plate. He flipped them, then pulled the cover off and handed it back to me. Fumbling with the light already in hand, I grabbed the rubber-lined pane with the other hand and shifted it back to Miss Bang who set it aside.

With the interior of the contraption exposed, we saw a collection of wires, cams and odd little engines packed into the case. On the right side of the machine a series of brass plates were strung together on a chain. As we watched, the chain of metal cards advanced, driven by a set of gears, and one of the thin sheets was pressed against a pin block. Pins extended through the holes in the brass, changing the cams engaged, and moving the arms of the drill head into a different configuration.

The professor reached in to try to examine the chain of brass punched cards, but as he touched it, it moved forward again and he pulled his fingers back to keep them from being caught up in the machinery.

He studied the odd combination of different technologies as the noise and vibration rattled our bones and a light dust continued to fall upon us from the roof of the tunnel. After a moment he stepped out from underneath the lurking spool. He took the glow tube from me and gestured for me to take his place under the spool. I moved into the cramped space, but was unsure what I needed to do. He tapped the machete hanging at my waist and gestured with one hand in a vague stabbing motion. I shook my head, not understanding what he wanted. He tucked the tube under his arm and tried again in the diminished light.

He pointed at the pin block and formed his left hand into an L shape, with his fingers bent flat, perpendicular to his palm. Then he pointed to the machete with his right hand and flattened his hand and passed it along the back of the fingers of his left.

I blinked for a moment before I understood his pantomime and nodded. The professor stepped back and held the tube up, lighting the inside of the drill. I drew the machete from its scabbard and angled it until it lined up parallel to the brass plates. As the plates released and the chain moved forward, I slipped the tip of the machete between the pin block and the brass card. When the card was clamped to the pin block, the blade of the machete covered the holes. None of the cams engaged, but a second later the sequence advanced again, and the blade of the machete was forcibly ejected as the machine moved the next plate into position.

My second attempt met with the same results as the mechanism ejected the blade again. Frustrated, I threaded the blade down between the brass cards, binding them both above and below the pin box. As the plates advanced, I pulled back on the pommel in an attempt to snap the chain. The cards advanced and the machete was trapped against the pin block. I pulled on the grip, to separate the links, but the blade snapped off at the hilt. Fragments of metal ricocheted around the interior of the machine, casting sparks as they bounced against the different components. My hands flew up to guard my face. The machine clanked along, drilling into the soil. We were down one machete and the machine was still going.

The professor waved his hands at me again, gesturing for me to come out from the back of the machine. We rejoined Miss Bang. She pointed towards the right side of the machine, then held her glow tube up and made a cutting gesture across it with her other hand. I looked at the professor. He considered for a moment, and nodded. We moved over to the side of the machine and Miss Bang pointed to a section of the hose next to the barrel structure, after it exited from the spool.

I drew my knife and grabbed the thick, flexible pipe in my left hand. I tried to cut through the hose in a single quick motion, but the walls of the tube were too thick and resisted the knife. I sawed at it instead. After a few seconds work, I managed to make my way through the outer surface of the hose and was startled by a sudden burst of steam. I let go of the knife and stood back, clutching my hand. Hot steam continued to shoot from the damaged pipe as the knife tumbled to the floor of the tunnel, disappearing into the fine dust.

Miss Bang took my hand and inspected it. I reacted fast enough to keep from being scalded by the steam and escaped with only a mild burn. I was incredibly lucky, but in order to cut through the hose, someone would have to place their hand in the path of the steam.

Resolutely, I pulled the pack of glow tubes off of my back and handed it to the professor, who accepted it with a confused look in his eyes. I then shrugged out of my stained jacket and began to grope around in the dust on the floor for the dropped knife. The blade slid down the curved tunnel wall and fetched up against one of the thick rubber wheels supporting the drill. I picked up the knife and proceeded to wrap my jacket around my hand to help insulate it from the steam.

Thus prepared, I stepped forward to saw at the steaming pipe again. Before I could start, Professor Crackle grabbed my arm and pulled me back from the device. He gently took the knife from my hand and motioned for me to go to Miss Bang.

I stood next to her and turned to see the professor take my place next to the drill and saw at the steaming pipe. I started towards him, but Miss Bang grabbed my arm in a tight grip and held me back. Hot water streamed from the tube onto his hands. He held on as the water burned his skin, sawing faster. Steam sprayed out in a wide arc with each cut of the knife, scorching his face and turning his skin dark. The professor was quickly wreathed in a cloud of steam, but he continued to work. Finally the tube severed and he stepped away from the spitting hose.

Professor Crackle staggered away from the drill, his skin above his improvised mask scorched and blistered. His hands shook and he was barely able to hold on to the knife. Miss Bang and I gathered him and guided him several steps away. It was clear the steam blinded his unprotected eyes.

Miss Bang gathered him into her arms and turned to me, looking at me over his shoulder. Her goggles distorted her eyes, and I was unable to read her expression. Not knowing how to help, I turned towards the drill.

With the pipe severed and the steam spitting out into the chamber instead of flowing through the odd barrel device, the noise of the machine quickly died down, but the drilling arms continued to move and render the packed earth into dust. I stood back in amazement and watched as the device continued to function.

"It's not steam powered," the professor's voice came faintly to my ears.

I turned to him. "Professor?" I called.

He turned at the sound of my voice. "It is getting quieter, isn't it?" he called over the dying sounds of the drill. "It isn't steam powered. If it were, cutting the line would have shut it down almost instantly."

Miss Bang held him at arm's length. His skin, which was puffy and blistered only moments ago, was rapidly returning to its normal appearance. In the green light of the glow tubes, I couldn't tell the actual shade of his skin, but it was lightening before my eyes. He lifted his free hand and flexed his fingers, then shifted the knife to the other hand and repeated the gesture.

"I think the device the pipe was connected to was a turbine, converting the hot steam into electricity. It must be full of electrical engines, and it must have a store of power it is using to continue its work. I may be able to find the source."

I let my jacket fall to the silt-covered floor in my shock. Steam burns were incredibly painful. The professor shouldn't have been able to stand, and his hands should have been all but baked through from the heat. How could he heal so quickly?

The professor propped himself up under the spools feeding out the drill's lifelines once again. He bent over the exposed components of the machine seeking a point of vulnerability. With a cry of victory he stabbed down with the knife, but a loud electrical crack turned his victory shout into a cry of pain. He stumbled back into the overhanging spool and slumped to the ground.

"Harmonious!" Miss Bang cried out, rushing to his side.

The machine ground to a stop, and the dust slowly settled to the floor of the tunnel. In the new quiet, I could hear the fear in Miss Bang's voice as she tried to rouse the professor. With a moan, he rolled his eyes and sat back up. "Just... just a small shock," he said. "I think."

We helped the professor back to his feet. I looked into the back of the machine and saw where he jammed my knife between two screws on the top of a large cylinder. I reached down and grabbed the grip of the knife, but when I tried to lift it out, I found it was fixed fast. In some way I didn't understand, the blade of the knife was welded into place. I resolved to let the experts handle electricity in the future.

"Professor, the steam, your hands, your face... How?" I stumbled, trying to form the question, but unsure what I had seen.

"I'm a fast healer," he replied dryly, but Miss Bang didn't let him get any further.

"A fast healer who takes foolish chances," she said, giving the professor a dirty look. "One of these days, Harmonious, you're going to take once chance too many and run into something your gifts can't deal with." In a quieter tone she murmured, "I hate it when you pull stunts like this."

"But not today, it seems," he replied. "In any event, we must make sure this device is truly deactivated."

With the drill head shut down, we removed the wadding from our ears. The steam pipe continued to spit and hiss as it vented itself into the tunnel. There was also a sound of air moving in a confined space. I traced the sound to the larger hose, which appeared to be powered from the other end. The floating dust in the air gathered towards the front of the drill, and pulled itself into a wide aperture facing the end of the tunnel.

"Professor? Something still seems to be happening here."

"What, my boy?" He joined me, examining the stilled workings of the drill. "Clever. I wondered how Scaleslea was dealing with the displaced soil from his tunnels. Since the drill pulverizes the dirt and rock to dust, he's sucking it back out again through the second hose." He tapped the conduit in question. "It will have to come out somewhere, but with a system like this, it could be miles away, or spread out so finely it is hardly noticed."

"Harmonious, we'd best be going," Miss Bang reminded him, rousing him from his admiration of the device.

"Hmm? Oh, yes. Yes, quite right. Let's be off."

The steam in the tunnel warmed the air very quickly, and my wet clothes felt clammy against my skin. I hefted the pack of light tubes again. Our task complete, we made our way back up the tunnel away from the drill head.

Chapter Twenty-One

Traversing A Tunnel

We trudged back through the tunnels as they wound their way under the streets of Prague. The path we carved through the dust on our way in made walking easier, but the reconstituted muck clinging to our legs made each step feel like dragging a lead weight.

We hadn't quite made it back to the point where we fought into the tunnel, when we realized our glow tubes were dying. We pulled two more from the pack and activated them, leaving the dying tubes in the dust lining the passage.

We returned to our entry point and found the rushing water in the adjoining tunnel had risen. A stream flowed in through the hole and carved a muddy track flowing away from us into the dark.

We followed the stream, and the increasing sound of rushing water, until we came to a place where a second tunnel split off, digging into the floor and creating a pit, which barred our forward progress.

Our stream poured itself out into the pit, but the roar of much more water came from the depths. One pair of hoses spanned the pit, while another pair emerged from the dust on the far side and dropped into the hole.

"It is louder than it was, Harmonious," Miss Bang said, pointing at the shaft cut into the floor. "The water is rising back up the tunnel."

"I wonder if the boats managed to stem the flow and cause the tunnel to backfill," he said.

"Wouldn't that be a good thing?" I asked.

"Not necessarily. If the flow is blocked completely, these tunnels could fill up very quickly. If the flow is only partially blocked, the pressure could build up until the clog is forced to clear and then..." he looked me in the eye, "it will be like getting sucked down a drain."

"So we'd best stay dry," I answered.

"That's the spirit!" he replied cheerily.

We took inventory of the equipment that survived our journey thus far. There was a dwindling supply of light tubes, two coils of rope, a grappling hook, a leather case containing a small hammer and some pitons, and the professor's signal gun.

I removed my belt, which previously carried my knife and machete and was about to discard it when Miss Bang stopped me. "The blades may be gone, but we may still be able to use the belt somehow, my lord." I detached the empty scabbards and replaced the belt around my waist.

We tied the grappling hook to the end of a rope. Miss Bang shrugged out of her canvas jacket, revealing a leather corset with a number of metal rings attached around the back and sides of the garment. The second rope we attached to two rings located on either side of the lacing in the small of her back. Since she was the lightest of us, she was going to have to try to traverse the hole on foot. If she fell, the safety line would let us pull her back up.

The professor cleared a space by his feet and pounded a piton into the floor of the tunnel. He then sealed the hammer and remaining pitons into their case and handed the package to Miss Bang, who secured it to another ring on her corset with a small metal clip on the side of the case.

I swung the grappling hook over my head and cast it across the hole. The hook dropped heavily to the floor of the tunnel on the far side and I slowly reeled in the cable. The smooth tunnel floor, however, did not provide a purchase for the hook. I wound it back in and cast it out once again. Once again, the hook slid across the floor when I pulled on the rope. I stopped after dragging the hook a few feet.

"If I keep pulling, I think it will continue to slide. I don't believe the grapple will set unless one of us is over there to set it," I said. "The surface of the tunnel is too smooth for it to anchor properly."

"I am afraid you are correct. It looks like we will have to try to use the steam cables to help Miss Bang across."

We dug into the dust and lifted the heavy pipes out of the dirt. The insulated hose was still under pressure and was stiff, but the evacuation tube was soft and collapsed easily. I hefted the steam pipe and dragged it to one side of the tunnel so Miss Bang could skirt the edge of the hole. It moved easily in the fine dust, and did not seem to be secured. I pulled on the tube, taking up what slack I could. It did not become taut, but the weight of the hose made it progressively more difficult for me to haul it in.

"I don't know how safe it will be, Miss Bang, but it will give you something to hold onto."

"Thank you. Hopefully I shan't need it."

Miss Bang took the steam tube in hand and walked up the increasingly steep edge of the hole in the floor. The professor handed out rope as she went. She carefully ascended the slope of the wall, crossing one leg over the other in order to navigate along the narrow edge.

"Carefully, Titania! Carefully!" the professor called out when she teetered along the edge near the top of the path. The fine dust slid from beneath her feet and drifted down into the pit. She shifted her grip on the steam tube until she held it in the palm of one hand extended out over the hole. She held the other arm out to balance herself, her fingers brushing the side of the tunnel. Moving in a slow and deliberate fashion, she wobbled past the apex of the tunnel wall and gently made her way down the other side.

"Well done!" the professor cried as she strode away on the far side of the hole.

"Thank you, Harmonious," she said as she picked up the grappling hook.

From somewhere about her person, she produced a large, ornate fan and, with several swift strokes, she cleared the dust from a spot on the floor of the tunnel. Making the fan disappear as quickly as she produced it, she placed the grappling hook firmly against the exposed earth and stood upon it, using her weight to drive the teeth into the soil. After several such attempts, she shook her head.

"I'm sorry, Harmonious, but the floor is just too hard for the grapple to dig in. I'll have to try the pitons."

She took a piton and the hammer out of the case and pounded it into the packed soil at her feet with several swift, sure strokes of the hammer. Miss Bang then removed the rope from the grappling hook and attached it to the piton at her feet. She stood and reached behind herself to the rope affixed to her corset.

"I believe we're ready. Who is next?" With a few deft motions, she undid the knot and dropped the cable to the floor in front of her.

Professor Crackle turned to me and said, "Your turn, old chap. Don't worry, it won't take a tick."

I dropped the steam tube and wound in the cord Miss Bang dropped. When I retrieved the end, I looped it around my own waist, sliding it under the pack of light tubes draped across my back.

"I believe we'll need some light over there," the professor said as he plucked one of the tubes from my back.

When Miss Bang indicated she was ready, he tossed it to her in a long, low arc, not tumbling end over end, but spinning straight on course like a javelin. She casually plucked the tube out of the air, nonchalantly activated it and stood it up off to one side. I could not think of any time where I witnessed such an athletic performance, and yet the quiet, graceful lady proceeded as if nothing exceptional transpired.

"Ready?" the professor asked as he picked up the end of the rope terminating at the piton at Miss Bang's feet. I considered the task at hand.

"Are we doing this right, Professor?" I asked when I realized my rope was anchored on the near side and my guide rope, which was in the professor's hands, was anchored on Miss Bang's side of the hole.

"Of course, my boy. Even if you fall, we'll be able to get you to one side or the other."

He looped the guide rope around his own waist and tied it off. Grabbing up the slack of my rope, he prepared to reel it out behind me as I crossed.

I approached the edge and looked down into the hole. It sloped away at a much steeper angle, but the sides were just as smooth as the other tunnels. Falling into the it would quickly whisk me away under the city to an uncertain fate. Or perhaps to a very certain fate. I could hear the sound of the rushing water in the distance.

The guide rope was easier to grip than the steam tube and considerably lighter. It helped me to maintain my balance as I climbed up the side of the tunnel in Miss Bang's footsteps, but the fine dust on the edge of the hole made it difficult for me to maintain my footing. Each time my foot slipped I bobbled on the edge of the abyss for several nervous seconds until I managed to regain my balance. My pace was much slower than Miss Bang's. In time I made my way to the steepest point of the ledge. I placed my foot on the top of the ridge, but the edge of the hole crumbled away under my weight. I hung there for a moment, windmilling my arms and trying to keep from overbalancing, but it was already too late. I lunged forward with my free leg, reaching for the next step past the apex. For a split second I hung there, a foot on each side of the abyss, teetering.

As my precarious balance failed, I grabbed the guide rope with both hands and pulled hard, leaping toward Miss Bang. I ran along the side of the wall away from the pit as I hauled franticly on the rope. Kicking up dust as I went, I ran out and came to a stop beside her.

"Well done!" the professor cried, "Excellent idea! Hand your pack to Miss Bang, I have a thought." I doffed the pack of light tubes and handed it over to her. "Good! Grab my rope." He twitched the guide rope tied around his waist and anchored at Miss Bang's feet. "Excellent. Now, take up the slack." I did so. "Now I'm going to come at you rather quickly. Take up the slack as fast as you can. You may want to run backwards as you do so."

Miss Bang started to protest, "Harmonious, are you sure..." but the professor took off, running up the side of the tunnel at a surprising speed, the tails of his coat flying out behind him, and clods of mud peeling off of his legs with each step. I reeled the rope in hand over hand, but couldn't take it up fast enough. I stumbled backwards as fast as I could, but he was still coming at me faster than I could take up the cable.

When the professor reached the apex of his run, where the soil was already crumbling, I reached the end of my rope. The cord tied around my waist was still attached to a piton on the other side of the gap. I had no opportunity to untie it before the professor started to cross. The shock of hitting the end of the line knocked me off of my feet. I lost my grip on the professor's lifeline as I fell to the ground.

I rolled myself over and groped in the dust for the dropped rope as the professor came rolling down the near side of the gap. He was already overbalanced and his feet came perilously close to the edge of the pit. Just as it looked like he might regain his footing, the edge collapsed underneath him, dropping him to the floor where he bounced and then slipped away into the hole.

My hand landed on the rope as it jerked away from me under his weight. I clutched at it and dug in my heels to keep from sliding off behind him. The professor's weight dragged me for several feet before I finally came to rest, but even then I could tell the slightest tremor would send me sliding for the pit again.

"Miss Bang, a little help?" came the professor's voice from the hole. She knelt by the edge of the drop and looked down.

"Just a moment, Harmonious!" she called, and took hold of the cable by her knees and heaved upwards. The raw strength such a delicate seeming lady brought to bear surprised me, but I was too busy to think upon it as I took up the slack she created and together we hauled the professor up.

When his hand came over the edge of the hole, Miss Bang grabbed it and lifted him bodily up onto the floor of the tunnel. Our crossings completed, we lay and panted on the floor of the tunnel and caught our breaths.

"Well," said the professor at last, "it worked."

The statement was so ridiculous we sat there laughing in the green light of the glow tubes for several minutes.

At last, we picked ourselves up out of the dust. I untied the rope from around my waist and from the piton on the floor. We couldn't untie the other rope from the far side, so the professor instead tied the end of it to the piton on our side, "Just in case."

Our other glow tubes lay forgotten on the far side of the hole, so the professor pulled another from the pack and activated it. He took it and scouted ahead, while Miss Bang and I gathered up the remaining equipment.

In short order, he disappeared around another rocky outcropping in the course of the tunnel.

"Halt! Stop right there!" A harsh voice came from around the corner. We looked up the tunnel and could see white light mixed in with the green of the professor's glow tube.

"Oh, dear," came the professor's voice.

Miss Bang handed the coil of rope and the grappling hook to me and spoke in a low whisper, "They'll be looking for me, my lord. The professor and I are too well known, especially by Lord Scaleslea." She pulled a fresh tube from the pack and pressed it into my hand. "Stay to the shadows and follow. Don't light the tube until you absolutely have to. We'll be depending on you to find us."

"What are you going to do, Miss Bang?" I whispered back.

"Why, get captured, of course," she said with a smile. She stood and hefted the pack of glow tubes onto her back and grabbed the lit tube from where it stood. She strode down the tunnel calling loudly, "Professor? Do wait for me, Professor, I'm not used to all this exertion." She turned the corner and added "Oh! Hello."

I crept up in the darkness to the rocky outcrop. Peeking beyond, I saw two armed men pointing guns at the professor and Miss Bang. They wore matching suits of an odd design. Each carried what appeared to be a heavy pack on their backs. A tube from the pack connected to a mask covering each man's face. A filter perhaps? Another cable ran from the pack to a helmet sporting a large light on its brow. Unlike a gaslight, the lamp produced a steady, bright white light.

I had never seen its like before.

I watched from the shadows, as the two men gathered the professor and Miss Bang and marched them up the tunnel ahead of them, leaving me behind in the darkness.

Chapter Twenty-Two

A Guarded Exchange

Paris is known the world over as the city of lights. In my experience, Prague should have been known as the city of darkness. I found myself in places with a decided lack of illumination with disturbing frequency. In the tunnels beneath the city, I found my light waning again as their captors marched Professor Crackle and Miss Bang away.

I followed the party up the tunnel. It wasn't difficult, at first. While other tunnels did branch off from the one I found myself in, the joining passages all seemed to merge in as we went.

In addition to the flexible tubes lying on the floor to run the drilling machines, I noted a pair of steel pipes hung suspended from the apex of these new tunnels. Every few feet, one or the other of the pipes sprouted a metal nozzle off to one side. While I couldn't fathom the purpose behind those odd bits of plumbing, they made it easy to navigate as long as there was a hint of light to see by. All too often there was only a hint of light.

The pipes coming from adjoining tunnels were invariably a fixed size, about three inches, and would join up with its mate from our tunnel which took on a larger diameter.

I determined my path by moving into the passage with the thickest pipe mounted on the ceiling. The most difficult part was managing to stay far enough behind my companions to avoid detection by their escort while still able to see well enough to follow along. At times, I crept along as quietly as I could in plain sight and prayed I didn't do anything to attract their attention.

Eventually, I ended up hanging back a bit too far and lost them in the darkness. With no glimmer of illumination ahead or behind I was forced to activate my single glow tube. As the chemical fire filled the tube, the influx of brightness seemed blinding to my light-starved eyes. I blinked back the tears and then cast around me, looking for footprints in the dust. After a few moments study, I was able to determine the direction of the walkers and follow along in their wake.

The tunnel proceeded to make a number of twists and turns around large rocky structures, demonstrating the reason I lost my companions so quickly. A few of these were sharp turns, which blocked all illumination quite effectively. I also came across the exhausted glow tubes the professor and Miss Bang carried, abandoned in the dust as their chemicals were spent.

I continued my solitary progress up the tunnel until I realized a white light shone ahead of me, outlining another rocky outcropping. I laid my glow tube on the floor and crept forward in the dimness until I could peer around the corner.

I eased my head around the edge of the stone to gaze down the tunnel. I squinted as my eyes protested, for just around the bend bright floodlights filled the passage, overwhelming my darkness-attuned eyes.

About fifty feet past the corner where I hid, the large tunnel abruptly ended in a smaller, roughly hewn space. At the end of the space was a wall with a heavy metal hatch set into it and a larger version of the strange white lights were set above the door and filled the space with steady illumination. Steps came down from a small platform below the hatch.

The floor quickly smoothed out from there as it blended into the larger tunnel. From above the entry a two-foot pipe exited the base and a smaller three-inch conduit emerged beside it. They were the source of the smaller pipes I saw mounted to the ceiling of the tunnels. I had no idea what such an impressive exercise of plumbing was intended to distribute, but I strongly suspected it would turn out to be something unpleasant.

Off to one side of the large hatch, another, smaller hatch hung open with several hoses running up out of the thick, loose dust of the tunnel to attach to a metal plate. These pipes were grouped in pairs; the larger extraction hose set just to the right of the insulated steam supply line. The plate appeared to have sockets for at least four more pairs of hoses to be connected. It seemed the entry could support up to ten devices, but only about half were currently in use. I wondered how many other similar portals stemmed from the underground facility.

In tracing the path of the drill's umbilici, I realized the thick dust, previously ubiquitous in the tunnels so far, ended abruptly, along with the footprints, several feet from the platform. It was the point where the drilling originated.

In front of the small platform, another of the strangely clad men stood on guard, one hand casually resting on the hilt of his sidearm. I wondered why someone would post a guard on an isolated tunnel beneath the city, which could only be reached from inside the base. Then I realized: we were the reason a guard was posted. We had found another way to enter the tunnel, and let the personnel in the base know it by messing with one of the drills. In response, they posted a guard.

A guard with a gun, and an unobstructed view of the only approach.

I slid back into the shadows and considered how to proceed. If I approached the man, he could easily shoot me before I got anywhere near him. If I surrendered to him, I would not be able to rescue my companions, but would instead share their fate. I needed a way to lure the guard closer, and a weapon to use against him. My glimpse around the corner failed to reveal anything I recognized as an alarm, but I wasn't sure the guard wouldn't be able to summon assistance.

I still had the grappling hook, but it would only be useful as a weapon at close range. I possessed the last coil of rope, and my one glow tube. I ran as quietly as I was able back to where the tube lay. The dust, which was such a bother up to this point, proved a godsend as it muffled the sound of my feet.

I realized I had one more resource in my possession. Grabbing up the lit glow tube, I continued down the tunnel until I came across one of the discarded ones left behind by the professor and Miss Bang. The tube was hefty, with a thick glass body. It would do as a weapon in a pinch.

I ran swiftly but silently back to the head of the tunnel, stopping well back to keep my dying light from being spotted. Kneeling down, I tied the end of the rope around the base of the lit tube. Taking the dead tube with me, I quietly made my way back to the stone providing the closest cover to the guard, trailing the rope behind me by the free end. I slipped over past the edge just enough to confirm the guard was still there. I couldn't see his face, due to the mask covering it, but his body language indicated he was alert. He seemed to possess the discipline of a professional soldier.

I took a moment to pause and gather my breath, and then proceeded to drag the lit glow tube closer to my position.

When I perceived the darkness receding, I risked another peek around the corner. The guard noticed the green glow and drew his pistol. He approached my position, moving some thirty or so feet closer. He proved reluctant to move around the corner, remaining within the lit area at the tunnel's end.

I needed him to move close enough that I could rush him before he could get off a shot. Even better if I could trick him to move past me so I could strike him from behind. I gave the rope one last jerk and dropped it, the tube rolling and clattering along the floor. From the corner of my eye I saw my opponent shift into a more aggressive posture, his gun held in both hands.

Unfortunately, it also put his attention much closer to my position. I needed to draw him into striking distance, but without making myself a target in his sights.

Slipping back behind the cover of the rock, I hefted the grappling hook, and tossed it underhand down the tunnel. I was pleased when it landed on the glow tube, shattering the thick glass with a loud crack and effectively extinguishing the light as the chemicals ran underneath the dust on the floor of the tunnel. Just the diversion I needed.

I shifted my grip to the dead light tube, holding it like a cricket bat. The sudden noise and the disappearance of the green light seemed to make up the guard's mind. White light sprang to life against the tunnel wall and the guard rushed around the corner leading with his gun and yelling, "Halt!"

Fortune smiled on me, for he stopped just past my position, his gun pointed into the depths of the tunnel illuminated by the light on his forehead, while I lurked in the shadows just behind his shoulder. I kicked out with my right foot, knocking the gun out of his hands, and followed up by bringing the dark tube down across the back of his head.

It shattered as it struck him, and he staggered forward. I dropped the broken end of the tube and rushed him, pressing my advantage. As he regained his balance, I threw a right hook, hitting him square in the face. Pain exploded up my arm, and I realized the mask over his face was hard metal, providing protection in addition to concealing his features.

He staggered back from the blow, but recovered as I clutched my bruised hand. He charged me, hitting me high in the chest and the two of us went rolling into the dirt.

The guard came up on top of me, holding me down with his left and raising his right to strike. The light from his helmet blinded me, but I reached across his face with my right hand and grabbed the side of his mask. Digging my fingers into the metal edge, I yanked his head to one side, pushing the light out of my eyes. He grabbed at my hand with both of his, trying to disengage me. I dug my fingers in harder, driving them past the edge of the mask and pulling with all my might. He threw himself back the other way to maintain his position above me, but ripped off his mask in the process. His dislodged helmet bounced against his pack, tethered to him by a length of double wire. The light flickered crazily around the space as it dangled.

I responded with a left jab to his exposed face. The blow over-balanced him and sent him rolling backwards. I jumped onto him and hammered his face with three hard rights and the fight went out of him. I stopped, panting in the half-light of the tunnel. I looked back towards the hatch, but there was no sign of activity, and no sound other than my own labored breathing.

I stripped the uniform from the guard and tied him up with the rope, looping the excess coils through his open mouth as a makeshift gag. The guard was slightly larger than me, but that allowed me to don his uniform over my soiled garments.

Hefting the uniform pack onto my back, I staggered towards the hatch, setting the mask and helmet into place over my face.

I immediately regretted doing so, as apparently my opponent had a penchant for a number of aromatic foods and an aversion to oral hygiene. I took a final inventory of my person and realized the sidearm was missing. A quick search using the helmet light let me fish the guard's semi-automatic pistol out of the dust. I gave it a cursory cleaning, and returned it to its place in the holster at my hip.

My disguise complete, I was ready to try my luck with the enemy base.

Chapter Twenty-Three

The Villain Revealed

The hatch resembled something from a naval vessel, and reminded me of the exit we found beneath the opera house, although this one was much better lit. A large central wheel secured the portal. I spun the wheel disengaging the bolts. A lever to one side released the final catch and the door swung open. I pushed my way inside to discover a long stone corridor. Muddy footprints led away from me, with scattered clods littering the floor. I sealed the hatch behind me, then assumed my most confident attitude and strode down the hallway as if I belonged there and was doing exactly what I was supposed to be doing. Doors branched from the wide hall at irregular intervals, but the trail proceeded down the passage.

I moved rapidly after my companions, trying to catch up with the guard detail. Unfortunately, when I rounded the first corner, I nearly ran over a pair of uniformed men busy mopping up the dirt from the floors. One of them stood aside to let me pass, the other kept up a stream of angry German under his breath as he leaned into his mop. I moved past them and kept my pace as I moved down the hallway. The trail hadn't just run cold; it was swabbed away.

I passed several other men going about their business in the complex, but they ignored me, engrossed as they were in their own tasks. Without a trail to follow, I wandered at random, glancing into rooms as I passed, with no idea how I was to find my companions. In due course, I came across a large dormitory, laboratories, massive boiler rooms, and other structures the purpose of which I failed to comprehend.

Signs in the complex were in English and German, but I could not decipher the terminology describing the areas the signs directed me to. Entire sections of the base were laid out by index numbers in some incomprehensible code. My bluff got me thus far, but I still had no idea where the professor and Miss Bang were taken.

"Hey! Hey, you!" called a voice. Perhaps I overestimated the success of my ruse.

Another faceless guard stomped up to me and growled, "What are you, an idiot?" He reached past my left arm and punched a switch on my backpack. "You'll drain the battery if you walk around with your headlamp on."

"I didn't realize it was on," I answered truthfully, trying to match the gravelly tones of the other guard.

"Don't let it happen again!" he growled. "Now get back to work." He stood with his hands on his hips, staring at me.

"Yes, sir," I said. Sweating beneath my mask, I strode past him, turned the first corner I came to, and stopped for a moment, my heart racing inside my chest. After a few deep breaths I managed to get myself back under control. I needed to figure out where to go next. I was hopelessly lost in the complex with no clue as to how I would find my friends.

So far, I only glimpsed rooms where the door was open as someone else entered or left, or where a window was set into a wall or door. Many, many more doors were a mystery to me, as I dared not try them. But it seemed I had no choice. If I intended to rescue my friends, I would have to begin poking my head into sealed rooms until I could figure out where they were being held, or until my presence was discovered.

I stepped out from my hidden corner and immediately ran into two more of the masked guards. The first one put his hand on my chest and pointed to the floor. "What is this? What is this?" I recognized the voice, this was the same man who had just upbraided me for leaving my light on. I looked down at my feet and saw a trail of mud and dirt on the floor leading right up to my mud caked boots.

I opened my mouth, but before I could come up with a single excuse, the back of my head exploded in pain and the world went black.

Two guards were dragging me down a hallway when I came to. The helmet and pack had been stripped from me, but I still wore the guard's uniform over my own clothes.

Unlike the rough stone corridors of the section where I entered the base, the floors in this hallway were polished to a high shine. The walls were covered with tile from the floor to chair rail height, and then with a dark wood paneling up to the raised ceiling. The same odd lights, which weren't gaslights, were present as well, but they were set in elegant sconces and chandeliers instead of the rough, simple, utilitarian lights I saw earlier.

They dragged me down the wide hallway to a pair of large double doors flanked by a pair of guards. As we approached, the guards reached for the handles and opened the double doors. They pulled me through the door, and threw me face down on the floor of the room beyond.

It was a huge chamber filled with all manner of strange devices I could not begin to understand. The room clearly wasn't a laboratory, although it was filled with row upon row of equipment.

Men in lab coats stood at several of the workstations, holding clipboards and making adjustments to the dials and levers in front of them. A few of them glanced in my direction, but then quickly turned back to their work.

A thirty-foot wide crevice ran the length of the room. The crevice itself was a rough gash, although I could see finished floors on both sides of the gap. A floor to ceiling glass wall sealed the near side. I could see a finished wall covered with heavy-duty switches, relays, and other electrical equipment on the far side. A single two-foot wide bridge connected the two sides. A glass door set into the wall provided access to the bridge, which was little more than a steel plank, lacking guardrails, or any other safety precautions. From somewhere nearby I could hear the sound of air moving, but I couldn't place the source.

The professor and Miss Bang stood next to the glass wall under the watchful eye of another guard who covered them with his pistol. The professor fidgeted at the restraint and I had the distinct impression he would much rather be sticking his nose into all the bizarre machines about the room instead of standing in place and waiting. In contrast, Miss Bang stood placidly and calmly, the very picture of patience.

At one end of the chamber, a large brass cylinder filled a corner from floor to ceiling. Set into the cylinder was an archway, and I could see a small compartment with a single padded chair beyond.

At the opposite end of the room, two large glass tubes were mounted on top of a strange device covered with knobs, dials, and levers. Dozens of small lights shone impossibly from the controls like a constellation of tiny red, green, and yellow gaslights. The tubes themselves, instead of being cylinders, were large glass cones with their points to the wall and a flat glass surface facing the room. Instead of being clear, the sides of the tubes were painted a flat black, while the flat ends filled with color, and showed scenes of the interior of a building.

With a shock, I realized the scenes were familiar. The interior of Castle Prague itself. And the images moved!

A tall man in a black suit stood in front of the control panel, watching this impossible view into the far off Castle. With his back to me, all I could tell of his features was that his hair was dark and thick and carefully cut. His posture positively radiated power. He held himself with a cold and regal bearing. While he stood no taller than I did, there was no doubt he looked down upon everyone in the room.

The guards stopped a few feet behind the man. "My lord, we found this one skulking around on the lower levels," the lead guard said.

The man made an adjustment to the panel in front of him, then turned to face the guards. He appeared to be in his mid to late 40's. He sported a full beard and mustache, carefully trimmed, with his beard beginning to grey at the point of his chin. A pair of glasses perched on his nose. He cast a measuring look over the guards and myself.

His eyes slid away from me, dismissing me as unworthy of his attention. Instead he turned to the professor. "After all these years, you're still putting your nose into your betters' business. Now you've taken to dragging your idiot pets along for the ride? This one was apparently too stupid to wipe his feet." He glanced at Crackle and Bang's equally dirty feet and sighed. "I suppose I should give up hope you might have learned by now if you're associating with such imbeciles. You continue to be a disappointment."

The professor took off his glasses and polished them with one of the scraps of his handkerchief. He replaced the lenses and looked back up at the dark man.

"Hello, Father," he said.

Chapter Twenty-Four

An Offer Made and An Answer Given

*L*ord Scaleslea replied in an aloof and forbidding tone. "You don't deserve to call me that. You have been nothing but a disappointment to me for decades. You had great potential once, but you never could see the big picture. You never saw our rightful place in the world. You don't have the stomach to do what is necessary to take back power from those who have usurped it from us. All of your potential has been wasted! You kowtow to those who should call us 'master'. You seek to curry their favor, although they only treat you with disdain. You are worse than the sheep you seek to protect. You are no son of mine."

"I see you haven't changed, Father. Still measuring the world against your own desires. You look down on these people because they don't measure up to your standards, but you ignore so much they create. You discount their courage and their loyalty. In the end *you* are diminished from it. They have so much more to offer than you give them credit for, Father. I wish I could make you see that. Then again, given your latest exploits, I suppose I'm not surprised. You could have done so much to help mankind, Father; instead you keep trying to tear down civilization." The professor sighed.

"If your so-called 'civilization' cannot withstand my little games, it doesn't deserve the name. As for mankind, those who are wise enough to follow my genius will reap the benefits. Those who fail to do so will find themselves among the harvested. Those who seek to steal my genius and use it for their own ends; those I will crush utterly. Thus it has always been." He smiled mockingly at the professor. "Another lesson you have consistently failed to learn."

"It isn't too late, Father..."

"Too late? To do what? To bend the knee to that bitch, Victoria? To throw away my honor and let her get away with everything she's stolen from me? I will bring about Hell on Earth before that happens." Scaleslea looked angry enough to spit.

"Why, Father, why? What is this grudge you've been nursing all these years? What is it you hold against the crown? We've battled across half the world and I still don't know what started this feud in the first place."

Lord Scaleslea's eyes shown with an inner fire as he answered the professor. "You dare to ask me this? Just one more sign which shows you have learned nothing. You were witness to her crimes and you don't even remember?"

The professor shook his head.

"Idiot. Surely you remember your mother, and the illness which took her from me?"

Professor Crackle looked stunned. "Mother? Yes, she had Goulet's disease. There's no cure."

"There WAS no cure!" he corrected, shaking a fist in the professor's direction. "I put everything I owned into research to find a cure. I spent the entire family fortune to save Caroline, and when everything was gone, and I was so very close, like a good little sheep I went to the Crown. Goulet's disease was rare, but the medical breakthroughs I'd made in the research warranted the additional investment. But they rejected me. First the Ministry of Science, and then Victoria herself. They caused Caroline's death."

The professor seemed shaken. "I... I had no idea, Father. I knew you were working, but..."

"But it wasn't enough!" The villain's lips curled into a snarl. "They didn't stop at taking my wife from me. I discovered a cure, but too late to save Caroline. They called it a tragedy. An unfortunate whim of fate. Then two years later when Victoria contracted Goulet's, what did they do? They invaded my labs! Confiscated all of my materials! They stole my research!

"Victoria killed my wife, but when her life was in danger, she took what she wanted and left me with nothing. NOTHING! I will not stop until I see her brought low. Until everything is taken from her as it was taken from me. Even if it takes me Eternity to do so!"

"Please, Father, surely this has..."

"Enough! You will cease to address me in that manner!"

"Very well, Lord Scaleslea," the professor answered. "If you persist upon this course, you know I will have no choice but to stop you. I cannot let the Crown Prince come under your sway, or let you kill him. You must cease this behavior. Let us end this feud between you!"

"You? Stop me? You overestimate yourself, boy. You're not up to the task. All you've ever been able to do is delay things. The world will soon recognize my supremacy. I will pave the way to a true peace. True prosperity. My empire shall unite the planet and let us reach forth from this tiny sphere to take on the cosmos! It is only a matter of time. And with each delay you create, the death toll escalates. You say you care for these chattels. If you truly cared for them, you would bring them into my fold. Only those who serve me will prosper in the end. The others are merely the price paid for progress. Their lives are more on your head than mine."

I could scarcely believe what I was hearing. Lord Scaleslea was the professor's father? And he was planning more death and destruction?

"You murderer! You killed my uncle! I swear I shall make you pay..." I struggled to my feet, desperate to get my hands on the man responsible for Uncle Randolph's death, but the two uniformed men held me fast.

"SILENCE!" Scaleslea's voice rang from the very walls.

One of the guards punctuated Scaleslea's command by driving his fist into my stomach, knocking the wind out of me. I doubled up and would have collapsed, but they held me off the floor in a grip like iron. The technicians ceased their work to watch our little drama play out in their midst.

"If your uncle got himself killed, that is his fault. I shall suffer no recriminations from an imbecile such as yourself. Do yourself a favor and hold your mouth while your betters are speaking."

I fumed and glared at him, but said nothing. There was no point pressing it any further when we were outnumbered and outgunned.

Lord Scaleslea made a single, sweeping gesture, dismissing the technicians. Silently, they gathered themselves and swept out of the chamber, leaving only the three guards, Scaleslea, the professor, Miss Bang, and myself.

Scaleslea cast a baleful look over the guards and their prisoners before speaking again. "Leave us. Return to your duties. I have nothing to fear from such as these." When the guard hesitated, he added, "Go!"

The guards holding me lifted me up, and threw me to the floor again, before they turned and marched out of the room. The remaining guard followed, moving across the room while keeping his pistol trained upon the professor and Miss Bang. He exited, closing the doors behind himself. The sound of the door latching was heard clearly in the room, despite the noise of wind on the other side of the glass wall.

I let out a small groan from the fresh abuse. My midsection still ached from its most recent battery. Scaleslea's guard was exceptionally strong. I took a moment to regain my strength, and Miss Bang crossed to kneel and assist me as the professor spoke up again.

"We have stopped your drill. You won't be able to undermine the castle without repairing it, and by then, Prince George will be warned about the attempt. He won't be an easy target."

Scaleslea laughed. "Victoria's lapdog will be insignificant after the next demonstration of my power. In fact, it might even be better for me if he is warned and survives while the whole city perishes. Then perhaps the people will see the Hanovers for the cravens they are."

Miss Bang spoke up for the first time. "The city! You can't!"

"Yes, girl. Prague has been useful in the past, but I have plenty of bases scattered throughout the continent. It will be easy enough to replace. If I dispensed with the princeling earlier, as originally planned, it might have made a sufficient demonstration of my might. Unfortunately, I was forced to delegate a portion of the assembly of my singers to an assistant, and his ham-fisted incompetence ruined that opportunity. At least I have the consolation he won't fail me again. Now, you've interfered, and I've decided upon a more... theatrical demonstration of my capabilities." A smile dripping with cruelty crossed Scaleslea's face.

"Even you cannot destroy an entire city," the professor protested. "Such an act would take an army."

"I have an army, you fool. But for this, I don't need them. I've already set the wheels in motion. You disabled one drill, but I have dozens. A network of tunnels runs underneath the city, expanded and linked together by my borers. By themselves, they're inconsequential, but I've already begun pumping a very special mixture into the tunnels." He moved towards the glass wall and gestured downwards. "Air, pulled from the surface mixed with a special fuel of my own devising. In liquid form, it is entirely stable, but as an aerosol... ah, then it becomes something very special."

"You're going to make the entire city into a bomb?" Professor Crackle was aghast.

"Going to? Ha! When I was told of your capture, I started pumping my mixture into the tunnels at high pressure, creating an extremely volatile mix. When detonated, the aerosol explosive will have a thousand times the destructive force of an equal quantity of dynamite. The tunnels will rupture and the blast will completely obliterate the center of Prague. The resulting tremors and aftershocks will cause the remaining sections of the city to collapse in upon themselves."

"NO!" I cried from my position on the floor. I pushed myself up to my hands and knees, preparing to rush him physically.

Scaleslea shifted his gaze to me for a moment, and then looked back at the professor. "I suggest you curb your dog before I put him down."

"You killed my uncle. I will not let you kill his city!" I stood with clenched fists.

Scaleslea looked over at the professor. "This pup is one of yours?"

"His lordship is another one of your victims, father."

"No, seriously, who is he? He doesn't seem to know when he's beaten. That's a quality I don't see very often." Scaleslea gave me a sidelong look.

"You want to know who I am?" I growled. Perhaps the tide had turned my way at last.

"I said as much. Out with it. What is your name?"

I told him.

Miss Bang gasped and her hands flew to her face, her eyes as big as saucers. The professor shook his head, putting one hand to his brow.

Scaleslea leaned his head back and laughed. I blinked at him in confusion. "You're the one!" he chortled. "I knew your grandfather. He really went through with it? Oh, my. What a mess your life must be. A life of being a running joke."

He turned to the professor. "On second thought, I think I like him. Not very bright, but he has spunk. I can use a man like that." Scaleslea turned back to me. "You could go far in my organization, young man. You already wear the uniform of my troopers; why not wear it for real? See the world under my banner and I will show you the corruption, which chokes the honest citizens of the world, and you will be able to stamp it out in my name. Under my service, I will show you freedoms such as you have never dreamed. To do as you will, and answer to no man, save myself. Come with me, and I can make you a prince among men."

I couldn't believe my ears. Lord Scaleslea, asking me to become one of his men? He claimed to be fighting against corruption? A champion of freedom?

Professor Crackle answered in my stead, "You expect him to side with the man who killed his uncle? Really, Father!"

"I? Oh, I think not. True, some lives were lost, but had things gone as planned they would have all survived. And so many more escaped unharmed. You truly can't blame me for those who were too slow or stupid to leave the building."

I found my voice at last. "My uncle was Randolph, Duke of Prague. He saw the prince to safety and then was crushed when he returned to help his people evacuate."

Scaleslea looked surprised. "Really? Consort Randolph was your uncle? I am sorry, but I didn't kill your uncle. His own heroism did. He put those lesser lives above his own and paid the price. A tragedy, really. But you needn't share his fate. In my service, you can be one of the rulers of Europe. What do you say?" A smile spread across his face.

Thoughts swirled in my head. Was it just an accident? Did Uncle

Randolph needlessly put himself in danger? I didn't really know any of these people. The Crown Prince didn't trust Professor Crackle. Who could I really trust? Who should I believe?

What if he really could do what he said? All my life I'd been a laughing stock. What if this was my chance to make something of myself? To have power. To make those who tortured me pay for their actions.

I looked at Lord Scaleslea. "What do I have to do?"

Miss Bang and the professor cried out. "No, my lord!"

Scaleslea's smile blossomed into a huge grin. "Excellent! All you have to do is pass one little test." He raised his voice and called for the guard outside the door.

One of the uniformed men stepped in and snapped to attention in front of Lord Scaleslea.

The older man moved over to the guard. "Your sidearm," he said, with his hand extended. The guard drew his pistol, reversed it, and placed it in Scaleslea's hand.

Gun in hand, he strolled over to me. "One simple test, to prove your loyalty to me, and that uniform is yours, along with all the privileges that go along with it."

I gritted my teeth. "What do I need to do?"

He placed the pistol in my hand. Grinning he said, "Kill the girl."

"What?" I asked.

"No! Absolutely not! Don't do it." The professor jumped forward placing himself between Miss Bang and myself. "Please, my friend, don't be a part of this."

"Restrain him." Lord Scaleslea barked. The guard grabbed Professor Crackle and pinioned his arms behind him. The man dragged the struggling Crackle off to one side, giving me a straight line of sight to Miss Bang.

"Tempting as it might be to have you shoot my sorry excuse for a son, that would ultimately prove to be useless. No, it will be much more effective for you to shoot her. Don't worry. Her pain will be over in an instant. While his shall linger on for years." The smile that covered Scaleslea's features was beyond cruel.

Miss Bang stood straight and looked at me calmly.

I looked down at the gun in my hand.

"Not having second thoughts, are you? While she is quite fetching, there will be other women. As many as you like. Besides, what have either of these two brought you but trouble? Dragging you along into danger? Risking your life unnecessarily? Surely you're better off without them." As he spoke, he crossed to Miss Bang and stalked behind her. He lifted her chin with one hand. "Such a brave face she puts on, eh?" He looked at me over her shoulder. "Time to make your decision."

I raised the pistol.

"Ah! There's the backbone I've been looking for," Scaleslea said as he moved a few paces away from Miss Bang. "Take your shot."

I pointed the gun at Miss Bang. I felt as if I was shaking through and through, but my hand was steady. I took careful aim.

Miss Bang looked back at me over the barrel of the gun. "Trust your heart, my lord," was all she said.

"No, my boy, don't!" Professor Crackle pleaded.

I blinked. My hand twitched, and I pulled the trigger.

Lord Scaleslea dropped to the floor like a wet sack of horse manure. The brass cartridge pinged as it bounced off the polished stone floor beneath my feet.

I'd fired guns before. Even gone hunting on occasion. But it was the first time I shot at another human being.

Miss Bang screamed, high and piercing.

"No, no, no!" the professor cried. Their voices came to me as if from a distance. My world was wrapped in fog. Everything seemed thick and slow, as if the world had turned to molasses.

The guard threw Professor Crackle to one side. His weight pitched forward as he pushed off with his feet, rushing me. He had hardly taken a step when my hand twitched again, another spent cartridge ejecting as the man sprawled to the floor at my feet.

The doors slammed open and the other guard burst in. He took in the situation in an instant and grabbed for his side arm. My arm moved of its own volition. The pistol barked. Two reports, and another body flopped to the ground.

I blinked as I realized what I had done. All I could hear was four brass cartridges as they spun and danced across the floor. My world turned red as two pools of blood welled out from a hole over each man's heart. My stomach rebelled and I doubled over, retching as time resumed its normal flow.

The professor ran to the door and looked outside. He closed the double doors and latched them shut. He went to each of the guards, trying in vain to help them as they twitched and bled out the last few seconds of life.

He sighed, and stood. "I hope you'll pardon me for wishing you weren't such a good shot." He eased the facemask off of one of the men, a thick dent marking the mask between the eyes where the bullet struck.

The gun clattered from my hand and I pitched forward on my knees. "Dear God, what have I done?" I gasped. I felt Miss Bang's hands lightly touch my shoulders as she knelt next to me.

"You've ruined my jacket, and one of my best shirts, you imbecile."

I looked up in puzzlement at the voice. I blinked my eyes twice, thrice, before the form in front of me registered in my brain. Scaleslea stood before us, fingering the hole in his shirt with a look of distaste.

"How? He was dead," I babbled. "I shot him." I watched as he pulled the flattened bullet back out of the hole in his shirt.

"Because," sighed the professor, "he is Eternal."

Chapter Twenty-Five

The Fall

"Eternal?" I repeated, dumbfounded.

"Immortal, indestructible, invincible, godlike, whatever word you choose. In the end, it makes no difference. As I told the guards, I have nothing to fear from such as you."

"But only the Empress is Eternal. Only she is blessed by God with life Eternal in the flesh." Scaleslea cut me off with a laugh.

"Dear God, you actually believed that rubbish? Just another good little sheep, reciting your catechism to the Eternal Anglican Church." He snorted. "Blessed by God? As if he'd have anything to do with that strumpet. If you're that gullible, I'm glad you couldn't pass my test. I'd hate to find that kind of stupidity might spread to the rest of my men."

I looked up at Scaleslea. He stood sneering at me.

"I will never become one of your lackeys," I spat. "I will fight you to my very last breath."

"Pathetic," he said. "You won't be breathing very much longer, in any case. Ah, well." He strode back to a large switch mounted on top of a nearby panel of instruments. "Thanks to your interference, I've decided to move up my time table. I intended to move a few prototypes of my newer projects to a different base before destroying the city, but I can easily re-create them. Did you like my starlings? They certainly liked you." He grinned again. "But now, I shall have to sacrifice this base and its contents. No matter. It is a small price to pay in the larger gambit. After all, I literally have all the time in the world.

"Prague, however, is out of time. I was going to give the city until dawn, more dramatic that way. Now I figure it will have about... an hour or so." He placed his hand lightly upon the switch.

The professor took a step towards Scaleslea. "You can't! There are thousands of innocent people up there. People who have done you no wrong!"

"Sheep who have chosen to follow the wrong shepherd, boy. They don't matter. As I have tried to tell you countless times, there will always be more sheep." He grasped the handle of the switch and made to bring it down. Panic leapt into my throat and mixed with the bile already there. I groped for the pistol on the floor.

"My lord!" Miss Bang cried out, but my hand closed around the pistol and I raised it again. The gun barked and Scaleslea jerked with the impact of the bullet, but held onto the switch, keeping to his feet. I pulled the trigger twice more. He jerked again, but held his position. I kept pulling the trigger as the ejected brass danced around me. He held on under the hail of bullets. Finally, the slide locked in the open position, the magazine's ammunition spent.

Scaleslea eyed me hotly and growled, "There is such a thing as too much spunk." He slammed the switch down, sparks erupting from the heavy metal plates as they completed the circuit.

The professor scrambled for the switch, grabbing the heavy wooden handle and struggling to raise it again. He pulled mightily several times. "Argh! The current has welded it down! I can't raise it!"

Miss Bang and I got up and ran over to the professor. We added our strength to his, but we were still unable to shift the switch. No matter how we tried, it resisted our best efforts.

"So predictable."

We turned to see Lord Scaleslea standing inside the room in the brass cylinder. "Enjoy the time you have left." He pulled a hidden lever and a stone slab dropped, blocking off access to the double doors to the hallway. "I'm afraid it won't be much. I'd say it was a pleasure, but there is no need to lie to the dead. Time for me to be off." He pulled another lever and sat down in the chair. As he secured the straps about himself a loud alarm sounded out through the base. He smiled as a thick brass door slid closed between us.

The professor ran over to the tube as an odd swishing noise rattled the brass cylinder from floor to ceiling. "Damn him! A pneumatic tube? A pneumatic escape system? Really?" He pounded on the brass door.

"Professor," I called, "that was your father?"

"Not now, my boy, we have other issues to tend to," he said, and ran back to the device Scaleslea just triggered.

"Lord Scaleslea *is your father*?" I insisted. "The man who has been terrorizing Prague, who tried to kill the Crown Prince and ourselves, the man you described as one of the most dangerous men on the planet, is your father? I think some kind of an explanation is due!"

He hesitated, glancing back at me. "If we survive this, I will gladly tell you all, but right this moment we have something less than an hour to disable a system we basically know nothing about or the entire city will be destroyed. I think under the circumstances we can postpone a trip down memory lane, don't you."

He reached into his jacket and brought out a familiar cylinder: an odd collection of tubes attached to a central hub. His hand darted back into his pocket and retrieved a tuning fork, which he attached to the hub. I remembered seeing him use the device, or something like it, in the dim light in the ruins of the opera house. The professor banged the edge of the tuning fork on the top of the machine in front of him and pointed it at one of the screws securing the rear panel. He twisted the tubes slightly and the screw in question backed itself out of the instrument.

"How did you do that?" I asked, unable to believe my eyes.

"Harmonic spanner. Very useful gadget, even if I do say so myself." He proceeded to remove all the screws on the panel and expose the interior of the device. Inside was a rat's nest of heavy cables and electrical equipment incomprehensible to me. The professor dove into it, tracing the mysterious windings of the cables and wires.

I looked to Miss Bang. She had moved to the glass wall and looked downwards into the rift. "Harmonious," she called, "there appear to be cables on the underside of the bridge."

"Mmmmhmmm," he grunted back with his head deep into the entrails of the device. If he actually paid any attention to what she said, he gave no sign.

Desperate to grasp what was happening, I turned to my other companion. "Miss Bang, do you understand what is going on here?"

"I believe so. Lord Scaleslea appears to have turned his entire base into a death trap, which may just be capable of destroying the city. Harmonious is -"

I interrupted her, "Is he Lord Scaleslea's son?"

She hesitated, and then answered. "Yes. They have been... estranged for some time. The relationship has been a source of some trouble for the professor for quite a while."

"Trouble? Trouble? Like being trapped underneath a city about to be destroyed, trouble?"

"I believe that would qualify, but I was thinking of the difficulties with the civil authorities, actually."

I blinked at her in surprise. Didn't she realize our lives were at stake? "We are trapped here. We can't get out in time!"

"Harmonious will find a way."

"You're confident of that?" I asked.

"Totally confident."

"Damn!" the professor shouted from inside the equipment, then something made a bang and he extracted himself from the machine, rubbing the top of his head. "Damn," he repeated, somewhat less enthusiastically.

"Harmonious?" Miss Bang inquired.

He climbed to his feet, still rubbing his head. "The cables for this equipment disappear into conduits under the floor. I cannot trace it back to the power source."

"Under the floor?" She gestured towards the glass. "Could they lead to the cables under the bridge?"

The professor bolted to the glass wall and bent to catch a glimpse of the cables strung underneath the bridge. Heavy bundles of thick wires traced lazy arcs underneath the narrow, railless bridge and disappeared into a conduit on the other side of the ravine.

"Yes!" he cried. "It must be a power station! He would have needed one close by in case he needed to make changes to the equipment. I have to go over there!"

We moved to the large glass door and the professor threw it open. As he did so, we were pushed backwards by a powerful blast of air from the ravine. Professor Crackle leaned into the mighty wind until he stood in the doorway and squinted up at the top of the rift.

"The current is coming down from the surface!" he yelled over the howl of it. He looked down, past the narrow bridge. "Of course! It is an air conduit! He used the natural crevice to funnel fresh air from the surface down to the lower levels. It probably feeds fresh air to aerate his explosive as well."

Miss Bang stepped up to the doorway. "Is it going to be safe to cross, Harmonious?"

"The wind seems to be constant. The crossing shouldn't be too difficult." He blinked to clear fresh tears from his eyes. "Although I do wish I had my goggles, still."

Miss Bang reached into a pocket in her loose trousers and pulled out a pair of the lenses. "Here, take mine."

"Thank you, my dear." He held the goggles up, examined them for a moment, and strapped them on. "This should only take a minute or two."

I looked down into the ravine. Far, far below us the light of a raging fire could be seen. The walls were rough, but straight. The ledge across from us appeared to be the only sizable indentation in view.

"Are you sure it is safe, Professor? It looks like an awfully narrow bridge."

"Not a problem, my boy."

He stepped out onto the bridge with the wind whistling around him. His frock coat snapped about his body as the gale battered at him. He paused for a moment to get a feel for the pull of the air as it swirled about. He leaned over a bit to steady himself, and slowly made his way over the bridge. His steps were stiff as he crossed. His coat wrapped about him, and he staggered, nearly plunging from the narrow walkway.

Miss Bang gasped and lunged forward, but stopped at the glass doorway. The rush of air coming through the door whipped her trousers about her legs and teased her hair from the careful bun holding it.

The uniform I took from the guard in the tunnel was made of thicker stuff and I hardly felt the currents as they pushed back at me. I tried to close the door to shield us from the blow, but Miss Bang would not allow it.

The professor steadied himself and continued forward. He shrugged and his coat billowed out behind him, pulling him backwards. He teetered on the edge of the bridge for a moment, before leaning forward and driving himself the rest of the way across in a half-jump. He landed hard against the heavy power equipment on the ledge and bounced back.

Miss Bang started again as the professor balanced on one leg and wind-milled his arms in a desperate attempt to keep from going over. His foot slipped and he dropped... and caught himself by grabbing hold of a large switch. Miss Bang and I both breathed a sigh of relief as the professor dragged his weight back up onto the ledge.

Steadying himself with handholds built into the front of the massive power transformers, the professor regained his feet and studied the stacked banks of heavy switches. He ducked down several times, trying to peer under the bridge at the thick cables dangling there and attempting to place them in relationship to the multitude of switches in front of him. After several attempts to determine how the power was routed through the hardware, he finally started grabbing switches and proceeded to walk from one end of the ledge to the other, opening switches as he went.

As he opened the circuits, the breeze subsided. The roar of the wind quieted down and the air calmed.

"That seems to have done it!" the professor cried.

He started back across the bridge, having a much easier time of it without the air howling about him. As he approached the middle of the bridge a new gust of wind hit us from above. We looked up, and suddenly the bridge was gone as a huge machine crashed down through the ravine, sweeping away all in its path, including Professor Crackle. No longer falling straight through the open shaft, the heavy device bounced back and forth digging huge chunks of rock out of the walls and creating a thunderous racket.

As loud as the noise was, Miss Bang's wailing drowned the crashing out as she tried to charge past me. I grappled with her to prevent her from flinging herself bodily into the chasm after him. She fought me and I could feel new bruises form as she battered and screamed for me to let her go. I dragged her to the floor and pulled her back from the open door. The whole time she continued to scream out the same word over and over, in a voice sounding like a lost soul being cast down to hell.

"HARMONIOUS!!!"

Chapter Twenty-Six

Into the Chasm

Since I met her at the opera, I wondered how I could get Miss Bang into my arms. Then suddenly I found myself lying on the floor with my arms wrapped around her and it was the furthest thing from what I wanted.

I expected her to dissolve into tears once she screamed herself out, but when her voice grew hoarse, she abruptly stopped fighting me and sat back, breathing heavily. She quickly brought her breathing under control and murmured in a low tone.

"Damn you, Harmonious, you do this to me every time!"

She cleared her throat and addressed me in a louder voice. "Thank you, my lord. You may release me now. You need have no fear that I shall fling myself into the chasm."

I searched her face. She met my gaze with a hot stare. I withdrew my hands from her, quite sure failure to do so would be to my great peril. I moved to a kneeling position, but kept myself between her and the open doorway.

"I am sorry for your loss, Miss Bang. It happened so fast..."

"I appreciate your concern, but we have to move quickly. We must find a way down the ravine." Her voice was rough, but she spoke with a cold conviction.

"Down the ravine? I'm sorry, Miss Bang, but he's gone. There's nothing we can do to help him."

"No! Harmonious is still alive. He's very resilient, but he needs us to help him!"

"He can't have survived. No one could. I'm sorry, Miss Bang, Titania, but we must face the fact the professor is dead."

She shook her head. "You don't understand. He has endured damage much worse than this. He can recover if we get him free, but if we leave him buried he may be trapped forever." Her brows furrowed and the heat in her eyes increased. "I won't believe he is dead until I see his body with my own eyes."

"Titania," I began, but she cut me off again.

"We *must* go to him!"

"There is still the issue of this doomsday device of Lord Scaleslea's, which is going to turn Prague into a pile of rubble! And us with it!"

"Harmonious will know how to deal with it. We must reach him. I know he is alive!

"How? How do you know?"

"Because..." She bit back her words at the last moment. She thought for a while, then sighed and continued. "Because he is like his father." I blinked dumbly at her as she scrambled to her feet, paced back a few steps and then turned to face me, tears welling in her eyes, barely restrained. "He is Eternal. That's the research I was working on for him. Trying to find a cure for his condition." A cure? For immortality?

She placed one hand upon her chest. "I hate it, but it is a fact. It keeps us together, but always apart. I know he's down there. He's hurt, but he's still alive. We must find him."

I stood and looked at Miss Bang. She was no longer the calm, proper, and reserved woman I met the other night. *This* Miss Bang crackled with fire. She was alight with a passion most mortals will never know.

"Very well. We will see what we can do, one way or the other. Alive or dead."

Tears fell from her eyes. "Thank you, my lord."

"Thank me when we get free. I supposed we must rescue the professor if he is to rescue us."

She wiped her cheeks with the back of a hand. "The device should also be down below. Harmonius said Lord Scaleslea must be using the shaft to feed air to the tunnels under the city." Miss Bang glanced in the direction of the double doors where we entered the room. The slab of granite stood implacably blocking the way. "We're not going to be able to get out the way we came in. It seems we have no choice but to go down the hard way."

I went to the open doorway and looked down into the crevasse. Clouds of dust obscured the view of the bottom, since there was no longer a strong, steady wind to clear the air. Whatever crashed down the ravine carved great chunks out of the walls, providing ledges and handholds. Some of them were oddly spaced, but it might be possible to make our way down using them. A few other places showed the stubby ends of supports and equipment, the remnants of structures driven down to the bottom of the shaft. It was possible there might be air ducts or other ways into the rest of the complex farther down.

I shook my head. "This is not going to be an easy climb." I silently wished I had not used the entire coil of rope to tie up the guard whose uniform I wore.

"No, it won't be. And with us locked in, we can't exactly pop out for proper climbing tools."

"I am surprised you can make jokes, Miss Bang."

"If you are done laughing, time is short. I suggest you help me search the room and determine what we can salvage for our climb. Of course, if you could uncover a hidden ladder or set of stairs it would help *ever* so much." While her words were tinged with bitter humor, her tone indicated she was serious.

I started to speak, but closed my mouth again as I realized anything I could say would only antagonize her further.

We searched the control room, trying every switch and cupboard door in the hopes of finding something of use. With the power connections severed, the controls were dead. We pulled the levers and spun the dials, but there was no noticeable effect for all of our fiddling and button pushing.

The cupboards were either locked or filled with an array of small parts, tubes and other bits to be used in maintaining the equipment in the room. We did manage to find a pair of short metal rods attached to electrical cables. We weren't able to discern their purpose, but tying the two cords together gave us a short length of makeshift rope, providing the cable could take our weight.

Miss Bang insisted we take the belts and guns of the two guards I shot. As I feared, both men died from their wounds. My accuracy in the heat of the moment proved deadly, as the professor said.

I started to feel sick again as we removed the gun belts from the bodies and checked them for spare ammunition. I reminded myself many more lives were depending on us being able to find a way down to the bottom of the shaft to disable the device meant to destroy the city. Lives who didn't even know they were in danger.

I suggested using the pistols to shoot out the locks of the remaining cabinets, but Miss Bang thought it better to conserve our ammunition in case we needed it on the way back up.

She put one of the gun belts about her waist, threading it through the rings of her corset, and tightened it to its farthest notch. It still hung loosely about her. We tied one end of the makeshift cord onto the belt as best we could with the metal rod attached to the end. The rod and the odd plugs on the opposite ends of the cord both proved to be too big to pass through any of the rings on her corset.

We tied the two cords together by the plug ends, and then Miss Bang tied the remaining end to the back of the gun belt I wore, tucking the rod into the belt to hold it securely closed. She looped the second gun belt through the first and made sure the pistol was securely snapped into its holster.

Thus prepared, we approached the door to the truncated bridge again. There was a brief debate as to who would go first. The matter was decided simply when Miss Bang pointed out the closest handholds to our entry point were beyond the reach of either of our arms. The only practical way to get to them was for one of us to swing out while the other provided an anchor from the bridge. Either way, we'd have to trust our lives to the strength of the cable and to each other's ability to hold on to the rock face despite the other's weight, but it would be much easier for me to swing the lighter Miss Bang from the bridge than vice versa.

We stepped out onto the stub of the bridge, Miss Bang leading the way. The end of the bridge curved down sharply where the metal sheared off.

I took up the slack of the cord and asked her again, "Are you sure you want to do this, Miss Bang?"

She looked back to me and replied, "I must."

She sat down on the edge of the bridge and swung her legs over the side. I braced my feet and took up some of Miss Bang's weight on the cord. Miss Bang grabbed onto the edge and leaned forward to slide herself off.

"Wait!" she cried, almost shocking me out of my wits. She leaned back and began to dig in one of her pockets. "Titania," she muttered to herself, "you're smarter than this. You're letting your emotions get in the way, again. You know better!" She pulled an ornate fan from her pocket, the same one I saw her use earlier in the tunnels.

"I don't understand, Miss Bang. How is your fan going to help?"

"By improving the quality of our climbing gear, my lord." She pulled a pin from the base of the fan and spread the individual blades of the fan apart. Then, with a quick motion she tore through the silk binding the pieces together and handed the freed blade up to me.

I took the proffered piece and was surprised by its weight. It was metal, pierced in several places as part of the elaborate design, and thicker than I expected. I tested the blade between my hands and found it rigid, with no perceptible flex to it. Before I could examine it further, Miss Bang handed another blade from her fan up to me.

"How are we to use these, Miss Bang?" I asked as she continued to tear the silk and separate the blades.

"Pitons, my lord! We don't have any rope to anchor with them, but we should be able to drive them into the rock face and give ourselves a better hold." She handed me another blade and I stuffed my growing collection into the front of my uniform. She continued tearing until the fan was completely disassembled. She shoved the remaining fan blades into the front of her corset for easy access and then prepared to drop off the edge of the short stub of bridge. "Ready?" she called.

I hastily drew up the slack of our makeshift rope and responded, "Ready."

Miss Bang slid her hips over the edge, holding on with her hands as I leaned back to counter-balance her weight. When she was sure of my stance, she slowly let go of the edge of the bridge, transferring all of her weight to the cord, and said, "Lower away."

I fed the slack cord out hand over hand, grunting slightly as she descended slowly to the end of its reach. She used her feet against the side of the ravine to orient herself so she faced the wall. The thick electrical cable cut into my fingers. I hoped the makeshift rope would be able to take the strain we were about to put on it. Miss Bang dangled perhaps a dozen feet below me, the only slack remaining being the short length of cable from my hand to the small of my back where the cord was tied.

"Ready when you are, my lord," Miss Bang called up. Did I detect a touch of impatience in her voice?

I didn't bother answering, but instead swung her, taking care to make sure she moved along the rock face, rather than into it. Each swing pulled another grunt from my lungs as the motion threatened to yank me from my perch and my muscles strained to compensate.

As she gained momentum, Miss Bang helped the process along by lightly running back and forth as she swung, touching only the tips of her toes against the rough walls. The muscles in my arms screamed with the effort of each swing, and my back ached when the ends of each arc threatened to pitch me off the edge of the bridge.

"Just a little bit further!" she called out as she reached for a handhold at the end of her arc.

I leaned down as she swung back, under the edge of the snapped bridge, using the bridge as a fulcrum to gain more power for the next swing. As she swung forward from that position, I pulled up on the cable, closing my eyes against the pain in my hands and arms. Then suddenly the cable went slack and there was no longer any weight on the end! I cried out in fear for my companion and opened my eyes.

Miss Bang stared back at me from a deep ledge gouged into the wall. "Well done, my lord!" she cheerily cried to me. "Give me just a moment to get myself settled."

I sat down heavily on the edge of the stub. "Take your time," I told her, panting slightly from my exertions. My hands throbbed.

Her feet firmly planted in a pair of gouges, she pulled two of the blades from her corset and drove each one into crevices in the rock to form handholds. Finally, she gripped these handholds and pressed herself flat against the surface of the rock wall.

"I'm ready."

"Are you sure about this, Miss?"

"I don't think I have much choice at this point. One way or the other, this is how we're getting down there. Come along."

I sighed and swung off the edge of the bridge, holding on with my hands. I looked past Miss Bang's position and tried to figure out where my arc was likely to take me. I figured I would only get one chance, and I needed to know where my handholds were going to be.

"Here goes nothing," I said, and let go.

My heart leapt into my throat as I dropped through the open air and traced an arc against the face of the rock. Unlike *The Argos'* debarkation platform, there was no hint of security in my descent. I could neither trust the cord connecting me to Miss Bang, nor be sure of her ability to cling to the stone with my body dragging her down as I swung.

The belt dug into my waist as I reached the lowest point of my arc, my weight fully supported by the tenuous link between us. I heard Miss Bang grunt with the effort of remaining anchored against the pull as I swung like a pendulum. My swing took me directly under Miss Bang, and I shot up the rock wall on the far side, propelled by my momentum. My hands scrambled as I went, hoping to find some outcropping where I could anchor myself.

I slowed as I reached the top of my arc, but my fingers only scraped the rock, failing to find a grip anywhere along the wall's surface. I started my return swing, dragging my fingers along the wall in an attempt to find a handhold by touch. My left hand caught the edge of a crack in the rock, arresting my movement suddenly, and my body pivoted oddly and alarmingly, around my grip. I dug in and swiveled to bring my right hand over to the same crack. My feet groped for a foothold and I tried to spot a likely location to place them as I dangled at the end of my tether. My right foot caught on a protrusion from the wall, providing some slight support and a chance to shift some weight from our tenuous lifeline. But it proved to be little more than a rough knob on the surface of the wall, not substantial enough for me to plant my feet and anchor Miss Bang's next swing.

"Hold on!" I called, "I don't have a proper grip yet."

"Neither do I," Miss Bang called down. Small chips of rock and dirt began to fall from above me. "Hurry!"

I cast about again in a panic, desperate for a more substantial handhold. I spotted a ghost of a ledge to my right. Digging my fingers into the crack, I pushed against the rough knob under my foot and reached out with my right hand. The indentation of the shallow ledge remained just past the reach of my questing fingers. I stretched and strained, attempting to walk my fingers across the rock face but just missed the ledge.

Reaching out one last time, I pushed off with my left hand, my foot slipping from the sparse grip, and dug my right hand into the ledge I sought. My heart pounded like a speeding engine. I did it! The ledge proved to be deeper than it looked, allowing me to lay my right hand down flat in it just as the fingers of my left hand popped out of the crack. My new grip was a good one, though. I felt a surge of confidence as I realized we might be able to make the climb to the bottom. Dangling from my right hand, I pulled myself up to plant both hands in the narrow space of the ledge.

At that moment Miss Bang's handholds pulled free from the rock face.

Chapter Twenty-Seven

A Hasty Descent

A shrill squeal filled the air as my weight came down fully on my right arm. Miss Bang plummeted past me, the fabric of her trousers fluttering as she fell. She reached for the wall, but inadvertently pushed herself away from it as she fell, dropping out into open space. When she came to the end of the cord binding us together, my body snapped downward from the added load. My fingers screamed with the strain of supporting our combined weight.

She brushed the wall with hand and foot as she fell, but instead of gaining a handhold, she managed to set herself spinning at the end of the tether. Dragging the two of us upwards by the force of my over-taxed right arm, I groped for a suitable anchorage with my left hand. Try as I might, I could not bring my left up to the same handhold. Miss Bang's spin pushed her away from the ravine wall, pulling me outward as well and sapping the strength from my muscles. We literally dangled by my fingertips, my arm fully extended.

I reached inside my uniform, fumbling for one of the metal blades. Desperate to find a new handhold, I drove the end of the makeshift spike into the face of the rock wall. It stuck into the shaft's surface, but when I attempted to put my weight on it the rock around it crumbled and my improvised piton pulled free. I reached back to try to set the blade a second time, but the rock of the ledge supporting my right hand gave way and we plunged into the dust cloud.

If freefall was akin to being held aloft by angels, that fall was something else. Screams and debris filled the air as we tumbled with no sense of up or down.

Our rapid descent ended a few moments later when the tether between us hooked on a broken support jutting from the side of the pit. The jury-rigged cable held despite the sudden tension, but it took the strain better than we did. I narrowly missed the support as I fell past it, and when our line caught, the gunbelt felt like it was going to cut me in two.

Our downward momentum turned into lateral movement, causing Miss Bang and I to slam forcefully into each other.

We hung, dazed, and caught our breath. As I looked downward, I felt relieved we stopped where we did. The shaft bottomed out another fifty feet or so below where we hung. A shattered engine littered the floor with pieces of twisted and broken metal. Smoke filled the shaft, making it difficult for me to see the debris clearly. Without a constant downdraft, the smoke from a huge boiler engine followed whatever path it could. Unless we could find another way down, a rather nasty landing awaited us a few stories below.

Miss Bang took a deep breath, and let it out slowly. The cable connecting us caught closer to my end leaving her hanging about a foot and a half lower than me. After pivoting around on the end of her line for a moment, she looked up at me. "Are you well?"

I groaned. My ribs hurt, and I'd nearly been torn apart. My friend's resilience surprised me. The last impact proved no matter how fragile she appeared, Miss Bang was a solidly built woman.

"In one piece, yes. I think it will be a while before I am well again. I am sure I will find I am one solid bruise. Provided we survive. I don't know where we can go from here. How about you, Miss Bang? Are you injured?"

"I am better than can be expected, I think." She leaned back to look up at me, or past me, and smiled. "But I think I know where to go next."

"Please tell me you have an option besides 'down, very quickly'."

"I have good news. It is now time for us to head up."

"You will pardon me if I don't see exactly how we are going to do that."

"I believe you will find this is because you are facing the wrong way, my lord." She grinned at me.

Wondering what she saw, I grabbed hold of the line supporting Miss Bang and steadied myself. I pulled on her rope and tried to climb up on her side of the support, when the cord suddenly shifted, re-distributing my weight.

Miss Bang squeaked at the sudden movement. I started to apologize, but she stopped me. "No, it's quite all right. I was simply startled. Go ahead and see if you can pull yourself up against the underside of the beam."

I pulled myself hand over hand, shrinking the loop around the shattered support and making Miss Bang drop farther below me. I tucked myself up against the short stub of the beam, doing my best to avoid the sharp ends where the metal was snapped off. Looking upwards, I saw a finished portion of the shaft wall above us, and the corner of an opening. I turned back to Miss Bang whose shoulders were about the level of my feet. "An access panel?"

"I think so. Or perhaps some kind of ventilation for the lower levels. Either way, it should give us access to the more finished portions of the facility, and let us get to the bottom of things."

"So how do we proceed?" I asked.

"You've made a good start already. Hold tight to the cable. Stay upright. I'm coming up." I took a two handed grip to the cable and held tight, just as Miss Bang reached out and grabbed my foot. She climbed up my body, using my clothes as handholds and planting her feet at the angles of my body as footholds.

Despite the unsteady, swaying motion of her climb, Miss Bang moved rapidly until she planted her feet on my shoulders and scrambled up onto the beam.

I experienced a moment of panic when I realized I was no longer supported by the counterbalance of Miss Bang's weight. Instead, the cable tied at my waist hooked over the beam above and held me as long as I could maintain my hold on the makeshift rope. After a silent moment, I heard the faint sound of Miss Bang fiddling with something.

"Is there a problem?"

"Not quite. It is a ventilation duct, but there isn't enough room up here for both of us. If I can get some of these vanes out of the way and squeeze my way through, there will be room for you to come up." She grunted softly. "Do you still have some of my fan blades, my lord? I dropped the ones I had in the fall."

I reached inside my uniform with my right hand and understood some of the pains I felt. As I withdrew the blade from within my clothing, I could see a sharp point piercing the silk at one end of the fan blade, and the fabric was stained a dark red. As I handed the blade up to Miss Bang, I realized I led with the wrong end earlier when I tried to drive the other blade into the wall.

"Excellent," she said, taking it from my hand. "Oh. Oh, dear. Just a few more moments, my lord. The first ones are always the most difficult. Things should speed up a bit now. Hold on."

I did little more than hold on, I reflected silently. The muscles in my hands and arms burned with the effort of holding myself in place. I heard her prying industriously at the vent and then a series of sharp snaps and small pieces of metal began to cascade past me into the pit. After a few moments, the flow of materials from above my head ceased.

A rustle of fabric came from above me. Miss Bang called down, "I'm through. Try to climb up."

How was I going to get on top of the silly thing when my weight kept positioning me directly below it? I craned my head to get a better view of the support.

The support appeared to be a steel beam about a foot or so wide. I groped blindly above me with my left hand, trying to find a grip so I could pull myself up. I managed to hook my fingers over the top and swung my right hand over to join my left. The cable slithered out of sight as I let go of it, sliding across the top of the beam to fall against my back. I heaved my body up, levering myself onto my elbows and chest.

Fresh agony shot into my chest from the blades still tucked into my jacket. Gritting my teeth against the pain, I kicked back to give myself enough of a swing to scoot forward more firmly onto the narrow beam. With my chest flat on the bar, the pain subsided a bit. I kicked my leg over the support and brought myself up to a sitting position. I looked at Miss Bang and let my arms relax from the sustained effort. She looked back at me from the other side of a small ventilation window, which she had completely cleared of the metal vanes directing the airflow.

"Well done, my lord."

"I am glad you think so. I am afraid I'm not in condition for this sort of exercise."

"Then why don't you come inside, and we can walk for a while?"

"I thought you'd never ask."

We crawled a few yards down the cramped confines of the air duct before finding a vent leading to a stairwell. Apparently, the section of duct we were in was meant to double as an inspection crawlway, because just past the vent the conduit narrowed considerably and the interior was full of sharp, unfinished edges. Neither of us fancied trying to make our way through such an inhospitable mess, so an exit was in order.

Despite the cramped conditions, Miss Bang kicked out the vent cover with three swift strokes. She untied the improvised rope from the gun belt around her waist and slipped out through the opening, dropping several feet down to a land in the midst of the stairwell. Following after her, I slid my legs out through the vent and looked down.

The shaft for the stairs appeared to be carved from the natural stone of the hill. Brass handrails were fastened to the walls. Instead of gaslights, long glowing glass tubes protruded from the walls to light the space. Unlike the professor's glow sticks, the tubes were thinner and glowed with a soft yellow light.

Miss Bang took a few steps down the stairs and looked back up at me, expectantly. I dropped the cables to the floor, then slipped out of the vent and landed heavily in the stairwell. The impact made my feet sting as I followed her down the stairs. I opened the uniform jacket and three more of the fan blades clattered to the floor, two of them stained with my blood. Miss Bang came and inspected my injuries, tearing the fabric of my shirt to expose the wounds.

"You're quite lucky, my lord. These are only shallow cuts. We don't have anything to bandage them with, but they look like they are closing on their own."

I looked down at the three wounds on my stomach. The blood was coagulating, and only a small trickle leaked from the edge of the wounds. The thought that any second Lord Scaleslea's device could detonate made a few drops of blood seem unimportant. How long had it taken us to get here?

"Very well," I said. "Let's go find the professor." We gathered up the three blades, I slung the extra gun belt over my shoulder, and made our way down the stairs.

We descended deeper into the complex, and the air became noticeably warmer and thicker. The smell of coal smoke tinged the air. We doubled our pace, realizing the air was only going to get worse before we could make our way out again.

Emerging from a pair of double doors at the bottom of the stairwell, we stepped into a vast, smoky chamber. Several large machines were arranged around a water tank the size of a small building. Black smoke poured from the base of the tank from openings positioned next to each of the machines. The machines, apparently fed from a reservoir on a floor above, rattled with a deafening grinding noise. The combustion chamber beneath the tank seemed filled with the very blazes of hell judging by the waves of heat and smoke coming from it. I deduced the machines were grinding coal into a fine dust so it could be burned at a high temperature. Even I knew enough to realize such an apparatus represented a wealth of energy to be harnessed, even from simple steam power.

I stared in awe at the enormous machine for a moment. When I came out of my reverie, Miss Bang had disappeared. I looked about for her and found her off to one side. Rock and debris lay scattered, and the remains of the device, which plummeted down the ravine, lay shattered. The finished floor of the room ran up to a railing, which was crushed by rock and other fallen equipment. What hadn't hit the rail lay at the base of the ravine, some twenty feet below. Miss Bang ran to the shattered railing and called out for the professor, although I couldn't hear her over the din of the grinders. I chased after her.

The uneven floor of the ravine looked as if someone employed a copious amount of explosives. Rock and twisted metal were strewn all over the ground. I saw no sign of the professor's body among the wreckage, and I feared he was smashed to pieces and scattered about the devastation zone. Miss Bang began to frantically turn over pieces of rubble, and I could see her calling out over and over again. I ran up to her and grabbed her by the shoulders.

"It's too late. There is no way he could have survived. Please, Miss Bang!" I screamed, barely making myself heard over the grinding of the machines behind me.

"You don't understand," she screamed as she fought with me, "He can't simply be killed. An Eternal can survive almost anything, but that doesn't help him if he's trapped. We have to find him!"

The whole world knew there was only one Eternal, Her Eternal Majesty, Empress Victoria. Unaging, invincible, and ordained by God to lead Her people to the redemption of all mankind.

But what the world knew was wrong, for there were two more Eternals: Lord Scaleslea and the professor. What did it mean? Did God have other chosen servants? Was some other force interfering in the affairs of men? If the Devil granted Scaleslea life Eternal, what did that mean for Professor Crackle? I felt well out of my depth. Was the world better off if we saved the Professor, or if we left him here? I tried to think practically.

"Very well," I yelled to her, "If the professor is Eternal, he's in no danger. But the rest of the city is. We need to stop Scaleslea's machine or the entire city will be destroyed. Besides, with those grinders going, he's never going to hear you calling. Help me shut them down, and I'll help you find the professor."

She stood up straight. "You have a point, my lord. I can barely hear you, I'd never be able to hear Harmonious answer me."

I let go of her shoulders. "We have an agreement?"

"Yes." She looked down, and then met my eyes again. "But first, I must ask a favor of you, my lord." Her voice was soft, although we still needed to yell to be heard over the racket. I leaned in to hear her better. "Earlier, I... I lost my head a bit. Up in the control room. I suppose it is a bit obvious that I have feelings for Harmonious. Please, don't let him know. If he knew, he'd send me away. He is a proud man. He thinks he is shamed by his exile, and by his father's actions. If he knew how I felt, he would send me away rather than have me share his shame. Or he would send me away because he didn't share my feelings. Please don't do that to me. Please don't say anything to him."

A powerful temptation welled up inside me. If the professor was Eternal and survived the fall, I had the power to separate him from this gorgeous creature with but a careless word. I looked into her pleading eyes. Those dark pools, so innocent, so vulnerable. And looking into her eyes I knew I could never bring myself to break her heart, for it was truly pledged to another.

I nodded, "Very well. You have my word. He will not learn of this from me." It seemed ridiculous to yell those words, which should have been spoken in much more tender tones.

"Thank you, my lord." She leaned forward and kissed my cheek. I could feel the heat rise to my face.

"Let's turn these damn things off, shall we, Miss Bang?"

We turned and picked our way out of the debris field and strode over to one of the feeder machines.

Chapter Twenty-Eight

The Eternal

The smoke from the furnace made us cough as we approached one of the stoking machines. From what we could see from the outside, it appeared to be a steam driven device. Instead of the flexible tubes, which fed steam to the turbine in the sonic drill we disabled earlier, metal steam pipes descending from the gigantic tank above us directly powered these machines. We circled the feeder machine twice, looking for some way to access the control mechanism. All the panels were firmly bolted in place, and we could find no sign of mechanical or pneumatic controls until Miss Bang traced the pipes back up to the tank.

She spotted a control valve high above the floor on the steam pipe near where it exited from the boiler. The only thing missing was a way to get to the valve. It was too high to reach, and did not appear to be accessible without a ladder. The only method available for us to reach the valve was to climb the pipe itself. The scalding hot pipe.

I pulled out a pistol and showed it to Miss Bang. She shook her head and motioned for me to put it away. It made sense. We had a limited number of bullets. We couldn't be sure we could disable all the machines before running out.

I considered the problem for a moment, but before I could come up with an idea, Miss Bang tapped me on the shoulder and motioned me to follow her. She led me over near the debris.

"Do you have a plan, Miss Bang?" I yelled in her ear to make myself heard.

She held up one of the blades salvaged from her fan. "Your knife was lost in the tunnels, and mine was taken when the professor and I were captured, but these will cut. We can cut strips of fabric from our clothing to help us climb."

I touched my chest briefly. "Indeed they will."

"Now we need something to cut." She considered the hem of her trousers dubiously.

I shrugged out of the uniform jacket and handed it to Miss Bang. "Here. It is too late for disguises, and the material is thick."

Miss Bang took the garment and examined it. "It will do quite well, my lord. I believe it even has some insulation built into it."

I removed the uniform trousers as well, relieved to have the extra layer off. I felt much cooler and the uniform caused my trousers to bunch up underneath the thicker fabric. Long strips of drying mud peeled off of my legs as I pulled off the outer covering. We sat down and proceeded to cut a series of long strips of fabric out of the jacket and trousers. I wrapped my hands and fingers with the first strips and headed back to the machine, leaving Miss Bang to complete the disassembly of the outfit.

I scrambled up onto one of the noisy coal-crushers and moved to the steam pipe, feeling the thrum of the grinders in the vibration through my feet. I grabbed the steam pipe and began to climb, wrapping my legs around the pipe and gripping it with them to keep from sliding back down. The pipe felt mildly warm in my hands, but the heat quickly began to burn through the thinner fabric of my trousers. I regretted giving up the extra layer of the uniform. I climbed franticly, trying to reach the valve, but the heat from the pipe quickly became unbearable against my legs.

The heat seared into my thighs and other sensitive parts. My grip failed and I slid down the pipe, hitting the top cover of the grinder hard, and skidding down the length of the machine towards the furnace. The heat and smoke pouring forth from the open hatch burned my eyes and lungs. I rolled to one side, tumbled off the machine, and sprawled clumsily onto the floor.

I pulled the steaming strips of cloth from my hands. My hands were red, and my calves and thighs stung from the heat. I looked back to my companion, but she was gone, leaving a small pile of fabric strips behind.

I spotted her when I heard one of the feeders shutting down, and looked up to find Miss Bang perched atop another of the steam pipes and quickly turning the wheel to shut off the valve. She took several long strips cut from the jacket and used them like a lumberjack's strap: her feet braced against the hot pipe, and the strap looped around the pipe and tied behind her back. As I watched she shimmied down the pipe and untied the fabric. She then jumped down to the floor and rolled, using her momentum to pull herself back to a standing position. She moved with the athletic grace of a dancer, despite the constricting nature of her garments.

I cursed myself for an idiot.

I went over the pile of fabric, but found Miss Bang's gun belt atop the pile. I may have been slow, but I knew a good idea when I saw one. I connected the three belts together and headed for the next machine.

Once I set the belts to the correct length, I found I could walk up the steam pipe relatively easily. I could still feel some heat through the soles of my boots, but the leather proved thick enough to protect my feet, and the surface of the metal was rough and provided adequate traction. Once I reached the top, the valve proved to be large and radiated enough heat so it was only warm, not scalding. It turned easily, and I made my way back down.

In that manner we shut off the remaining stokers. Miss Bang proved much more adept at scaling the pipes than I and quickly outpaced me at closing off the valves. As each machine ground to a halt, the noise abated until the final one came to a shuddering halt and there was silence in the chamber. As she descended from the last machine, Miss Bang began calling out the professor's name. Her voice rang out in the eerie quiet of the large space.

We made our way towards the blasted ruins at the bottom of the airshaft. She continued to call out. I followed after, unsure of how we would find the professor in such chaos, or how grievous his wounds would prove to be. Miss Bang said Professor Crackle was Eternal, but I still found it difficult to believe. Surely there was a limit to the punishment he could take. What if he reached that limit?

The smoke still issuing from the furnace behind us became thick and black. I found myself coughing in response and my eyes were beginning to burn. If we did not find the professor soon, I would have to persuade Miss Bang to begin our ascent before the foul air overcame us.

True to my promise, I made my way into the debris field and scouted about for signs of Professor Crackle. Shattered stone and twisted metal made for unstable footing and obscured the larger fragments from view. I looked for telltale signs of blood, but dust and smoke did a fair job of concealing them. Miss Bang prowled aggressively through the scene, flinging small bits of debris out of her way and overturning larger pieces with a manic strength fueled by her desperation to find the professor.

My feet slid on the rough footing, sending me tumbling down the uneven slope to fetch up against the side of some mangled chunk of machinery. The impact extracted a grunt from me and, more surprisingly, a pained groan from nearby. I pulled myself to my feet and called out, "Professor? Where are you?" Could it be true? Could he really be Eternal? Did he survive the fall the way Scaleslea withstood the flurry of bullets? My mind spun with the possibilities.

The groan repeated itself, weaker than before, and I followed the sound, running around to the other side of the smashed machine. Sliding my way to the far side, I found the professor's battered form pinned beneath the wreckage. Still alive, he was in obvious pain, with his eyes clamped shut. While the professor was covered in dust and debris, there was no sign of blood anywhere. He could barely breathe from the weight of the wreckage pinning him down. I called for Miss Bang, threw myself against the shattered piece of machinery, and strained to raise it from him. I heaved with all my might, but could barely shift the hunk of metal. When I was forced to ease it back down, the professor groaned again.

"I'm so sorry, Professor. We'll get you out of there as soon as we can."

Miss Bang skidded around the corner of the broken device and dropped down onto her knees next to the professor. "Harmonious! Oh, Harmonious!"

She pushed at the mass of metal with one hand, as if expecting to simply brush it away, but it defiantly stayed put.

"It's too heavy, Miss Bang. We'll have to find some other way to free him. It's a miracle he's lasted so long. Try to make him comfortable. I'll see if I can figure out some way to pry this thing off." Miss Bang didn't answer me, and I wasn't sure she even heard me. I looked over the battered floor for something I could use to free the professor.

I staggered back to the broken railing where the mass of the rock and machinery landed. Surely something in the mess could be used to help us free him. Unfortunately, the other pieces of the device were little more than bent and twisted fragments. The bridge where the professor stood and the support beams beneath it snapped off on the way down, and were crushed out of shape. But the raised floor of the boiler room was bordered by a brass railing and it might prove to be useful.

While the rails directly under the fallen debris were hopelessly mangled, there were other segments, which appeared to still be intact. I climbed back up the slope and checked the surviving rails for one I could wrest from its supports. The first pipe I came to slid from its place easily, but it proved to have been bent at one end. It would not be sound for the entire length of the pipe, but if I could find nothing else, it would have to do.

I tossed the bent pipe down the slope and moved on to the next piece of brass tubing. It proved to be securely fastened to its supports, as were the next two pieces of railing. I ran to the other side of the blast zone to try the rails there. The support rocked drunkenly; the bolts securing it to the floor were partially sheared off and failed to hold the post firmly. The pipes forming the rail appeared to still be straight and true, but despite how I tried to jiggle and shift them, I could not coerce a single one of them to slip free.

In frustration, I kicked out at the loose support. The brass rocked on the stripped bolts, and the impact sent a jolt of pain up my leg. I hopped on the other foot, trying to regain my balance and grabbed onto the loose rail in an attempt to steady myself. My good foot skidded on loose gravel scattered over the floor and I slipped. I clutched to the rail as I fell, trying to check my fall, but it spun under my hand, dumping me unceremoniously to the floor.

I cursed, and grabbed the rail again to lever myself up, but it twisted again, causing my grip to slip from the brass.

No, it didn't twist. It turned!

I shoved myself back to my feet and grabbed the brass rail with both hands. I spun the rail in its socket easily. Looking at the end of the support I saw the railing was threaded and screwed into the supports. I rotated the rail rapidly, unscrewing it. I let out a yell of triumph as the heavy brass rail popped free.

Using the pipe as a support, I made my way back to my companions. Professor Crackle's condition was unchanged, and she was quietly crying, the tracks of tears streaking down her face. She wiped some of the dust and dirt from his face, exposing deep bruises pooled beneath the skin. She looked imploringly up at me, but her tone was one of command. "Help him!"

"I am!" I assured her. I dug the brass pipe down underneath the broken chunk of equipment, placing it alongside the professor's body. With the pipe set, I shifted my hands along to its far end and hauled upwards again. I saw the block wobble as I pushed against my brass lever and it encouraged me to more energetic efforts. I wedged my body beneath the pipe and pushed again, walking up the length of the lever. I was able to lift the rubble pinning him, but was only marginally farther than with my bare hands. I put all my strength into one last push and called to Miss Bang in a hoarse grunt, "Pull him out!"

Miss Bang slid her hands deftly under the professor's shoulders and tried to tug him free, but try as she might, he remained wedged beneath the heavy hunk of machinery. My feet began to slip and I was no longer able to keep the machine aloft. It came back down on the professor, squeezing a strangled cry from him. Miss Bang cried out in sympathetic pain, but deftly pulled her hands from beneath his shoulders, keeping them from being trapped beneath his body.

I lowered the pipe and tried to dig it deeper in for a better mechanical advantage, but was unable to achieve any appreciable improvement. I looked to Miss Bang. "I don't know if I can free him! I can't lift the wreckage high enough. It's too heavy, and we're running out of time!" How much time did we have left? Did we manage to delay Scaleslea's device at all?

"Wait," Miss Bang said. She wiped her hands over her eyes, clearing her tears and smearing dirt on her face in the process. She looked at the professor for a moment, and then scanned the surrounding debris, gathering large flat stones and other items to herself. "Try again! Just lift it as far as you can and hold it."

I walked back to the end of the pipe and levered it up again, raising the broken machine slightly over the professor's damaged chest. Miss Bang sprang into action as I pushed the lever up, shoving the larger rocks and chunks of metal underneath the machine and packing smaller pieces in around the larger ones to keep them in place.

"Now let it down, as gently as you can," she said.

I stepped back, lowering the machine as slowly as I could. As the weight came to rest on Miss Bang's improvised support, I could hear the crunch as the stone and metal shifted slightly under the pressure. The smaller pieces popped out of the structure and rained down, but after a moment, they stopped, and the larger pieces held, preventing the machine from lowering further. With the device propped up for the moment, I set the base of my lever again, sinking the pipe a few inches deeper than before.

She assembled more scraps to build up her support. "Again!" she cried, and I shared the hope I heard in her voice as I heaved again, raising the broken apparatus and holding it while she shored it up with more debris. After a few more repetitions, we managed to lift the machine far enough for Miss Bang to pull the professor free.

He groaned again as she dragged his body across the loose stones and out from beneath the wreckage. As his feet cleared the rubble, I dropped the machine onto the cairn Miss Bang built and turned to look at him.

He was a bizarre caricature of a human being. There was no sign of blood, but his clothes were tattered and torn. His chest had been crushed, and his legs bent in odd directions, the bones clearly broken. A normal man would have bled out from the internal injuries alone and cast loose his spirit to the hereafter, but Professor Crackle still clung to life. He was in tremendous pain. If that was what it meant to be Eternal, it was a foul curse indeed. There was no way we would be able to carry him out without causing him more harm.

Miss Bang stroked his cheek gently and called out to him. "Harmonious. Please wake up, Harmonious."

I started towards her, when the professor gave a great shuddering gasp.

Instead, I took a frightened step back as the most hideous transformation came over him as he gulped for air. The professor's chest rose back to its accustomed place as his lungs filled. I could hear the snap and crack of bones, as his ribs slotted back into their proper places.

He spasmed, and his arms and legs moved of their own volition. They bent and twisted, jerked and bounced, a sharp snap punctuating each movement. Each limb shifted from its mangled position and writhed back into its accustomed shape.

His gasp mutated into a cry of anguish as his crushed body swelled before my eyes, becoming more solid and healthy with each second. The bruises on his face faded from an angry, mottled purple to red, then pink, and then disappeared completely. As suddenly as it began, the transfiguration ended. Where a wreck of a man lay moments before, Professor Crackle appeared whole and hearty once more.

"Dear God Almighty!" I cried, "How can this be? How are you still alive?" I was never a great believer in the supernatural, but what I witnessed left my faith shaken to its core. Could such a metamorphosis be the work of God? Or was something more sinister responsible for the professor's condition? Surely no science known to man could explain the horrific transmogrification I observed. The Eternal Empress continued unchanged from year to year down the decades, but I never heard of anyone testifying to seeing such a transformation.

The professor put a hand to his face, then his chest and legs. "I appear to have lost my glasses," he said. Miss Bang helped him to rise. He fairly sprung to his feet. "And Manqoba is sure to have a fit when he sees this suit."

"Is this what it means to be Eternal?" I gasped, remembering what Miss Bang said about her reasons for believing, for knowing, the professor would survive the fall.

He squinted at me and nodded. "I am afraid so. It is not without its drawbacks. If you have ever envied the Queen for her long life, you should take some solace in the thought she just as likely envies you for your mortality. If we manage to escape, I will explain in more depth, but for now there is much we must do and little time. If I know my father, his device will have a number of back-up systems to ensure it won't fail, and I've been out of the game for a while."

Without warning, the machines clustered around the boiler suddenly surged back to life. The noise of coal being crushed and funneled into the furnace filled the room once more. I turned to see black smoke belching forth from the furnace again.

Chapter Twenty-Nine

Into the Works

After all the trouble we'd taken to turn them off, Scaleslea's coal grinders had turned themselves back on, creating a terrible racket, and causing smoke to belch forth from the boiler anew. We were far enough away from them to talk, but only just.

"I don't understand," Miss Bang said, yelling to be heard over the noise of the machines. "We shut off the steam pipes. How can the machines be running again?"

"I thought as much," answered the professor. "Lord Scaleslea *has* developed a new form of power. He built these machines to use both traditional steam and this new energy source. We can't just shut off the steam, and we don't know enough about his new system to effectively sabotage it. We can't stop it."

"If only we had a stick or two of dynamite," Miss Bang replied.

The professor turned to her. "That would be helpful. A small blast would let us contain..." He broke off, blinking as if stunned, and turned back to the massive machine, studying it and tracing pipes upward to the ceiling. "There may be a way we can stop it. We'll need to get above it, first.

There must be stairs around here somewhere."

We scrambled over the rubble, clambered back up onto the main floor, and sprinted to the stairwell, the professor leading the way once Miss Bang showed him the direction to go. Not only was he restored in form, he seemed filled with rekindled vigor.

We pounded up the stairs to the next level of the complex. Emerging through the double doors from the stairwell, we found ourselves in a long hallway. The professor set off down the hall, and we followed in his wake, unsure if we were going in the correct direction, but trusting to his instincts.

Rounding a corner, we found him struggling with a heavy door. "Locked!" he cried, giving the doorknob one last shake. He reached inside his tattered coat to pull out his harmonic spanner. What he retrieved was a crushed ruin. The gadget was dented and cracked, and it bent at an odd angle in the middle. "Dash it all! The harmonic spanner is ruined. We will have to find another way around."

I reached for my pistol and realized I left the guns and the gun belts on the floor below when we went searching for the professor. "I left the pistols downstairs. Let me get them and we can shoot the lock out."

"No, there is no time."

"Just a minute," Miss Bang said. "Let me try." She reached into her hair and withdrew a pair of what appeared at first to be exceptionally long hairpins. I only got a glimpse of them as she moved to the door, but each one ended with small metal prongs. She inserted the ends of the pins into the locking mechanism and pried about. After a few seconds of fiddling, she opened the door and returned the pins to their former place.

"Well done," the professor cried as he pushed past her through the door.

"Wherever did you learn to do that?" I asked Miss Bang as I held the door for her to enter.

Smiling, she replied, "A lady must have some mysteries."

The room beyond was filled with pipes and pumps and conveyors running in a dozen different directions. Every few feet there was a large box liberally speckled with gauges, switches, levers or wheels. The professor dove into the tangle of equipment, running from box to box giving each a quick inspection before moving on to the next.

"What are we looking for, Professor?" I called, unsure how we could assist him in his search.

"Scaleslea's device is pumping a gaseous explosive into the tunnels beneath the city at high pressure. We need to shut off those pumps at the very least. Better still, reverse the pumps, and bring all the explosive back here!"

"Harmonious, won't that cause the system to rupture?" Miss Bang asked.

"Exactly!" A huge grin covered his face.

"What are we looking for, Professor?" I repeated.

"Pumps, my boy! Big pumps! With large pipes attached to them. It will take a lot of power to push that much fuel into the tunnels, regardless of its current form. The more fuel dispersed, the more pressure in the tunnels and the harder it will be. He's got to have some very large pumps to deliver his explosive. Spread out and give a shout if you find something."

He turned and dodged back into the nest of pipes and equipment. Miss Bang and I shared a glance, then shrugged and followed his example, moving along separate paths as we delved into the maze.

I came upon a set of metal stairs and followed them up to a catwalk crisscrossing over the equipment below. The nest of pipes continued at the higher level, but was easier to navigate across the catwalk. I wandered along the metal pathways, desperately trying to make sense of the jungle of plumbing around me. The room was filled with the chugging sound of pumps, the rise and fall of enormous pistons. As I moved forward, the noise of the pumps got louder, drowning out the footsteps of the professor and Miss Bang searching below.

I hurried forward, following the sound and came to a row of monstrous pumps, with one pump stacked on top of another so a single set of controls was on the floor, and another at the level of the catwalk. Gigantic pistons drove the pumps, and next to each of the units was a large cylinder labeled with warnings in several languages.

"Professor! Miss Bang! I think I've found something!"

"My lord?" came Miss Bang's voice from below me.

"Where are you?" the professor's voice came back.

"Up here! On the catwalk." I called, leaning over and waving my arm to draw their attention.

The professor appeared from the tangle of pipes and looked up at me. "Well done! Good thinking, following the sound of the pumps."

"Now we've found them, what do we do?" I asked him.

The professor squinted up at me. "Look for a big wheel up there. There should be a gauge near it labeled 'flow rate'. When you find the right valve, turn it all the way closed. The gauge should drop off to zero. There should be one wheel for each pump. Have you got all that?"

"I hope so, Professor." I looked uncertainly at the strange devices around me.

"You'll do fine!" he replied.

I went to the largest wheel I could see and examined the box of instruments next to it. The surface was covered with several round gauges, and a large tube with a floating indicator in the middle of it. While I could read the numbers on the gauges clearly, I couldn't make heads or tails of the labels on the faces of the dials.

"Professor!"

"Have you found it?" he called between grunts as he pulled at a valve below me.

"I'm not sure. I found a large wheel attached to a bunch of gauges, but all the dials are gibberish. I don't know if it is the right one."

"Gibberish? No, it's labeled in Bohemian."

"Professor?"

"Yes?"

"I can't read Bohemian."

I could hear Miss Bang conferring with the professor below me, but I couldn't make out their words over the noise of the pumps.

"My boy?"

"Yes?"

"Just close every valve you can put your hands on. Shut everything down."

"That I can do!"

I seized the large valve in front of me, grabbing it with both hands, and turned it vigorously until it reached its stop. Looking over at the panel of gauges, I noted the floating indicator already dropping to the bottom of its tube. The other dials were moving separately, some rising, some falling.

I moved to the next valve and repeated the process, franticly spinning the wheel until it shut. I was on the third box when I discovered a series of smaller valves underneath the main box and stopped to close those as well.

As we proceeded to shut down the various valves, the tone of the pumps changed. The devices continued to run, but they slowed in their progress. It became easier to hear as the chunk, chunk, chunk of each piston slowly wound to a stop.

I called down to my companions, "All done, Professor! I closed every valve I could find."

"Well done!"

"Now what do I do?"

"Look for a large lever. It will be a locking lever. There should be one for each pump."

"A what?"

"A lever with an extra handle on it. You have to squeeze them together to change the position of the lever."

I looked at the row of pumps I just shut down. Each did have a large lever with the extra handle on them. "I see them. What do I do with them?"

"Throw them the other way! What else?"

I moved down the row, grabbing the handles, squeezing until the mechanism released, and then pulling the lever towards myself until it wouldn't move any farther. As I proceeded, Miss Bang and the professor were doing the same to the controls for the pumps on the floor below.

"That should do it," the professor said as he pulled the last switch.

"What happens now?" I called down to them.

"Now, we open all those valves we just shut down!"

"What?"

"Yes, my lord," Miss Bang chimed in, "You can't just throw an engine into reverse. You must stop it first."

"Exactly! We should have all the pumps reversed, so we want to throw those valves wide open. Set it to pumping back towards the base as fast as it can."

He launched into action, spinning open the valves in front of him, and Miss Bang and I followed. About a minute later, the pumps were cranking back to life and throwing off a terrific noise in the process. They ran much faster than when we arrived. I noticed the indicator in the glass tube dancing near the top of its run. Deep inside a section painted red.

The professor yelled up to me. "With the pumps running in reverse, pressure will build up inside the system until it destroys itself. It should build up rather rapidly."

"And then what?" I responded.

"Why, a rather sizable explosion. Should do quite a number on the base, I would expect."

Miss Bang joined in our little exchange, "How long have we got before it goes, Harmonious?" Even over the noise of the pumps, I could hear the anxiety in her voice.

The professor pulled out his pocket watch and consulted it, but found it destroyed as well. "Oh, I should think only a handful of minutes. Perhaps ten at most."

I stared at him in shock for a moment. It took us more than ten minutes to descend to where we found the professor. Could we climb that distance and more before the base exploded?

I was pulled from my reverie by the sound of running feet. Specifically, Miss Bang's feet racing back through the forest of pipes and pumps for the hallway. I sprinted back down the catwalk, the metal walkway clanging loudly with each footfall. A second later, the professor could be heard bringing up the rear.

Chapter Thirty

An Exit With A Bang

We spilled from the jungle of pipes into the hallway and ran to the stairwell. Miss Bang reached the door first, grabbed the handle, and pulled. The door shook in its frame, but remained resolutely closed. I grabbed the handle, as Miss Bang stepped to the side. I hauled at it, pounded on the door, but my best efforts failed to grant us entry to the stairwell.

"It's locked!" she cried.

"Can you open it, Miss Bang, as you did with the other door?" I asked.

"No time!" cried the professor as he ran past us, "It's a big facility, there's got to be another way up. This way!"

Miss Bang and I ran after him. At the end of the hall we turned left, into a stretch of corridor filled with doors on both sides. I wondered at the size of the facility as we ran. It was much too complex. Much more than would be needed to destroy the city. How long was Lord Scaleslea operating out of Prague? How many other plots did he carry out, which failed to be recognized as the work of his devious mind?

We hurried down the corridor, checking each door as we went. I could feel the panic rising in my throat as door after door proved to be locked. I almost cried out in joy when we came to a door in the middle of the hallway, which swung open at the touch of my hand, but it proved to only be a small water closet.

We reached the end of the row without finding another unlocked door, turned right, and sped down a long corridor only sparsely populated with rooms. The third door to the left proved to be propped open by the handle of a discarded piece of scientific equipment. The professor pushed open the door and we scampered inside. We found ourselves in a large laboratory, laid out in a familiar manner. It gave me a distinct sense of deja vu.

"Harmonious?" Miss Bang sounded just as surprised as I felt. Her eyes roved around the room. Each workspace was laid out with great precision, and dedicated to a different scientific pursuit. One dedicated to biology, another to chemistry, and a massive Holyfield Industries generator standing at the far end of the room.

The professor moved over to another workspace covered with tiny cogs and tools for assembling clockworks.

"He always did insist on having a workspace laid out just so," he said as he picked up a partially assembled wing attached to the body of a small clockwork bird.

"More clockwork budgies of doom?" I asked as I stepped next to him. He nodded, but I scarcely noticed as I caught sight of the next workspace. "Professor? What is this?"

He looked over my shoulder, and pushed past me to take in the new workspace. The bench was covered with unfamiliar equipment, most of which appeared to be small painted blobs with wires sticking out of both ends. The professor picked up a small, lacquered board covered with a variety of different blobs, connected together with wire and traces of metal bonded to the lacquered material. A metal cylinder was attached to one end with two more wires. As the professor turned it, something shifted and several small blobs attached to the board lit up green and amber.

"Remarkable! This is his new technology! Imagine what we could build if we understood it!"

"Harmonious," Miss Bang called from behind us. "Did you see this?" She stood next to a metal tube some ten feet in diameter, which ran from floor to ceiling. An oblong opening on the side facing us sprung from the floor up about seven feet tall, and four feet wide. The opening was sealed with a smooth arc of metal about half an inch inside the outer tube. A series of switches were mounted on a box to the right of the opening.

"Is that...?" I started, but the professor interrupted me.

"A pneumatic tube! Of course! He would have an escape route nearby in any part of the complex. No matter how sure he is of his success, he always has a contingency plan. Naturally it would include an escape route."

"Can we get out the same way, Professor?"

"Let us see." The professor examined the switches. He flipped them in rapid succession, trying different combinations, but his efforts failed to produce a reaction from the tube. It remained well sealed.

"Damnation. He must have done something so once one of his escape pods was activated, the rest of them were disabled." He paused, and then pried at the cover of the switch box. "Miss Bang, a screwdriver, please."

Miss Bang moved quickly among the workbenches to retrieve the tool for the professor. I moved up next to him.

"Do you think you can repair it?" It took us much too long to find this laboratory. Surely the explosive vapor would detonate soon.

"I don't know, but it does seem to be our best chance. If I can get this working, we can escape. It is much better odds than running down the halls trying to find another stairwell. At the very least, if we can get inside, it should give us some protection from the blast."

The reminder of the imminent explosion sent shivers down my spine.

Miss Bang returned and handed the professor a screwdriver, which he immediately used to pry the cover off of the switch box. From what I could see, the interior of the box was packed with thick cables connecting the switches to other bits within the tube. The professor pried at it for a moment then declared, "It seems to be in working order, it just needs a source of power."

Miss Bang grabbed my arm lightly. "My lord, assist me, please?" She led me across the room to the Holyfield Industries generator at the electrical workbench. Opening a cabinet in the base of the machine, she pulled out two coiled cables with thick metal clips at the end and placed a clip into each of my hands. "Take these to the professor. Make sure you do not let the clips touch."

I dragged the cables across the room, pulling them out of the cabinet as I went. The ropy cables were heavy, with an unfortunate tendency to kink, causing me to stop and have to shake them out. The professor took the black clip from me as I approached and clamped it onto the metal frame of the switch box. He then took the other, red painted clip and carefully connected it to one of the bolts on the backside of the switch plate. He did this several times until he felt satisfied the red clip would not touch any other part of the box.

I hurried back to Miss Bang who unscrewed the two large metal balls positioned prominently on the front of the machine. She attached the clips at the opposite ends of the cables to the threads, which previously sported the heavy spheres. As she reached up to grab a lever on the device, I noted she wore a pair of thick rubber gloves several sizes too big for her.

"Are you sure you know how to operate this device, Miss Bang?"

"Yes, my lord. It is the same model Harmonious has in his laboratory. I have worked with them extensively." She pulled down on the lever and the two clipped mounting points swung in opposite directions until they were well over six feet distant from each other.

"What more can I do?" I asked.

"Give a shout if anything sparks," she said as she went to a series of valves and gauges on the side of the machine. She opened one valve and the needles on the gauges jumped up immediately, and I could hear a rush of steam somewhere deep in the machine. She opened the valve slightly wider and jumped back with a scream of her own as steam jetted at her from the base of the valve.

After the scare of the unexpected venting, Miss Bang took a moment to catch her breath. I went to make sure she was unhurt when I noted the wheel of the valve still turning and gaining speed.

Leaping to Miss Bang's side, I hooked my arm around her midsection and pulled her away from the machine, moments before the steam-driven wheel and valve stem shot forth from the device, embedding itself in the far wall of the laboratory.

The temperature in the room rose rapidly as steam rushed from the ruined valve. Miss Bang and I pulled ourselves off the floor.

"Thank you, my lord. A most timely rescue."

"You are quite welcome," I replied.

"Are you two quite all right?" The professor asked.

"None the worse for wear, Harmonious," Miss Bang answered.

As we exchanged words a low hum began to grow in the room, hidden under the hiss of jetting steam. I realized it was the sound of a turbine, hidden deep in the electrical workstation, spinning up to full speed.

"Excellent. But we don't have much time. Once one of those pipes ruptures, Scaleslea's explosive gas will fill the complex quickly. The slightest spark or flame will set it off. If the gas gets down to that monster of a boiler on the level below, the whole thing will go up. If this doesn't work, we'll either be steam cooked or flame broiled. All in all, I'd rather be somewhere else. Switch on the power!"

Miss Bang pointed, and I grabbed an open lever on the far side of the device and slammed it closed. Sparks jumped from the switch, and from the box next to the professor, and the expanse of metal blocking the tube slid open to reveal the chamber inside.

We stumbled into the tiny chamber, and round tubes set in the ceiling flickered and began to glow in an eerie pale light. The air in the small chamber was refreshingly cool, but rapidly growing warmer. The room was decorated with a single large chair, bolted securely to the floor and fitted with a number of straps to hold the occupant firmly in place.

"I should have known," said the professor, "He only thinks of himself. He probably never considered letting anyone else escape with him." The professor pointed to the seat. "Sit, my boy."

"But surely Miss Bang..." I began.

"We have no time to argue, sit!" He punctuated his words by shoving me into the single chair. Before I could protest, he grabbed Miss Bang and pushed her into my lap. Miss Bang's soft form against my own body brought about an immediate stirring inside me. Reminding myself we were all very likely soon to die did not help matters much, nor did the fashion in which Miss Bang settled herself on top of me before she strapped the both of us to the chair. She seemed to have a much better grasp of what the professor had in mind than I did.

"What about you, Professor?" I asked.

"As you have seen, I'm much more resilient than you are. I only hope

I don't hurt the two of you too much if I should bounce around the cabin." He took a firm hold of one of the straps fastening us down. "All secure?" he asked, and at Miss Bang's nod, he slapped a large button on the side of the chair.

Nothing happened.

The air in the room beyond was thick with steam and white vapor poured into our small chamber as the broken valve and the turbine screamed their twin songs.

"Damnation!" the professor swore. "Something has gone wrong with the system."

The room shook and we heard a distant explosion. How close was it? How soon would there be more?

"It's time to go, Professor!"

"I know!" He dashed to the hatch, examining the telltales set into the inside of the chamber to the right of the hatch, then the opened the switch box in the room beyond.

As I waited helplessly for the professor to solve our latest problem, I cast my gaze upward and noticed several wide, flat glass disks arranged in a grid on the wall above the door. Images played on the inside of each of these, as if they were portholes into another area, just like the two odd glass cones in Scaleslea's control room showed images from inside the castle.

Two were filled with crazily dancing lights, one looked into what appeared to be an armory; several others showed views of machine rooms filling with gas from ruptured valves and pipefittings. As I watched, one of the pipes in a porthole blew itself apart and the view changed to the crazily dancing lights as the room shook with another explosion.

Strangest of all were two portholes depicting perfectly calm scenes inside a well-appointed house. One scene was a view of a desk in an opulent study. Hands appeared from either side of the viewer and flipped through the papers upon the desk. The overall effect was as if I was looking out of someone else's eyes. No, not out of his eyes. The angle was wrong. Somewhere slightly lower. Very strange.

The other showed a moving view, as if walking down a corridor. It struck me, as the scene was eerily familiar, and yet I could not place it. The motion stopped at a pair of large, darkly stained doors, and a hand rose to knock on the dark wood.

"I think I have it," the professor called, interrupting my examination of the viewports. "There is too much power in the system, and the interior mechanism seems to have shorted out. But I should be able to switch it from outside."

"You are not staying behind, Harmonious!" Miss Bang commanded.

"Never fear, my dear, I simply need to throw a switch."

The room shook again, and another viewport turned to those strange lights. "Then hurry!" she answered.

I looked up to the two odd portholes, and suddenly knew why the views seemed so very familiar. The moving view stopped in front of a desk, with the Crown Prince seated, going over some paperwork. My eyes leapt back to the other viewer, where a uniformed figure could be seen standing at the end of the desk, his face hidden beyond the edge of the porthole. But the uniform itself was very distinctive: an officer of the Imperial Guard, and a well decorated one too.

"No! Wait!" I cried out as the view began to tilt upwards to reveal a silver gorget. A second longer and I'd see the face of the traitor in the Prince's retinue.

Heedless, the professor flipped the switch sending up another shower of sparks. He dove back into the chamber with us as the metal door slid shut, sealing us inside. An invisible hand pressed Miss Bang and myself down into the seat as the chamber shot upwards inside the pneumatic tube.

We scarcely adjusted to the first sudden burst of acceleration when a monstrous explosion sounded, shaking the chamber from side to side, and we were slammed harshly back against the chair by a stronger burst of acceleration. Metal screamed around us, and the entire chamber went dark as the power failed. A high scream sounded in the small chamber, but I knew not who voiced it, or how many of us joined in. We experienced a series of harsh jolts and my head cracked against Miss Bang's and I knew no more as our steam-driven projectile propelled us upwards to our salvation. Or our doom.

Chapter Thirty-One

An Incomplete Escape

The feeling of something warm and soft pressed against my hand brought me back to awareness. I flexed my fingers slightly and was rewarded with a gentle pressure of more warm softness against my lap and chest. I tried to snuggle against the pressure, but found myself unable to move further.

Two things began quietly nagging at the back of my head. The first: while I seemed to be laying on my right side, my right arm was swinging freely in open air. That didn't make sense. The second was a sharp pain on my forehead where Miss Bang's skull knocked against mine.

My eyes shot open with the sudden realization of what was in my left hand. I blinked in the dim light streaming through the open hatch of the escape vehicle. Miss Bang and I were still firmly attached to the chair in the middle of the chamber. The floor was angled up almost perpendicular to its usual position, suspending us in midair. As I became used to my peculiar vantage point, I realized the capsule was embedded in the ground, laying on its side. The orientation may have helped save our lives, for the open hatchway was filled with earth, leaving only a small gap along the top for the thin light to filter in.

Had we struck full on the opening, we would surely have both been turned to bloody pulp by a column of packed soil. As it was, the hatchway was more than half blocked by dirt and a number of sods spilled onto the side of the cylinder below us.

Miss Bang, being in a somewhat more precarious position, appeared to have instinctively grabbed my left arm and was holding it fast to her chest. Her muscles must have locked into place, because her grip had not lessened when she lost consciousness.

I gently opened my hand and attempted to disengage my arm, but her grip on the limb only tightened. I raised my right arm up and wrapped it around her to provide additional support, and attempted once more to extricate my left, but still she refused to let go. She truly had a death grip on my arm.

"Miss Bang?" I called gently, her ear scant inches from my mouth. "Time to wake up, Miss Bang. We have a busy day ahead of us. Miss Bang?" I continued my gentle but insistent calling, but she still did not rouse. "Do you suppose I might have my arm back, Miss Bang? Miss Bang?" I gently shook her, patted her face with my free hand, even raised my voice, but she remained quite insensate and retained her impressive grip upon my trapped limb.

I took stock of our current situation. Mostly embedded in the ground. Miss Bang unconscious. Suspended in the air in the small escape pod, and myself only able to use one arm. There did not appear to be a way to release us from the chair without sending the two of us tumbling to the bottom of the capsule. My choices were constrained to remaining in the chair and waiting for rescue, or Miss Bang's return to consciousness, or to devise some manner of lowering ourselves in a controlled fashion. Given the first two options did not require action upon my part, I occupied myself pursuing the third.

With my free hand, I felt around to determine the nature of the restraints binding us together. Two straps passed over our shoulders to join at some point in front of Miss Bang. I found a third strap along my right side, and surmised another mirroring it from the left. Tracing along the waist strap with my right hand, I discovered it clipped into a large buckle, which connected to a strap between our legs. The shoulder straps clipped into the same buckle as well. Gently probing with my hand, I noted a single, large button crowned the buckle. The feature was so prominent I feared I might accidentally set off the release in my explorations.

I considered our situation. If I released the buckle, Miss Bang would slide off of my lap to the floor, but I would fall over the chair's arm and land on top of her. With her grip on my arm, there seemed to be no way I could prevent myself from falling with her, and no way I could hold on to her and prevent both of us from tumbling to the metal below. The fall wasn't far, but it would be enough to hurt, and given Miss Bang's non-communicative state, I worried such an action might do her additional harm.

As pleasant as her proximity was, certain aspects of such closeness became disturbingly... uncomfortable. And would be even more embarrassing should we be discovered in such a state. I ruled out waiting for rescue as a viable option. A man can think of glaciers only so long. As much as I intended to remain a gentleman, I could feel my body betraying my thoughts. I needed to free myself from the chair.

I tried to think of a firm... ah, a fixed point I could attach myself to in order to prevent the sudden inevitable surrender of ourselves to gravity. If my left arm were free, I believe I could have held onto the upper arm of the chair, but with it captured, my options were limited. The only thing holding us in place were the straps of the harness, and with those released...

I gaped for a moment as I realized my error. I thought when I disengaged the harness the straps would just fall away, detached from the chair. But the reality was they would remain fixed to the chair, but only the buckle end of the harness straps would be freed. I would still have an anchor, albeit not a fixed one.

Dropping my left shoulder, I twisted my left arm around in Miss Bang's grasp until I could grip the strap crossing over our right shoulders instead of resting my hand upon her, ah... chest. Taking a firm grip upon the strap, I reached for the release button with my right hand and pressed it.

Nothing happened.

I pressed the button again, but the device did not disengage. The button moved, but only slightly before it hit a plate in the interior of the mechanism. Frustrated, I pounded on the buckle, but it still would not let go. All I accomplished for my anger was a bruised hand and a wounded ego.

When I regained my temper, I reviewed the problem. The button was large and smooth, but the edges were knurled. Gripping the edge with my fingertips, I turned the button experimentally. It moved slightly, before hitting a stop. Reversing the direction, I turned again...

Miss Bang and I tumbled head first from our perch. Just as I realized we were falling, my grip upon the strap checked our descent and spun us around, ripping my arm free of Miss Bang's grip as we fell. My legs smacked into the wall and my shoulder screamed at almost the same moment as I felt a popping inside the joint and Miss Bang fell on top of me. Momentarily blinded by the pain, I released my grip and we slumped to the curved wall of the escape pod, sprawling in the dirt scattered below. My shoulder felt like it was yanked from the socket.

I failed to realize my chosen anchor point was on the lower portion of the chair. Instead of keeping us from falling, I insured I would pivot around Miss Bang and land first. With her on top of me. Idiot.

I tried to shift myself out from under the unconscious Miss Bang, but when I moved, the motion jarred my injured shoulder, causing me to cry out in pain. I was no longer strapped to the chair, but I was just as trapped as I was before.

We lay there for a few minutes as I struggled to come up with a plan for extracting myself from beneath Miss Bang. As I considered my options, the pain slowly receded and I could pay more attention to my surroundings. From my new position at the bottom of the capsule, I could see through the gap at the top of the hatch to the blue sky above. The blast must have ruptured the escape tube and tossed us out onto the surface. I breathed a relieved sigh. Being lost above ground was a much better situation than being embedded in hard packed earth somewhere beneath the city, even if we were mostly jammed into the dirt.

As I watched the sunlight across the clouds herald the morning, something dark moved across the blue of the sky.

Was it a person? Could it be one of Scaleslea's men, or perhaps a rescue team from the town, or even *The Argos*? It was a chance, but Miss Bang was still unconscious and might need medical attention. Then again, I was feeling a need for medical attention myself. I hoped for the best and called out to the form.

"Hello? Is anyone out there? Some assistance, please?" I paused and listened for some sign of a response. At first I heard nothing, but then there was a faint sound. A footfall? I called again. "Anyone there? We could use some help here! Hello?"

I heard the crunch of running feet over scattered debris. A dark shape blotted out the sky beyond the entry of the capsule. Hands tore at the earth, expanding the thin gap at the top of the hatch. Two pairs of hands made short work of clearing a hole, which was then filled with a familiar face lit by a strong bluish light.

"I have to say, I don't think I've ever been so glad to see someone before in my life."

Tinka's dirt smeared face frowned at me. "If you're makin' fun of me, you toff, you'll be lucky if all I do is leave you in this hole." She was clearly angry, but for the first time, I saw her as she was: a young woman, capable in many ways, but somewhat unsure of herself in others.

I smiled back at her. "Miss Tinka, I owe you an apology for my earlier..."

"Stuff it!" she interrupted. "No time for that rot. She alive?"

I looked at my other companion, who breathed shallowly. "Miss Bang is in need of medical attention, and I believe I am as well. Can you help us?"

Tinka's head disappeared from the hole, and I could hear her shouting to someone else, her voice strong and commanding. Her hands tore at the hole again, widening it until she slid into the capsule. She came to a stop next to us. With the larger entry more light bled down into the capsule and I could see despite the low level of illumination. Tinka pulled something from a large pocket of her vest. The item proved to be a small glass cylinder. She twisted a metal disc on one end, causing the cylinder to flare up with the same bluish light that illuminated her features a moment ago when she first peered into the capsule. I shielded my eyes with my right hand and asked, "Good heavens! What is that thing?"

"Aetheric luminator," she said, gesturing with the hand holding the device. She braced her upper left hand against the chair still protruding into the center of the capsule and examined Miss Bang with her two lower hands. "Father made it for me. Real good for doing repairs. He used to have one built into his cane, but he lost that one at the opera." She glared at me for a moment as if it was my fault, before returning her attention back to Miss Bang.

I realized, despite her extra anatomy and the covering of grease and dirt, she really *was* just a slip of a girl.

"Tanya's still breathing. She doesn't seem to be bad off."

"Yes, but I've been unable to rouse her. She took a bit of a blow to the head."

"Then we'd better not move her until the stretcher party gets here. What's wrong with you?"

I sighed. "I wrenched my shoulder trying to get us down from the chair."

"Us?"

"The professor strapped us both in before he started the escape sequence. Then the complex exploded. We got a bit banged up in all the confusion."

Tinka panned the light around the small pod. "So, where is Father?"

Tinka's crew soon arrived to dig out the pod. They dropped a stretcher down to us, strapped Miss Bang to it, and gently lifted her out. Someone fashioned a sling for my arm. Miss Tinka helped me into it and secured my injured limb. She was surprisingly gentle. I climbed out on my own, with only minor assistance. By the time I reached the surface, a medic roused Miss Bang with smelling salts.

The Argos hung very low over us, half filling the morning sky. I finally realized how incredibly large the ship actually was with it looming over me in dawning light. It appeared to be the size of a respectable estate house. Or perhaps a tad larger.

Two debarkation platforms hung from *The Argos'* wide gondola. The first was the one I already knew; the second was a larger, longer version used to lift sizable cargo to the airship. I wondered why we had not used this one when we descended into the ruins of the opera house. I reminded myself to ask later. The larger platform sported three supporting cables instead of one, and appeared much more stable.

The capsule was almost completely buried at the end of a long trench, the earth displaced by the formation of the trench collapsed under its own weight, almost entirely concealing the pod. Debris littered the surrounding terrain. Blasted trees lay scattered about, surrounding a large, smoking hole to the west. Aside from the aftermath of the blast, we appeared to be in a wooded park. Two smaller airships circled the center of the blast, although given the distance it was unclear if they were trying to fight the fire, assess damage, look for survivors, or something else entirely.

I moved to the stretcher, where Tinka and a crewman who appeared to be a medic treated Miss Bang. She tried to sit up repeatedly, but they kept pushing her back down. "We've still got crew out looking, Tanya. You can't go help them search, you're wounded."

"I've got to go look for him, Tinka!"

I joined in the discussion. "Miss Bang, you know if anyone could survive the blast, it is the professor. He's much more resilient than either of us. *He's* probably out looking for *us* at this moment. Our best bet is to remain here, by *The Argos*. He'll come home presently."

"But he wasn't in the capsule!"

"He must have fallen out when we were blasted clear of the pneumatic tube. You know he's indestructible!"

Tinka turned a wide-eyed look upon me. "You were escaping in a pneumatic tube?"

"Our options were limited."

"What were you thinking?"

"It was better than being blown up." I turned back to Miss Bang. "In any case, I don't think it matters what you and I would like to do, Miss Bang. I believe we are going to pay a visit to the prince."

The ladies looked at me quizzically. In answer, I pointed to several off-road jitneys, which pulled up alongside us and disgorged Imperial troops. The brave young men of the Empire advanced upon us, their lightning rifles pointed in our direction, turbines humming loudly.

I raised my right hand above my head. "I hope you gentlemen will forgive me if I surrender with just the one hand."

Chapter Thirty-Two

A Traitor Amongst Us

Once more, I was led off to my uncle's study under an armed Imperial guard. Miss Bang was taken into the care of a military doctor to ensure she would not suffer any ill effects from the concussion she received in the blast. I wondered what became of the professor, and if Lord Scaleslea made good his escape.

I did not have long to wait on the first score. As the guardsmen opened the doors to my uncle's study, a figure jumped up from one of the couches, and was immediately thrust back into it by the four guardsmen surrounding him.

"Professor!" I cried, and ran forward, but was likewise restrained from getting too close to my companion. Instead, I was placed in a chair facing him.

"I am so glad to see you, my boy!" The professor was dirty, and his clothes were likewise a mess, from the repeated crushing and battering of the last few hours. His glasses were still missing, as was the right sleeve of both his jacket and shirt. The exposed arm was dirty, but seemed otherwise in perfect condition.

"We thought we had lost you, Professor! How in heaven's name did you get out of the capsule?"

"I fell. When the base exploded, the shock wave blasted everything in the upper levels out into the open air." He lifted his hands together in a tossing gesture in illustration. "The pneumatic tube got us high enough, so we went out with the rest. I tried to hold on, but once the capsule was blown free, it tumbled and I bounced around inside it like a loose ball bearing." He dropped one hand to his lap and placed the other to his temple. "I swear I will never look at those games where you have to get those little steel balls into all the holes in the same way ever again."

"That is a very unusual comparison, Professor. You make me almost glad I was knocked unconscious and don't remember it."

"Consider yourself lucky on that score, my friend. Eventually, I fell out the open hatch. It seems Lord Scaleslea never designed the thing to have a door at all. It simply turned within the tube to provide a seal. Once we were tumbling free in the air from the blast, it was only a matter of time before I found the opening and we parted ways." His hands came back together and then drew two separate arcs in the air.

"It wasn't the most comfortable landing, but I do have a tendency to bounce back, as you know."

I remembered the gruesome scene at the bottom of the ravine. "Yes, as I've come to realize."

He grabbed the tatters of his coat and lifted them in the air. The left side of his jacket came away in his hand. "Of course, my wardrobe is much the worse for wear. I hope the two of you weren't hurt too seriously. I tried to avoid hitting you. How is Miss Bang? Is she wounded?"

The professor's words were relatively calm, but the expression on his face, and the way he hunched forward as he asked, betrayed his deep concern for the lady. "Miss Bang is well enough. She got a bit of a knock on the head from all the bouncing around and it took a while for her to regain consciousness. She's with the guard medic. We believe she will be fine, but the doctor is making sure."

He collapsed back onto the couch in relief. "Thank God. I was so worried for the both of you."

"We came through it, Professor. Battered but whole. But now we have a more important issue. You never got a good look at the interior of the capsule. There were these glass disks attached to the interior wall. When you connected the power, they lit up. It was like some sort of magic window..."

"Nonsense! There is no such thing as magic. Only scientific principles, insufficiently understood."

"That is what I'm trying to tell you! These disks didn't light up a solid color. There were images, like looking through a glass into a different room."

"Really? Sounds fascinating!" The professor shifted to the edge of his seat, but then leaned back slightly when his guards started to reach for him. They subsided when it was clear he did not intend to rise.

"Most of them showed scenes inside Lord Scaleslea's base. I saw the explosions in other parts of the complex. But two of the viewers showed different scenes, Professor. They showed..."

The doors burst open interrupting my tale as Prince George stalked in, trailed by two more Imperial Guardsmen.

"You have gone too far, this time, Crackle," the prince shouted as he dropped into my uncle's chair, throwing a handful of folders down on the desk. "What in heaven's name possessed you to destroy a Bohemian National monument? With the duchess traveling abroad, and on top of the duke's death and the destruction of the opera house, the local authorities are in an uproar. You've hit these people in their collective national pride. There is going to be a stiff price to pay for this kind of nefarious conduct."

"Your Highness, I didn't know where the base was located, and I had little choice in the matter of its destruction. I thought it was preferable to limit the destruction to just the base, rather than have it take out the entire city." The professor stood slowly out of respect for the prince, but very carefully kept his place to forestall any reaction from the Guardsmen.

The prince's two bodyguards drew their lightning pistols and the characteristic hiss of compressed gas sounded as they engaged the tiny turbines concealed within. The room filled with an ominous hum as they built a charge. The Guardsmen showed no emotion as they raised their weapons and pointed them at the professor and myself. Staring at the projector rods as they glowed and sparks jumped between the rods, I felt the small hairs on the back of my neck stand upright. I'd never seen lightning pistols in person. While the army's lightning rifles were well known, only the royal bodyguard carried those powerful sidearms. I did not like them pointed in my direction.

The prince ignored his Guard's display of strength. He addressed the professor, leaning forward and punctuating his statements by jabbing his index finger down upon one of the folios in front of him.

"Oh, come now, Crackle. You expect me to believe you destroyed a national monument, no, TWO national monuments in an attempt to prevent your father from detonating a bomb capable of eliminating the entire city? The Empire has the most advanced technology on the planet. Such a device isn't possible. If it was, it would be so huge it would be impossible to conceal."

"I beg your pardon, Your Highness, but the device *was* concealed. Buried in tunnels beneath the city, controlled from a secret base Lord Scaleslea constructed beneath the monument. He undermined the city, weakening the bedrock with his tunnels and poising it so it could be demolished at his whim. I had to prevent that from happening, sir!"

The prince was not impressed. "And all this just happened to take place during my visit to Prague, after Scaleslea took months of effort establishing a base to destroy the city?"

"No!" My voice sounded strange in my ears as I joined the conversation. "I beg your pardon, Your Highness, but Lord Scaleslea built his base, undermined the city, and purposely destroyed the opera house as part of a plot to demonstrate his power to the Empress. These events were deliberately timed to coincide with your visit to the city."

"Don't be ridiculous. I wasn't even coming to Bohemia until about a month ago. I don't care what kind of technology you claim Scaleslea has access to. There is no way he could have built a base from scratch in less than a month. Besides, this is a secret visit. There is no way he could have even known I was to be in Prague. I see it was a mistake for me to have you associate with Crackle. He has been a bad influence on you. Or perhaps you're more gullible than I thought."

My cheeks reddened with anger at the prince's insult, but I kept my voice even as I replied. "No, Your Highness, there is a much simpler explanation. You have a traitor in your midst. An agent who has been secretly working for Lord Scaleslea and reporting your every move to him. This intelligence allowed Lord Scaleslea to choose the time and place of the assassination attempt against yourself. You only came to Prague now because he was ready for you, and because his spy planted the suggestion."

The prince studied me intensely. When he spoke, his voice was very low and his tone was grave. "That is a very serious accusation. I hope you can prove it."

I swallowed, realizing with the destruction of Scaleslea's base, all I really had to go on was my eyewitness account.

"Well?" The prince looked impatient. The hum of the lightning pistols buzzed in my ears.

"Your Highness, while the Empire leads the world in the realm of scientific exploration, in the past week I have seen countless examples of technology I could never have dreamed of before I came to Prague. If you examine the escape capsule Miss Bang and I used, you will find the interior of the capsule holds a number of glass disks. When we were escaping Scaleslea's base, I saw several images on these disks. Two of those images, in particular, were very important. One was the view of a man walking down the halls of this castle, entering this office, and coming to stand in front of this desk while you sat behind it. The other view, showed the contents of the desk, and the man standing before it. While I do not claim to understand the technology, it is the reason I know you have been betrayed. I have seen the face of the traitor."

"Good lord!" exclaimed the professor. He leaned towards the prince, squinting in an attempt to see clearly in the absence of his glasses.

The prince's face turned a deep shade of crimson. "Are you suggesting, sir, that I am working against the interests of the Empire? That I would throw in with Scaleslea in a bid for power and fake my own death?"

"What? Um, no, no, Your Highness! Not in the least!"

"Then I suggest you choose your next words most carefully, or I shall be sorely tempted to have you summarily executed!"

My heart raced. What did I say? Why was he so furious?

The professor came to my rescue. "I do not believe my companion intended to impugn your character, your highness." The prince snorted. "But if you take his account at face value, disregarding the technical details, which in themselves would make a fascinating study..."

"Get on with it!"

"Yes, Your Highness. From my companion's description, it would appear Lord Scaleslea has developed a new kind of camera, very small and easily concealed, and capable of sending images continually over a great distance. It sounds like what he would have needed to maintain control of the clockwork birds he used to attack us in the park the other day. Unfortunately, your scientists destroyed that device. But given the size of those devices, and the necessity to make them move and behave as natural animals, a simple camera device might not be very large at all. Indeed, it should ideally be wearable. A piece of jewelry perhaps?" The professor squinted at the prince again. "Your pardon, Your Highness. Do you wear that cravat brooch very often?"

The prince's hand went to a large brooch pinned to the silk about his neck. To my eye, it appeared to be a small rendition of the royal coat of arms. "I have several of these pins. I wear one of them just about every day."

"Perhaps if I could examine it more closely, I might be able to settle the matter decisively. Would you mind, sir?"

The prince scowled, but took hold of the brooch with one hand, the other digging into the fabric of his cravat. A moment later, he placed it on the desk and gestured for a guard to convey it to the professor's hand.

Taking the item carefully, the professor thanked the prince, then kneeled down next to a small table. His guards shifted positions to keep him contained, but he ignored them, being wholly engrossed in the examination of the jeweled object. Holding the pin in one hand, he peered at it, bringing it close to his face as he patted the tattered remains of his clothing.

"Ah... I seem to have lost most of my tools. Do you think I could borrow a letter opener? There's a good chap." I was not sure if the professor was addressing myself, or the prince, or perhaps the room in general. He concentrated so fervently on the brooch he was no longer fully aware of his surroundings. The prince gestured absently, and the same guard plucked a small replica of a sword from the desk and placed it on the table in front of the professor. "Ah! Thank you. Perhaps you could speak to Miss Bang about arranging a cup of tea," he murmured as he pried at the back of the pin.

"My prince?" one of the bodyguards began, his weapon still spinning up in a dull drone of menace.

"No, let him proceed. All he can do is ruin it, but if he finds something it could be very important."

We stood, watching, as the professor continued to fiddle, making small noises as he worked. After about a minute, he let out a louder, "Ha!" which was punctuated by the rattling sound of a small screw dropping to the surface of the table and rolling. The prince and I leaned forward to get a better view of the tiny screw, which was joined by a second, and a third.

The professor angled the letter opener and pried around the edges of the pin. He was soon rewarded for his effort when the brooch separated into two pieces in his hands. The jeweled metal front was a hollow shell. Two thin wires traced from a tiny box packed in behind the crown of the coat of arms and led to a grey blob in the bottom. The blob was mounted to a small lacquered card covered with more painted blobs like the ones we saw in Scaleslea's workshop.

The professor held the two halves out to the prince in the palms of his hands. "I do not believe this is the work of your usual jeweler, my prince."

The Crown Prince stood and leaned over the desk at the device in the professor's hands. Without taking his eyes off the device, he barked out a command, loud enough to be heard in the hall beyond.

"Major Lawrence! Come here at once!"

The door to the study opened and a uniformed officer entered, closed the door behind him, and approached stiffly, coming to a stop several feet from the desk. "At your service, My Prince."

"Major Lawrence, have this device taken to Doctor Roche..." The prince didn't get any farther, as I interrupted him.

"That's him! That's the man I saw! He's the traitor!" I cried, pointing at Major Lawrence in his heavily decorated uniform, with a silver gorget around his neck.

Chapter Thirty-Three

The Weapon

Several things happened almost at once.

The prince protested my accusation, but his bodyguards moved on their own. Almost as one, they shifted their humming guns to train them on the major, and the closer guardsman interposed himself between Major Lawrence and the prince.

The major stood stock still, only a slight narrowing of his eyes indicated he noticed their change of target. His eyes darted as he took in the tableau of the prince and his guards, the professor and myself with our guard details, and finally the partially disassembled brooch in the professor's hands. That last detail seemed to decide him as the moment his eyes lit upon the dismantled piece of jewelry, he turned towards the interposing guardsman, opened his mouth, and screamed.

It was not a scream to ever come from the throat of a mortal man, but a harsh, keening note. A banshee shriek from the depths of hell, it rose in pitch until it passed beyond the realm of hearing and became a palpable presence in the room. The automaton at the opera house produced a note that shook the very walls. This note was like a punch: solid, powerful, and fast.

The professor and I reflexively covered our ears with our hands as every bit of glass in the study exploded. The windows shattered, the crystal covers of the gas lamps rained down upon us in sparkling shards. The bar in the corner of the room erupted as the decanters detonated one after the other like a series of grenades. The prince dove to the floor behind the desk, covering his head with his arms to protect it from the volley of glass. The professor's guards scrabbled for their side arms, and two of my guards did as well, while the other two rushed the major directly.

The bodyguard interposed between Major Lawrence and the prince, never got a chance to react. When the major screamed, the poor man's head exploded, unable to withstand the tremendous wave of sonic force that tore through him, and splattering the room and those present with his blood and brains. My entire body vibrated in an odd sensation akin to being narrowly missed by a speeding jitney, or being a rat in the mouth of a large terrier, shaken within an inch of one's life! What had Scaleslea given to the turncoat? A sonic scream? A devastating sonic weapon, which worked only at close range? How does one dodge an invisible weapon?

The dead man's partner didn't flinch, but pulled the trigger on his lighting pistol. The weapon discharged into the major, a blinding shaft of electricity leaping across the room with a deafening crack, small tendrils of flashing current reaching out from the bolt into the air around it!

The traitor flew backwards into the wall, black traces striping up his uniform where the mighty burst of electricity burned through his thick wool coat and into his flesh. A single shot at such close range should have been more than enough to kill a man, but he bounced off the wall and righted himself as though the blast was only a gentle shove. The defector seemed disoriented for a moment, which gave the two men rushing him the opportunity to close and clutch him by the arms.

Major Lawrence spared a glance at each of them, still betraying no hint of emotion, and grabbed the two guardsmen one after the other and flung them across the room as if they were ragdolls. The first man slammed into a bookcase and fell to the floor behind a couch, followed by a shower of books as the broken shelves disgorged their contents. The other man was less fortunate. His body sailed overhead and passed through one of the windows, splintering the empty sashes. He fell to the courtyard below.

Ejecting the gas magazine and discarding his spent lighting pistol, the prince's remaining bodyguard dashed forward, reaching for his fallen comrade's still-humming pistol. In his off hand, he held a second pistol, which hissed and vented gas as it built up a new charge. The small weapons were deadly in the extreme, but were only capable of firing a single charge per cylinder of gas. He scooped up his partner's gun, but as he brought the weapon up to fire, Major Lawrence stepped forward and stiffly backhanded the bodyguard; the mighty blow snapped the poor man's neck with a loud crack and sent his body sprawling on the floor.

The other six guardsmen, the professor's detail and the last of mine, chose not to close ranks, but raised their standard issue pistols and fired a volley of bullets into the major. The professor and I dropped to the floor to clear their lines of fire. Bullet after bullet struck Scaleslea's agent, but he stood fast through the buffeting of lead. Some bullets tore through his flesh, leaving bloody trails in their wake, but others ricocheted off of metal buried beneath the skin, striking sparks as they were deflected.

The major screamed again, emitting a single prolonged screech instead of the sharp blast he used previously. A turn of his head felled two of the firing gunmen as ragged slashes appeared across their chests. The remaining guardsmen stood their ground and continued to fire. Major Lawrence advanced upon them, still shrieking, until one by one they dropped to his sonic weapon, falling as the directed blast of energy shattered bone and turned flesh to liquid. The last man, seeing what happened to his comrades, took cover behind a settee. He got off one final shot before he, too, was taken down as the officer took a final step forward and his sonic shriek punched a hole through both couch and guardsman in an explosion of stuffing and blood.

I looked in horror at the carnage around me. Falling to the floor kept me out of the direct line of fire, but I was far from untouched by the lances of sound blasting over my head. My ears buzzed, and I could feel drops of blood sliding down one side of my face. I wasn't sure if the blood was mine. My arms and legs felt weak with fatigue. My vision swam and I couldn't bring objects into focus, but my eyes were drawn inexorably to the figure standing over me.

Major Lawrence, looked the very part of the monster. No longer the starched and pressed soldier who entered the room, but instead scorched and bloody, both uniform and flesh rent, he resembled a demon, or a creature out of a nightmare. He ceased his screaming as the last guard fell, and turned his eyes to the professor and myself. His cold gaze chilled me to the bone. As he locked eyes with me, I thought the end had come upon me at last.

Instead, he turned to face the prince, who huddled behind the desk. The creature, for that is what the major was, opened his mouth to scream once more, but instead of a blast of sonic death, twin gouts of blood and steam erupted from the side of his neck adding the scent of seared blood to the smells of alcohol, charred wool, and cooked flesh already in the air. He opened his mouth a second time, with similar results. It seemed the final soldier's bullet caught the major in the throat and caused sufficient damage to disable his banshee wail.

He hesitated, but only for a moment. His primary weapon disabled, the creature advanced, stepping around the desk to get to the prince and finish him off by hand.

For a moment, I thought of standing and throwing myself at the monster, buying the prince a few more seconds, and perhaps the chance to break for the door and escape. I was prepared to do so, when I spotted a still-humming lighting pistol dropped by one of the bodyguards, only a few inches from my hand. The projector rods crackled and sparked, showing the weapon was fully charged and ready to fire. I grabbed the pistol, hoping the device operated in roughly the same manner as conventional firearms, and scrambled to my feet.

The major cornered Prince George behind the desk and was reaching for him when I slid over the desktop, sending papers, pens, and other assorted keepsakes and paraphernalia flying in my wake. I dropped to my feet, planted the gun against the traitor's spine and pulled the trigger. The thunder crack was deafening as the over-charged bolt of electricity from the tiny gun blew a hole clean through the assassin's torso and burned black scars into the dark paneling of the wall a few scant inches above the prince's head. The blast shoved me back, knocking me head over heels and depositing me across the room. My ears rang from the repeated discharges of lightning and gunshots at close range. I lay dazed, trying to gather my wits.

When I regained my senses at last and sat up, Prince George was thankfully still unharmed, staring in shock at the carnage around him. The room reeked of ozone, blood, roasted meat, alcohol, and offal. The professor was examining the major's body, which still smoldered in several places, including the ear and eye on the right side of his head. I put my hand to my head, hoping to quiet the pounding therein, only to realize the pounding was from additional guardsmen beating on the locked door. With one final crash, the doors gave way and a troop of Imperial Guardsmen stormed in, their weapons at the ready.

The professor and I raised our hands above our heads, excepting my injured arm, which protested painfully at the attempt. The prince raised a single hand and commanded, "Stand down! The situation is... under control."

Chapter Thirty-Four

An Issue of Ownership

The professor and I were quickly whisked away to the sickbay and were attended by a military doctor while Prince George was taken to see his personal physician by a squad of bodyguards.

Professor Crackle was naturally unhurt, although it took a bit for the doctor to assure himself of that fact. The man couldn't understand how the professor could be physically untouched, when his clothing was so thoroughly destroyed. In the end, he gave up and handed Professor Crackle a surgical gown to cover his tattered clothing.

When my turn came the physician found plenty of injuries to catalog and treat. He assured me my shoulder was not dislocated, but instead I tore my rotator cuff. He could not do anything about the ringing in my ears, but he gave me hope it might only be a temporary condition. Time would have to suffice for the many bruises.

When my treatment concluded, I made two discoveries. First, a guard summoned Professor Crackle away while the physician examined me, and second, Miss Bang and Tinka were waiting in a curtained bay in the infirmary.

"My lord! What happened? We heard sounds of a battle, but no one would tell us what was going on." Miss Bang sat up on the bed where she was resting and her brows knit together in worry. "Where is Harmonious?"

"I'm surprised he didn't see you before he was summoned away," I replied. "I guess there was a battle. Prince George's majordomo turned out to be an agent for Lord Scaleslea. We exposed him, and he tried to kill the prince."

"Oh!" Tinka protested. "I missed the fight!" She glared at me angrily.

Miss Bang shot her friend an admonishing look. "Were there many casualties? It sounded horrific."

I sat on a stool on the opposite side of the bed from Tinka. "It was horrific, but it could have been much worse. Many of the guard gave their lives today, but the prince is alive, and I don't think he was seriously harmed."

"And Harmonious?"

"Not a scratch. One of the orderlies told me a guard collected him while I was being treated."

"You worry too much, Tanya," Tinka told her friend, her face full of compassion. "Nothing hurts Father."

Miss Bang sighed and raised a hand to her forehead. "I know. I keep fretting something will come along that can hurt him. Or his power will begin to fade. I know it is stupid, but I can't help it." She dropped her hand to her lap and frowned. "I should know better. I do know better."

I described the clash to the pair. I tried to spare them the particulars of the various deaths, but Tinka kept insisting on more detail, while Miss Bang listened attentively to my account. The young rigger obviously regretted not being able to take part in the fight, though I doubt she would have fared any better against the major than trained soldiers. Miss Bang was clearly more interested in the technology implanted into the man's body.

"One thing I don't understand. How did you know Major Lawrence had betrayed the prince? Had you seen the man before?"

I could feel my cheeks flush and I dipped my head to hide the fact before answering. "Not exactly. Do you remember the odd glass tubes in Scaleslea's command center?"

She nodded. "Yes. Some new kind of compact cinematograph, I believe. I think I heard one of the technicians refer to it as a see-artee. Or something like that."

"Yes, of course, it was like a small cinematograph screen. Except in color." I shook my head at my stupidity and sighed. "In any case, there were several of these screens in the escape pod we commandeered. Right when the professor finally activated the system two of those screens were showing me images from inside the castle."

Tinka snorted. "Yeah, roight! Why would it play a film from the castle?"

"It wasn't a film. Somehow Scaleslea found a way to send the images across the city so he could spy on the prince."

"That would be a powerful technology, indeed. What makes you say that?"

"One screen showed me the prince's papers on his desk. The other showed me the view from a man entering the study. The two images were in synchronization with each other. They were live."

"And you saw the major's face, my lord?"

I could feel the flush returning. "Not exactly. It was a bit of a bluff. The professor activated the capsule before I could see the man's face, and then the base exploded."

"Then how could you be sure you had the right man?"

"You flippin' lied! Ha!" The girl jabbed a finger in my direction.

"Tinka, hush! My lord?"

"I recognized his uniform."

The ladies blinked at me.

"My lord? Shouldn't his uniform look the same as any other officer?"

I shook my head. "No, Miss Bang. Enlisted men are issued common uniforms, but officers have to make a better impression, so they provide their own, tailored to fit. Most officers will have their tailors include a few embellishments to make them look more impressive. And all military men wear insignia to indicate their unit and their accomplishments. If you know what you're looking at, you can practically read a man's history from the front of his uniform. And he was the only officer I'd seen wearing a silver gorget."

"Did you serve, my lord?"

"Ah, no. But I went to a military academy as a boy. In any case, I recognized his uniform."

"Quite a gamble," Miss Bang chided.

"Yes," said the professor as he walked into the bay, "but one that paid off handsomely."

"Harmonious! We were wondering where you had gotten off to." Miss Bang's tone was politely curious. I carefully schooled my expression to keep from exposing her effort to hide her feelings from her colleague. Tinka didn't bother. She just grinned at the two of them.

"Just a little chat with the prince. I have good news! If they are quite done with you here, we can all return to the ship. I, for one, am quite ready to go home."

"Prince George is finally satisfied you had nothing to do with the attacks?" Miss Bang asked as we walked down the wide hallway towards the courtyard.

Tinka walked along at her side, unnecessarily supporting Miss Bang with her right arms. The girl was not willing to fully accept the doctor's word Miss Bang was in no danger from the minor injuries sustained in our hasty escape from the destruction of Scaleslea's base.

"Yes, my dear," the professor replied, "Major Lawrence's attack demonstrated conclusively to His Highness that his staff was infiltrated by an enemy agent. It seems, given my past, the prince didn't think I was capable of the level of subtlety required to suborn and modify one of his men without being detected. Given the evidence, he is satisfied the episode was entirely Lord Scaleslea's doing. I'm still trying to decide if I'm insulted by the implication that I lack subtlety. In any case, I am glad to no longer be under suspicion."

"So, the major was a real person, not like those things at the Opera House?" I asked.

"I'm still not quite sure what we saw at the opera house. I don't think we'll ever be able to recover any of the remains at this point. Given what we saw with Major Lawrence's case, they may have been real performers who were altered by my father and made into weapons, or they may have been very clever replicas, much like the attacking ornithoids."

"You mean the clockwork budgies?"

"They weren't budgies, my lord," Miss Bang interjected half teasingly.

Tinka didn't quite suppress a giggle.

The professor continued on. "Indeed. The bird's behavior didn't show the same level of sophistication as Major Lawrence. He was more than just a clever mechanical. He was either a man who was surgically modified to allow Scaleslea to monitor everything he saw and heard, or he was an absolute masterwork of the builder's art. I have never heard of someone combining both biological and mechanical components into such a remarkable simulation of life. Not to mention a particularly grizzly sonic weapon. I wish the prince would let me examine the remains further, instead of packing them off to that Ministry oaf, Roche!"

"I thought Doctors Roche and Ricks were scientific advisors to the prince. What ministry do they work for?"

"Oh, they are his scientific advisors, but they work for the Ministry of Technological Security. The MoTS. Their charter claims they're supposed to catalog and examine new technologies to determine if they are safe for use by the citizens of the empire. In reality they take practically everything anyone else invents for themselves and suppress any hint of new discoveries. It is quite frustrating for a scientist to make any respectable progress with them around. Then again, I suppose they're better than the peculiar people from the other ministry. That lot seems to think everything is haunted! Such rubbish!" The professor shook his head.

"Which other ministry?" I asked.

"I don't know, my boy. They won't tell me. They simply insist they work for a secret branch of her Majesty's government and investigate odd occurrences. Some of their people are quite capable, but when they show up everything that isn't nailed down simply disappears and is spirited off to their warehouse. They have no respect for personal property."

The guards at the end of the hall snapped to attention at our approach. They drew open the double doors, allowing us to exit into the courtyard. A dark shadow hung over the yard, covering it entirely, and the twin embarkation platforms of *The Argos* hovered inches above the cobblestones on either side of the courtyard's center. A number of guardsmen were swarming over the larger platform, attempting to shift the battered cylinder of the escape capsule off of the platform and into the courtyard.

The professor strode up to a young officer supervising the process. "Excuse me, my good man, but whatever is going on here?"

The lieutenant gave the professor a sidelong look, taking in the borrowed gown covering his tattered clothing. He opened his mouth, and appeared to be about to give the professor a dressing down, when his eyes flicked to Miss Bang, Tinka, and myself. Something clicked in his mind at the sight of Tinka, and he checked his reaction and responded civilly, "I take it you are the owner of the airship, sir?"

"Yes, I am," the professor answered.

"We should be able to return your ship to you momentarily, sir. Your crew has been released, but we needed to use the ship to move some pieces of... um, interdicted technology." The young man looked concerned, as if he thought he might have divulged too much.

"I can understand that, but why in the devil's name did your men seize my ship in the first place? And what are you going to do with that equipment?"

"They arrested us and the search party *The Argos* sent out to find us, Professor. I guess they seized the ship as well," I said.

Tinka piped up, then, although her voice was quiet, almost shy. "I told the men to cooperate, Father. I didn't want to waste time fighting the guard when we needed to find you. 'Sides, they had more men for the search."

"Most reasonable, Tinka, but it doesn't explain what you're going to do with this equipment, Captain."

"Lieutenant, sir. The apparatus has been classed as dangerous weapons and forbidden technology, sir. We're taking it into custody on behalf of the Empire."

"But it needs to be studied, young man!"

"The Empire has men to do that, sir."

"You don't understand..."

"Professor," I interrupted, "Don't badger the poor man. He's just doing his duty. Perhaps tomorrow you can petition the prince to let you study some of what they find. After all, you are probably the best person to make sense of it all."

"I doubt that, sir," the officer answered. The professor bristled and he hastily added, "Not your capabilities, sir. I wouldn't know about that. But this is all under Her Eternal Majesty's Dangerous Secrets Act. No civilian access, sir. Military personnel only. Not even the MoTS have access."

"Bureaucratic rubbish!"

"Not my call, sir."

I sighed. "Let's not argue with the man, Professor. I'd really like to get cleaned up, now."

"Very well," He replied dryly. "I am certainly in need of some fresh clothes."

"You and your party are cleared to return to the ship, sir." The young officer sounded almost apologetic.

"Thank you, Lieutenant." The professor's voice still held an edge of coldness.

We proceeded to the empty embarkation platform and signaled our readiness to ascend. The platform rose slowly and steadily, providing us with an excellent view of the city. Prague spread out before us, a beautiful example of old Europe.

The city was strangely peaceful. One had to know exactly where to look to see the signs of the recent destruction. I found it somehow reassuring, and yet disturbing at the same time. The city lost two major landmarks in less than a week. Surely it was worth a little upheaval?

"What is wrong with this thing?" the professor groused.

"I would surmise the operator isn't exactly familiar with the controls," suggested Miss Bang.

Tinka snorted. "Guardsmen are too timid to run a bloody lift," she said.

I imagined most people were too timid to run a lift the way the professor does, but instead I asked, "Professor, why didn't we use the other platform when we went to investigate the ruins of the Opera House. It would have been much more convenient for all the equipment we needed to carry."

"Isn't it obvious? The cables are much too short. In order to land us in the bottom of the pit, the ship would have been scraping the rooftops. It wouldn't exactly have been a clandestine operation." He pulled impatiently at the signal cord in the lift tower. "Come on! Speed it up, man!"

I couldn't help but smile at his frustration. I put my hand over his and said, "We've had plenty of hurry the past few days, Professor. For once, just enjoy the view."

We ascended in silence for a few minutes, each wrapped in our own thoughts. I reflected on all I endured in the past few days. How much my life changed from that fateful night at the opera!

"Professor, I still have some questions..."

"Yes. I know. If I can beg just a little more forbearance from you, I will do my best to answer them. Can you give me until tonight? After dinner, perhaps?"

"Very well, Professor."

Chapter Thirty-Five

A Confidence Shared

As I followed Professor Crackle to his cabin after dinner, I wondered about the questions I had been asking. He promised me answers, but did I know what to ask?

"I have an excellent brandy..." the professor said, rummaging in a cupboard for a bottle and a pair of snifters.

It was my first visit to the professor's cabin. It sat in the traditional location in the rear of the ship, carried over from the days of sailing ships. The back wall of the suite was covered with windows, angled due to the curve of the hull, and commanded an excellent view of the town.

I walked along the rail, looking down at Prague in the deepening twilight. The streets below were lit by gaslight, the light slowly snaking along the twisting streets as the lamplighters made their rounds. With the city wrapped in shadow, the scars of the past few days' events were smoothed away and it was much easier to believe in the illusion of peace among the rolling hills of Bohemia.

The common people went about their lives and counted themselves lucky to have avoided involvement in the tragic loss of the opera house, or the disaster which destroyed the Vitkov Hill monument. Or perhaps they sat angrily in their homes, taverns, and other meeting places, cursing the loss of the monument, for it was an important symbol of Bohemian pride.

The local government had not released any cause for the disaster yet, what with the duchess traveling and the duke tragically killed in the collapse of the opera house. Imperial troops from the local garrison closed off the park surrounding the monument to allow royal investigators to survey the site and determine its safety. Perhaps the citizens of Prague believed it the result of some natural disaster?

At the thought of Uncle Randolph, a wave of sadness washed over me. So much happened in such a short amount of time, with hardly a moment to catch my breath, much less think about my uncle's death. In that quiet moment, it began to sink in. I had only known him for a few weeks, but I found I missed his lectures. For some reason I couldn't remember any conversation with him which didn't end up as a lecture. He was family, and he died a hero, giving his life for the sake of his subjects. How would I tell Mother about her brother's death? And that I failed to capture his killer?

I learned so much in the past few days, saw so many fantastic things, and my world became a much more dangerous place because of it. I envied the common citizens for their ignorance. Little did they know the architect of the past week's destruction, Lord Scaleslea, still roamed free. The mercenaries who served him poured into the streets to lose themselves in the crowds, blended in with the common citizens, and made their escape as well.

Where would all those men go? Would they make their way to another of Lord Scaleslea's bases? Seek out some other villain's employ? Or perhaps scatter to the winds? I doubted we would ever know.

"Here we go!" The professor's approach interrupted my dark reverie.

I gratefully accepted the snifter of amber liquid he held out to me. One of the few things I learned from Uncle Randolph was brandy was excellent for brooding. I inhaled the bouquet of the liquor, took a small sip, and mentally agreed with the professor as the liquid rolled around my tongue. It was indeed an excellent vintage.

"Sit down," he said, crossing to a pair of overstuffed chairs facing the windows. "I am sure you have a lot of questions."

I sat in one of the chairs and gave one more glance out over the city. "I do, Professor, but now we come down to it, I'm afraid I don't know quite where to start."

"Perhaps you should begin at the beginning."

"I'm not sure where the beginning is, Professor." As soon as the sentence was out of my mouth, I knew it wasn't right. I did know where to begin. "Is Lord Scaleslea *really* your father? Who is he? Why did he attack the Crown Prince?"

The professor sighed deeply and adjusted a fresh pair of glasses to a slightly lower place on his nose. He looked through the lenses into his brandy as he swirled it around in his glass. At last he took a small sip, held the liquid on his tongue for a moment, swallowed, and began his tale.

"My father is Edward Thomas Alexander Crackle, the sixteenth Baron of Scaleslea. He was one of the greatest scientists of his time, but after my mother's death he became increasingly withdrawn and critical. I think he could not deal with the thought he was helpless to prevent her death, despite all of his scientific expertise. He became obsessed with gaining power and control over the world, both in the scientific and political sense."

He sighed again. "I never knew why it weighed on him so heavily. Not until the other day. I can't imagine how it must have felt, to know he came so close to finding a cure. To ask the crown for help, have them refuse, and then have your research taken away because the person who denied you aid now needs your findings. I finally understand why he became so angry."

The professor took another sip of his brandy. "I guess, in the end, it broke him. Now, he is a dangerous madman, who lacks the scruples to use his genius for the betterment of mankind.

"As for the attack on Prince George," The professor's face sagged, leaving him looking much older, as if years of weariness were just laid upon him. "I suppose it is his way of striking back at the queen for the wrong he suffered. She is much too well defended for him to get to her now, so he lashes out at targets he can reach. Unfortunately his reach gets longer every year."

"So what kind of scientist is he?"

"My father has several doctorates in different disciplines, although I've never had the patience to complete such work. These days it would be much harder to find peers for anything I might put forth as a dissertation. And most likely the MoTS would suppress the whole thing."

"If he was such a shining light of the scientific arts, why is it I've never heard of him before?"

"His papers were all discredited. His madness drove him to treachery. He attempted to assassinate the queen, thinking it would clear the way for him to take over the Empire. Or at least I thought it was his motive. Now... Now I think it might have been a desire for vengeance. Or perhaps he thought it was somehow justice, to kill the woman who took away the cure meant for his wife."

He shrugged and gestured with his free hand. "When he escaped custody, he became an outlaw. Technically, he is no longer a lord, as his titles were stripped from him. The estates of Scaleslea were never large. The name became a national shame and fell into disuse. Place names changed, and the lands of Scaleslea are mostly forgotten. I imagine it is much like what happened to your family's estates when your great-grandfather decided to make an insult of his lands and family."

I laughed bitterly. "Great-grandfather made my family's name all but unspeakable in polite society. Our tenants simply pulled down the old signs and never put new ones up. Quite a number of people get lost trying to navigate through the estate to this day. Sometimes I wish the old man was still alive so I could tell him what a mess he has made of my life."

"I felt that way for many years, my boy. But in the end, he is my father. I hate the things he does, but when you get down to it, he is a very sick man. He needs my help, not my hatred."

"I don't know how you can be so forgiving, Professor."

"In some ways, it is actually harder to hang on to the hate."

We sipped our brandy in silence for a few minutes. The sky outside was black and the only light came from the streets below. At long last, I spoke, giving voice to a question I almost feared to ask.

"Professor, how is it possible Lord Scaleslea and yourself are Eternal?"

"How is it possible for anyone to be Eternal? If we truly understood that, we might be able to find a cure for the condition. Although I am sure it would become a weapon as well."

"That doesn't exactly answer my question. How did you and your father become Eternal? Were you born that way?"

"I am sorry. I don't mean to be evasive, but I don't fully understand how it happened myself. I can tell you what I remember, and perhaps it will be enough."

"I suppose it would be a start."

"Very well. In some ways it was an accident, although when you get down to it, it was ultimately my father's fault, and the downfall of our house."

"It has something to do with your father's attempt on Her Eternal Majesty?"

"Yes, although she was simply Her Majesty at the time."

"I don't follow, Professor."

"I'm sorry, I'm wandering a bit away from my story. As I said, it all started when my father was a scientist of great reputation and one of the shining lights of the Empire, despite some vocal conflicts with the crown. I was proud to follow in his footsteps as a scientist, and I hoped to win my place in society with discoveries of my own. I was experimenting with optics at the time. I made a breakthrough in high energy applications utilizing crystallized carbon refractors..."

"In what?"

"Focusing beams through crystalline lenses."

He waited for comprehension to dawn on me, but it failed to come.

"Shooting rays through diamonds," he said at last. While this sort of science was still well outside of my field, it was at least a concept I could grasp, albeit feebly. Apparently it showed upon my face, as the professor continued with his story. "As you can imagine, the research was horribly expensive. My father arranged an audience with the Queen..."

"You mean the Empress."

"Well, yes. Although in those days, the Empire was not her primary domain. But if I can continue, I think it will all make sense to you." He waited to see if I was going to interrupt him again, but I returned the floor to him with a gesture of my empty hand and raised my snifter to my lips again to remind me to keep quiet.

"My father arranged an audience for me, so I could present my findings and make a plea for additional research funding from the Crown. He suggested the best way to make an impression was to take my equipment with me and give a live demonstration for Her Majesty. I did not know it was all part of his plot to assassinate Her."

He took another sip of his brandy. "Father used my equipment to smuggle in a high-energy weapon of his own devising. At the time, he was performing aether experiments, or at least that was what he told me. He built a small, portable energy projector, which he intended to use to kill the queen. I thought he was finally proud of my accomplishments, but it was simply an excuse to secret a weapon into the palace."

I leaned forward in my chair. I could hear the pain in the professor's voice. I wanted to say something, but before I could come up with the right words, he continued his story.

"I was still setting up my equipment for the audience, when Victoria decided to come inspect the proceedings. I was explaining the construction of my device when Father pulled out his weapon. The guards tried to stop him, but before they could reach him, he fired. I didn't understand what was happening at the time, but I knew I could not allow him to harm Her Majesty, so I threw myself in the path of the beam. I was holding one of my crystalline lenses at the time, and apparently it intersected the path of the beam, splitting it in a dozen different directions. The room was filled with a blinding light, and we all collapsed."

Professor Crackle stared off into the distance. His eyes were pointed out over the city, but I knew he did not see it. He stared into the past. The silence grew thick between us.

"A moment later, three of us stood back up, Her Majesty, my father, and me. The energies unleashed destroyed his weapon and shattered much of my equipment. The guards and assistants in the room were all dead. For some strange reason, only the three of us survived. I don't think we'll ever know why."

"But, the three of you are Eternal. Wouldn't that be the reason why, Professor?"

He waved his hand in my direction. "Not exactly. I don't know if the queen was Eternal before the accident, but I know for a fact my father and I were mere mortals before the incident. I have considered the possibility she was Eternal beforehand and somehow the accident passed that capability onto Father and myself. Or perhaps the three of us became Eternal in that moment. I really don't know. In any event, Father and I were changed. Possibly forever.

"More guards rushed in from the surrounding rooms. I surrendered, but my father would not give up so easily. His weapon was destroyed, so he threw himself from a window and somehow managed to escape the palace."

"Dear God," I said in a whisper.

"Indeed," the professor agreed. He sighed again before continuing. "I was questioned and put on trial as an accomplice to my father's treason. I maintained my innocence and, in the end, there wasn't sufficient evidence to implicate me in his plot. I was acquitted, but the queen could not abide the thought of allowing the son of a traitor to remain. Perhaps she feared he might find a way to use my presence to make another attempt at her life, or to suborn me to his cause. I was exiled from Britain because of my father's crimes. I appealed. Begged for some way I could prove myself loyal to the Crown. Victoria said if I wished to prove myself loyal, I should bring my father before her to suffer the Crown's justice."

"The Empress set you to hunt down your own father?"

"Yes. I was banished from England's soil, but if I ever wanted to go home again, clear my family's name and reclaim its lands, I would have to return my father to be tried for treason."

"What did you do, Professor?"

"What else could I do? I gathered what resources I could and left for the continent. I took employ in research labs and universities. I learned to teach. And I looked for signs of my father's whereabouts."

"And he was hiding here, in Prague?"

"Oh, no. At least, not at first. He traveled around quite a bit. Gaining allies and causing mayhem here and there. I managed to track him down several times, but he always seems to slip away from me at the last moment. I keep chasing him, and he keeps slipping away."

"I thought the Empress being Eternal meant she discovered the secret of eternal life. She would never age. Then this happened. I shot Lord Scaleslea, but he got back up again as if it never happened. You burned yourself disabling the drill, but the burns healed in a matter of moments. You were crushed under those rocks, but when we dug you out your body repaired itself before my very eyes. I know it is because you're Eternal, but it still doesn't make sense. It was like magic."

The professor snorted. "There is no such thing as magic, my boy. But in this case, I will agree with you. I have been studying what it means to be Eternal for more decades than I care to count, and I am no closer to understanding the forces governing my own body than I was that first day."

He sighed. "And it is difficult being both researcher and test subject."

"So there are only three Eternals?"

"Four, that I know of, actually, but that is a much longer story, and one of which I don't know all the details."

"Four Eternals? All my life I thought it was only Her Etern... ah, Empress Victoria," I said.

"As far as the world is concerned, Empress Victoria is the only Eternal. Her state is the sign of her divine right to rule. Even the Vatican recognizes her condition as a blessing from God and places her authority second only to the Pope, despite the schism between the Catholic and Anglican Churches. They don't even understand how it is a curse to be Eternal."

"A curse, Professor?"

He drained the last of his brandy and rose to refill his glass, speaking as he went, "To be Eternal, is to be frozen in a moment of time. Locked, mentally, emotionally, and physically into who and what you were at a single instant.

"My father is trapped in the height of his madness and arrogance. He believes he is superior to all other men and only he is fit to rule. He seeks to bring down the Empire so he can reshape it in his own image. And so he can have his vengeance on the queen.

"Victoria is caught in her anger and outrage at my father's treachery, and her grief at Prince Albert's untimely death. An assassination attempt about a year before struck down the Prince Consort. For most of the year she remained in seclusion, grieving. Father used Albert's memory and his love of science to arrange the audience. She still believed, or I should say believes, in Albert's dream of better living through science, but she fears it as well. She is determined to bring order to the world, but she cannot abide true progress, even while she continues Albert's programs of scientific exploration. She cannot rest, or forget the pains of the past.

"It must be hell for her." The professor looked at the brandy for a moment before continuing.

"As for me, I am trapped in the body of a young man, full of adrenaline, fearlessly throwing himself into danger. All energy and confidence, but no focus. I cannot have a life or a family. I am dogged by a sense of urgency. A frenetic need to do something. It is only in times like this, after I have given almost everything I have, when I can feel something else. For a little while, I can remember what it is like to be a living man." He returned to his chair as he spoke, snifter refilled. "But it won't last. By morning, I will be my old self again. My young self. What little clarity I have will be gone."

"Professor," I could scarcely hear my own voice as I spoke. Consumed by the awe of it all, I could not raise my voice above a whisper. "Prince Albert died in the middle of the 1800's. Victoria has been on the throne for over a hundred years. How old are you?" The Empress had been Eternal all of my life, and all of my father's life. If what the professor was telling me was true...

"I was born in 1836. I was 28 years of age in 1864 when my father attempted to kill the Queen. It wasn't until a later, more public assassination attempt led Victoria to adopt the title of the Eternal Empress and began to use the religious and political clout being Eternal gave her to assert her will upon other nations. Now, every nation is either under her sway, or is nervous lest they provoke her wrath. Once, Britain was the undeniable superpower. Now, it is Victoria, and only Victoria."

He sipped his brandy again, and smiled wryly. "But I suppose I've avoided answering your question again. I apologize. Sometimes there is so much history I cannot keep from getting lost in it. Let's see. This is the year 2010. That would make me... one hundred and seventy-four years of age. Or at least I will be come October."

"One hundred and..." I gaped. "You've been chasing your father for a hundred and fifty years?"

"Not quite. But close enough as makes no difference. Mind you, at first, years passed before I could find any kind of a lead. The world is a big place, and at the time neither of us possessed much in the way of resources. It was many years before I could afford my present home. But I find it suits me much better than being tied to one place."

"You never married, Professor? Never had a family?"

"Once. Many years ago. It was a harsh lesson to learn, my boy. Marguerite, my wife, and I were naive enough to believe we could make it work, but we were soon disabused of the notion. We never had children. I'm sure that was my fault in some fashion, either due to my condition, or to too many hours taken up in my work. At first, it was enough for her to be with me, even without children, but in the end, she was the one who left. It is only a matter of time before a woman gets tired of a man who remains ever young and vital while she continues to age. In the end, she was faced with a simple choice: to move on or lose her sanity. So I let her go."

"What happened to her, Professor?"

"She married a widower, and was accepted as mother by his children. I don't know if she bore him any children of her own, but I know she was happy and fulfilled. She died many years ago, surrounded by her family. I attended her funeral."

The tone in his voice gave me pause. "You still mourn her, Professor?"

He looked at me, and nodded. "Yes. And No. I still think of her, and miss her presence, but I would not have denied her the life she so wanted. You could say I mourn the life we could have had, if only my condition wasn't pulling us apart. If I continued to age, in mind if not in body, I suppose I could mourn her properly. But my body is still that of a young man, and it is hard for a young man to mourn the past. No matter how much one may see, a young man cannot help but look to the future. And that is one last way I have done her an injustice."

The professor's pain evoked a sympathetic ache in my own chest, although I could not fully grasp it. I thought of my uncle, whose life was tragically lost at the Opera House. I still didn't know how to deal with his loss. I had that vague sense of wanting to *do* something, but did not know what. What must it be like to suffer a loss and be unable to feel it?

"You never found love again, Professor?"

"Love? Oh, I wouldn't say that, my boy. A man cannot live without love. But I never again committed the folly of thinking I could share life with a woman in that way. It would be a disservice to the lady. Even if a woman could overlook the fact I am so very much older than she, which some can, given my appearance, I can have no permanent relationship of that sort. I remain where I am, and they must eventually continue past me. Perhaps one day I may discover a cure for my condition, which will return me to mortality without ending my life immediately. Then, perhaps. But for the time being, I may indeed find love, but I cannot act upon it. One way or another, I must honor the lady, and let her go her own way. You could say I am a confirmed bachelor."

"I'm sorry, Professor. I wish I could help, somehow."

He smiled, briefly. "It's quite all right. You must remember, I've been living this way since well before you were born."

I stood, placing my snifter on the small table between the chairs. "You've given me much to think about, Professor. I believe I shall turn in for the night."

"Good night. I hope I've managed to answer your questions. It has been a long time since I've talked about any of this to someone. It has been... refreshing. Sleep well."

"And you, Professor."

"I thank you, but I don't sleep much anymore."

Not knowing what to say, I turned and made my way to the door of the dark stateroom. I looked back at the professor when I found the door, and saw him standing at the window, gazing down upon the city. As I let myself out into the hall, I heard him speak again.

"Goodnight, Titania, my love. If only I could do justice by you."

With that thought echoing in my head, I silently closed the door.

Chapter Thirty-Six

An Unexpected Invitation

H ealing was slow in Prague.

The buildings surrounding the site of the opera were evacuated to ensure they wouldn't collapse into the hole, which filled with water. The papers debated over the likelihood that the opera house would be rebuilt, or if the site would become a memorial pool or garden.

Vitkov Hill was closed while engineers determined the steps necessary to rebuild the monument. I suspect this was a cover to allow the remains of Scaleslea's base to be fully explored and demolished, but I couldn't get anyone to confirm my suspicions.

The Argos was ordered tethered to the castle grounds until the prince's staff could positively determine if any additional traps or forces remained in the city.

And there was a state funeral.

"It was very good of you to stay for the funeral, Nephew," my Aunt Katerina, the Duchess of Prague, said as I walked her from the carriage back into the castle.

We buried an empty casket that morning, as Uncle Randolph's remains were never retrieved from the debris of the opera house. He was given full honors and hailed as a true protector of the Bohemian people. Throughout the entire ceremony, Aunt Katerina maintained her composure in front of her people, but I could tell her control was at its limits.

"It was the least I could do, Your Grace, after I failed to bring his killer to justice."

"Nephew, we are still family, you don't have to stand on formality when we are alone."

"I'm sorry, Aunt Katerina. The morning's proceedings put me into a more formal mode, I suppose. I regret it took Uncle Randolph's death to make me realize what he was trying to do for me."

The Duchess patted my arm as we walked. The family guards opened the doors ahead of us and we entered the castle. "Prince George told me what you did. I know things did not turn out the way you expected, but you acquitted yourself well. I'm sure Randolph would be proud of you."

"You really think so?" I looked over at my aunt. Her eyes were full of tears, but they also shone with pride. My eyes felt a little misty as well.

"I do. You have made great progress from the young man who arrived a few weeks ago. I shall be sure to write your mother and let her know how much you've grown."

"Oh, dear. Must you?" I didn't feel much like the young man who set off from England with the excitement of being on his own for the first time in his life. I also didn't feel I had grown much. I knew the events of the past two weeks changed me, but I needed time to understand how. Nightmares still plagued my sleep. Even waking, I could still see Lord Scaleslea's guards dropping to the floor. I shoved the image from my mind as she answered me.

"I must. While she will mourn the loss of dear Randolph, I think she will be very pleased with you."

We walked in silence for a bit, each lost in our own thoughts. Duchess Katerina finally broke the silence.

"Have you made arrangements for the next leg of your tour?"

Damnation. I was so wrapped up in current events, I hadn't thought about continuing my journey. I let out a sigh. "No, I am afraid I haven't. To be terribly honest, I haven't had the luxury of thinking that far ahead."

"Then you should see about making your preparations. It is very important for a young man to plan for the future. You are already overdue for your visit with your Aunt Phyllis. I am sure she will understand the delay, but it would not do to keep her waiting overlong for the pleasure of your company, no?"

I recognized the tone of familial and royal command, and quickly took the hint, lest it be applied again. "No, that would not do." Especially considering Aunt Phyllis was much more of a stickler for proper forms than Mother. No one ever kept her waiting. Not if they wanted to hear the end of it. "I shall have to see what arrangements I can make to repair my schedule. With any luck, I shall be on my way within the week."

While I knew it would appease my other maternal relations, I was not particularly thrilled with the idea of spending much time in India with Aunt Phyllis.

"Excellent." I wondered if Aunt Katerina was actually more interested in being rid of me. While she was absent for the majority of my visit, it would not be the most pleasant memory for her. Before I could say anything in response, two soldiers in the uniform of the Imperial Guard rounded a corner and spotted the two of us.

They approached to a respectful distance, and for the first time in my experience with the Imperial Guard no one was pointing a weapon at me. The men braced to attention, and then one of them spoke. "Your Grace, my lord, Prince George requires His Lordship's presence in Saint Vitus Cathedral. The pleasure of Your Grace's company is also requested."

My aunt somehow grew taller as she addressed the messengers. "What is the nature of this summons? The house is in mourning."

"Yes, Your Grace. Prince George regrets the intrusion, but it involves business His Highness must clear up before his departure. Only His Lordship is required to attend."

I touched Aunt Katerina's arm. "I can deal with this myself. You need not be bothered."

She shook her head. "No, Nephew. George is up to something. I want to know what it is. You have suffered enough from his suspicion." To the guardsmen she added. "You may inform the prince we will be joining him directly."

"Yes, Your Grace." The two men bowed and retreated the way they came.

When we were alone, my aunt turned to me and asked, "What do you think he wants?"

"I assure you, I have no idea. I thought the whole matter was resolved. I thought I'd finally gotten on his good side. Or at least off of his bad side."

"I suppose the simplest way to see what he is up to is to let him play it out." She tapped a finger thoughtfully against her chin. "Come. The sooner it is over, the better. I did not need this today of all days."

The duchess led the way to the cathedral, and I hurried to keep up.

We arrived in the sanctuary of Saint Vitus Cathedral to find Prince George with a platoon of his guardsmen. The prince was clad in a full dress Army uniform, which was positively covered in gold braid and decorations. So much so, I could barely make out the rank insignia for a full colonel. Likewise, the other soldiers were in their dress uniforms and each sported a fine collection of decorations. The prince waited for us between two rows of soldiers each wearing a blue sash or blue medallion around their necks.

The sound of our footsteps echoed off of the high gothic walls as we entered at the transept and turned towards the high altar. I saw Professor Crackle and Miss Bang, seated to one side and escorted by more guards. Opposite the professor, a group of scribes and officials were seated with one of the priests, discussing something in hushed tones.

"Your Highness," Duchess Katerina called out as we approached, "may I ask what business you have with my nephew? I thought we resolved all the questions before us."

"Ah! Our guest of honor arrives at last. Thank you for coming, Your Grace. I think you will be pleased when you see what I have in mind. Your kinsman is in no trouble, I assure you. Quite the opposite. If you would take a seat with the other guests we can begin." He gestured to an empty seat beside the professor.

The duchess looked at me, took my hands in hers, and leaned close. "Play along, Nephew. The prince can be a schemer at times, but this seems like too much theatre. He's being clever, but I don't think he means you harm. I will be here to intercede if necessary."

I thanked her, and she took her seat besides my companions. As ever, Miss Bang was the picture of composure, while the professor fidgeted in his seat, looking comically like a small boy trying to wait quietly when he really wants to be running around looking at everything.

"Come, my lord. We have a place reserved for you here." Prince George pointed to a spot on the floor in front of him.

My heart stuttered as the crown prince directed me to stand before all assembled. My knees wanted to buckle, or to turn and run, but I took a deep breath and stood up straight. I tried to emulate the effortless calm Miss Bang exuded. With measured steps, I walked forward to stand before Prince George.

He smiled, and it sent shivers down my spine. My aunt was right; he was up to something.

The prince's voice took on the tone of a practiced orator. "The Empire expects much from the service of its citizens. In this way the Empire remains strong, and peace is preserved."

He paced around me as he spoke. "But there are times when a citizen goes above and beyond even the Empire's high expectations. In those instances, the Empire owes a debt. It is one such debt we are here to repay today."

He thrust an arm out in my direction. "This man, while under suspicion of crimes against the Empire, exposed an enemy agent who successfully infiltrated my own retinue. And when that agent sought to assassinate me, this man risked his own life to bring down the killer."

Prince George stopped in front of me, turning to face me.

"In cases such as these, the Crown has a particular honor to bestow upon such a benefactor."

At these words, the soldiers at the end of the two lines stepped forward. One carried a short padded stool, and placed it on the floor between the prince and myself. The other soldier took a position to the right of Prince George and presented a sword to him, hilt first.

My eyes went wide as I realized what he intended.

"Oh, no! No, Your Highness, you can't! I can't! To enter my name in those roles would sully the entire order! Please, I beg of you..."

"SILENCE!"

The echoes of the prince's outburst came back to us from the high stone walls, but no other sound was to be heard.

The rasp of metal on metal as Prince George drew the sword seemed almost deafening in the silence.

He pointed the sword at me. "You are not permitted to object." The point of the blade dipped down towards the cushioned riser on the floor. "Now kneel. And shut up."

I hesitated for a moment.

"Now."

My throat felt swollen and my heart pounded like a steam engine. I couldn't let him besmirch an entire knightly order with my blight of a name, but how could I refuse a royal command?

Unable to see any way out of the situation, I knelt upon the riser, and prayed for deliverance.

"Much better." The prince stepped closer to me.

"Do you swear your loyalty to the Eternal Empress? To take no action against the Crown, and strike down all those who would take arms against the Empress, the Crown, and the British Empire?"

He had just commanded me to silence, what was I to do?

"You may answer."

I swallowed the lump in my throat. "I... I do."

"Then by the power invested in me by her Eternal Majesty, Victoria, Empress of the British Empire, I do hereby dub thee," I felt the tap of the blade on my right shoulder, then a moment later on my left. "Sir Richard Blasphemy."

"But... that's not my name!" I gasped, heedless of the prince's command to be silent.

He leaned in close to me and replied quietly. "No. It's your title!"

I looked up and saw the crown prince grinning like a Cheshire cat.

Chapter Thirty-Seven

A Passage to India

In the early years of the Eternal Empress' reign, Victoria wanted an honor that she could confer upon those who provided particularly valuable services to the royal family. While the empire had a number of other honors and orders, each of these required approval by parliament. To avoid the need for such approvals, she created the Royal Victorian Order, a knightly order under the direct control of the royal family.

An order into which Prince George inducted me.

"Knight Commander of the Royal Victorian Order! Well done, my boy, well done!" The professor pumped my hand vigorously as he congratulated me. It was all I could do to hold on to the emblems of my new office. I clutched to my side the patent acknowledging Sir Richard Blasphemy as a Knight Commander of the Royal Victorian Order, the pin of the order, and the presentation case for the other emblems of the order. I wore the emblems themselves, a Maltese Cross on a blue ribbon trimmed in red and white, which bounced as it hung around my neck, and the Maltese Cross on a blazon, which was pinned to my coat front.

"I'm so happy for you, Sir Richard," added Miss Bang.

"Thank you both. I'm shocked by the whole thing, but I'm still not sure I can accept the accolade."

"You can." Aunt Katerina approached after leaving the group of officials gathered to witness the ceremony. "I was right. Prince George was being clever, and quite proud of it he is, too."

"In what way, Your Grace?" asked Miss Bang.

"He finally found the loophole in Sir Richard's great-grandfather's will." She turned to me. "It seems your ancestor overlooked one thing when adding his inheritance codicil. He never considered you might gain new titles in your own right, so he made no provision against them."

"But how does a title help me?" I asked. Never having expected to gain a title other than through inheritance, I never bothered to study the process or its implications.

"After you saved his life, Prince George realized he could knight you. But he needed his lawyers make sure there wasn't any requirement to knight you with the same name you were given at birth. It seems using an honoree's given name is simply tradition, and not a requirement."

The professor laughed. "Very clever indeed. By knighting you, he was free to give you any name he wanted without endangering your inheritance!"

"And 'Sir Richard Blasphemy'?"

"I suspect that was his sense of humor. You have to admit your given name is blasphemous." He looked at me over his spectacles, and grinned.

I shook my head. "Why would the prince go to such lengths? Surely my little problem is unimportant to him."

Miss Bang inclined her head. "Not exactly, Sir Richard. While the prince certainly has other matters to attend to, I overheard one of his aides saying the business with your name and your father's has been a thorn in the administration's side for a long time. It set a bad precedent, and they needed to find a way to defuse the potential social unrest that might be caused if more parents started calling their children rude names, if you'll pardon the expression."

"I'm actually quite used to it."

The duchess nodded to Miss Bang and added, "In addition, it gives him bragging rights. He can now claim to have outfoxed one of the smartest lawyers in the past century."

"And lastly, it is a favor to you, my friend. After all, you did save his life. A prince is permitted to show his gratitude."

Aunt Katerina smiled. "I am happy for you, nephew, but it has been an otherwise trying day for me. Would you walk with me for a bit?"

We took our leave of the others and left the cathedral, crossed the courtyard, and entered another wing of the castle. We walked down one of the private hallways where she stopped me, and turned me to her. "I did not miss the fact you tried to refuse the honor when you realized what Prince George was up to. That it was not for your sake, but for the other members of the order. That is a very mature attitude, my dear nephew. A truly noble gesture." She startled me when she stepped forward and hugged me.

I stood, uncertain what to do for a moment, before returning the hug. I heard a sob and a small sniffle and realized my cheeks were wet. "One day I am sure you shall be a great leader of men. You do us all proud." Another sniffle and she released me and stepped back. "Would you do me one small favor, Nephew? Would you be so kind as to let your friends know they are also free to leave? We appreciate the aid they have offered in the light of the recent disaster, but their presence in the skies of Prague is no longer required."

A very polite way of saying some citizens noticed all of the recent mayhem happened when a particularly large airship started lurking above the city, and it would be much easier to restore order if the ship and its occupants would kindly move on. I admired my aunt's diplomacy.

"Certainly, Your Grace. I shall inform them as soon as I return."

"Thank you. I... I wish to be alone now." She patted my arm one last time, turned, and strode away. She moved rapidly, but I could not help notice her cheeks were also wet.

I fitted the goggles over my face, stepped up onto the embarkation platform and strode to stand next to the central tower. I took a firm grip of one of the brass handholds with my left hand, then snaked my right hand into the tower's lattice and tugged the cord dangling there twice. I withdrew my hand and grabbed the brim of my bowler just in time before the platform shot up into the air towards the waiting *Argos*.

I smiled as I rocketed upwards. It was good to have the professor's crew back at their stations again. While the ride was short, it was undeniably exhilarating.

The platform slid smoothly into the embarkation room of *The Argos* with a slight bump. I doffed my hat and strapped the lenses around the bowler's crown for safekeeping. I always considered wearing the protective lenses atop one's headgear to be a silly affectation before, but I realized it was actually a fairly practical way to carry a bulky set of goggles.

Hat in hand, I stepped off the platform and headed for the control room door.

I was surprised to find Tinka manning the controls of the lift. She was uncharacteristically clean, considering every other time I'd seen her she was covered with a layer of dirt, soot, or grease. Once over my initial surprise, I took a good look at her. She was a rather pleasant looking young woman with a slight, athletic build, and an additional pair of arms. Just at the moment, she looked comfortable with herself, confident in her ability, and I couldn't help but smile.

As she became aware of my regard, she stiffened visibly, her self-doubt taking over. She ducked her head and slid her lower set of arms behind her back to hide them.

"Miss Crackle! What a pleasure to see you again. I hope you are doing well today." My cheery tone, and the realization I was genuinely pleased to see the young woman, surprised both of us.

She looked behind herself, knowing no one was there, and cast a confused look at me. "Who are you talking to?"

"I'm terribly sorry. Miss Bang told me Professor Crackle adopted you. I just assumed you'd taken his last name. I'm afraid I don't know your full name, Miss."

"It's Tinka." She stared at me the way one watches a snake, or some other strange animal, which might do something dangerous at any moment.

"Just Tinka?" I asked.

"Isn't that good enough for you?" She bristled visibly as she spoke, and all four of her hands tightened into fists. I admired the fire in her eyes.

"More than good enough, Miss Tinka. I simply wanted to be sure I understood properly." She relaxed slightly, but still regarded me with suspicion. "I hoped I would have the chance to make things up to you for our previous misunderstanding... Well, MY misunderstanding." I paused to let her speak, but she simply stood and glared at me in silence.

"Anyhow, it seems I shall be leaving Prague soon, and I may not be afforded another chance to speak with you. Please accept my apology. My behavior at our first meeting was uncalled for and inappropriate. I hope you can find it within yourself to forgive me and we might perhaps meet on better terms in the future." I bowed to the young lady.

She studied me, trying to make sense of my words. "You're apologizing."

"Yes, Miss."

"To me?"

"Of course. You are, after all, the wronged party."

She gazed intensely at my face. I waited calmly for her response. "You mean it, don't you?" She seemed puzzled.

"Yes, Miss, I do." I kept my tone soft and even.

Her brows furrowed and her lower left hand rose, jabbing a finger at me. "Then why did you turn my men against me?"

"Miss Tinka?"

"You said something to my men and they... they wouldn't continue carrying out the orders I gave them." Guilt flickered across her face for a moment, but her anger was clear.

"I'm sorry, Miss, but I don't know what you're referring to. I've hardly said two words to any..."

"Don't give me that! You said something before you went down into the ruins. What did you say?"

Oh. I remembered a conversation with one of the Riggers before we descended into the tunnels beneath the city. "All I did was tell one of your men my name, Miss."

"So what is it? What's your name?"

Oh, damn. How was I going to get out of this one? "I'm afraid it wouldn't be appropriate, Miss. My name is not..."

Her hands roughly grabbed my arms and I found myself raising my chin to keep it away from the point of a dagger, which suddenly appeared in her upper right hand. "Tell me your name, or so help me, I will gut you like a trout!" The fire in her eyes blazed like a furnace.

Clearly having no other choice, I told her my name.

The fire in her eyes dimmed and they widened until they were like saucers. She didn't move, but I could feel her grip on my arms loosen.

"That's your name?" she said with a strange fascination in her voice.

"Um... yes, Miss, at least it was until earlier today."

A huge smile blossomed across her face. "Oh, that's choice! That's just smashing!" She actually giggled.

"If your curiosity is satisfied, would you be so kind?" I looked pointedly down at the blade still under my chin.

"Oh." The blade disappeared, and she released me, taking a moment to smooth my jacket down with her hands. She giggled again.

"You're not offended, Miss Tinka?" Her reaction confused me, being completely unlike any other reaction to my name I'd ever experienced.

She blinked. "Oh, no. That must be the best name ever."

I was taken aback. She actually *liked* the atrocity of a name my great-grandfather foisted upon me? "If you say so, Miss." She didn't reply, but simply stood, grinning at me. "Does this mean you accept, Miss Tinka?"

"Accept what?"

"My apology."

She blushed, and dropped her eyes. Her voice when she spoke was small and quiet. I strained to hear her. "Oh, yes. Thank you."

"You are welcome, Miss Tinka."

She seemed flummoxed for a moment, waving her arms aimlessly in different directions before she could compose herself again. "Did... did you come up here just to apologize to me?"

"Not entirely, Miss Tinka, I do need to speak to the professor. May I come aboard?"

"Oh. Certainly. I'll show you where he is." She started towards the door to the lounge, but paused as I added my hat to a rack otherwise filled with the professor's top hats, all sporting multiple pairs of goggles.

I crossed to the door and opened it for her and we stepped through into the lounge. Closing the door on the other side, I offered her my arm and she paused, staring at it for a moment, as if she thought I'd pull it away. Then she gently took my arm with both of her lefts. She looked at me, expecting some kind of reaction. I smiled back at her, and gestured with my left hand.

"Shall we go?"

We proceeded across the floor of the lounge, arm in arm, and from the corner of my eye, I thought I could detect a smile crossing her face again.

"Hello, my boy," the professor called as he spied Tinka and myself entering the salon where he and Miss Bang were taking tea. "To what do we owe the honor?"

Tinka and I shared a glance. Neither of us was surprised to find the two of them together. It was actually a little amusing the way they sat at opposite ends of the settee, stiffly holding themselves apart while trying to stay as close as possible.

"I bring you a message from the duchess, Professor. She thanks you for your assistance, but now the emergency is over, she says you are free to go. Personally, I suspect she would prefer you found somewhere else to park."

Tinka drifted forward and stole a few biscuits from the tea trays on the table. Taking her prizes in hand, she circled behind the settee.

"We can certainly accommodate her," the professor replied.

"How is your aunt holding up, my lord? She wasn't very talkative at your knighting ceremony."

"She is managing well enough, Miss Bang. She knows affairs of state will not wait long upon her grief, and she is dealing with them as best she can. Her marriage to Uncle Randolph wasn't just a marriage of state; she truly loved him. That was why she shared her title with him, making him the duke instead of the ducal consort. But she has a strong sense of duty, and she loves her people almost as much."

"It can be very hard to lose someone so close to you," the professor said. Miss Bang looked as if she wanted to say something in reply, but she covered her thought by taking another sip of tea.

I continued on, "It would seem now is also an appropriate time for me to take my leave of you. My aunt has reminded me I am past due for the next leg of my tour and I shall have to make travel arrangements in the very near future. I wanted to thank you, Professor, Miss Bang, for all of your help in these trying times. I am not sure how I would have survived without your friendship." I stepped forward and shook the professor's hand.

"Nonsense!" he cried as he pumped my arm in return. "It has been our pleasure to make your acquaintance."

"Where are you off to next, Sir Richard?" Miss Bang asked. Tinka peered over her shoulder at me as she nibbled on her biscuit. She seemed very child-like in her open curiosity.

"The next stop on my itinerary is a visit with my Aunt Phyllis and her husband in India. I believe he is a colonel with the Raj, but I'm afraid I have quite forgotten his name." A fact my aunt would surely take me to task about at great length.

"India! Oh, excellent! I haven't been to India in at least a decade."

"Ooh, Father, could we stock in some curry?"

"I hear the gardens in New Delhi are absolutely wonderful to behold, Harmonious."

Everyone was talking at once; I could hardly make sense of what they were saying. "Wait a moment! What are you all talking about?"

"Why India, of course. It should be a grand trip!"

"Well, yes, but why are you all so excited because I'm going to India?"

"We're taking you, of course! You are in need of transport, and we are in need of a new destination. Two problems that amply solve each other."

"You mean to take me to India?"

"Certainly! Our pleasure. It seems the least we can do for holding you up for so long."

"And we'll make better time than any commercial liner," Tinka added around a mouthful of biscuit.

"Professor, you realize this might mean you'd have to endure my Aunt Phyllis?" I did my best to convey the proper sense of dread and unpleasantness at the prospect.

"I have faced such dangers before, I assure you. We have already braved many dangers together. How could I send you alone into peril?"

Miss Bang gave the professor a look of censure and responded, "I am sure your aunt is a delightful person, Sir Richard. I shall look forward to making her acquaintance."

Tinka bit off more of her biscuit and muttered, "I'm staying with the ship." I could not keep the smile from my face.

"Professor, I don't know what to say. You don't have to do this."

"Pish and tosh! It is nothing. Besides, it will get us off of the duchess's lawn, now won't it?"

Laughter filled the parlor and I grinned at the thought of a new adventure opening up before me.

But that is another tale.

The End

About the Author

Doc Coleman is a blogger, podcaster, voice actor, and writer. A guest spot on Galley Table's second episode opened the door of podcasting, and Doc Coleman stepped through. He soon became a regular on Galley Table, produced his own podcast: The Shrinking Man Project, and became a guest co-host on The Writer's Round Table. Most recently, he has taken over the Balticon Podcast, and will be continuing the tradition of news, panels, and interview at Balticonpodcast.org.

Discover Doc's stories in The Ministry of Peculiar Occurrences' Tales from the Archives, the Way of the Gun Bushido Western Anthology, and the Steampunk Special Edition of Flagship magazine, and The Perils of Prague, the first book in the series The Adventures of Crackle and Bang.

Find out about all of Doc's projects at Swimming Cat Studios (http://SwimmingCatStudios.com).

When he isn't juggling projects, making a living, or mainlining podcasts, Doc is a gamer, an avid reader, a motorcyclist, a home brewer and beer lover, a fan of renaissance festivals, and frequently a smart-ass. He lives with his lovely wife and two cats in Germantown, MD.

Want to know more about us?

The Author - Doc Coleman

Doc Coleman is a writer, podcaster, and voice actor. His work has been featured in the *The Ministry of Peculiar Occurrences Tales from the Archives* podcast and short story collections, *The Way of the Gun* anthology, and the Steampunk Special Edition of *FlagShip* Magazine. His most recent release is *The Perils of Prague, Book One of The Adventures of Crackle and Bang*. Want to get the most up to date information on what Doc is working on and releasing?

Website: http://SwimmingCatStudios.com
Facebook: https://www.facebook.com/scaleslea
Twitter: https://twitter.com/Scaleslea
Questions? Email him at: Doc@SwimmingCatStudios.com

The Illustrator/Designer - Scott E. Pond

Scott E. Pond is an illustrator, artist, graphic designer, humorist, photographer, and author. His artistic and graphic design work can be found in works by New York Times Bestselling Author Scott Sigler, award winning novelist and screenwriter Matt Wallace, Parsec Award winning author Paul E. Cooley, Bram Stoker Award nominated-novelist Jake Bible, Campbell Award winning author Mur Lafferty, Scott Roche, Sue Baiman, Kate Sherrod, M. Jandreau, Escape Artists audio fiction, and many others. You can experience some of his dark and wacky nuggets of wisdom from the mental recesses of his mind in his coffee-table book, *Mental Graffiti*. Want to get the most up to date information on what Scott is working on and releasing?

Newsletter-mailing group: http://www.scottpond.com/newsletter/
Website: http://www.scottpond.com
Facebook: https://www.facebook.com/scottepond
Twitter: https://twitter.com/ScottEPond
Questions? Contact him at: http://www.scottpond.com/contact

The Editor - Jennifer Melzer

Jennifer Melzer is an author, poet, and editor. One of her best-known works is *The Goblin Market*. Her most recent release is *Boys Don't Cry*. Want to get the most up to date information on what Jennifer is working on and releasing?

Website: http://jennifermelzer.com
Facebook: https://www.facebook.com/jennifermelzerauthor
Twitter: https://twitter.com/jennybeanses
Questions? Contact her at: http://jennifermelzer.com/about-me/contact/

CPSIA information can be obtained
at www.ICGtesting.com
Printed in the USA
LVHW021739250719
625327LV00004B/560/P

9 780998 015101